A PIMP'S DARK LOVE

WRITTEN BY GHAD

First edition—remake of *Serving Ice Cream.*

ISBN-13: 978-1-0691070-0-8

Dedication

In a dark world where money rules, many do immoral things to live lavishly. I wrote this book to depict that at its finest.

The sex trade has become glamorized in this day and age, while many are oblivious to the true depths of it.

This story goes out to those who've walked that underworld to understand the pain and heartaches that go hand-in-hand with the glory that it's all done for...and for those who've been dragged through it and never had a chance to truly embrace the glories of a game that's glamorized only at the surface.

*"Everything is beautiful and ugly in its own way
...just goes to how you understand it."*

A Note on Perspective

The narrative alternates throughout, with Gelato's first-person perspective capturing the ruthless, gritty mindset behind the lifestyle, while third-person scenes through other characters add a more formal lens, bringing the raw truths of that world into clearer focus.

PROLOGUE

3:40 A.M.

After a good night at the strip club in London, Ontario, Tanya returned to a motel in Saint Thomas. She freshened up and changed into a comfortable grey sweatsuit before settling in to relax. Her work for the night was done, and she'd return to the club the next evening. Exhausted and ready for sleep, she lay in bed when her phone began to ring. It was an unknown number.

"Hello, who is this?" Tanya answered.

"It's me. I'm here," a male voice said.

"Daddy?" She recognized him immediately. "Why're you calling from a different number?"

"I got a new burner phone. But, yeah, what's the room number? I'm here."

"Oh, okay. I'm in room one-twenty-seven," Tanya confirmed. "You wanted a room on the first floor with a backdoor entry, right?"

"Yeah, that's good. I'll see you soon."

The call ended, and Tanya set the phone down. She couldn't resist smiling. It was going to be an interesting weekend. It wasn't unusual for Tanya's pimp, who was also a dope boy, to leave Toronto and sell drugs in smaller towns. He would set up shop near whichever city Tanya happened to be working in. They had once enjoyed that time together, but things were different now.

The vigorous knocking on the back sliding glass doors made Tanya rush over and pull the curtains aside. A man dressed in all black stood outside wearing a light jacket, gloves, and a cap pulled low. His entire appearance should have made Tanya wary, but she was used to him being incognito. She unlocked and slid the door open. He stepped inside and walked past her as she relocked it. He sat on the room's only sofa and looked up at her. Tanya could now see his face clearly—a slender man with brown skin, a fading haircut, and a moustache with chin hair.

"What's up?" Tanya asked. "Why're you looking at me like that?"

He smirked. "I can't look at you?"

Tanya sat back on the bed and flipped through the channels. "You just haven't looked at me like that in a while."

"How am I looking at you?"

"That look you make when you wanna fuck," she said, holding back a smile. "It's been a while."

"I haven't seen you in so long 'cause I been busy. I miss you, though."

"Really?" She did not buy it. "You've been busy? But you always find time for the three other bitches. Don't you see Crystal like three times a week?"

"I'm guessing you feel a way that I haven't kicked it with you for months?"

"Kinda." Tanya sighed. "Sucks when you still working for a guy you don't even get to see."

He didn't answer, and the room went quiet. The TV stopped on a music channel, pop music filling the air. Tanya spoke again.

"So where's your bag of clothing and stuff? Aren't you staying out here for the weekend to sell your drugs or whatever?"

"My bag's in the car."

"Should I go get it for you?" She needed a breather from the awkward moment.

"Nah, it's all good."

"Okay." Unsure of his tone, she tried again. "Are you gonna at least take off your jacket and stuff? Like, get comfortable?"

"I'm good."

Tanya sank against the headboard, defeated by the awkwardness. "Daddy, is everything okay?"

He thought for a moment before asking his own question. "Tanya, have I ever done you wrong for no reason at all?"

She stared at him, unsure why he was asking. "What do you mean by that?"

"Well..." He paused. "I know I be hard on you sometimes and maybe you hate me because of that."

"Daddy, I know I'm hard-headed and maybe that's why you're hard on me. I just don't like when you put hands on me." She lied. "But I don't hate you for it."

"So why you still hard-headed if you know it pisses me off?"

"I dunno." Tanya thought about it. "I just don't like always being told what to do. I chose to be in this game with you because I like you and all, but I'm a free-spirit type of bitch and sometimes like to do my own thing."

"Do you think it'd be best to leave me and maybe do your own thing?"

The question caught Tanya off guard. It was strange enough that he was having that kind of conversation with her. It sounded like he was offering her a way out, but maybe he was just testing her. No pimp let his breadwinner go that easy.

"No. I'd never leave you. I love you and got too much invested in you to wanna leave you."

He didn't respond, lost in thought. Tanya stayed calm, sure he had bought her lie.

"Okay..." he finally said.

Then silence. Whatever connection they had once shared was gone. Now they struggled to hold a conversation. She knew if they didn't loosen up the weekend would be long and awkward. Giving in to sex would be the best ice breaker. "Daddy, get comfortable and come keep me warm in bed."

"Okay, sounds good. Umm, get my stuff from the car for me. I'ma hit the shower."

Tanya got off the bed. "Where's the car parked?"

"Right out back." He stood and unzipped his jacket.

She grabbed her light coat and slipped on her sneakers, then went to the sliding door. As she pulled the curtains aside and began unlocking it, a cold object touched the side of her head. She turned and saw the gun in her face and the malice in his eyes.

"OH MY GOD!"

The gunshot sent Tanya into darkness. Blood sprayed the wall as her body dropped lifeless. He tucked the hot gun into his waist, slid the door open, and calmly left the room.

GHAD

GHAD

CHAPTER ONE

◆

My birth certificate said Angelo. I never knew my father. He got killed in the streets of Toronto a month after I was born. Some mafia debt gone wrong, and they came to collect his life. All he left me with were the Italian genes and the last name Russo. My Haitian mom had to leave Toronto and raise me in Montréal with her sister. That's where I grew up. Only child. Single mother. Low-income housing.

I made my name in the streets of Montréal with some guys I grew up with. We started off selling crack as kids, moved to credit card scams when we got older, then switched to pimping when that wave hit Montréal in 2002. At seventeen, a mixed-breed young fella with a slick tongue, already pulling women older than me, getting in their heads and owning them. By eighteen, I moved out my mom's place in the ghetto and leased a condo for myself. The name Gelato Icy started ringing through Montréal's streets. By twenty, I had four elite thoroughbreds in my stable. My closest friend and I moved back to my birth city, Toronto, where our girls could chase that big-city money. The game in Toronto was way more glamorous than Montréal. The rules were real, the pimps were known, the bad-bitches were about it, and the tricks came in all kinds. Didn't take long before some of my girls drifted off to better pimps in the city. I was young and untamed. Still hadn't learned how to secure my stable. That's something an older, seasoned pimp once told me.

Things turned for the worse when my mother back in Montréal died of cancer. That loss sent me on a downward spiral. I became lost and picked up the habit of using drugs and alcohol to bury my pain. Bombay Sapphire kept me at peace with my Jinns, MDMA lifted my spirit, and Percocet numbed whatever darkness I kept bottled up. Eventually, cocaine became the drug of choice because it did it all and kept me alive—feeling like a vibrant pimp in the big city.

Five years later came the moment of meeting my solid bottom bitch, Sierra. A Persian babe, nineteen at the time. That day, me and my pimp partners hit a college pub in Waterloo to hunt for fresh meat. Sierra was that out-of-town chick from the boonies with a broken family, all the right highlights for a girl ready to be turned out. When she met me, she saw the big-city life she'd dreamed about. I was 265 pounds of muscle, 6'2", full sleeves tatted, braids hanging to my back. My designer and jewellery game were flawless, and my three partners looked just as sharp. We were the Benz Brothers. That night, Sierra got a taste of how Toronto pimps partied. Didn't take much. cheap drinks, college music, and our presence alone had them lit. She ended the night in a hotel with me where I fucked those big-city dreams into her body and soul. By morning, she was down to cut her classes and leave to Toronto with her new king. My closest partner had his own catch from that night, so we both left Waterloo that afternoon in our separate Benzes while the other two stayed behind to party another night.

Back in Toronto, things with Sierra moved fast. We had brunch at my downtown condo then met up with my partner and his girl for a double date that carried into the night, when the city lights came alive. Within weeks, Sierra still hadn't gone back to Waterloo. Her family gave up on trying to pull her back, they had their own problems, and she was grown. After being settled into her own Toronto apartment, she learned exactly what her new king was about—The Game. She met my other girls, joined in on the orgy nights, and built a tight bond with my ebony girl, Foxy, who was the bottom bitch then. They worked together at the same club where Foxy schooled her on how to be a live bitch and turn tricks. Sierra took the name Skye Icy. My stable got stronger as my game got tighter, no longer relying on just my looks.

Over time, Skye became the new bottom bitch. She had my heart beyond the game. When I bought a condo by the lake, I leased another one nearby for her. She was the only one living close. Even though a pimp needs his own space, I needed Sierra near me when my vices got heavy.

GHAD

CHAPTER TWO

◆

Friday, June 8, 2018 – 10:39 P.M.

At thirty-three weighing 250 pounds of muscle, the six-pack was gone and a gut was settling in. Being older now, I had retired the braids for a wave cut and a neatly trimmed beard. All them years in the game had me bossed up, rolling into the Sherway Gardens condos in my Bentley GT soft-top. Smelling like Jean Paul Gaultier and money. Had on a Breitling watch and a couple of gold rings, with extra diamond weight on the left pinky. Designer T-shirt, belt, and jeans over high-top kicks. My thick signature chain hung with a huge pendant on my chest—a gold bowl with ice-cream scoops of different coloured diamonds. Everything about me showed glamor and glory.

I got on the phone and called my closest partner, Smooth Darken Caesar. He answered on the second ring.

"What it do, playa?" His pimp slang hit with that Congolese accent and raspy voice.

"I'm downstairs," I said.

"Shit, son. Come upstairs, then. I ain't even ready to roll out."

"What's taking you so long?"

"I'm still getting dressed, playa. Just come up so we can fix our face."

I left the Bentley parked out front knowing the stay upstairs wouldn't be long, then headed into the building. The concierge clocked me and buzzed me through the security doors. I gave him a quick nod by the front desk, then headed for the elevators. Took it up to the 22nd floor, walked down the carpeted hallway to unit 2202, and knocked.

Smooth opened the door quick. He was a dark-skinned, six-foot, pudgy dude in Balmain jeans and a Versace belt, no shirt. The Caesar cut fit his rounded face, already showing the wear of a seasoned alcoholic.

"What's up?" I greeted.

"Just here, playa." He closed the door behind me.

We went over to the marble dining counter where my interest was. "Need to fix my face," I said, grabbing the curled-up hundred-dollar bill by the pile of cocaine.

"Do your thing, pimpin'," Smooth said.

A card was already on the counter, perfect for lining up three rails that went straight up my nose one after the other. It was clean, top-quality coke, what we called Designer-Dope, or D-D. Smooth took the card and bill from me, did a few rails himself, and we both stood there a moment appreciating the high.

"Yeah, man, I'm feeling right," I said.

"Hold up, I'ma bring more out so we can hit a couple more." Smooth walked off toward his bedroom.

He went out of sight into his room, so I called out, "Hurry up and get dressed, too." I took a seat on one of the stools at the counter and waited for Smooth. The coke rush ran through me. This was the kind of live life I had with my partners, Friday nights rolling through strip clubs to check on our girls. We always made appearances for any solo bitches thinking about choosing up on us, because hitting the clubs was clockwork for real pimps in the city.

Smooth had been my right-hand since we were kids in Montréal. We met when his family came fresh to Canada from Congo, and he ended up in grade school with me. He was dark as fuck, so all the kids called him Darken Caesar. He spoke French and no English, which didn't matter much since French was the official language of Quebec. I learned English from my mother, who spoke it at home. Smooth picked it up being at my place so often. We both got into the game at seventeen. I had it easy luring girls with my looks while he had to work twice as hard. He got the name Smooth for being a slick talker. When we moved to Toronto, the English he'd learned came in handy, and his accent mixed with that smooth talk made Toronto girls weak for his foreign suave.

"Alright, let's fix all the way up and hit the road." Smooth came out his room dressed in a silk Versace button-up and heavy on the cologne. Gold necklace, gold Rolex, gold bracelet, gold rings with ice on the left pinky. He dropped a small baggie of cocaine on the counter for me to set up more lines while he went to his bar cabinet for a bottle of Courvoisier and shot glasses. We were leaving the condo on a wave of liveliness with the *ism*. PGO—*Pimpin' Going On.*

We were doped up when pulling up to Atlantis in our separate Bentleys at midnight. Smooth Darken Caesar kept strong in the race with me. He had the same Bentley GT as me, except mine was white on tan and his was black. We parked out front, engines humming low, two kings stepping into a kingdom. Atlantis only hired premium strippers, and my girls were part of that lineup. We walked through the heavy front doors and breezed past security like we owned the place. They knew better than to ask big pimpin' studs like us for IDs. The club glowed neon, music pumping with a naked girl on stage working the pole. Men filled the tables, some right up front, others chilling by the bar where pimps liked to post up. Strippers in skimpy outfits worked the floor on hustle mode. They'd slide up to the tables to drink with the men and work their charm till a trick was made. Upstairs was the private area where they took tricks, and a lot more went down up there than lap dances if the price was right.

The club was packed. Scanning the room for my girls, Diamond and Velvet, I didn't see either one. Instead, I caught sight of a brown-skinned pimp with a low fade, mustache, and a patch of chin hair. Full Gucci tracksuit. He was at a side table with another dude in burgundy. I couldn't place the second guy, but could tell you all about the pimp in Gucci.

Preeme. He was the little brother in the squad, youngest at twenty-eight. We met when I was twenty-one and still fairly new to Toronto, and he was only sixteen. Back then, home was in Mississauga, and he worked at a pizza shop near my spot where food was a regular grab. One night when I came in at the end of his shift he asked me for a ride home. From that ride we got cool, and of course, he was fascinated with the idea of me being a real pimp. Preeme grew up in Regent Park after coming to Toronto from Nova Scotia when he was nine. He knew a bit about pimping but grew up in Toronto with the gangster mentality. As a young rebel, he had run-ins with the law and got kicked out by his mother after doing a one-year bid. The poor kid was just a juvenile that needed direction. I took him under my wing, gave him a place to stay, and a job as security for my stable. He had a gun—illegal—and a legit driver's licence, so all he needed was a car to be mobile. Then Preeme learned the game from me. Before he was even old enough to step into a strip club, he did the expected and found himself an older bitch to pimp.

Known for his guerrilla-style pimping, Preeme built a ruthless reputation. Dominant, controlling, aggressive, and physically abusive. Once a girl gets comfortable being in your stable, she eventually tries to test your authority. Preeme being 5'8" and only 140 pounds didn't help him much in using intimidation. Raising his voice and puffing his chest just didn't cut it for the scrawny guy, so he had to remind bitches he had man strength by applying it. Besides, he already had a violent temper from the gangster life he lived in the streets, and that had many pimps respecting him. Stories of Preeme regulating other pimps and shooting to kill floated around, and most were true. I personally knew of a time he shot another pimp in a strip club parking lot just for talking slick to him. Shot the man in the face, and that dude was lucky to live. Then there was the time two guys robbed his working-girl at a hotel. Word hit the streets about who they were, and a week later one of them made the news—gunned down in his condo's underground parking. The second one showed up days later, found dead in a downtown apartment where he was dealing drugs. The cops didn't solve either case. They had no real evidence, but word on the street was Preeme did both.

The latest story about Preeme that kept everyone on edge, especially the girls, was the one that hit breaking news and got him locked up. He murdered one of his girls for planning to betray him. Preeme was twenty-four when it happened. He had about four solid girls working for him at the time. Losing a bitch wouldn't have phased him, because he was doing well and could always find another. But his girl then, Tanya, made plans to leave him and told her new pimp, Ricky, about Preeme's 200K cash safe. Of course, Preeme was known, so Ricky thought twice about making a move like that. Instead, Ricky showed respect to the game and reached out to let Preeme know Tanya was a dangerous bitch. Preeme kept that to himself for a couple days till he got her somewhere out of town and blew her brains out. The story went viral on social media and had too many people talking who had no business talking. Then word on the street reached the cops. With no hard evidence against him, Preeme beat the case after waiting two and a half years in jail for trial. During that time, he lost all his girls except his bottom bitch, Crystal, A Portuguese beauty respectable for her hustle and loyalty. She's still the only one with him, since other girls are too scared to work for him. But Preeme had no desire for any other girl anyway. He couldn't bring himself to trust another bitch again.

My attention switched back to the liveliness of the club when Smooth asked, "Who's that at the table with our boy Preeme?"

"Not sure." Looking at the dude in the burgundy tracksuit as we walked towards their table, I said. "He looks familiar."

Preeme noticed us coming and got up to greet us with brotherly hugs, then gestured to the dude at the table. "Y'all remember my homie Jiggy, right?" Jiggy got up to greet Smooth and me before we sat down, but he stayed on his feet like he wasn't planning to stick around. Hearing his name, I remembered who Jiggy was, though not knowing him personally outside of Preeme. From what I knew, he was an all-around hustler, a solid source for Designer-Dope. Preeme dealt with him in the dope game, then Smooth and I would get our ounce or two off Preeme.

"Alright, fam, I'ma get going," Jiggy said to Preeme. He chugged the rest of his beer, then saluted us before leaving the table.

He was far from the table when Smooth said to Preeme, "You gotta be careful with them menz. I hear he's shady as fuck, jacking people and shit."

Preeme raised an eyebrow and said bold, "Jack who and take what, from who? Not me."

I chuckled at Preeme's raw statement, then asked, "What brand was the burgundy tracksuit he wearing? The suede style nice."

"Neeshy. It's the brand on a wave right now."

Smooth added, "Yeah, I think I heard of it before. I been seeing a couple cats wearing it in the city. It looks dope."

"Yeah, I could fuck with it," I agreed. And in that moment my dopamine levels started craving a fix so I asked Preeme, "You grabbed some Designer-D off Jiggy?"

Preeme nodded.

"Okay, cool. Let me get an ounce when we leave here."

The pretty, fully clothed waiter came to take me and Smooth's order. We both ordered Grand Marnier on ice, and she was gone.

My eyes swept over the vibrant place again, expecting to spot my girls by now. I asked Preeme, "You seen my bitches here tonight?"

"Yeah, I saw Velvet earlier." He asked, "You got Diamond and Skye here too?"

"Nah. Just Velvet and Diamond. You already know I keep the young two together and let Skye do her own thing 'cause she rather work solo."

"True, true," Preeme said. "The mains never like working in the same club with the next girls on the team."

Smooth added, "They like feeling like they on a different level than the rest. Only time they like working with a next broad in the stable is when they training 'em, and that's 'cause it reinforces their title as the bottom bitch. Pimping could be easier if some of these hoes didn't have a damn ego."

We all laughed at the truth in that, and the waiter came back with our drinks. Smooth gave her a forty-dollar bill and fanned her off to keep the change. We cheered with Preeme's beer bottle and drank. He asked Smooth, "Any of your many bitches in here tonight?"

"Nah, I got 'em spread out all over the province. And I think a few out the province too."

"How you even keep track of all those bitches?" Preeme asked, shaking his head like he'd never understand it.

Smooth gave his usual laugh and answer. "I don't. I keep tabs on my boss hoes, Alize and Star, and they keep tabs on the rest of the stable. All I gotta do is spend time with each paying hoe every now and then." He chuckled. "And that keeps me hella busy sometimes."

Smooth's stable had a rare but familiar setup. He kept no less than ten girls and usually had over fifteen. Sometimes he'd even forget about the ones working out of town till they came back to the city with money for him. Two ebony prime girls, Alize and Star, were his bottom bitches. They were basically sister wives, twenty-eight and twenty-six, running the stable together. With their years in the game, they handled everything—lining up schedules, sending girls to clubs and hotels, keeping the money flowing, and getting it all back to their pimp, Smooth. They still worked the game themselves too, bringing in their own cash for their king. Having boss-bitches and a big stable like that was every pimp's dream. But the flaw with a setup that size, built by the pimp and his boss-bitches always recruiting, was that not every girl was Smooth's taste. Still, they stayed as long as they brought in something, even if it wasn't much. A big stable also meant too much estrogen, too much drama, so girls came and went quick.

Me, I preferred the baddest bitches only, even if that meant having fewer. The three I had were solid, dime thoroughbreds, and they made me a killing. Still, keeping my eyes open for new ones was always the sport.

A hand on my shoulder surprised me, but I kept my cool. That touch and the scent of a woman was familiar. "Hey, Daddy," she whispered in my ear.

I looked over my shoulder and saw Velvet's pretty face. Almond-shaped green eyes, a nose piercing, and plump lips. Her tanned skin had a sexy glow under the club lights, and her wavy brunette hair looked rich and shiny. She stepped closer to the table, right by my side, and greeted Smooth and Preeme with soft handshakes.

Smooth complimented her, "Girl, you look like money." She smiled, knowing she was a real breadwinner.

At twenty-one, Vanessa, better known as Velvet Icy, was my petite bad bitch, standing 5'4", though her six-inch heels gave her more height. She wore a scandalous two-piece outfit and weighed around 115 pounds. Slim body, perky silicone D-cups, and a natural bubble butt from daily squats. She was Italian with a quarter Caribbean in her, which gave her that natural tan. On her right rib was a detailed panther flowing down to a bunch of roses on her thigh. Around her neck was a platinum choker with a small pendant—a purple diamond ice cream scoop on a yellow gold cone—representing me, Gelato Icy.

She sat on my lap and reached into her small purse, pulling out a stack of money to put in my hand. I shoved it in my pocket and said in her ear, "Looks like a good night, huh?" Her expensive perfume had her smelling exclusive, like my girls always do.

"A bit over a thousand already." She flirted, "It's always a good night for me when Daddy shows up."

I tried holding back my smile so my partners wouldn't catch me getting big-headed, but they weren't even paying us any mind. Their eyes were on the girls walking around the club. I asked Velvet, "Where's Diamond?"

She gave me that worried look and I knew right away something was off. Velvet sighed. "Diamond's in the changing room…stooped."

"You gotta be kidding me."

Diamond crashing at work was something I'd been fed up with. My blood was boiling, but Velvet tried to calm me down. "Don't be mad, Daddy. She made a lot of money tonight. She just crashed, like, only an hour ago." She kept pleading Diamond's case. "She spent most of her time upstairs with tricks and they kept buying her drinks, so she got kinda tipsy and did a bump of D-D to stay focused through the night. Then that bump led to a couple more, and yeah. But she made over two thousand already."

Diamond probably did make good money before crashing, but Velvet always covered for her. They were teammates, basically best friends. I recruited them separate but around the same time two years ago. Back then the only other girls in my stable were Sierra and a Colombian chick named Sugar who left months later. Diamond and Velvet were both young and vibrant so they clicked fast. I helped build that bond by leasing them separate pads in the same condo in Mississauga. Got them both matching 3 Series BMWs, different colours. They were a strong duo, loyal to me, but it was always expected that one would cover for the other.

"Go to the back and call Diamond out for me," I said to Velvet.

"Daddy, to be honest, I don't think she could even walk straight right now."

"You gotta be kidding me." Getting up quick brought Velvet off my lap and onto her feet too. My partners looked over wondering what was up, so I said, "I'ma be back," and stormed off towards the changing room at the back of the club. The door read: *Employees Only*.

The rage was mine, the Designer-Dope just turned it up a notch. I strong-armed the flimsy changing room door open and stepped in as it swung shut behind me. My eyes scanned for Diamond. Frightened faces stared back. Some of the girls sat at mirrored stations doing makeup, a few were scrolling on their phones, and two peeked out from the shower stalls. They looked shocked to see a man in there. Or maybe they were just on edge seeing me, Gelato Icy, a pimp known to crack down on bitches. Every head turned towards the one girl sitting at a corner station. She was out of it, staring at herself in the mirror, vacant, oblivious to me. I walked over and grabbed her platinum blonde hair, yanking her up onto her heels.

"Oh my God!" Diamond shrieked. The other girls froze, knowing better than to step in as I spun her around and slapped her across the face. "Dumb bitch."

She staggered for a few seconds, dazed, before falling back into the chair when released. Her eyes fluttered, lost, trying to piece together what just happened. When her mind finally caught up, she looked up and recognized me. "...Daddy?" She broke down right away, sobbing with her face buried in her hands. "Daddy, I'm so sorry."

Disgusted, I told her, "You're a mess."

"Daddy, I-I'm so s-sorry," she stuttered with teary eyes, all messed up from too much dope and alcohol in her system.

Dianna, also known as Diamond Icy, was my next twenty-one-year-old girl on the team. At 5'11", she weighed a thick 190 pounds, with a curvy body and a flat stomach she kept through diet. Her big breasts were natural, wide hips, thick thighs, and that jiggly booty she was sitting on right now. She was purely Canadian, pale skin smooth as milk, with small eyes that showed her Native genes. She wore a one-piece stripper outfit that hugged every curve of her body. Around her neck was her platinum choker, repping me, with the ice cream scoop in pink diamonds. If it weren't for the tears ruining her mascara and the redness on her left cheek from my slap, she could've passed for a Covergirl model. But right now, this bitch was a hot mess.

"Daddy, I-I'm so sorry. I know, I-I'm s-sorry. I'm s-so fucked up, Daddy," Diamond pleaded senselessly. "I don't know how...how this. I messed up but...Daddy, I made money." I couldn't make out half the shit she was saying through the sobs, but she reached into her purse and pulled out a thick stack of cash for me. Her phone, makeup, and a few other things spilled out with it. I took the money from her hand and shoved it in my pocket while she scrambled to pick up what fell to the floor. It was clear she couldn't work the rest of the night in the state she was in. "Just get your ass changed and go home," I said.

"Buh-but I can work, Daddy. I'll make muh-more money."

Diamond used the chair to help herself up but wobbled in her heels. She leaned toward me, looking for support. *Dumb bitch!* I delivered a fierce backhand that sent her falling over the chair, with everything in her purse flying out. Two security bouncers stormed into the changing room but froze when I turned to face them. Known for laying out bouncers with my good hands, and these two had no desire to get physical with me.

"Gelato, you have no business back here," said the white one.

"Please, just leave the club, or we'll have to call the police," the black one added.

Behind them stood a stripper with her hands on her hips and a pouty face. Clearly the one who ran out to call for security. A typical renegade bitch who didn't like pimps. "Flake-ass hoe," I said to her when walking towards the same door I came in through. The bouncers stepped aside so I could leave, and the renegade bitch kept her distance, knowing I'd pimp slap the shit out of her if she got in my way. Stepping out the room, I came back into the club with the bouncers trailing behind me. I went straight to the table where my partners sat, Velvet waiting by my seat looking nervous. She knew things hadn't gone well for Diamond in the changing room. Ignoring the bouncers trying to escort me out, I stopped to speak with her. "You and Diamond came here in separate cars or one?"

"Umm, one. One car, Daddy." Her voice was shaky.

"Okay, well she's done for the night. Get her ass home. And you call it a night too."

"Are you sure I should end my night too?" Velvet hesitated, careful not to sound like she was going against my word while I was heated. "...I have a trick waiting to see me at his place later tonight. So, umm...should I just get Diamond home safely and then see my trick?"

"Yeah, do that."

The bouncers were nudging me to keep it moving, so my partners Smooth and Preeme got up from the table. It was time to roll out. The three of us walked out of the club with our chests high, eyes on us from all corners. The bouncers followed behind until we were fully out of the building.

GHAD

CHAPTER THREE

Saturday, June 9 – 4:15 A.M.

The party run ended at Sierra's lakefront condo, just down the road from mine. Having my own set of keys to all my girls' places like a pimp should, I scanned the fob to get into the underground parking. Sierra didn't know I was coming by tonight, but I figured she'd be home after work. After finding a spot in the P2 visitor's area there was no rush to step out the car. I reached for the glove compartment and pulled out the Bentley's thick manual, already chalked up with Designer-D residue from the rails Smooth and I had done in the car through the night. It had been a long one. My partners and I had hit a few other strip clubs after leaving Atlantis, then Smooth and I met with some other pimp colleagues at a downtown nightclub and shut it down with a wild bottle service show. That move brought all the thirsty girls our way. Some bad bitches looked tempted to choose up on real pimping, but they held back. Most of them knew who we were, and they weren't ready for the level of the game we played at. Just the usual outcome whenever we showed up in a club.

Couldn't help the thrill kicking in while pulling out the baggie of Designer-D and pouring a few crumbs onto the manual. At least a quarter of the ounce was gone for the night, and stopping now wasn't a thought. I used a bank card to break the crumbs into fine powder across the page. Once it was laid out, it looked like more than expected. *Who cares.* I rolled up a hundred-dollar bill and snorted the whole mountain. Then kicked back in the Bentley's seat as the coke rushed through me. Designer-Dope. The kind that separated the elite from the fucking squares who'd be sleeping at these hours. These were the vampire hours, where immortals lived, and I was a god in this realm to bitches. A real live pimp named Gelato Icy.

My mind raced with all kinds of thoughts. I felt good, then slipped into that other feeling—a state of overthinking when high on Designer alone. Scrolling through my phone made for the perfect distraction, leading me to the text Velvet sent earlier. She said she got Diamond home safe and even brought her up to her pad before heading out for her trick appointment. That had me thinking about Diamond. Lately, she'd been overdoing the drugs and alcohol to the point of crashing out at work. Maybe I was to blame, glamorizing the use of Designer-D to my girls. The way I carried myself gave the idea that it was normal to lose focus because the life was about being lavish, fun, and faded. But Diamond would be crazy to think she could do what I did. We weren't equals. I could turn-up on drinks and Designer whenever and however I wanted because I was a pimp, a gentleman of leisure. She was a bitch who was supposed to be getting me paper and only got to party on my level, with me, when I allowed it. A talk with her would be necessary.

Paranoia kicked in when a car came down into the underground and parked close to me. I quickly dusted off the manual and shoved it back in the glove compartment, then tucked the baggie of Designer-D by my nuts inside my Versace boxer briefs. The random white guy stepped out of his Mercedes and headed into the building. He looked like an average Joe coming back from a Friday night out in the city bars. There was no reason to be paranoid. It was just the mountain of Designer-D messing with my head. I needed a moment to get myself together. The time read 4:56 a.m., and ten minutes would pass before deciding to go up into the building.

The sound of little paws on the hardwood rushed toward me as I stepped into Sierra's unit. Chocolate was at my feet—a purebred French bulldog with a brown coat and black face. His stumpy tail wagged wild, excited to see me. It wasn't long before his partner in crime, Vanilla, strolled out from the short hall to my left. She was a purebred serval, an exotic African wild cat with big ears and a golden coat marked with bold black spots and a white belly. Looked like a cheetah, just smaller and slimmer. Her meows were sharp, and so were the long fangs that flashed each time. Crazy thing was, this wild cat got along just fine with Chocolate.

I crouched to pet Chocolate's big head while Vanilla brushed against my leg, purring. I showed her some love too. Chocolate bolted off for his squeaky toy and came back with it in his mouth, ready to play. Vanilla sat by my side giving him that bougie look, like, *buddy, nobody's trying to play with you right now*. I ignored him, kicked off my shoes, and called out for the one person who hadn't come to greet me. "Sisi, where you at?"

"I'm in here!" Sierra shouted from behind the washroom door. "Give me a second!"

Moving down the hall to my left, the sound of the shower filled the space. "Why you showering?!"

"Just got back from work not long ago!"

"But it's past five a.m., so didn't the club close around three?!"

She said something I couldn't make out, so stepped closer to the door. "Say that again?"

Her voice came clearer this time. "I hosted a VIP bachelor party tonight. Club closed at three, but Upper Brass stayed open for the private party."

"So how long you stay after?"

"Party ended, like, an hour after closing—" She paused, catching on. "What's with all these questions?" Then came the callout. "Are you on Designer?"

I ignored the question and walked back to the living room, sinking onto the couch. The shower cut off a moment later, and her voice came sharp from the washroom. "Are you high?!" I leaned back on the couch, eyes on the ceiling and pretending not to hear. The washroom door creaked open. "Oh, so you're avoiding me, huh?" she called down the hall when she didn't see me waiting there.

Stayed quiet, hoping she'd drop it, and instead of coming my way, she went into the bedroom. A slow breath slipped out, one I hadn't realized I was holding, relief washing over at not having to face her yet.

Sierra's pad had the typical open-concept layout of most Toronto condos, where the main entry brought you by the kitchen to the right, or sometimes the left. The living room was straight ahead, with a long dining counter separating it from the kitchen area. Lounging on the sectional leather couch, the glass wall to the balcony was on my right, showing the bright lights of Lakeshore Street and the dark water of the lake under the moonlight. The infamous Toronto skyline used to be part of the glory, but constant construction in the area had new condos now blocking that view.

Vanilla showed up at my feet and hopped onto the couch beside me, her head high like a lioness by her king's side. Chocolate appeared next with his toy in his mouth, ready to play. I kept ignoring him, leaned my head back on the couch, eyes on the ceiling again, thinking about nothing. A space cadet, not noticing the footsteps coming from down the hall until Sierra was already in the kitchen. With the dining counter blocking part of my view, only her upper half could be seen. In a tank top, her devious pretty eyes glancing at me while she moved about the kitchen making drinks.

"What?" I asked her, defensive.

"Why are you so edgy?" She rolled her eyes. "You're obviously high."

"How you mean? You're over there staring at me, so I'm asking what's up?"

"Nothing's up." She smirked. "Is it an issue that I'm looking at you?"

"No, but it's just weird."

"Or you're just too high," she said, coming from the kitchen with a glass of coconut Cîroc on ice in each hand.

She came towards me as I looked her over. Sierra, also known as Skye Icy, was my Persian queen. She had that natural desert tan and stood 5'7" with a video vixen body. The white tank top showed her raw, perky nipples through the fabric, and the black booty shorts hugged her slim waist and curvy hips. The belly piercing caught the light, but her face was the real dime piece, flawless, with the kind of beauty that could rival Kendall Jenner, even without makeup. Her long jet-black hair finished the look. Around her neck was the platinum choker with the ice cream pendant, repping me, her gold cone holding three layers of vanilla-coloured icy scoops. She was levels above the rest in my stable, my bottom bitch.

Sierra shooed Vanilla away to take the spot next to me on the couch and pulled the centre table closer to set the drinks down. Vanilla strutted off in a pissy mood to the other side of the couch to lie down on her own. Chocolate had to move out of the way too. He dropped the toy from his mouth and went to lie next to Vanilla.

Sierra asked me, "How you been?"

"Good, like always."

I picked up my drink and cheered her before we both took a sip. She crossed her legs and looked sassy sipping her drink. I smiled. "I miss you, mami."

She playfully rolled her eyes. "You only miss me when you're on Designer."

"No, that's not true." I moved in for a kiss but got nothing. "So you're just gonna leave me hanging?"

Sierra gently pushed my face away. "I'm sure you got plenty of kisses from all types of girls while partying tonight, so you'll be fine."

Brushed it off and took another sip of my drink. "Anyways, how was your night?"

"Made a bit over three thousand. Most of the cash is in the room, and the rest was e-transfer, so I'll have to send it to your account."

"The VIP party must've been lit."

"It was whatever. Just another night at work." She changed the topic. "What's new with you? I haven't seen you in, like, two days. What you been up to other than getting high?"

"Cut that shit out." She started to annoy me. "I'm high, and what? You got something you wanna get off your chest?"

"Yeah, actually, you're high and I don't like it. You know this." She went on. "Is there ever a night you don't get high and go out wasting money on thousand-dollar bottles? It's like you're losing focus."

"I stay focused," I told her.

"If that were true, then you'd stop going out every weekend, turning up, blowing money recklessly, and using the excuse that you're trying to recruit a new bitch. Like, have you even been saving towards investments for us?"

"I'm always saving towards investments."

"So tell me, what's next for us?"

"Well..."

She always chose this time to interrogate me. Always while I was high. Still, had to give her something solid to get her off my back about how I'd been living lately. "Well, I plan to get a tanning spa business going for Velvet and Diamond. Hopefully in another year—"

"I'm not asking about them, Angelo. I'm asking about us."

"If you'll let me finish talking," I said. "Anyways. I'll own at least forty percent of the tanning business so that we'd be getting a piece of their legit earnings when they're out the game and focused on that business. And then, I'm thinking of buying us a big house that we'll move into. You'll give up your lease here and I'll sell my condo to make a big flip for more money to use towards buying a good franchise company. Then you can come out the game when I breed you up." I smiled at her. "We've held it down together for some solid years, mami, I'm feeling to have you pop out some babies soon."

"Oh, really?" Sierra wasn't convinced. "You've been saying this for over three years now. Tell me, how much do you even have saved up for these plans?"

"I dunno. Maybe a hundred K?"

"You don't even sound sure," she said. "And why is it only a hundred thousand that you have saved up? I know everyone in the stable brings in good money on a regular basis, so shouldn't you have saved a lot more than a hundred after all these years?"

"You forget that y'all bitches be high maintenance with expensive shit, and your bills be high as fuck?"

"Or maybe you just been blowing most of the money on popping bottles and getting high as fuck!" she fired back. "You can't even use us as an excuse, because the money one girl brings in a good week is enough to cover everyone's monthly bills, and could even get her a nice purse on top of that."

"Well, it's not always a good week!"

"Angelo, you got two girls and me, so one of three is more than likely to have a great week, if not two. And there are four weeks in a month before bills show up."

She made her point. But we were both caught off-guard by the sound of growling, and our attention turned to Vanilla, who was annoyed with Chocolate trying to mount her behind. She turned to him and hissed hard, showing her fangs, then swiped at his head with her paw. She held it up and extended her claws to let him know the next swipe would draw blood. Chocolate backed down right away. Sierra and I laughed. That moment helped cool the argument that was starting to heat up between us. Silence settled as we sipped our drinks.

Sierra and I had been together for years, and our relationship was nothing like the usual dynamic of a pimp and his bitch. What we had went deeper than that. Sierra had been by my side through thick and thin, pulling me up during times I'd fallen to my vices. Losing my mother years ago felt like losing a part of myself, so I used drugs and alcohol to mask the pain. All that did was spiral me into another mess of addictions and mental breakdowns. While other bitches left me during moments of weakness, Sierra came into my stable committed to giving me strength, and that made her my bottom bitch. She proved herself true to her word. Sierra's focus went beyond money; she was there for me emotionally, trying to be that woman who mattered, a woman beyond the game. She loved me and understood me for the man I was behind the cloak of an infamous pimp. I confided in her because she was someone I trusted. She knew me better than anyone, my best friend.

This woman had my heart and cared for it right. And because of that, she never accepted or tolerated the addictions that made me weak.

Once promised her I'd only touch Designer-D socially. But lately, she'd been fed up with my nightly runs with the boys, and that's what started most of our arguments. But I hadn't shown up here to fight with her, so leaned over to Sierra for a kiss, my gesture of surrender. She leaned in and met my lips with hers. We shared a long kiss, then pulled back and stared at each other, just happy to have each other.

"Wanna do a line with me?" I asked.

She rolled her eyes. "Sure. I might as well get high too, since I can't even hold a serious conversation with you right now."

I chuckled. "Yeah, good idea."

"I'll get a plate," Sierra said, getting up to head for the kitchen.

Her Brazilian butt lift was a sight, peeking from the bottom of the booty shorts. Her cheeks jiggled with each step, hypnotizing with the sway of her hips. I took off my chain, then struggled a bit to pull off my fitted D&G T-shirt and got comfortable. Topless now, showing my tatted chest piece of detailed Greek gods and skin sleeves of exotic women and creatures. Sierra came back with a clean plate in one hand and the Cîroc bottle in the other. She set both on the centre table and sat back down beside me. We did rails off the plate and drank together.

Having Sierra on a Designer wave with me was comforting. It seemed safe enough to start talking again, so I said, "Would you believe Diamond was out of it again tonight?"

"Not hard to believe at all. It's been happening a lot more lately. But at least Velvet is still straight. Weird how they're besties and always around each other, but they haven't picked up on each other's habits."

"Yeah," I agreed. "You'd think Diamond would learn from Velvet to keep focused when working."

"Actually," Sierra said, "I mean it the other way around. I'm surprised Velvet hasn't picked up on Diamond's bad habits. Whether at home or work, you'd think if one is turning up, then the other would join."

I thought about it then asked, "You think maybe Diamond's becoming worn out in the game?"

"Could be. But she's only been in a tad bit longer than Velvet. They're always around each other, same environment, same energy. If Diamond's turning up a lot because she's worn out, then Velvet should be close enough. But clearly, Velvet's still straight and focused."

"Maybe Diamond's just weaker," I said. "You see, that's why I gotta find a new bitch to fill her spot when she falls out."

"Or maybe your ass should focus on the bitches you already got and realize that the poor girl might be going through something." Sierra looked at me. "Poppa, you need to spend some real one-on-one time with her and figure out what's going on with that girl."

"Why don't you play the big sister role and talk to her, then?"

"No," Sierra said flat. "I think Daddy time's what she needs. And I mean actually spend some days bonding with her. Don't just show up at her place and dick her down thinking that fixes everything." She said it straight. "Over the years it's like you've lost your suave and compassionate ways. Nowadays you just use your dick as your only game for one-on-one Daddy times with these girls."

"And you've been distant from these girls too," I said in my defense. "You don't hang out with the other bitches like you used to years ago. I think you should start bonding with them again. That way they'll open up to you about what's on their mind."

Sierra gave me that unimpressed look. "Isn't that supposed to be your job as the head of the stable?" She smirked. "Or do you wanna swap roles and work at a male club somewhere, turning tricks while I play the pimp and keep this stable intact?"

"Relax!" The idea of me becoming a male stripper irritated me. "I'm just saying you should spend more time with the other girls like you used to."

Sierra replied, "And I'm saying you should stop wasting time and money at nightclubs with your friends and play your position with your girls like you're supposed to."

There was a casual silence, so Sierra reached for the bill and plate to hit more rails. After her lines, she was passing the plate over to me but somehow fumbled it. She caught it before it fell, though some of the dope spilled onto her cleavage. "Shoot!" she said, setting the plate down.

"Wait." I stopped her from going to clean herself up, and said, "Leave it. I'll handle that."

Sierra gave me a sly smile. "Okay, poppa. Clean me up, then."

I leaned in close. Her scent mixed with Designer-D on her skin, pulling me in. I brushed my nose against her and breathed it all in, then used my lips to clean the rest. She liked it, so my lips brushed her skin again, slow and deliberate. And I didn't stop there. My mouth stayed on her cleavage as I tugged her tank top down, letting one full breast spill free. My tongue circled her areola, slow and deliberate, then flicked over her hardened nipple before I drew it between my lips, sucking gently. Sierra's hand slid along my face as her breathing turned heavy. She lifted my head, our eyes locking for a beat before our lips met. Our tongues tangled as she leaned back into the couch. I moved between her open legs, still kissing her while grinding against her. My hand slipped into her shorts and found soft, warm moisture between her thighs. I teased her slowly. Felt her getting wetter under my touch. Then I pushed two fingers inside her, easing them in deep. Our kiss broke when she lost herself to the pleasure, soft moans slipping out as my fingers worked inside her. I left her lips for her neck and took my time, sucking slow like a vampire on warm skin.

Sierra said to me, "Papi, let me do a line off your dick."

I came off her and stood, dropping my pants and boxers to my ankles while Sierra pulled off her tank top, with both round breasts out to play. She kneeled in front of me. She picked the bill up off the floor, then used the card to scoop some designer D from the plate onto my already hard dick. She snorted what she could, then dropped the bill and grabbed my dick, licking off what remained along the shaft. She focused on the head while her hand worked the rest. Sierra tried to take it all into her mouth but only managed two thirds before she started gagging. She looked up at me with a filthy smile, then went back to sucking what she could handle. I would've liked some eye contact from her, but her eyes stayed closed as she slurped and sucked me off, lost in her own pleasure. She enjoyed having my dick in her hands and mouth too, like it belonged to her. My attention drifted to Chocolate and Vanilla, still curled up at their end of the couch, cuddled together and minding their business like they were asleep. What Sierra and I were doing was beyond their understanding of play.

I tilted my head back, closed my eyes, and let myself sink into the sloppy blowjob. I was in no rush. Whatever Sierra and I were about to get into, what was left of the night belonged to us.

CHAPTER FOUR

Saturday, June 9 – 5:33 a.m.

Vanessa preferred working at strip clubs, where the game still held its appeal. The real money came from extras, each dancer setting her own rates. As one of the premium girls under the Icy brand, she was far from cheap. A handjob went for $50 with a condom, a blowjob cost $200, also with protection, and full sex started at $600 for one round within thirty minutes. Gelato set those rates to attract high-end clients, though that often meant older men.

Now one of them was between her legs. Ralph, a sixty-one-year-old Irishman, his once-red hair faded to grey, worked his tongue with the eagerness of a man chasing youth. The sight of his balding head and sagging body made Vanessa's stomach turn. She kept her eyes closed, trying to enjoy it as best she could.

Ralph had paid $500 for five hours of her company and $1200 for two sessions, $1700 in total. She had three hours left to play the charming guest in his home, but the thought of another round drained her. Even with the prestige of being a high-end escort, encounters like this left her feeling stripped of more than clothes. The past two hours with Ralph had been spent drinking, and Vanessa had enough wine in her system to loosen her up for the session. The only part she could stand was his mouth between her legs. She kept her eyes closed, thinking of the man she wished was there instead.

When the oral play finally ended, she opened her eyes to find Ralph's wrinkled face smiling up at her. She gave him a playful smile in return, pretending to look forward to what came next.

Ralph was already naked and on his knees, erection ready, condom in hand, waiting for Vanessa to do her part. The sight of his aged, wrinkled body and sagging gut reminded her what this really was. A client and a prostitute. Even with the status of being a high-end escort, servicing men like him always left her feeling degraded. The only reason she hadn't walked away after countless days and nights of this work was because of the man she did it for, Gelato Icy. He loved her, valued her, and claimed her with pride. She loved him too, and that love kept her in the game.

Ralph waited for her, and Vanessa got on all fours with a soft smile. She took the condom from him, unwrapped it, and used her mouth to roll it on with practiced ease. Then sucked on him with practiced intensity, the way a porn star might. Ralph's snarling moans turned her off completely. The old-man scent, thick and sour, had her fighting the urge to throw up the wine she'd just had. Her eyes stayed closed, blocking it all out and focused on the only thing that could carry her through—her king, Gelato. In her mind, it was his ice cream bar in her mouth. The one man who always felt right. Lost in that thought, she said, "I love your dick, Daddy."

"You suck it so nice," Ralph said in his snarling voice, snapping Vanessa out of her fantasy ice cream world. She stopped and lay on her back, wanting to get it over with. A small motion urged Ralph forward, and a wide smile crept across his face as he moved between her open legs. Vanessa quickly spat on her fingers to lubricate herself, preparing for the unwanted penetration. He entered her and let his weight settle on top. With his face close to hers, he snarled in her ear while moving gently in and out. Vanessa wrapped her arms around him to make him feel wanted, keeping her eyes shut. Her mind drifted elsewhere, focused only on the man she truly desired—Gelato.

When Vanessa joined the game two years ago, she knew it'd mean sleeping with undesirable men. What she hadn't known was whether she could endure it. Her lead teammate, Sierra, once told her, *'You have to own every session with a trick like you're a sex goddess, draining the life and riches out of these mortal men.'* That mindset worked for a while, especially with clients who were at least tolerable. For the dreadful ones, Sierra advised her to think of Gelato. At first, it helped. But over time, each unbearable session chipped away at her dignity, and now, two years later, the Gelato method was losing its hold. No amount of alcohol could loosen her up enough to embrace a session with thoughts of him anymore. How could it, when she saw her clients more often than she saw Gelato himself? Lately, she hadn't seen him at all. Other than his brief stops at the strip club, his presence in her life had faded. It wasn't fair. She missed him, craved his time, his affection. Maybe if she could have more of that, it'd make the game easier to bear. She made a quiet note to tell him how she'd been feeling, hoping he'd still care enough to listen.

For now, Ralph kept humping on top of her, and Vanessa's thoughts of Gelato were no match for the old man's stench and the feel of his damp skin pressed against hers. Nausea crept up, forcing her to switch positions. "Baby, I want you from behind," she said, her voice steady despite the urge to gag.

The doggy-style position allowed her to face away from Ralph's body, sparing her from the full force of his smell. Vanessa added more saliva to herself before he entered from behind. She kept her eyes closed but moaned with seasoned seduction—just enough to arouse Ralph and get him to finish faster. Vanessa focused hard on the thought of her king, Gelato Icy, pounding her from behind, his massive hands gripping her small waist. Her bottom lip drew between her teeth as she slipped deeper into the fantasy, beginning to enjoy the feeling brought on by her longing. She moaned louder, and the man began humping faster with purpose. It was going smoothly until he let out a loud snarl of a moan, snapping Vanessa out of her fantasy and back to the reality of Ralph. The only good news was that he was finished. It was finally over. For now.

Ralph left the room to dispose of the semen-filled condom in the washroom. Vanessa remained on the bed, wondering if he'd have the stamina for a second session. Exhaustion lingered as she hoped he'd be too tired for the night, though it hardly mattered. Ralph was a regular who could afford to see her again, like so many other old men. As long as she stayed in the game, they'd keep coming. Men who saw her as nothing more than a woman with a price. A prostitute. Vanessa wiped away the tear that trickled down her face just as she heard Ralph returning to the bedroom.

GHAD

CHAPTER FIVE

◆

Monday, June 11 – 11:25 a.m.

I spent the whole weekend at Sierra's place, drunk in love and Designer-Doped up. Our only sober moments were waking up in the mid-afternoon to grab something to eat, then going right back to the foggy abyss till night. Sierra missed a busy weekend of work because of it. Nothing a bad-bitch of her standing couldn't make up for on Monday.

My plan today was to spend some quality time with Diamond, like Sierra suggested. Besides, Diamond had texted me Saturday morning apologizing for messing up at work the other night. I appreciated her stepping up, but it wasn't anything major. Diamond was always quick to apologize whenever she slipped up. It was part of her routine now. A problem that needed my attention.

Velvet also called earlier this morning, practically begging to see me tonight since she had the night off. So my first plan was to catch up with both Diamond and Velvet together. But when I called to make arrangements, Velvet was at the salon getting her hair done, and Diamond said she'd be busy with a trick later. So the new plan was to spend the day with Diamond and see Velvet in the evening. Then another call came through from my partner Whitey, who was back in town after being out west for so long. We planned to meet by the lake to catch up before carrying on with the rest of my day.

I pulled up to the lakeside on Marine Parade Drive in my Bentley GT and parked by the nearest meter. Preeme's silver Corvette and Whitey's white Maserati were a few cars ahead. I stepped out in black Jimmy Choo sneakers, Burberry shorts, and a black V-neck. The big bowl of ice cream hanging from my neck glistened under the bright sun. Had on my Breitling watch and a few gold rings, extra diamonds flashing on the left pinky as usual. I dropped some coins into the parking meter, placed the ticket on the Bentley's windshield, and headed across the open grass toward the lake. People were walking their dogs, families had picnics going, and a few couples sat up ahead on the rocky shoreline. The spot my partners and I always chose was deeper near the wooded area, and the weed smell hit me the moment I stepped onto the dirt path into the bushes. There were voices but didn't see anyone at first, so I pushed through the tall shrubs to reach the other side. Standing on the rocks were Preeme and Whitey. They were smoking, not noticing me behind them, the lake splashing at their feet.

"What's good?" I greeted them by surprise. They both turned quick with startled looks, and Preeme pulled a gun off his waist. With my hands up, I said, "Chill out, man," and laughed. "It's just me."

Preeme chuckled. "Fuck you doing?" His words were muffled by the weed blunt between his lips. "You shouldn't be creeping on menz like that, big homie." He shoved the big handgun back on his waist and covered the handle with his shirt. He had on Gucci sneakers, fitted jeans, and a silk button-up shirt. A big maple leaf diamond pendant hung from his neck on a thick gold chain, an icy bracelet on his wrist, and a pinky ring shining. I gave Preeme a brotherly hug and caught the scent of Creed on him, keeping the embrace loose, not trying to trigger that gun on his waist. A firmer hug went to Whitey, who I hadn't seen in forever. "What you dealing with, man?" Couldn't tell what cologne he had on, but the scent carried power and spice.

"Just here, dawg. Bizzack in the big city," Whitey said. "Feels good to be home."

"You been gone for almost a year, right?"

"Yeah, bro. You missed me, eh?"

"Of course, man," I joked. "You my favourite white boy."

Whitey laughed. "Dawg, you frontin' like you ain't half white. We could pass for half-brothers."

We all laughed, and Preeme passed me the blunt, but I waved it off. "Nah, I'm good. You know weed ain't my thing," I said. "I been turnt up all weekend on Designer-D."

"You need to cut back on the Designer-Dope, bruh," Preeme said, handing the blunt over to Whitey.

I told him, "Don't worry 'bout all that. I'm good, man." Then turned to Whitey again. "What's good with you, though? Haven't heard much since you been gone."

"Things are looking good, bro," Whitey said with a grin, taking a long drag from the blunt and exhaling slow. "Things looking real good, bro."

"I can clearly see that," I said, eyeing Whitey. For a thirty-five-year-old Hungarian guy standing 5'9", he carried the urban swag better than most black guys in the city. He rocked a full Puma tracksuit with matching kicks.

No chain, just a thick diamond bracelet on his right wrist, an iced Audemars on his left, and a pinky ring shining. His eyes were ocean blue, his goatee dirty blonde. The sides of his head were shaved clean, the top gelled back into a ponytail that hung to his shoulders.

He said, "I been getting shit right out west, dawg."

"Shit must be more than right by now," I said. "You been going out there with your girls for years. This time you been gone almost a year straight. You must be doing more than pimping."

Whitey took another pull on the blunt and passed it to Preeme, then blew out a thick cloud of smoke. "I started a massage parlour in Calgary. That's what I been building these past few years, and it's officially up and running now."

"No way!" Whitey flipping his game into something legit caught me by surprise. "You serious, man? You telling me you pimping legally now?"

Preeme laughed. "I couldn't believe it when he told me, too."

"Dead serious," Whitey confirmed. "Been running about four months now. Got Chanel holding it down. She already got over twenty girls on schedule."

"So you telling me you got over twenty bitches legally hoeing for you in a spa out in Alberta right now?" I asked, impressed.

Whitey grinned. "C'mon, dawg. Legally speaking, I run a business with many masseuses who give thirty-minute full-body therapy sessions for a hundred a client. Forty percent goes to whichever girl does the service. Anything else behind closed doors ain't nothing Chanel or I know about. We just glad to be running a legitimate spa with gorgeous masseuses."

Preeme laughed, "Sounds like some serious pimpin' going on under corporate covers."

We all laughed, and I asked Whitey, "So Coco fully out the game now and managing the spa, huh?"

"Yessir. She bossed up now fo' real."

I was happy to hear that Whitey's bottom bitch for twelve years, a Filipino chick named Chanel, or Coco, was out the game and running the legal spa with him. That was something I'd like to do with Sierra someday. Impressive how Whitey had been working on this quietly for years, and with dedication, he made it happen. A pimp turned legal and recognized by the government as a tax-paying businessman. That was motivation for me.

I asked, "So, what's the spa called?"

"Consational."

Preeme caught it quick. "Coco's name and sensational in one word." He took a long pull on the blunt.

Whitey nodded. "Y'all don't hesitate to send your girls to work there when they're out west. I get high-end clients passing through regular. The girls be milking them at premium rates, easy. It gets so busy that they don't even bother trying to steal clients to see them outside the spa. Everyone's happy with the setup."

"Yeah, I'ma have Crystal check it out when she does her run out west. Most likely this winter," Preeme said, passing what was left of the blunt to Whitey.

We went quiet, taking in the sound of waves splashing against the rocks. I pulled out my phone and snapped a pic of the lake with the CN Tower skyline in the distance. I posted it on Snapchat with the caption: *This Moment Right Here.* Sitting there with my partners in the game, I felt that moment. One of us had elevated to new levels. It happened to be the white boy, the one everyone figured would flip the game legal first anyway. But it meant something to us because he was our brother in the game. A game we played with heart and dedication.

Whitey grew up in Toronto with his uncle and aunt after both his parents died back in Hungary. His grandma sent him and his siblings to Canada when he was nine. His uncle was in a Hamilton biker gang, so Whitey was raised in a home where crime paid the bills. He was a smart kid who took the street route early, selling drugs through his teens before stepping into pimping at nineteen.

We met when I was twenty-two and he was twenty-four. I had one of my old girls working out of a hotel near Pearson Airport, booking tricks from online ads. I was at the hotel bar waiting for her to finish when Whitey sat beside me. We got to talking, and it turned out he had a girl working upstairs too. I never cared much for the few white pimps I'd met in the game, but Whitey's swag and energy reeked of live ism. He was solid. We vibed quick, and by the end of that night our girls finished work at the same time so we could all party at a downtown nightclub. That's where Whitey became my guy. Days later, I introduced him to Smooth and young Preeme, and he became part of our circle.

For some reason, Asian and Black girls, usually the light-skinned ones, always loved Whitey. His game was more structured than most. He worked with incalloutcall escorts and ran his stable like an agency. The bottom bitch acted as the receptionist, handling all calls and texts from the girls' online ads. Whitey kept things professional, avoiding girls with too much emotional baggage. Instead of taking all their earnings like most pimps, he worked on a percentage basis. Coco, his bottom bitch, was the only one he went all-in with. The rest stayed on the split. He preferred escorts over strippers and always played the game straightforward, never shying away from calling it what it was—the sex trade. That was how he kept it real and ran his pimping for years.

My mind came back to the moment on the rocky shoreline with Preeme and Whitey. Both their eyes were glossy red, and Whitey flicked the last bit of the blunt into the water. I asked, "Y'all heard from Smooth today?"

Whitey replied, "I spoke with him in the morning. I wanted to meet here with him too, but he says he's out in Niagara."

"He knows about Consational?"

"Yessir. Told him about it on the phone since he couldn't be here to hear about it. Says he got bitches in Alberta right now, so he gonna have them check it out sometime when work in the telly and club is slow. My spa stays busy all week."

I was sincerely happy for Whitey, proud even, thinking how far he'd come and how solid his move was out west. Before I could sit with the thought, my phone rang. I pulled it from my pocket and saw the caller was Maria. Some girl I'd just met at the club the other night. I answered, "What's good?"

Maria's soft voice came smooth through the line. "Hey, what's up with you? I sent you a couple messages last night. Didn't you get them?"

"Yeah, I saw the text. Was gonna hit you back but got caught up with some things."

"Oh, okay." She asked, "So what you doing tonight?"

"Might be caught up with something again. Why, what's up?"

"Nothing really. Just wanted to follow up after meeting you the other night. But if you're too busy then it's okay. Sorry for bothering you."

"Nah, cutie, you ain't bothering me."

There was a pause. Then Maria spoke, "So am I gonna get to see you again? Because I don't see the point in keeping your number if we don't plan to follow up or anything."

"Chill out, cutie. You ain't gotta do all that," I said. "Hold on a second, let me think."

A moment was needed to reflect on my plans for the day, to see where I could squeeze Maria in. I for sure couldn't cancel tonight with Velvet since she had practically begged to see me. That left the other option of bailing out on Diamond for the day. I said to Maria, "You could be ready in thirty minutes?"

"Woah. Thirty minutes is kinda rushed, don't you think?"

"Were you not just about to delete my number if I didn't make time for you?"

Maria laughed then said, "Okay, so where we going?"

"We'll go for lunch."

"I could be ready in an hour."

"Text me where I'll be picking you up from," I said. "I'll text once I'm on my way in about thirty minutes. Then you'll have another thirty to be fully ready when I arrive."

"You're so calculative and assertive." Maria giggled. "But okay. I'll be ready, boss."

A smile came to my face that Maria couldn't see, and I said, "I'll see you soon, cutie."

"Okay. I'll text my address now. Bye." She ended the call.

Whitey smirked and asked, "What chick got you big headed?"

"Some bitch I met at the nightclub on Friday."

"She down to get live?"

"I don't even know, man. But we gon' find out in an hour." I was still smiling.

"I'll never trust any bitch from the city. They dangerous," Preeme said, and I already knew why, remembering his story with Tanya. I had another question for him instead. "You got a bounce on you?"

"Bruh, didn't you just grab a bounce on Friday?"

"Why you studying me like I'm asking for free shit or something?" I shot back. "Is there a limit on how much Designer one person could buy in a week or some shit?"

Preeme chuckled. "It ain't even about that, big homie. Just hoping you ain't grabbing all that to turn up on again. For real, that's a lot, bruh."

"Chill. I didn't turn-up on all that from Friday. There was some left. I gave it to Sisi to take with her to see her trick today," I explained, then got defensive. "Even if I'm turning up a lot, don't be watching me, man. Focus on yourself."

"Whatever you say, big homie. I'm just saying, it don't look right that you getting saucy in all that dope glamour. Only your bitches should be doing that when they with their turn-up tricks."

"He's right," Whitey added. "We getting older, dawg. We all need to cut back on the turning-up."

"We?!" Preeme cut in. "Menz better miss me with that talk. I ain't ever fuck with that shit. So don't be saying *we*." He said, "I'm good with just smoking my gas."

"Man, send me the bounce and let me get going," I cut in, tired of the talk. "I gotta pull up on this Maria bitch and see what she tryna get into."

Preeme replied, "I got nothing on me. I'ma have to deal with you in my car."

"Okay, so you leaving now too?"

"Nah. But I'ma deal with you then circle back here to smoke another one with Whitey."

"Okay, cool."

"A'ight," Whitey said to me, "I'll see you again before I fly back out. I'ma be around a couple more days to figure out how to ship my Mazi out to Calgary."

"Wait, you relocating out there completely?" Knew Whitey had bought a place in Calgary a year back, but never thought he'd close his chapter in Toronto. "So you selling your spot in Liberty Village too?"

"Nah, not doing that. We gonna list it on AirBnB when we staying out in Calgary so that me and Coco still have a home whenever we come back here. Only shipping out my Mazi and her Jag to Calgary because that's basically our primary home now. We'll just rent cars whenever we staying down here."

"Okay, that makes sense."

"Yeah, so we'll all link up a couple more times before I leave again."

"Okay, sounds good." I pulled Whitey in for a brotherly hug before walking off with Preeme.

CHAPTER SIX

Monday, June 11 – 12:04 p.m.

"Fuck me harder," Sierra moaned.

Heat rolled off the man on top of her, his body already worked up as he lay between her open legs, humping away. Her arousing request pushed him over the edge, driving him to pound into her harder with punishing authority. Sierra only played the part, letting the man believe she enjoyed the sex as much as he did, and now the role was giving her more than she'd bargained for. The relentless pounding pressed past pleasure and into pain. Being a sex Goddess meant Sierra always knew how to regain sexual dominance, so the solution came to her quickly. She pulled the man closer and wrapped her legs around his waist, limiting the space he needed for those hard, driving thrusts. The shift gave the man the impression that her desire for him was the reason she drew him closer. A slow kiss landed on his sweaty neck, and his strokes softened inside her. Relief spread through Sierra as the pressure eased, creating the perfect moment for controlled Kegel grips. Her inner walls tightened around his penis, giving him more pleasure and turning the act into something he read as pure desire rather than strategy.

"*Ouuu...baby,*" Sierra moaned softly. "I love how your dick feels inside me."

The man replied with a howling moan of his own as he finished, loading into the condom inside her. Sierra continued doing Kegels, ensuring he enjoyed every bit of the pulsing sensation at his climax, to the very end where she felt him going limp.

He let out a deep breath as his weight settled on her, then he whispered in her ear, ""You're so amazing."

Sierra responded with a light kiss on his cheek.

At thirty-six years old, Benjamin owned a few car dealerships passed down through his family's fortune. Standing at 5'6" and weighing 200 pounds of flabby fat that sat mostly around his gut, with a huge nose centred between bulging eyes and a thinning mop of hair, he knew his money was the only reason a woman as gorgeous as Sierra would look at him with any interest. After meeting her at the strip club last week, he arranged a late breakfast today, prepared by personal cooks at his mansion in Ancaster, Hamilton.

Sierra's sassy game was beyond anything Benjamin had ever experienced with a high-end escort. He paid $450 for three hours of her company, just eating and socializing, and Sierra negotiated $1000 from him for the one sexual encounter he had just enjoyed. Before the bedroom, she had him savouring every moment of their social time just as much as the sex, helped by her impressive social skills that allowed her to slip into effortless, natural conversation. The warmth in her demeanour had Benjamin convinced she might have been genuinely interested in him, as if the two of them had met under different circumstances and their date was something fuelled by mutual attraction. The experience pleased him so much that he gladly tipped Sierra an extra $550.

Sierra went to the room's massive washroom with all her belongings and freshened up quickly in the shower. She came back out fully clothed in the bright Flavia Maxi dress she had arrived in, a piece that complemented her tanned skin and hugged her incredible body. Her Birkin bag was already in hand, and she was ready to leave Benjamin behind in the big mansion. Still, Sierra understood the importance of leaving the right impression with a wealthy client, so her goodbye carried a flirtatious edge. She kissed Benjamin on the lips and placed her hand across his hairy chest before slipping away, leaving him standing alone in his robe at the mansion's main foyer.

"I'll try to see you again this week," Benjamin called after Sierra.

"Anytime, hun. Just give me at least a day's notice," she said over her shoulder.

"I'll let you know by Wednesday for sure," he added. "I'll call or message you."

At this point, separation anxiety had taken hold of Benjamin, which Sierra found cute in a way. Yet she knew her job was done and had to leave. No glance was given back as she chucked the deuces. "I think you should go inside and get yourself together before your wife comes back from her trip."

Once outside, the mansion's large front doors closed behind her while she descended the stone steps surrounded by the beautiful garden. Her white CL Benz coupe waited in the roundabout that circled an angelic fountain. Sierra slid into the driver's seat, reached for the Cartier glasses inside her Birkin bag, and set them on her flawlessly dolled face. Inside her bag, the little baggie of cocaine that Gelato had left with her caught her eye, and relief washed through her that Benjamin hadn't asked to party this early in the day. Clients who avoided that request were always her preference. She hated the fog that came with getting high, especially when it meant dealing with a client who was even more awkward once he was gone off it.

The Chris Brown playlist connected through the Bluetooth, and Sierra put the Benz into gear before driving towards the front gates to leave Benjamin's estate. Music bumped through the speakers while the drive stretched toward her condo an hour away, the routine already forming in her mind—a gym session, a shower, then a quiet moment to reset before making a killing at the strip club for the night. Sierra was a true breadwinner in the game and she knew it. She'd started her day with a gourmet breakfast and worked $2000 out of the entire ordeal like a real bad-bitch.

Control was what she loved most about the game, especially the way she could finesse men who believed their riches made them powerful. And to think, she once wanted to finish school, pursue a career in business, and work for men like Benjamin, believing that was the best way for a woman in society to earn a good income. But that was many years ago. Eight years since Sierra met Angelo, and the life she once lived had changed completely. She was nearly finished with her second year of Business Marketing when she met her prince charming the day after her 19th birthday, May 14, 2010, at a pub night celebrating with some college friends.

Angelo and his friends from Toronto were in town partying as well, and it felt like a gift from the Universe to cross paths with him that night.

Sierra was raised in a small town near Waterloo and had never been to Toronto or met such vibrant people from the infamous city. Everything about Angelo felt like a glamorous urban movie and she wanted to be part of it. A handsome man with a warm personality, he was someone she trusted easily. There were no second thoughts the next day when she cut class to see how his movie-like life continued in the major city. Angelo kept it real and upfront about his lifestyle in the game, which allowed Sierra to appreciate the truth of what she'd be stepping into if she chose to be with him, a pimp. Yet the game wasn't what people depicted it to be. It was different and surprisingly alluring. Society painted it as filthy, but Angelo drew it out in a way that made the lifestyle seem tasteful and almost sensible.

Sierra got down with the game not just for the money and luxury that came with it, but for the promising idea that as long as she stayed true to Angelo, he'd be hers forever. Angelo also made it clear that she'd be sharing him with the other girls in the stable, a new reality that demanded an adjustment of both her mind and her heart. Even so, being part of a family with other girls helped her feel more comfortable with her decision to get down with the uncanny program. From then on, Sierra was determined to become the baddest in the stable, carrying the mindset of someday earning the bottom bitch title.

In the early stages of her new life, Sierra sometimes thought about her family back in the small town she had left behind. Long before Angelo entered her life, she'd been living in a broken home filled with tension and unresolved issues. Before Sierra moved out to live on campus in Waterloo with OSAP support, her parents had divorced because her father had married another woman back in Iran. Her relationship with him had always been distant. He worked constantly to provide for the family, yet Sierra knew he loved her and her younger brothers. Her father kept a roof over their heads, food on the table, and clothes on their backs. The divorce was simply an issue between her parents, something she understood without attaching emotion to it. Sierra couldn't bring herself to blame him for leaving, especially knowing how difficult her mother could be. Being the eldest and only daughter often put Sierra in the woman's path. Comments about ageing and beauty sharpened the tension, feeding Sierra's belief that her mother envied her youth. The former beauty queen, frustrated that her best days were behind her, took those frustrations out on Sierra while the younger brothers got away with everything.

Campus living became Sierra's escape. Her father had disappeared, her brothers were getting arrested often, and her mother was slipping further into instability. Curriculum breaks filled her with dread because they meant returning to that house. One summer, her mother's anger escalated until it turned physical. By the end of her second year of college, Sierra faced another summer at home, but then her prince charming, Angelo, arrived and pulled her away. She never returned to Waterloo or her hometown after that.

Memories of her younger brothers came and went. They had been young when she left for good, and she hoped they'd straighten out as they grew older. Sometimes the thought of checking in on them crossed her mind, but not now, not while she was navigating her own responsibilities in the underworld.

As for her mother, the woman made a few attempts to stay in touch during the early months after Sierra left. Calls came in asking about her safety, but those efforts faded once Sierra made it clear she had no intention of finishing college. Sierra believed there was no point in wasting more years in school when other, faster ways existed to reach the finer things in life. Her mother may have eventually heard the rumours in Waterloo that Sierra had left for Toronto with a pimp and was up to no good, but Sierra could care less.

Her past life mattered even less now, after years of establishing herself as one of the baddest women representing her lover, Angelo, the infamous Gelato Icy. She was Skye Icy now, the bottom bitch in a stable of premium bad-bitches.

CHAPTER SEVEN

Monday, June 11 – 1:28 p.m.

I called Diamond to cancel our plans for the day, told her there'd been a change without giving any real reason. She didn't seem bothered even though she hadn't had quality time with me in over a month. And this wasn't the first time I'd cancelled on her, so the guilt sat heavy. Tried telling her to skip work tonight and join Velvet and me for a trio night, but she didn't think cancelling on her trick was a good idea. She had an overnight lined up with one of her loyal regulars at 6 p.m., dinner at some expensive restaurant included, so she wasn't about to bail last minute. Fair enough. Nothing less than a grand would come from the overnight anyway, plus another six hundred depending on how many times they fucked for the night.

I carried on with my day, pulling up to a condo in Scarborough with the Bentley's top down. Maria came out in cute Louis Vuitton flats, tight jeans, a cropped Louis Vuitton shirt that couldn't button all the way up because of her huge breasts, and a Louis Vuitton purse in hand. At twenty-three she stood at 5'6", weighing around 135 pounds. Her curly dark hair framed a pretty Latina face and a Marilyn mole. Once she got in, I took in her beauty, and all she had for me was, "You're kinda cute."

We rode around looking for a good lunch spot. Most of the ride was spent dealing with her excitement over rolling in a Bentley. It was her first time. And it would be her last if she didn't cut the social media nonsense. First she begged me to put the top up just so she could drop it again at a red light for Instagram. I did it once. Then she tried getting me in one of her videos. I refused and warned her to put her phone away or our day would end right there.

A patio table at Earl's Bar and Restaurant was where the ride brought us. I ordered steak with a beer and Maria got fish tacos with wine.

"So," I said, "You're tryna tell me you're a bartender and that's how you getting your bread?"

"Mmhmm…" she replied with a mouthful.

Didn't buy it. "I never knew bartending money could afford condos."

Maria swallowed before answering. "I don't own it. I'm renting."

"Oh, okay." I cut into the steak.

Maria sipped her wine, then asked, "So are you gonna tell me how you got yourself a Bentley?"

"I work hard. With horses," I said. "Fine mares."

"Oh, wow. You breed horses?"

I chuckled. She clearly didn't catch my drift. "Nah, haven't bred any of them yet."

"So do you race them?"

"They're not in the type of race you're thinking."

She rolled her eyes. "Okay, can you just keep it real and tell me what it is that you do?"

Took a sip of beer and smiled at her. "I'll keep it real when you keep it real with me."

"How am I not being real with you?"

"You telling me bullshit 'bout you living lavish on bartender money," I said, stuffing my mouth with more steak.

"Bartenders make good tips," Maria said. "Renting a condo and having expensive things don't mean I'm living lavish."

"What's lavish to you, then?"

"A Bentley."

"You got a car?"

"Nope." She took another bite of her taco.

"Interesting. So, you got designer bags and clothes but no transportation to get you to and from your full-time bartending job?"

Maria laughed it off. "Like, why are you investigating my life?"

"Because it don't make sense."

"You don't make sense," she shot back playfully.

"I make money."

"So do I," she replied.

"So keep it one hundred like a brown bill and don't be dropping me brown shit." I ate another piece of steak.

She paused before saying, "Why don't you just tell me what you think I do?"

I washed down the food with beer and got to it. "I think you tend to a lot more than the bar for your tips."

"What exactly do you mean by that?"

"I think you be turning tricks for the tips."

"Well, that doesn't mean I can't still have a legit bartending job too." She didn't deny it. Then she thought for a moment and said, "But why are you so interested in how I'm getting my money? Seriously, why does that matter so much to you?"

"Listen here carefully, cutie." I dropped my knife and fork and sat back, settling into my live element. "If you turning tricks, then I can't be entertaining your shit unless you down with paying me the chips. How you getting your bread could either be a conflict between us or a common interest."

Maria took a sip of wine but kept her eyes locked on me. "What do you mean by that?"

"I'm live, baby."

She took another sip, nerves showing in the way her hand tightened on the glass. "I still don't get what that means."

"It means if you turning tricks, you in the game. And if you ain't in the game with me, you not someone I entertain. This could be our first and last outing."

"What if I was legit only working a bartending job and didn't see tricks?"

"Then you'd be a square. And I'd be cool teaching you the game myself. I'd put in the time to turn your life in my direction."

"Hmm..." Maria narrowed her eyes at me. "So you're a pimp?"

I leaned back, relaxed and in control. "Live, EA Sports. We in the game."

She twirled her wine, thinking hard. "What if I don't want to be in the game with you? We can't just be friends?"

"A solo bitch in the game is a flake-ass hoe. And I don't fuck with flakes."

"Ok…but what if I already got a man?"

"A man or a pimp? Two different things. Which one you talking about?"

"Well…I have a guy I'm working with in the game, but he's definitely not my pimp."

"He popcorn simpin' on you if he ain't claiming the title. But answer this—if you got a pimp already, why you here sitting across from me?"

Maria set her wine down and crossed her arms, eyes dropping from mine like she knew she was cornered. Meanwhile, I was close to leaving the table. She either got real with me or she got left.

"Okay…so," she finally admitted, "I used to bartend at a restaurant, and some older men would ask me to go on dates and back to their place for good money. I got scared going alone, so I'd give the address to some guy I knew, and he'd stay close by."

"What guy?"

"Just someone I was talking to. Not a pimp."

"What's his name? And what exactly does he do?"

"His name is Marvin. He's a dope dealer known as Marvel," she said, then carried on. "Anyways…it was Marvel who told me to post online to find more clients. And that's how I got in the game three months ago, doing outcalls. I quit my job and started taking tricks full-time. Now I check into hotels for a couple days taking incalls, and Marvel comes by sometimes to make sure I'm good."

I nodded. "That basically means you're in the game with this Marvel guy."

"Yeah, I guess, kinda." Maria took a sip of wine. "But I post my own ads and do everything myself. He doesn't know much about the game. I'm only still with him because I'm scared of pimps."

"Scared of pimps?" I wasn't sure if I heard her right.

"Yeah. I'm scared of pimps."

It made no sense. "How you scared of pimps but got this Marvel guy rolling with you like one? Even though he's really just a simp."

"I'm scared of real pimps." She tried to explain. "Marvel told me stories of solo girls getting robbed, faces cut open, kidnapped, raped, all types of shit by serious pimps. That's why I stay working with Marvel, so that I'm not a solo bitch on the radar."

I had to laugh. "Sounds like that popcorn-simpin' dude is just a shade-tree."

Maria frowned. "What's a simp, anyways? And a shade-tree?"

"A simple-ass guy trying to be a pimp. And a shade-tree is that simp-ass dude you hiding under for cover, making it seem like you really got a pimp."

"Well, yeah. I was afraid that if real pimps, like you, found me in the game and I didn't have a man around, I'd be in trouble."

I chuckled. "And what makes you think I'm one of the real pimps you gotta be afraid of?"

"Because I heard about you, Gelato. You and your friends are big pimps. Everyone in the city knows that. Especially that pimp in your circle that kills his girls. Isn't his name Prime, Promo, Perimeter, or something like that?"

"Preeme," I corrected her and chuckled. "He's not out here killing bitches. That's just bullshit people be spreading."

"Well, there's a lot of stories on him. I hear he's really crazy."

I steered the topic back on track. "Never mind all that. But listen. Everything you're saying doesn't make sense." Couldn't understand this girl's logic. "If you knew I'm a real pimp you're supposedly scared of, then why'd you give me your number and now sitting here with me?"

Maria blushed, shy with her answer. "I heard about you and creeped your Instagram before, but Friday night was my first time seeing you in person. I thought you were really cute. Then when you invited me and my girls into your booth, you were very friendly and cool. Nothing like the big scary pimp I thought you'd be."

I took the compliment in silence, finished the last cold piece of steak, washed it down with beer, then looked at her with a smile. "So what you want from me?"

"I honestly don't even know." Maria stared at the last piece of taco, then looked up and smiled too. "Could you get me a Bentley?"

I laughed. "I dunno if you're ready for all that." Then got serious. "You feeling to choose-up and pay the fee to get down with me?"

"Maybe. But I don't have a lot of money to pay you any type of fee. Marvel takes all the money I make."

"And what does he do with it?"

"He makes sure my rent and bills are paid. And takes care of me, somewhat."

"Sounds like he doing what he supposed to be doing, then."

"Yeah," Maria said, but she didn't look happy. "I think he has another girl, though."

"What's wrong with that? That's part of the game. The dude tryna grow his stable."

"It's a girl that doesn't work in the game. She's a square," Maria clarified. "He uses my money to take care of her, too."

"Oh. Well, now, that's some sucka-shit."

"Yeah, tell me about it." Maria went on, venting everything. "He always made me think he wasn't a pimp and more like my man. Always telling me stories about how there are scary real pimps out there that would come for me if we broke up. But he takes my money, controls me, and always puts his hands on me when he gets mad. That's basically all the shit pimps do, so I don't know why I'm still with him when he's behaving just like the real pimps—"

I cut her off. "Cutie, that Marvel character sounds like a cartoon and nothing like a real pimp. The dude been brainwashing you and ain't even being true to the game. He shouldn't have a square girlfriend on the side while you in the game turning tricks, only for him to buss the bread down with some square bitch. That's some sucka-shit. He telling you bullshit about real pimps just to keep you scared and stuck with him. But really, he probably knows you'd do just fine with a real live pimp."

"Yeah...I think so, too." Maria smiled. "You don't seem scary at all."

"Believe it or not, I never kidnapped a bitch in my life."

"Really?" She looked surprised.

"Dead serious. What the fuck am I doing that for? Every pimp deals with flake-ass hoes differently. The most I'd do is knock out a flake-ass hoe if she in the strip club getting between my bitch's bread. But I'm not out here looking for these flakies. Especially not to cut up their faces and all that crazy shit. Maybe some next pimps into all that, but they prob' just some savage cats who ain't got much going on in the game. I just be focused on being true to my game and keeping my stable strong."

She listened, so I explained further. "For example, I don't entertain a square bitch who ain't tryna be down with my stable because that's disrespectful to myself and my stable. That sucka-shit is not familiar and only leads to failure."

"Makes sense." Maria giggled. "I now know why you said you work with mares." She sipped more wine and gave me that smile. "Well, I'm glad I got to meet a real pimp. A good one."

"That's the whole point of the term *choosing-up*. Every bitch has the right to choose the pimp she feels comfortable with."

"So what happens if I choose you?"

"First thing, I give Marvel a call and serve his simp-ass."

"Serve him?" she asked. "What does that mean?"

"Gotta make it clear to him that you're moving on with me."

"What's the point of that? He's only gonna get mad."

"He gon' feel a way, of course, but that's how the game goes." I added, "Even though I feel like this Marvel character is nothing close to a pimp and probably wouldn't respect a serving, I still gotta stay true to the rules of the game."

Maria hesitated. "How 'bout I just disappear with you one day and he doesn't need to know?"

"Nah," I refused. "I'm not a sucka-playa."

"Okay. But I don't know how he'd handle this."

"Don't worry about all that," I assured her. "Leave it to me. You just focus on putting together some racks for the choose-up fee." A waiter passed and I signalled her for another beer. Maria finished her wine quick, and the waiter knew to bring her another glass too.

"Do I really have to pay a fee to get with you?"

"Yeah."

"But how am I supposed to save up a couple racks when Marvel shows up every night to collect all the money?" She paused, thinking. "I mean, I guess I could lie about the amount I make some nights and put that to the side for you."

"Do what you gotta do, cutie. I'll be looking forward to five thousand."

"Wow. That's a lot." She was wide-eyed. "So every girl has to pay five thousand dollars upfront before getting with you?"

"Yup, any bitch already in the game who knows of me. If she knows me then she knows my worth. I usually ask for ten to twenty thousand, but you getting a big discount because I feel you and you my type." The waiter brought our drinks and cleared the table. I drank some beer, then looked at Maria. A blush crept across her face.

She asked, "So what makes me your type?"

We carried on our date, flirting and getting to know each other on a more personal level. If Maria was a square girl, the date might've had this vibe the whole time. But from the beginning, it was clear she was in the game. That was why the pimpin' had to get laid down early.

CHAPTER EIGHT

Monday, June 11 – 9:11 p.m.

After lunch with Maria, I dropped her home. She looked disappointed that I wasn't coming upstairs for more drinks. Her eyes said it all. She wanted to get dicked down, but that was never happening for free. Not with a girl already in the game. She could talk about choosing-up all she wanted, but she wasn't getting a taste of this ice cream until the fee was paid.

In a city full of big pimps, my name stood as one of the major brands, so a choosing fee was necessary. Too many girls left their weak-ass pimps chasing hype and status, hoping to jump to a name-brand stable without proving a thing. The fee kept the choosy-Suzy types away. The only time I waived a fee was when I really wanted a girl on my team, because she was too bad to pass up. Turning out a square who knew nothing about the game was the other exception. Maria was somewhere in the middle. Fairly new to the game, and she was the type of girl I would've pursued on my own. That was why she got the discount she did. But I needed a fee from her to prove she was serious about leaving that simp and stepping into my world for real. Good chemistry at a lunch table wasn't enough to earn a place in my stable.

I spent the rest of the day cruising the city with Preeme and Whitey before heading to Mississauga for the night. Velvet and Diamond lived in the same building, the twin Marilyn Monroes. Two tall curving condos shaped like cola bottles. I Took the elevator up to Diamond's pad on the 43rd floor first. Every bitch in my stable had a hidden safe in her bedroom where she stacked nightly earnings when it wasn't e-transfer. Only necessities were allowed to come out before the money reached me, whether groceries, getting their nails or hair done, or whatever basic needs made sense. Everything else was covered by me. And since I'd been distant on Daddy-time with Diamond and Velvet lately, slipping into their pads to hit the safe kept things smooth and avoided questions I wasn't tryna answer yet.

Diamond's safe came through with $4980, a decent haul for the weekend. Then it was down to the 35th floor, to Velvet's pad. No creeping there. She was expecting me.

The layout of Velvet's place was identical to Diamond's and furnished the same way. A small kitchen sat to the left when stepping in, and a hall to the right led to the bedroom and washroom. The living room up ahead was huge. Its left wall separated the kitchen, curving into a dining area by the balcony. The glass wall along the balcony stretched wide, wrapping around the dining and living room, with the curved balcony extending toward the bedroom side.

Velvet had made shrimp Alfredo pasta, so we sat down to eat when I arrived an hour ago. She decided to freshen up while I kicked back on the couch. The Burberry shorts stayed on, but the shirt and chain came off so I could relax in just a wife beater. A tequila bottle and a plate of Designer-D lines waited on the side table. Velvet had asked me not to start the party without her.

This was her Daddy-time, and she wanted every moment to count. To pass time, I replied to a few messages from Maria. She had been blowing up my Snapchat ever since I dropped her home, asking questions and trying to stay in conversation. I hit her back here and there, nothing serious. She wasn't getting my full attention until she paid the choose-up fee and earned the right to be upgraded to real access. And whatever little back-and-forth we had would end the second Velvet came out ready.

When the shuffling in the bedroom stopped, Velvet came out with her wet and wavy brunette hair tied in a ponytail. Her pretty face was lightly made up, the diamond in her nose ring catching the light. A tank top struggled to contain her D-sized breasts, her perky nipples showing through. Grey yoga tights framed her petite booty, and the small ice cream choker on her neck represented me as always. Velvet poured two shots and passed me one. We took them, set the glasses aside, and she slid onto the couch beside me with the Designer plate in hand.

"Okay, Daddy, it's time to turn-up," she said with a grin, and we got into the rails.

I couldn't remember the last time we were together like this, but tonight was something we both needed. I missed my hot little Italian-Caribbean babe, and she definitely missed me too. Earlier, while we were eating at the dining table, Velvet told me how she'd been feeling. She missed me and was upset that she hadn't spent time with me in over a month. Things had changed from how I used to make time for her at the beginning of our relationship. We used to have movie nights, fancy dinners, vacations, and sometimes blended her and Diamond's time with me into trio days and nights. That was all at the start. Spending time together eventually settled into a weekly thing, and was still something she always looked forward to. But over the past few months, everything shifted. I had only seen her once every two weeks, if she was lucky. And now she hadn't seen me for a month. Velvet feared that, over time, she wouldn't be seeing me at all. That wouldn't work for either of us. She only got into the game to be with me, and not having time with me was starting to discourage her from continuing in the game.

Vanessa came from a wealthy family in Oakville, and outside of me she had no reason to be in the game. She was a student at Ryerson University when we met in the Eaton Centre Mall food court. I approached her with the right swag, said what needed to be said, and kept her intrigued. Once she learned about my lifestyle, I told her straight that we couldn't keep seeing each other unless she got down with me in the game. Her young and vibrant attitude made her open to trying something new, so she stepped onto the program.

Being the spoiled rich girl with no filter, Vanessa told her parents the raw truth about dropping out of school to be with me, along with a watered-down version of how she'd be working in strip clubs. Her Italian mother fainted on the spot. Then her Italian-Caribbean father kicked her out of their mansion with threats to hire a hitman if she ever used the family name while stripping. There were rumors of a second hitman lined up for me, but I never gave it much thought. Couldn't imagine the proud, legitimate businessman risking everything on a murder charge. He was better off accepting the loss of his daughter to a pimp. Which he eventually did.

Vanessa had been mine as Velvet since then. She was the perfect addition, a brunette Barbie doll in my stable. After six months together she went from a B-cup to a D-cup, fitted to the look I wanted for her. And the love I had for her stayed the same through those two years. So when she opened up during dinner tonight, I actually listened. Her concerns made sense. I promised to be more attentive and more available with love and affection. Saying she'd see me daily would've been a lie, but meeting once a week was something I could guarantee.

Tonight was about us. We killed half the tequila bottle and nosedived a ski slope of Designer-Dope. Velvet's bubbly personality always came with down-to-earth jokes, sarcasm, and her flirtatious ways. She was in her comfort zone, finally with the man she'd been waiting a month to feel again. Clothes still on, she lay on top of me on the couch, her chin resting on my chest as she looked up at me. I stared back into her green eyes and gave a groggy smile.

"Eww, you're ugly," she joked.

I stuck my tongue out at her, and she sprang forward like she meant to bite it.

I scoffed. "You were really gonna bite off my tongue?"

"Maybe, or maybe not." She giggled. "You should've left it out to find out."

"Nah, you're crazy."

"Crazy for you." Velvet pressed her soft lips to mine.

We kissed gently with our eyes closed, and our tongues slow danced. She sat up to take off her tank top, then came back down and eased herself upward until her perky nipples met my lips. Velvet splayed her boobs across my face. With her tits in my mouth and something else on my mind, my hand slid down her tights. She had no panties on. Her light moans told me she loved how my fingers met her moist pussy. I peeled off her tights and she moved with me to get them all the way off. She stayed sitting up on me, naked now, and helped me roll off my wife beater. Velvet then slid off me and impatiently pulled off my shorts and boxer briefs. I sat up properly on the couch while she kneeled in front of me, ready to suck me off. Velvet grabbed on like a slut who'd been starving for dick. After a few seconds of sucking, she took it out of her mouth just to admire it. She kissed and licked the tip, those green eyes staring up at me like a little whore. Then she closed her eyes and went back to work. A dirty little bitch, and a bad one too. Always making me proud.

I stood up and lifted her light body all the way up, placing her legs over my shoulders with her crotch in my face. Thank God for the living room's high ceilings. Her giggles turned into soft moans while she held my head to steady herself, and I buried my face between her thighs, eating her pussy like I owned it. It was wet and sloppy dining for several minutes until my arms felt the strain of holding her up. I lowered Velvet, and she hooked her legs around my waist while her arms settled around my neck. I entered her. My hands held her small waist as I lifted her, moving her with a steady rhythm. Velvet let out a soft moan and leaned back, her hands barely resting on my shoulders as she trusted me to carry all of her. She was lost in it, completely giving herself over to me. I moved her small body with more force, and her voice broke into loud cries that filled the room. She couldn't escape, and melted even deeper into the moment, her reactions growing stronger with every thrust of my control.

I held her close as I carried her down the hall and into the bedroom, never breaking the moment between us. At the edge of the bed, I set her down gently while I stayed standing in front of her. I moved with her on the bed, my hands pressed firmly against her breasts as I kept control of the rhythm. There was a sharp intensity in Velvet's eyes when they met mine, and the way she touched herself only pulled me in deeper. I kept my pace slow, giving her room to feel everything. Her green eyes held onto me like she was lost in the moment, completely taken by the pleasure running through her. Her moans rose sharply, and then her body released in a sudden, powerful rush of warmth that soaked my skin. I looked down at the way pleasure surged out of her, her hand moving with fierce urgency while I kept a slow, steady rhythm.

Her chaotic release kept splashing against my lower body while pressure balled up in me, like I was seconds from exploding. Velvet must've felt what was coming, because her hand moved quickly, gripping me firmly at the base with full intention. She kept her firm hold as she lifted herself upright, her control steady while she brought her face closer. A deep pulsing tension gathered within me under her grip, tightening with a mix of pleasure and edge. And the moment she released me, everything rushed out at once. It got messy on her face as she jerked the cum into her mouth. She looked up at me, smiling, then licked her fingers clean..

"It's been so long," Velvet said, "I had almost forgotten how good real ice cream tastes."

"I forgot how quick you turn the place into a water zone."

She blushed. "It only happens when I'm with you, Daddy."

I smiled too. "Come on. Let's hit more rails and drink. You gon' need to refill that water gun if we'll be at it all night."

Velvet laughed. "I love you, Big Daddy."

"I love you too, baby."

GHAD

CHAPTER NINE

Tuesday, June 12 – 1:12 p.m.

Dianna and Vanessa hadn't seen each other since that night at work when Dianna overdid her coke and alcohol. Their schedules hadn't aligned over the weekend while both were busy with work, though they kept in touch through messages. Vanessa sought no apology from her. Still, those were the first texts that came in, so Vanessa assured her it was all okay and they moved on. The situation had happened many times before, and Vanessa knew it wouldn't be the last. Even so, she never minded being there for Dianna because their bond ran too deep. Today finally aligned as a day off for them both, and they planned to spend it together, like always.

Dianna and Vanessa sat on the patio at Moxies by their condo. The weather was nice. They both looked amazing in Prada shirts and sneakers, sexy jean shorts, nice jewellery, and their Icy chokers. Two premium ladies, indeed, a busty blonde and a spinner brunette. Most of the men on the patio couldn't resist looking their way from time to time. Even men seated with their women stole quick, surreptitious glances at the duo. The girls both had a plate of steak salad, with chicken wings in the centre that they shared, along with a bottle of wine on the table. It was their girl's day out and they were enjoying it. Vanessa told Dianna about her night with Gelato, sharing how wonderful it felt to finally spend time with him after waiting over a month. No jealousy touched Dianna. She knew she had gone just as long without seeing him. A small pout formed instead as she admitted how much she wished she had been there too, imagining how wild a trio night would have been.

"I do miss him, though. That big dick of his," Dianna said.

Vanessa laughed. "I barely got any sleep. We were up all night, until four in the morning."

"What time'd he leave?"

"Around seven, I think. I got to cuddle and rest with him for a few hours."

"Damn, babe, you should've kept him for a few more hours until I got back from my client." Dianna took a slow sip of her wine, her voice softening with playful want. "Have Daddy put me to bed too."

Their laughter drifted across the patio, then Vanessa said, "He was in a rush to go. He got a call from Smooth.""

"At seven in the morning?" Dianna's brows lifted. "Where do you think he had to go?"

"Probably off to hang with his boys. Apparently, Whitey is back in town for the week. And we both know how that's gonna be."

A small eye roll followed. "I guess I won't be seeing him this week for sure, then," Dianna said.

They both took a moment to eat their salad. Vanessa had something on her mind that she had been meaning to get Dianna's opinion on. She sipped some wine and waited for Dianna's attention before asking, "Babe, I've been thinking of stopping my birth control so I could get pregnant for him."

Dianna almost choked on her food but managed to swallow and let out a laugh. "Girl, you're crazy. He'll tell you to abort it."

"And what if I don't?"

"Then…I don't know. But he'll definitely beat your ass." Dianna paused with her wine glass in hand, thinking. She drank and then added, "And I don't think Skye would be happy with you if you did that."

"Why would it matter so much to her?" It didn't seem fair to Vanessa that Sierra would be bothered by something like that if Gelato belonged to all of them. "She could just have a baby for him too."

"Yeah, but," Dianna explained what Vanessa already knew, "Skye is the bottom bitch, so I think she's supposed to have more entitlement to Daddy than us. And if you got pregnant and had his baby, then that's like a cheat code to always have him in your life even if you decided to not be in the game with him anymore."

"Well, he doesn't have to be in my life. I just want his child. I'll just go back to living with my family and raise the child on my own." She took another sip of wine and said, "Or, after having the baby I could just continue working for Daddy when the baby is old enough for babysitters."

"I don't know, Vee." Dianna felt stressed just talking about it. "Either way, Skye is entitled to having his child first. You should really think about this and not do it. Things would get really crazy."

Vanessa didn't have a response, so they both stayed quiet. Each took a wing from the centre to eat. As they chewed, their eyes met, and they both laughed.

"You're fucking crazy, Vee. How long have you been thinking of this plan?"

"Last night when I was laid in bed with him. He's just so sexy, and I want his child."

"Good dick just got you losing your mind, babe." Dianna mused, "It's been over a month since I got that good dick. Shit, I might lose my mind when I finally get a taste of it too."

They both laughed hard, loud enough to turn a few heads on the patio. Some men took the chance to really look at them this time instead of sneaking glances. The girls went back to eating. Vanessa still thought it would be a good idea to have Gelato's child and believed Dianna simply didn't understand her. Meanwhile, Dianna saw it clearly. Vanessa was a spoiled brat raised in a rich home with entitlement, and she didn't understand that life didn't bend for her wants.

Vanessa asked, "When's the last time you even saw Skye?"

Dianna thought about it while chewing, then swallowed and answered, "That night we all went out for her birthday. Last month, no?"

"Yeah, I know. But, like, other than birthdays and family gatherings, when was the last time you went to lunch or shopping with her?"

"I dunno. Why?"

"I feel like she's been distant from us the past year."

"I wouldn't say that," Dianna disagreed. "She looked super happy to see us at her birthday party that night."

"Yeah, but at the end of the night, she didn't want us to join her time with Daddy. She used to be down with us all messing around together, but when was the last time you even got to have fun with her?"

"Oh, c'mon." Dianna rolled her eyes and laughed. "It was her birthday, Vee, maybe she just wanted to enjoy Daddy alone. And you know she gets super busy with work, so maybe she don't always have the same free time we do to hang out with us."

"That's true. But I just remember how we used to hang out all the time when we first met. Me, you, her, and that Sugar girl. Then Sugar left for whatever issues she and Daddy were having, and now it's like Skye drifted away from us."

"Yeah, Sugar was so fake, though. I don't think she really liked us. I'm even glad Daddy let her go," Dianna said. "But Skye always been cool. I think she just gets super busy, that's all. But she definitely did make more effort at the beginning to hang with us, and I think that was just to build good relations with us. I still get good vibes from her even though we don't see her as much anymore. She always comments and stuff when I post my new nails or whatever on Snapchat."

"Yeah, I guess you're right. She still connects with us that way."

"Exactly. Skye is perfectly fine, babe." Dianna added, "If you ask me, I think you're just the one going crazy, tryna have Daddy's child and all."

Vanessa laughed a bit but wasn't over the topic. "How come she doesn't work the same clubs with us anymore? I saw Crystal at the club the other day, and she was telling me that she works the same clubs with Skye, Alize, and Star all the time. Sometimes they all even plan it together."

Dianna shrugged and drank some wine. "Remember, Crystal is Preeme's bottom, and Alize and Star are Smooth's bottoms, so I see it as just the bottom bitches linking up. I feel no way about it, and you shouldn't either." She went on after another sip of wine. "They're all older than us, with years in the game. Skye obviously has more in common with them and probably prefers to work with them. Me and you click better because we're young and gettin' it, so fuck them old hoes."

Dianna chugged the rest of her wine, and Vanessa laughed, doing the same.

Vanessa said, "I miss Chocolate and Vanilla, though. Those two furballs are too cute."

"Yeah, I know. I love seeing Sierra post them on her snaps and stuff. We should tell Skye to leave them with us for a week or two."

"Vanilla looks like she's getting bigger every time. I think her lion bloodline, or whatever, is gonna have her growing bigger. But Chocolate still looks small and adorable. The poor guy probably won't get any bigger."

Dianna laughed. "That's so true. Poor little guy. I miss him the most."

Vanessa picked up the wine bottle to refill both their glasses while Dianna ate another wing. They were partners in crime, always had each other's backs, and kept the friendship pure by staying honest with each other. A golden bond.

Vanessa cheered Dianna and asked, "So what's the plan tonight?"

"Let's turn-up and go to a nightclub," Dianna suggested and sipped her wine. "Did Daddy leave you with any D-D for us? I finished mine days ago and been meaning to ask him for some, but after Friday I'm kinda scared to."

"You should've just asked him because you did have tricks to see on the weekend."

"True. But just didn't want him to think I woke up the next day thinking about turning up." Dianna scoffed. "I mean, he collected the money from my safe last night and didn't leave any D-D, so I'm guessing he wants me to lay off it even if I'm with a trick."

"Well, you're wrong, 'cause he left me with some to give you too." Vanessa smirked. "But he did say to give it to you only if you're seeing a trick that asks for it."

"Wow." Dianna playfully rolled her eyes. "So you're in charge of me now?"

"Yup." Vanessa bit her bottom lip because what came to mind turned her on. "I'll be in charge of you tonight too."

A little heat rushed through Dianna at the thought. She blushed and sipped her wine. "So we're not going to the nightclub tonight?"

"Umm...We'd have to ask Daddy about that one. And he'll probably say no. So most likely not. We should just catch a movie together or something."

That was a fact. Places like nightclubs were off limits, not without Gelato. The nightclub vibes were different, and he couldn't have his girls in that type of environment without him. It was one thing to not permit them getting wasted in the vibrant setting of a strip club, because he had the justifiable reason that they needed to stay focused at work. But there was no telling what they would do on their day off in a nightclub, with no real reason to not get wasted, surrounded by prowling city hustlers and pimps like himself. He had allowed the two girls to attend a few nightclubs in the past, over a year ago. That was only because it had been a girl's night out including Sierra, who he trusted to be more mature and able to handle the two other girls and herself in that environment. Every other time Dianna and Vanessa asked to go on their own to a club, he refused. Over time, they accepted that his answer would likely never change.

After finishing her salad, Dianna suggested, "We'll turn-up, go bowling, catch a movie, then we'll go home to turn all the way up, and have sex."

"You just wanna turn-up." Vanessa chuckled. "But sounds good to me. It's always more fun eating each other's pussies when we're lit."

"Exactly. Then you'll fuck me good with your strap-on," Dianna added, and they cheered to that.

Vanessa finished her salad and joined Dianna on the wings. Every now and then they checked their phones to reply to clients and make arrangements for the week. From the looks of it already, they would be doing a duo tomorrow evening with one of Vanessa's regulars. They planned to work the strip club together on Thursday and Friday night. The weekend would be busy for them both, as usual, seeing their separate clients. Even those Thursday and Friday plans were never guaranteed. Either one of them could get booked for those hours, which meant the other would be on her own. So they made sure to hang out every chance they got, even if it was only a few hours at the gym before going their separate ways for work.

Dianna sipped her wine and let the question she'd been dwelling on slip out. "Do you think your father would really let you return home if you got pregnant?"

Vanessa didn't have to think hard about the answer. "Even if my dad didn't want me back home, my mom is an Italian mother. She'll accept anything just to have me back home. When my older sister got pregnant in high school my dad kicked her out. But when she broke up with the guy a few months after giving birth, my mom took her back in. With the baby and all. My dad was mad but couldn't do anything about it. My mom's really the one running the show in that house. And she has a big heart. Always forgiving."

"Yeah, but you became a stripper and left home with a pimp."

"And I'll always be her daughter," Vanessa said. "She's probably been praying for things to go wrong with me and Gelato so that I return home. If I hadn't changed my phone number and all that, I'm sure my mom and sister would be messaging me sometimes just to check up on me."

"You're lucky," Dianna said and grabbed a wing.

"Why do you say that?" Vanessa grew concerned. "Do you sometimes think about leaving Daddy, and the game or something?"

"No, no. Absolutely not. But, like, it must be nice to know that your family still cares about you, no matter what you do in life."

Vanessa grabbed the last piece of chicken and ate without a response. She knew Dianna's story. Life had been much harder for her growing up. As much as Vanessa could talk about her good upbringing and family fortune, she knew better than to rub it in Dianna's face.

Dianna grew up in the Parkdale area of Toronto with her white mother, Courtney. They lived on baby bonus money and welfare. Dianna's biological father was an Aboriginal man who had been gone since her birth. Courtney used to say, "Don't be surprised if you ever come across one of the drughead men in the area and he looks like you." In other words, Dianna's father had most likely become a junkie.

When Dianna was twelve, Courtney found love again and had a man named George living in the small house with them. The welfare and baby bonus money couldn't take care of all three of them, and George had no intention of seeking employment, so Courtney took a night shift at a cash-paying factory. George was more than just a lazy forty-year-old living off Courtney. There was something darker in him. When Courtney worked nights, the house felt smaller, and Dianna felt the shift in his attention. Boundaries blurred early, long before she had the understanding or power to stop it. His presence in her room became normalized under the excuse of keeping each other company in a rough neighbourhood. He framed it to Dianna as nothing more than having each other's backs. Inappropriate closeness turned into harm she carried alone. She never told anyone. After all, George was the only person she had to protect her in that tiny house in a bad area. Their bond mattered, even when it meant keeping secrets.

When Dianna was fifteen, Courtney still worked nights at the cash factory, and George had moved from inappropriate touching to full-on sex with her. Over years of inappropriate encounters with George, Dianna had grown used to his attention, and by fifteen, being with him felt almost inevitable. Most of her high-school peers were already sexually active with people their own age, but Dianna's secret involvement with older, experienced George had shaped her understanding of intimacy. It fed something in her, a growing drive she didn't fully recognize yet. She accepted it. Even found herself drawn to it.

There came a time when Courtney and George were expecting a child together, and Dianna, at eighteen, was expecting one as well. Courtney did not care much about her daughter's pregnancy, but everything changed when word spread that George might be responsible. Instead of confronting the truth, he pushed Courtney to blame Dianna. In his story, Dianna's looks and youth made her the one who had to be seducing him, not the other way around. The depths of Dianna's affairs with George had grown so deep that she no longer remembered how it all began years ago. What stayed with her was the guilt she carried for enjoying sex with her mother's man.

Dianna had an abortion while living in a shelter after being kicked out of her home. Courtney gave birth to Dianna's half-sister months later. She never got to meet her. Dianna had turned nineteen and slipped into the sex trade with a Caribbean guy. It worked in her favour that he was more attracted to her than interested in profiting off her, so she rarely saw clients and lived off his drug money. That comfortable situation lasted for about two years until Dianna lost the guy to murder. With nobody left to depend on, she ended up back at the women's shelter. Not long after that she met Gelato Icy at a little food shop in downtown Toronto. The way he had parked a foreign car out front and stepped out glistening told her enough. She didn't doubt him for a moment when he said, *"I know what to do with a gorgeous young woman like you."*

Vanessa drank the last of her wine and said, "Okay, babe, let's get out of here and start turning up in the car. I got the D-D in my purse."

Dianna's face lit up with excitement. "Yes. Let's get it!"

They waved to the waiter for the bill so they could get on with their day of fun activities and their night of freakiness. While waiting, Dianna and Vanessa took a cute picture together and posted it on Snapchat with the caption, *"Girls' Day and Night #IcyBabies."*

Sierra was one of the first to view it and reacted with a kissy face emoji.

At this point in their lives, most of their friends and acquaintances on social media were other girls in the game they had met through strip clubs or somewhere along the way. The rest were clients who couldn't get enough of them and joined the fan crowd. Their lives and the people in it revolved around the game, the glamour, and the stable they considered a family. With Gelato Icy as their king.

CHAPTER TEN

Friday, June 15 – 5:45 p.m.

Cloudy skies showed a high chance of rainfall with warm weather. I rolled with Smooth in his black Bentley on the Gardiner Expressway towards Highway-427 to Mississauga. We kept the coupe's top down, designered up as usual in both clothing and headspace. Our jewellery pieces dazzled, with Smooth wearing his platinum wrist medallion of a pimp seated on a throne. Prime pimping was in the air today. Maria paid me the five thousand choosing fee last night, so I had her pack up and leave the Scarborough condo she was at. I checked her into a suite at Westin Harbour Castle and fucked her for the first time. She was now awaiting me while I sorted things out to get her properly situated.

Marvel got the courtesy call this morning, letting him know that Maria chose-up to me. The next step was to meet like men for a proper serving. He got upset, cursed and threatened me, then hung up. An hour later he called back asking what the meet-up was even for. As far as he knew, the serving was that phone call I had given him. I broke down the honour behind doing it face-to-face, explaining why it mattered. A sit-down made things clear on both sides, stopped any bullshit a bitch might play between two men, and gave us the chance to talk about my gain and his loss of Maria in a way that kept the game solid. Both of us are to prosper with or without the bitch. *Pimps up, hoes down.* He then decided we'd meet at a decent restaurant on Dundas Street in Mississauga. I told him to reach out to a solidified pimp to act as his witness for the serving, because I would be pulling up with my partner, Smooth Darken Caesar. Marvel had no ties to any real pimps in the game, which I already expected. But he claimed he was a big man and didn't need anyone standing on his behalf. He would come alone.

We took a corner booth in the busy restaurant, the music and people chattering around us loud enough to muffle our conversation. Smooth and I sat on one side of the booth while Marvel sat across from us. Each of us had a glass of Hennessy on the rocks, and a plate of nachos sat in the middle to share. Smooth was the only one interested in eating.

"...Yeah, she paid the fee yesterday, so she's with me now," I concluded to Marvel.

"She was mad that I have an actual girlfriend, and that's why she's leaving me?" Marvel asked. He was a 5'8" dark-skinned dude with shoulder-length dreads and a tough face.

"That might be part of it. But really, she chose-up to me because she feeling my ism. She wants a man who keeps it real."

"Okay, then send her back to me and I'll start being real with her."

"It don't work like that, man. The bitch chose-up, and she staying with me now."

"Then what's the point of this sit-down?" Marvel asked, "Weren't we supposed to talk so you can help me with this situation?"

"Yeah, man, but you confused. I'm putting you on game, showing you where you messed up. Letting you know your flaws so you can tighten up your shit and have better game for the next bitch. A hoe turns eighteen every day, man. You'll be alright."

"So basically you got me here to waste my time, eh?"

Smooth spoke to Marvel. "Playa, listen up. Pimpin' Gelato is here to put you on game with this good serving." He broke it down for him. "You out here loving square bitches and shit when you had a fine ass hoe breaking her purse for you. That's some sucka shit. You need to tighten up your game, son. You gon' self-destruct with that simpin'."

"Fuck y'all niggas talking 'bout?" Marvel snapped, frustration all over his face. "Y'all ain't no real pimps. Y'all some wannabees. Mind your own business and don't be telling me how to run my game. Just send my bitch back and we good."

"Mind my own business?" I laughed. "But your bitch just became my business. Looks like my pimpin' speaks for itself." I leaned in a bit. "If you were more of a gentleman at this table, I might've given you a playa's hand and dropped you the five thousand she paid me, just so you ain't fall on your face from losing the bitch."

"Okay, so give me the money," Marvel demanded.

"Playa, you ain't even acting right 'bout this serving," Smooth told him. "You getting all emotional and shit. You not giving pimpin' Gelato some game back on the bitch."

"Isn't he supposed to be a big pimp? Fuck he need game from me for?"

Smooth explained, "You gotta let Gelato know about Maria. If she lazy, if she got bad habits, anything he gotta watch out for so he could do right with her."

"Yeah." Marvel screwed up his face. "You gotta watch out for me!"

I looked at Smooth and spoke in French. "Ce mec est un putain d'idiot." *This guy is a fucking idiot.*

Smooth laughed and replied, "Oui. On perd notre temps avec lui." *Yeah. We're wasting our time with him.*

Marvel looked back and forth at us. "Why the fuck are y'all talking in a different language for?"

Smooth scoffed. "It's looking like no pimping going on over here, so we gon' roll out, son."

"Yeah, 'cause y'all ain't ready for some gangsta shit."

Smooth and I slid out the booth, leaving a hundred and fifty on the table to cover the drinks, nachos, and more than enough for the waiter's tip. Marvel kept running his mouth the entire time. Straight signs of an ignorant street cat with no real direction in the game. These were the type of fools who would never reach their peak in any kind of hustle, too small-minded and too prideful. It was a shame. He could've peeped real game today that would've helped him tighten up and move smarter, but he let his ego run the show. A serving was supposed to elevate a pimp. Losing a girl to another man, sitting across from him to hear his criticism, then giving him the information to guide the same girl you lost? *Damn. Now, that's sucka-free*—the kind of honour that earned glory from the pimp gods. And Marvel was nowhere close to worthy of that.

He kept beating his gums while we walked off, and his last words caught my attention. "Trust me, I'll find you and smoke you. I'll get my bitch back, you fuckboy!"

I wanted to turn around and punch off his face, but Smooth put a hand on my shoulder to keep me moving. By then half the restaurant was staring, disgusted by the names Marvel threw after us. "You fucking pimps. Women abusers. Kidnappers. Rapists."

That was it. I spun around on Smooth and cut straight back to the booth. My fist cracked across Marvel's face and dropped him cold on the table. Gasps hit the room and a waiter shouted, "I'm calling the police!"

Smooth and I rushed out and jumped into his Bentley. Not the cleanest getaway, since no witness would forget a car like his, but we weren't sticking around to make explanations.

Smooth dropped me off at my condo by the lake, then went his way. A change of look felt necessary, so a Hugo Boss sweatsuit went on before I hit the road again in my second car, a silver Range Rover Sport. Rain started coming down hard as I headed toward the Westin Harbour Castle in downtown Toronto. My phone rang and Marvel's name showed. I picked up. He jumped straight into threatening me and running his mouth, but all I wanted to know was whether he had cooperated with the police. Marvel took offence, swearing he was no rat and insisting he left the restaurant right after the incident. Right after he regained consciousness, is how it sounded to me. He kept ranting with more wild threats, so I cut the call. He tried ringing back a few times, but I let it go. Eventually he stopped.

Parking wasn't something I felt like dealing with when I reached the Westin Harbour, so valet made the most sense. Inside the luxurious lobby, I headed to a common seating area and pulled out my phone to make a call. Rich businessmen moved through the place in steady waves, and the thought crossed my mind that Maria could work the lobby and catch a few tricks. But she was new to my program and didn't know how to run a play yet. Last thing I needed was her approaching the wrong man and getting reported for soliciting where she shouldn't.

Sierra picked up. "Hey, Poppa, what's up?"

"Hey, mami, what you getting into?"

"Just getting ready for work. I'm doing Pro-Club with Crystal tonight. Then I'll leave there around midnight to see one of my tricks in Woodbridge."

I couldn't wait to tell her the news. "I just served Marvel. Maria's officially with us now."

"Okay, cool."

"You don't sound like you care."

She was sarcastic. "Oh, you got Maria officially on the team now? Wow. Good for you, Poppa. Congratulations." Then she got real. "But I'm busy now. What do you need me to do?"

"You need to come meet her and welcome her to the stable. Maybe skip the s-club, meet Maria, then go see your trick at midnight."

"I'm not missing the club," Sierra refused. "I'm focused on getting this money so we can stack up more for our plans, and you're asking me to come play host to your new guest."

"New guest? Bitch, are you dumb?!" That stirred me up fast, and I had to check myself in the public setting. My voice dropped, but the energy stayed sharp. "This new bitch gon' be bringing in more money to stack, too."

"More like money that has to be invested back into her living and expenses, because you obviously gotta get her situated and happy first. Then we gotta hope she sticks around and fully settles in before her extra money can even be considered profits."

"The fuck?!" Her response annoyed me. "Listen. I got a new bitch on the team, and it's your job as the bottom bitch to walk her through the game."

"Yeah, and it's your job to focus on the bitches you already got and maintain them. All this time you still haven't spent time with Diamond. And the poor girl is probably just dying for some attention from you."

"I've been busy."

"Yeah, busy with your friends and your new bitch."

"Whatever." I wasn't about to argue with Sierra on the phone. "So are you coming to do your part and meet Maria?"

"Not today. I'm going to work to make money for us, because I stay focused on what we got. I'll think about the new bitch another day. Angelo, I'll talk to you later. I gotta get ready. Love you. Bye."

She hung up. There was no point calling her back. I took the elevator up to Maria's suite on the fifteenth floor. When I stepped inside, she was lying in bed on her phone but jumped to her feet with excitement when she saw me. She had on only a D-cup bra lifting her jiggly breasts and booty shorts hugging her nice ass. Inked cheetah prints marked her outer left thigh, running up and wrapping around to her butt cheek. Maria greeted me with a hug and a quick kiss before settling back on the bed. I took the single sofa beside it.

"What were you doing?" I asked.

"Nothing." She sighed. "Just bored, skipping through Snapchat and Instagram." Then she asked, "So how did the meeting with Marvel go?"

"As you said, he couldn't handle it."

"You see. I told you so. If I didn't change my number and delete him off Snapchat today, he'd be hounding me right now."

"Yeah, he's a nutcase. Now I'm thinking of how to get you working without risking him finding you. Some OT strip clubs should be good."

"Okay, good. Because I'm scared of seeing him, too," Maria said. "But remember, I haven't worked clubs before. Aren't I supposed to meet your bottom bitch first so she could show me the ropes?"

"You'll meet her, eventually. Skye's busy these next few days."

"Okay. So what's the plan? When do I start? Where do I start?"

Maria was excited about everything that had me overwhelmed at the moment. With Sierra refusing to step in and tune up the new girl for the strip club, everything felt more complicated than it needed to be. Was I really expected to program Maria for club work on my own? It had been years since I handled that myself. I'd grown used to having my bottom bitch introduce any new girl to the clubs. The other option was to keep Maria doing what she'd already been doing with her service-provider postings. That would mean dyeing her hair a different colour to change her look, and taking fresh pictures so Marvel or any of his people wouldn't recognize her ads.

Most working-girls in Ontario posted on the same common sites, charging anywhere from eighty dollars for a half-hour to three hundred for an hour. Full sex. Sometimes multiple rounds.

Not with my bitches. I took pride in staying above all that and couldn't imagine settling for those prices. My Icy-branded bitches had to hold a higher value, but pulling in tricks willing to pay six hundred for a single round on those websites was rare. There were a few high-end platforms where girls like mine could post at those rates, but the traffic was weak, almost pointless. The strip clubs were always the best play for high-end services. Maria could still make good money there, even with two-hundred-dollar blowjobs for tricks who couldn't afford her full menu. That was why Sierra's training mattered. Maria needed the clubs, and I needed Sierra to get her right for them.

My next option was to put Maria with a reputable high-end escort agency. That came with territory, since they would use my girl to make their money and break me off a percentage. They would become the pimp in that arrangement, and I was not a fan of that.

"So what's the plan, Daddy?" Maria cut into my thoughts.

"Oh...umm..." I fumbled a bit, trying to line up an answer. "I'm thinking. Give me a second."

"Shouldn't you have it all figured—"

"Shut up, bitch." I needed silence. "Let me think."

"Sorry, Daddy." She went quiet and slid her attention back to her phone.

A long breath left me as I slouched into the sofa. Not much came to mind, and the quiet must've made her nervous. She tried to make up for it the only way she knew. "Daddy, you want me to suck your dick while you think?"

"Sure. You could help me with that."

Maria tied her hair up and slid off the bed, kneeling in front of me. She got straight to it, no warm-up. A few minutes of her amazing brains had my head clearing in the best way.

Alberta popped into mind. Rates for online postings were higher out there, so Maria could hold my Icy prices without fighting for tricks. Then Whitey's spa clicked in right after. That was the answer sitting in my face. Sensations and everything in me turned up a notch, and I released it all. She swallowed it with a proud little smile. I smiled back, tucked my dick away, and went to my phone. Maria climbed back on the bed in good spirits, happy to be useful.

I explained Maria's situation to Whitey and told him the plan was to get her working in his massage parlour.

Whitey broke it down. "As well as walk-ins, clients could call ahead and book whichever masseuse they want from our website. He shows up and pays a hundred bucks to my spa for the massage, and an extra forty goes to the masseuse. We document everyone's work and issue weekly paycheques, so your girl could also claim taxes for working at Consational as a legit masseuse."

"Okay, that's cool," I said.

Whitey moved on to what mattered more. "The massage happens in private rooms, and that's where the extras go down, behind my back, of course." He chuckled. "The girls charge anywhere from one-fifty to two-fifty for blowjobs, and five hundred to six-fifty for full service. We only hire premium girls, so nobody charging anything less. Your girl will definitely make money because it gets busy here."

"Sounds good."

He added, "Oh. And there's an off-the-record agreement where every girl shows gratitude to the spa by giving fifteen percent of their extra earnings for the day. But no worries. I'll let you keep everything your girl makes. I ain't tryna stomp down on your pimping, my dawg."

"You a real one." Then I asked, "You flying back out there on Sunday, right?"

"Yeah, in two days. I already got the shipment of my cars sorted out, so I'm ready to leave."

"Okay. So me and my girl, Maria, gon' fly out there too."

"That's bless. You guys could even stay with me and Chanel at our condo out there. We got a guest room."

"Nah, I don't wanna be all up in your space. I'ma just book an Airbnb. Text me the spa's location so I can get a nice place near that area."

"A'ight, bro, I'ma do that now."

We ended the call and I turned to Maria, who smiled at me. She hadn't heard Whitey on the line, but she could tell I had everything figured out now.

"We're flying in two days?" she asked.

"Yeah. I only do first-class," I bragged.

"Oh my God! I've never been to Alberta and never flown first-class, ever."

"Yeah. You'll like it. But I'ma need you locked in on the money we travelling for."

"Oh, for sure, Daddy. I'ma work hard and make you happy." She added, "I do Greek, too, so I know I can charge extra for that."

"Okay, cool. We'll tax an additional three hundred for the backdoor entry."

She giggled. "I love how you put my rates so high. It makes me feel expensive."

"The Icy brand be expensive, baby," I said with confidence. I made another call, this time to Smooth.

He answered, "What it do, playa?"

"Just here with Maria. What's good with you?"

"Parked up the Bentley and kicking it at one of my bitches' place."

I chuckled, thinking back on what happened with Marvel. "The fool called me saying he didn't stick around to talk to cops. That means we might be good."

"That simp a joke. He need to leave the game alone."

"Right?" I moved to what I really called about. "I'm trying to fly out with Whitey on Sunday. What you saying?"

"Man, I ain't saying fuck all. I'ma go back to Montréal tomorrow to visit my mom and family. My older sister booked tickets to check out some carnival with my nieces and nephews, so I'm gonna join them with my son."

Smooth had always been mama's boy, going back to Montréal often to see her. If my mom was still alive, I'd probably be heading home often to see her too. The other reason Smooth travelled back so much was his four-year-old son.

A couple years back, some girl from Montréal thought having Smooth's kid would be her way out the game, while still keeping him tied to her. She had the baby and ran back to Montréal to live a square life, and Smooth cut her off the moment she stepped away from his pimpin'. He kept solid ties with his son and couldn't care less about the bitch. She tried running to the courts for child support and failed because Smooth was a pimp with no documented income. Everything he owned stayed in his mother's name. Years ago, he made the smart move of having her get into real estate to wash the fortune he brought in. As far as the courts were concerned, Smooth was a broke man driving his mother's luxury cars and staying in her homes around Canada. The only time his baby momma ever saw money was when it willingly came from his mother. And Smooth's son stayed laced in all the finer things a child could want.

Smooth asked me, "You is flying out with the new bitch to work Whitey's spa?"

"Yeah, that's the plan."

"I had one of my hoes already out west working, and I had her check out that spa real quick. My bitch bad, but she couldn't compete with the premium hoes in that spa. Coco playing no games. She ain't hiring nothing less than a nine of ten. I'ma have to send my elite strikers up in there if I'm tryna get involved." Smooth scoffed. "But your new bitch definitely a premium. She's good to go." There was a pause before he added, "If you gon' be out there for weeks then I might meet you out there."

"Not sure how long I'll be, but I'll let you know once I'm there."

"Alright, pimpin'. Peace out."

Maria had questions the moment I hung up. "How long will we be out there? And when do I get to meet everyone else in the stable?"

"I haven't decided how long we'll be yet. But you'll get to meet the team when we get back."

And I truly hoped Sierra would be ready to take the new girl under her wing. Just a week or two of training Maria for the strip clubs, then I'd have Maria working the ones outside the GTA instead of hiding her out west. Worst case would be having to teach Maria the ropes myself. That would mean sitting in the clubs on the nights she worked, watching her moves and giving pointers. Not something I wanted to be doing. And that method would never be as effective as Sierra actively working by her side.

Maybe Velvet or Diamond could step up and train Maria.

CHAPTER ELEVEN

Friday, June 15 – 10:19 p.m.

Preeme had planned to meet the young pimp in the strip club's washroom, but he said he'd be outside shortly instead. That left Preeme waiting outside Midway Invader in Mississauga for a young hustler who sold cocaine to strippers and clients in the club. It was a hustle Preeme once ran himself at nineteen, so respect came easily for the young pimp's extra grind.

In his silver-on-black, tinted Corvette Stingray, he sat parked a few cars down from the main entrance, angled toward the wall and walkway that led to the front doors. From that position, he could watch everyone leaving and entering the club. He would have shown up in his Acura TSX, but he already had drugs on him when he got the call, and it wasn't convenient to drive all the way to his condo downtown just to switch vehicles. Still, he noted that next time he would. The Corvette had pedestrians stopping to stare, and that kind of attention was the last thing he wanted.

An old C-Class Benz pulled into the lot and parked a few cars down. Three black guys stepped out and headed toward the main entrance. The two taller ones dressed in outdated thug attire, baggy hoodies and jeans. The driver's style was different, less baggy and carrying a modern edge. As they passed, all three stared at the Corvette, their eyes lingering through the clear windshield once they noticed Preeme in the driver's seat.

He stared back. The twins kept walking. The driver, darker skinned with shoulder-length dreads, a swollen eye, and a hard face, slowed and screwed up his expression at Preeme. Instinct had Preeme grip the gun tucked at his waist. The dread kept glaring before finally moving on to catch up with the twins once he realized he'd fallen behind.

Nothing about the stranger sparked recognition. With the number of people Preeme had shot and killed, he couldn't say for certain that he knew the friends of those he should be watching out for. That was one of the reasons he avoided social media or anything that exposed him. Most people only knew his name, the stories that followed it, and maybe that he had ties to Gelato. Very few knew his face, the cars he drove, or his connection to Crystal. There weren't any pictures of him anywhere. Not a trace for the public to see. He would not even appear in a group photo when out with friends. If he slipped into a shot, they knew better than to post it online. Preeme made it clear he'd rage war over something like that. The least they could do was respect how he chose to live—a name without a face. Even the young pimp he had come to see had known him for years only as the dealer, Lucky-Loo.

A quiet urge to step inside crept up on him, a need to read the energy that dread would bring if they crossed paths again. He preferred knowing what was coming, with a chance to control it, rather than taking things lightly and risking his life later. Just as he opened his door to get out of the Corvette, the passenger side door swung open. Preeme whipped his gun off his waist and spun to his right, aiming it straight at the intruder.

"Fam, chill." The person threw his hands up and backed away from the door. It was the young pimp he had come to meet. Preeme lowered the gun and cracked a smile. The guy slid into the seat, his chest still heaving.

"What took you so long, lil' homie." Preeme asked.

"My bad, fam. Fuck." He was still shaking. "That's why you popped off on me?"

Preeme chuckled. "Nah, nah." He tucked the gun back at his waist. "Some weird menz walked past my ride eyeing me hard. A dread man."

"You talking 'bout Marvel? I just passed him on my way out. He's always screw-facing everybody. Probably just hating on your car."

The name registered, but that conversation was for someone else. Preeme reached into his pocket and pulled out a bagged ounce of cocaine. The young pimp handed over a fat stack of bills, mostly green.

"Sixteen hundred," he said.

"I believe that." Preeme shoved the cash into the cup holder of the centre console. The young pimp started to open the door, but Preeme stopped him with a question.

"That Marvel man always be eyeing people?"

"Trust me, fam, that's just him. I see him in the clubs chippin' work sometimes too. All he does is stare at niggas with his face screwed up. It's nothing."

"A'ight, lil' homie. Hold it down."

"Yeah. One." The young pimp stepped out and headed for the main entrance.

Preeme hit a few buttons on the car's temperature system and a mechanical stash box in the dashboard opened. Inside the hidden compartment sat a bag with about half a kilo of cocaine, a small digital scale, and a few wads of cash. There was still room for more, including a slot in the roof of the compartment designed to stash his gun. Preeme took the $1600 from the centre console and placed it inside, then closed it up. He kept the gun on him and pulled out his phone to make a call.

"What's good?" Gelato answered.

"Yo, big homie. The dude you were supposed to serve today, his name was Marvel, right?"

"Yeah, I served him. Ended up rocking his face."

The dread's swollen eye now made sense to Preeme. He chuckled. "Why'd you do that?"

"Fool was acting too sick."

"He's very dark with dreads, right?"

"Yeah. Got a tough face on him too," Gelato confirmed. "What's got you asking?"

Preeme explained his brief encounter with Marvel. Then he added, "My lil' homie was telling me not to take it personal. Said the man just be screw-facing anyone he doesn't know."

"Yeah, man, don't pay no mind to that fool. He don't know you and just moving sick for no reason."

"A'ight. I'ma holla at you tomorrow, if anything."

"Okay, cool."

Preeme ended the call, started his Corvette, and backed out of the parking spot. He got back on the road and right back to business. The night would end at Pro Club where Crystal would be, and he'd only admire her from a distance. He'd never say a word to her in public, not in a place where analytical eyes were watching. That was the understanding Preeme and Crystal had for years. She always appreciated when he showed up to silently accompany her in the clubs. No one would think he was there for her unless knowing them both personally

After walking past the sleek Corvette, Marvel asked his young boys, "Y'all know the nigga in that car?"

"Nah," one twin answered. "But that's a sexy car, stil'. He probably a big pimp."

Marvel scoffed. "He was gripping up his waist. Tryna front on me like he got a stick."

"Maybe he does," said the second twin.

"These pimps ain't 'bout shit but girls. They'll get smoked," Marvel said, patting the pistol tucked at his waist. It belonged to the twins.

They reached the club entrance just as a young black male came out and walked past them. Marvel made sure to grill him too. Losing Maria still stung, and he pegged him as just another girl-snatching pimp. The guy clearly wanted no problems and didn't look back as he passed.

Marvel and the twins went through the heavy entrance doors and another set that opened into the strip club's busy ambience. The lights were low, the music loud, and the place crowded. Marvel used the pause to remind his young boys of the plan. "We'll just chill for fifteen minutes to see if she's in here. Then we'll cut to a few more strip clubs in the area."

The twins nodded.

Gelato was a major pimp who'd rather have a gorgeous girl like Maria working strip clubs than chasing clients online. That meant if Marvel wanted to find her, he'd have to keep checking the popular clubs in the GTA. He would cross paths with her sooner or later. He felt it. Marvel knew Maria in ways that made him certain he could bring her home. All he wanted was that one chance to speak to her.

GHAD

CHAPTER TWELVE

◆

Sunday, June 24 – 11:42 a.m.

I'd been in Alberta with Maria, now Magenta Icy, for the past week while she worked most days and nights at Consational Spa in Calgary. Every shift she pulled in nothing less than $1500, right on par with the premium girls in that spot. When we landed in Calgary, I'd given Magenta the first day off so we could tour the city with Whitey and Coco. She started work the next day, and Thursday became her dedicated day off so she could have a full day and night of Daddy-time. Still, every morning she woke up next to me in our luxury Airbnb, which meant she got dicked down daily, morning if not night. Magenta fell in love with this pimping.

Morning light spilled through the edge-drop glass wall of my bedroom and woke me with a light hangover. I'd returned to Toronto last night, leaving Magenta in Calgary to keep working at Consational until I was ready to go back for her. My place was a two-bedroom plus den corner suite. From the front door, a long hallway ran past the den and guest washroom before opening into a wide living room, with the kitchen on the left split by a long dining counter. A thick marble pillar stood in the corner of the living room, catching sunlight the same way it glistened at night. The balcony wrapped the entire suite, giving views of the city and lake from both bedrooms. Waking up in this king bed was a reminder of why I kept everything looking legitimate. Through the right resources and fraud, I had a personal training business registered under my name for proof of income, and with good credit the mortgage approval came easy. Every year my fraudulent accountant filed false receipts for tax season, letting me claim a portion of my pimp money through that business. But owning my condo and keeping the lifestyle smooth didn't mean things were problem-free.

The night came back in pieces. Sierra had come over and the argument started as soon as I mentioned her needing to train Magenta in the strip clubs. She refused, saying I was focused on the wrong things and not bonding stronger with the team we already had. I was drunk and lit on Designer-Dope through the whole back and forth, so clear arguments weren't happening. The Designer had my hormones running instead, all horny and active, so I fucked Sierra to sleep before the night got any more heated.

Sierra wasn't next to me in bed when I woke up this morning. She had either slipped out early or was somewhere in the condo. I threw on boxers and stepped into my private washroom to brush my teeth quick. A shower crossed my mind, but music was playing in the living room, so I figured Sierra was out there and headed that way. In the kitchen, Sierra stood at the stove with her hair tied up in a bun, wearing the comfortable clothes she kept at my place. She looked good, focused on what she had sizzling in the pan. Without looking over she said, "I fried some eggs for us. I'm just finishing up with this steak for you."

Two plates of omelets were already set on the dining counter, waiting.

"Oh," she added, "And I'm not sure if you knew, but the milk in the fridge was spoiled so I threw it out. We'll just have orange juice instead."

"Okay, cool," was all I said.

I reached over Sierra's head for the cabinet, grabbed the Advil, poured a glass of water, and swallowed two pills. It was only a light headache, but I needed the clarity if I planned on finishing the argument from last night. I sat on a stool on the other side of the dining counter and settled in by my plate. Chris Brown played from Sierra's phone through the living room speakers, and I watched her move around the kitchen in the R&B ambience.

She asked without looking back at me, "You gonna start eating without me?"

"Nah. I'm waiting."

"On your steak?"

"Nah. On you," I said.

"Okay. That's nice. Your steak should be ready in five minutes."

I didn't respond to that. Something else needed addressing. "So what we gonna do about Magenta?"

Sierra sighed, lowered the stove's heat, then leaned back against the counter, facing me with her arms crossed. "I don't know, Angelo. That's for you to figure out. I already told you where I stand."

"You know you're changing on me, right? The way you're moving."

"I'm not changing up on you or moving any different. I just don't want to waste my time with new girls you're chasing."

"Chasing?" The word didn't sit right. "I'm turning bitches and working them. Fuck you mean by chasing?"

"Like I been telling you. You're not focused on what you already got and always looking for new girls. Girls I then gotta waste my time training. Then a year or two later they're gone. Sometimes even months. All because you don't focus on maintaining them in the team."

"So you should be helping me maintain them."

"I can only do so much, Angelo. You're the pimp. It's on you to keep them in the stable, happy, and focused, while managing the money."

"Exactly. And that's why getting this new girl is good. That's more money coming in."

"Really? That's what you think?" Sierra turned around to flip the steak, then back to me with her arms crossed again.

"Yeah. That's what I know," I said.

"Okay, so tell me this." She pressed me. "Magenta made about fifteen hundred each day she worked, so that's at least six thousand. But you came back to Toronto with zero dollars. What happened to the money?"

"I had to cover the Airbnb bills, the rentals, and shit we needed. Then I took her shopping and some outings with Whitey and Coco. Then I had to pay for my flight back down here."

"You see what I mean?" Sierra's voice sharpened. "You're always overspending on luxury rooms, spending too much on the girls, doing pointless first-class flights, and of course turning up and blowing money in clubs. Always the same routine when you get a new girl. Always the same shit when you're trying to recruit more. It's always a loss when it comes to new bitches. Then when you're done putting on the show, some don't even stick around long enough to start making us real money."

"Relax. I ain't ever putting on a show. I spend a lot on my girls because a bitch is entitled to enjoy the wealth of the life we living. The lavish lifestyle is just part of my campaign. You know this." I added, "And I do save money too."

"Okay, so maybe spending on a girl in the stable is fine. It keeps them happy to work harder, I get it," Sierra said. "But all that other shit is nonsense. A few months from now you're gonna stop paying attention to Magenta in search of a new bitch, while blowing money recklessly on your lifestyle. Not caring if she's happy or not." Sierra shook her head. "That's money going down the drain and a girl ready to leave because her pimp stops spending time for her."

"But don't I always make time for you?" I shot back. "Want me to see you less so I can spend more time with the others?"

"If you want. That's up to you." She shrugged like she didn't care, but we both knew she wouldn't want that. Then she said, "Or you can cut back on your partying and lavish lifestyle. I bet then you'll have enough time to see everybody and save us a whole lot of money."

I was done with arguing. "Listen, this is not a discussion. I'm flying Magenta back from Calgary next weekend, and you're gonna train her."

"No, I'm not," Sierra snapped, looking me dead on. "Get Velvet to train your new bitches from now on, 'cause I'm done with that. I'm focused on making money because you're blowing more than you save. In fact, I might have to start saving my money on my own."

A bitch of mine holding back money was like spitting in my face. As if I wasn't man enough, much less enough of a pimp to be paid everything, as the boss who handles everything. Sierra's statement was an extreme level of disrespect to my pimping and my alpha status to the whole stable.

I got up off the stool and walked around the dining counter towards her. Fire was in my eyes. "Have you ever held back money from me?"

"No." She stared at me, looking dead in my eyes without fear as I got closer. "But I just might have to start doing that since you ain't stack—"

I landed the rudest gorilla palm across her face and her whole body flew. Sierra bounced off the fridge and dropped to her knees. Ice from the maker scattered across the floor from the impact. My palm throbbed from the slap and she sobbed on the floor, holding the left side of her face. Still, I stood over her, half-naked in my boxers like a savage, ready to crack at whatever other stupid shit came out her mouth.

Sierra whimpered. "...I'm sorry."

Her voice and those words told me she'd been humbled, snapped back to her senses. She got the reminder she needed. This was a pimp and hoe thing, and she'd stepped out of line.

Sierra picked up the ice cubes off the floor while I went back round the counter and sat on my stool. She dropped the cubes in the sink and wiped her tears, then checked the steak. After turning off the stove, she plated the food, then came around the counter with it. Eyes down the whole time, quiet and small. A bad-bitch who'd just been disciplined.

She sat on the stool beside me where the next omelette waited, still not looking my way as she picked up her fork.

"What about the orange juice?" I asked, voice even.

"Oh, s-sorry." She stuttered, jumped up for the fridge, poured two glasses, and came back.

We ate in silence. I kept glancing at the red side of her face swelling out. I wasn't happy with what I'd done, but I had no regrets. Sierra was my bottom bitch, my woman, everything, and still needed a check sometimes. It got out of hand, yeah, but she'd challenged me on training a new girl and even talked about holding back her money. That shit couldn't slide. It wasn't like I put my hands on her often, but there were moments like this where she needed a reminder who ran things. Her pimp—*Gelato fucking Icy.*

CHAPTER THIRTEEN

Sunday, June 24 – 2:22 p.m.

Sierra and Gelato had eaten brunch together at his condo hours ago, in silence. The closest thing to a conversation was Gelato asking about her plans for the day, and Sierra giving short replies about a late-night arrangement with one of her regular clients. Their fight still hung in the air, heavy and unspoken. After hand washing the few dishes rather than using the dishwasher, she cleaned up the kitchen and made her quiet exit to get ready for her day. Still, she forced herself to give Gelato a respectful goodbye kiss before leaving. Gelato told her to put ice on her face when she got home so the swelling would go down before she saw her client.

It was an awkward departure for them both, and not their first physical fight. Something they'd likely get over sooner rather than later. After Sierra left, Gelato freshened up for his day. Red Café played through the sound system while he hit lines of cocaine at the dining counter every so often. This was his way of reviving his energy after the fight with Sierra. He couldn't allow himself to feel bad about what he'd done because that would make him a man unsure of his pimping. The coke helped numb his emotions and kept him from dwelling on anything.

After combing out his beard he threw on designer clothes, shoes, his Icy chain, rings, and Breitling watch, then left his luxurious unit to hit the road in his white Bentley convertible.

Vanessa's place was Gelato's first destination. After collecting a good week's money from the bedroom safe, he sat on the couch doing coke lines on her special plate. Vanessa was more than happy to have him over because this was the second time she'd seen him within the month. It wasn't the weekly visits he'd promised, but at least he was making the effort. Especially to see her first thing after returning from a week's travel. It was a good look on him.

Gelato hoped Vanessa would do some lines with him, but she declined because she'd be working the strip club tonight. Vanessa wasn't one to risk losing her focus at work by getting high. "You already know how that shit goes, Daddy." Curled up next to him on the couch in sweatpants and a T-shirt, Vanessa gave a small shake of her head. "It starts with one line now, then I'll be doing lines all day and night. I'll be all messed up. And I'm not trying to be way out of my mind at work."

Gelato nodded. He appreciated Vanessa's focus with work. A thought formed to commend her, but being too high kept him quiet, nodding again without meaning to.

Vanessa then said, "So are you gonna come to the clubs I'm working at this week, Daddy? I always do good when you show up at work."

"I might be going back to Calgary soon," Gelato replied. He told her the news. "There's a new girl on the team. Her name's Magenta."

Vanessa lit up. "Oh, wow! How long she been around?"

"About a week?"

"Oohh, so that's why you been in Calgary. Working with her." A pause followed. "So why didn't you tell me about her?"

Gelato shrugged. "I'm telling you now, no?"

"I guess," Vanessa chuckled. "When do I get to meet her?"

The questions started to wear on him, chipping at his high. Even so, Vanessa's joy was real, and she always welcomed another sister in the family. Gelato replied, "Yeah, you gonna meet her soon. I'm thinking about having you train her."

Vanessa's eyes widened with excitement. Then a flicker of confusion. "What about Skye? Isn't that her job?"

The questions would not stop. Gelato leaned into another line of coke even though he knew getting higher wouldn't help. What he really needed was a break so his mind could level out. Clear thinking rarely came when dancing with cocaine demons.

Vanessa asked again, "Isn't Skye supposed to be the one who trains the new girls?"

"Don't worry about that," Gelato finally answered. "Magenta will be rolling with you and Diamond more anyways, so it's better for you two to train her."

Vanessa nodded but kept a dull expression. The excitement Gelato expected wasn't there. He wondered, "Why don't you look happy anymore." He worried the question would lead to a conversation that needed him to think, something that would mess up his high.

"Diamond," Vanessa said. "I don't know what's going on with her."

"What you mean."

Vanessa sighed. "She's been distant the past week. Other than working at the same club yesterday and Friday, I haven't seen her at all."

"She's probably been busy with her tricks—"

"Yeah, I knew you'd say that," Vanessa cut in. "But we live in the same building. She'd at least make an effort to hang out any free time we both had. Even when I message her to meet me downstairs in the gym, she's not interested. And at work, she was acting weird with me. I think something's up with her, Daddy. You need to check on her."

"She was acting weird, how?"

"Sh-she-she..." Vanessa stuttered, paused, then settled on, "She wasn't really talking to me much."

Gelato analyzed everything for a moment, and all it did was ruin his coke high. Dianna going a week without socializing with Vanessa wasn't the end of the world. Vanessa had a clingy nature and grew up spoiled, thinking the world revolved around her. She expected everyone to be attentive to her, always. Dianna probably just needed time to herself and didn't know how to tell Vanessa. This wasn't something that needed Gelato's immediate attention, especially not when it would complicate his high.

He tried to shut it down with, "Don't worry too much about it. You'll be busy with Magenta from now on."

Vanessa nodded, looking pleased enough with his answer, but her mind was far from settled. There was more behind her complaint than Dianna not wanting to hang out. Vanessa wasn't about to tell Gelato everything. Only she knew Dianna had cancelled on a client a few nights ago because she'd gotten too high on coke during the day, for no reason, and wasn't in the right state to leave her home. Then, just Friday night, Vanessa had walked into the changing room and caught Dianna popping Percocet with another girl. It became talk among the dancers that Dianna had picked up a new habit.

Vanessa wasn't going to rat on her best friend. Their loyalties ran deep. But she owed Gelato loyalty too, which was why she tried again to cue him that something was wrong.

"I'm not worried about not seeing her as much, Daddy," she said, ignoring the fact that his face was in the plate doing another line. "I'm worried about her well-being. I really think you should try and see what's up with her. She hasn't been herself this past week. You should talk to her and feel her out."

The conversation was getting deeper than Gelato could handle. He did another line hoping the fog would pull him away from Vanessa, or at least shut her up. When he looked up, she was still there, curled beside him on the couch, her bright eyes fixed on him, waiting. She didn't care that he looked doped-out. She was determined to keep talking. The pressure weighed on him, so he set the cocaine plate on the side table and moved in on Vanessa. A lovely smile lit her face as she realized what he was doing. It dawned on her that he wasn't in the right mind for this conversation, so he was using sex as a way out. And she didn't mind.

Before their lips met, Vanessa whispered seductively, "Daddy, I want you to fuck me good and fill my cookie with a lot of ice cream."

Gelato would give her whatever she wanted. He might've been coked-up and not thinking straight, but there was nothing about Vanessa's request he'd question, even sober. As far as he knew, she was still on birth control.

CHAPTER FOURTEEN

Sunday, June 24 – 4:12 p.m.

Two rounds of wild, sweaty sex with Velvet helped drain the Designer-D out of my system and put me back in a decent state of mind to deal with Diamond. Some of that come-down had me in my emotions, feeling a touch of guilt about the way I slapped Sierra earlier, but not enough to make me call and apologize. I wasn't sorry for what I'd done. I just felt bad that it had come to that. I wasn't heading to Diamond's place because of anything Velvet complained about, either. I needed to collect whatever cash Diamond had stacked while I'd been in Calgary.

I hadn't texted to say I was coming, so I wasn't sure if she'd be home or at work. Reaching her unit, I let myself in with my key, focused on getting to the safe in the bedroom. Diamond was home. Caught her getting ready for a 6 p.m. trick. She was sober and could see I was the one coming off a sloppy high. Funny how the tables flipped since our last time together at the strip club, when she'd been the mess on Designer-Dope and alcohol. At least now I didn't look completely gone, since most of it had sweated out of me downstairs with Velvet.

I sat on the edge of the bed while Diamond stood at the mirrored dresser, dolling up her face as we caught up. Her bodacious, perfectly round ass pushed against the purple French-cut panties, and the matching bra held her DDs high and firm. Diamond was carved like a sex

God's favourite. A natural body that women like Cardi B paid surgeons for.

She turned to look at me every so often, those distinctive Indigenous eyes locking on me before she faced the mirror again. Watching her from behind was just as good. Ink covered parts of her back, tribal stars on her shoulder blade running down her spine in a squiggly line before ending in a lotus on her lower back. And, of course, the ice cream choker sat snug around her neck, matching the big bowl of scoops hanging from mine.

Diamond spoke about how she missed me and was glad to have me over, even though our time wouldn't last long because she had a trick to see soon. I apologized for not coming by in so long and told her I would've last week if I hadn't gone to Calgary. I mentioned the new bitch, Magenta, and Diamond was happy about the news of another sister in the family. After catching up, there were more important things to get into. I asked what she'd been going through that had her overdoing Designer-D and alcohol. Her honest answer was that she wasn't going through anything at all. She just enjoyed the Designer-D high too much. Diamond took full accountability, spoke on it maturely, and apologized for behaving like a coke-head these past couple months. She needed to cut back on that stuff and promised not to disappoint me again. I accepted her apology and left it there. There wasn't much more for me to say, especially since I'd shown up fresh off a toxic high myself.

I asked next if everything was good between her and Velvet. Diamond gave me a concerned look at first, but once I explained how Velvet felt neglected, she laughed and said she loved Velvet, and that would never change. She went on to explain that she'd just been busy with a new trick who'd been seeing her a lot this past week, and the rest of her free time went to catching up on sleep. Turns out my judgement was right. Velvet had been whining about nothing serious.

Diamond was always understanding and never complained about anything, no matter what we went through or how long it had been since she last saw me. Perhaps it was easier for someone who hadn't grown up with much to be satisfied with how life was now. I may have been rough on her at times, but her life had been a lot rougher, so the luxury she lived in now felt like a blessing in its own way. That didn't excuse the times I'd dealt with her harshly, but I appreciated the type of humble bitch she was, fully accepting my pimping. Diamond had nothing to complain about. She only told me to come back earlier tomorrow when she'd be free because she needed me to dick her down. According to her, that was all she'd been missing and needed to get her mind straight again. Hearing that turned me on, had me wanting to fuck her right then and there, real quick, but she didn't want to ruin her makeup and end up taking longer to get ready for her trick.

We were talking about her birthday plans when Diamond turned to me and said, "I honestly don't know what I wanna do. Why don't you just plan it for me?"

"It's your big day, baby. You gotta let me know what you want and I gotta make it happen."

"Okay, Daddy. I have about two weeks, so I'll let you know in a couple of days." She turned back to the mirror and focused on her eyeliner.

Her fat ass kept pulling my eyes back every time she moved, bulging out those French-cut panties. Crazy how it stayed that big and jiggly with no stretch marks, no cellulite, no hint of bad fat at all. The sexual frustration pushed me up from the bed. I moved in behind Diamond, my hand sliding to her waist as I reached to pull her closer. She felt my touch and tried to push me off, her voice tense. "Daddy, no. I gotta get ready—"

I grabbed the back of her neck, a handful of her silky platinum blonde hair in my grip, and forcefully bent her forward. My other hand dug into my zipper and pulled my dick out.

"Daddy, I'll be late if we do this now," Diamond said, her voice thick with arousal. She wasn't resisting anymore and dropped the eyeliner on the dresser.

I slid her panties to the side and felt that fat pussy already warm and wet for me. So I shoved my hard dick right into her. Deep, rough and hungry. Diamond stayed bent over with her arms braced on the dresser as I dug into her from behind, my grip firm on her waist. Her fat pussy gripped me just right, soft and wet, watching her ass bounce with every stroke, round and hypnotic, and my chain swinging over her back while she held that arch like she knew what I liked.

She creamed, off-white cum oozing over my dick while I kept stroking. Her moans pushed my arousal even higher. I felt like a champ, surging into a quick roaring victory. My legs trembled as I released all that pleasure.

We went quiet, both of us breathing heavy, while the last few drops leaked out into her warmth. Surprised me, how much I still had left in me after dumping two full loads in Velvet not too long ago.

"I don't think my trick's into Boston cream," Diamond joked, still bent over with me going soft inside her. I let out a quiet breath and pulled out, tucking my cream-slicked dick back in my pants. She said, walking off to the washroom, "At least my makeup didn't get ruined."

I went to the kitchen for a clean plate, came back into the bedroom, and sat on the bed. With the plate on my lap, I took out the baggie of Designer-D from my pocket and grabbed a bank card to begin setting up lines. The bathtub water stopped running, and Diamond came back out with her lower half bare and freshly rinsed, her top still dry with the bra on. She watched me hit a line with interest before turning back to the dresser to finish her makeup.

Four rails in, I finally said, "Here, babe."

She turned to see me offering the plate and rolled bill but shook her head. "No, Daddy. My trick is expecting me at six sharp, and it's gonna take me a while to drive with all this bad traffic. I gotta stay focused on getting ready so I can leave soon."

I figured she was only refusing because of the talk we'd had earlier and now wanted to show me she was focused on work. The Diamond I knew never turned down a chance to turn-up with me, so she wasn't fooling anyone. I got off the bed and brought the plate over to her at the dresser. I told her, "Text your trick and cancel with him. You're mine tonight."

Diamond met my eyes and caught the intensity behind them. She bit her bottom lip and I could see her wanting to give in, but she stayed firm. "Daddy, please, I wanna go get this money for you."

Hearing that was nice, but she didn't understand how I felt. Having her pussy already reminded me of what I'd been missing. One round wasn't enough and I wanted more. I needed her. And with the Designer-Dope running through me again, I wanted the night to keep going. I planned to drown us both in that foggy abyss.

I took her wrist firmly and looked into her small eyes, asking with force, "You love me?"

Biting onto her bottom lip again, Diamond breathed heavy. She loved the aggression and the intensity I brought. Her eyes stayed locked on mine, already soft with submission. "Yes, Daddy. I love you, always."

"Good," I said. "I love you, too. And miss you." Her wrist was still in my hand and her pulse jumped against my grip. I lowered my tone, stern but calm. "Cancel your trick."

I let her go and she quickly grabbed her phone off the dresser, fingers tapping fast. "I just told him something came up and I can't make it, so I'm waiting to see what he says. He normally responds quick—"

I took the phone from her hand and tossed it back onto the dresser. "Do a line with me."

We hit rails from the plate on the dresser. Each time Diamond bent over to take a line, her pussy was right there, glistening from the steam of her bath. It had me watching her with straight hunger. She looked too good, bent over and offering herself without even meaning to. The way her body moved under the light had my blood heating up again. I drew her up from the dresser and kissed her aggressively, sliding her bra off to free her pierced nipples. Then I led her to the bed, ready to have my way with her. These rounds would last much longer now that the Designer-D had me numb and charged.

We were both naked, going at it hard in missionary. I had one hand around her throat, the other smacking her face between strokes. Then I flipped her over, put her in doggy. Her fat ass stayed high while her face sank into the mattress. I pounded her from behind, slapping her cheeks as they jiggled under my grip. Somewhere in the madness, I swung my left leg over her back and planted my foot against the side of her head, holding her down while still stroking deep. The dominance and pressure was real. Hands on her waist for balance, my right leg braced as I kept drilling her from behind. This shit felt different, but every time I took control with Diamond, I ended up unlocking some new moves. She was a sexy giant like me, and dominating her was how I reminded her we weren't equals. I was the man—a pimp. She was my bitch, moaning and bawling out my name because she loved every second of it.

At some point we shifted sideways. I stroked her slow from behind, her head locked under my arm. Her moans came out broken, stifled by the way I held her. She couldn't let them out right, just soft gasps fighting to escape as I kept her tight against me. Her round ass cushioned my pelvis as I stroked into her creamy pussy. Sweat dripped off both of us, soaking the sheets. I breathed heavy in her ear like a beast, keeping her in submission. Her moans came out like cries. I had control of her, and a growing urge to conquer her in other ways. I loosened my arm from around her neck, spit on my fingers, and ran it between her ass cheeks, right through the crack.

Slipping out of her pussy, I shifted up to find the tighter hole. My dick pressed against her closed-up backdoor. Diamond gripped the sheets, bracing for the invasion. I leaned in and whispered in her ear, "Bitch, don't shit on my shank."

"Never, Daddy," she whimpered.

She gasped for air the moment I forced myself into her tight little asshole. A moment of grace was granted, letting her body settle into having me inside. Then I started stroking slow.

Picked up a steady pace.

Her cries hit the air like tears in a love song, but that wasn't stopping me. I locked her neck back in my arms, and now she was struggling to breathe too. I bit her ear like an animal, loving how her perfume and the scent of her hair filled up my face.

Diamond started tapping on my arm, hoping I'd ease up on the lock. She couldn't breathe. She was shit out of luck. That nut was coming fast in her tight ass, and the surge of pleasure shot through me hard enough to make my whole body spasm. I clenched up on her neck.

She might've passed out in the headlock before it was all over.

I let go of her and sighed, like a beast easing out of battle. She came back to life, gasping like she'd been pulled from deep water. The round was done, but I wasn't. Just needed a breather, a second to collect myself, then another hit of Designer-Dope to charge the demon back up.

For the rest of the night, I didn't just fuck—I performed. I preached with dick. Baptized her in lust. Turned that room into a chapel, and her body into my altar. By the time I was done, I wasn't just a man no more. I was a sex God.

And she?

She was the offering.

CHAPTER FIFTEEN

Sunday, June 24 – 11:53 p.m.

The bright lighting over Sierra's washroom countertop gave her a clear view in the mirror as she worked to cover the redness on one side of her face. The swelling and pain had gone down after hours of icing when she got home, enough to make the damage manageable. All that was left was contour and blush along her cheekbone, just enough to blend the irritation into her skin. She'd done this before. There were times she covered hickeys from Gelato, moments that once came with quiet giggles and small smiles. Those markings had felt different. Good times and bad times both came with hiding Gelato's marks. This time, there was nothing to smile about.

Sierra couldn't bring herself to be angry with anyone but herself when she thought about what had happened earlier. In her mind, it was her fault. Everything that went wrong with Gelato always circled back to her. This could've been avoided if she'd remembered what she signed up for. She'd let herself forget that no matter how much she loved him, or how much he claimed to love her, Gelato Icy had been a pimp the day she met him. She'd chosen him as his bitch, and that truth never changed. The bottom bitch was still just another girl in the stable. If Gelato felt disrespected or crossed, discipline came the same way it would with any other girl. That was exactly what he'd done today.

Sierra became the golden girl from the moment she entered Gelato's stable. Staying on her best behaviour left him little reason to put his hands on her. At most, he used brute strength to pin her by the neck against a wall when she slipped up over something minor or gave him attitude. Discipline rarely came her way. After five solid years of loyalty and minimal correction, the bottom bitch position opened up, and Sierra had the seniority to step into it. Even before then, a deeper bond had formed between her and Gelato, built on understanding and companionship, something the other girls resented. Watching previous seniors take the title and eventually leave only strengthened her resolve. Sierra meant to hold the position until the end.

Stepping into the role came with pressure she hadn't fully anticipated. As Gelato's main representative, she took on a secondary management role and spent far more time at his side. More proximity meant more conflict. When she messed up, violence followed. Gelato justified it by saying his emotional investment ran deeper with her, that frustration and anger hit harder because she was his closest woman. Once, he broke her nose while beating her badly. He'd been drunk and coked up, and Sierra accepted that incident as something beyond his control. He apologized, and that mattered to her. After that, he learned to rein in his anger, especially when under the influence, and she learned to give him as little reason as possible to touch her. Still, he did again. That was the last time, until today. Sierra remembered every detail of it.

The whole team had gone on vacation to Punta Cana the year before, along with Smooth and a couple of his girls. There was a day when Gelato and Smooth stayed in bed after partying too hard on their private excursions the night before. That left Sierra, Dianna, Vanessa, and Smooth's girls wandering the resort with nothing to do while waiting for their men to wake up. A group of American guys noticed the women gathered by the pool, drinking and laughing without men around. They invited them to join a private yacht cruise just off the resort. Normally, the girls never spent time with men who weren't paying. But vacation came with different rules, or at least that was what Gelato and Smooth claimed whenever they fooled around with random women while travelling. Seeing it that way, Sierra, Alize, and Star agreed to lead the others onto the yacht.

Nothing happened beyond drinking and dirty dancing. Still, the Americans assumed things would eventually turn sexual if they kept the drinks flowing and the mood light. That illusion ended once Gelato and Smooth woke up, looking for their girls. Messages went back and forth and the girls were honest about being on a yacht with friendly guys, and promised nothing else was happening. It didn't matter. Gelato and Smooth snapped. The girls begged the Americans to turn the boat around and rush them back to the resort.

When they arrived, Gelato took Sierra alone into his hotel room. He beat her until she lost control of her body and pissed herself. She couldn't leave the room again until the swelling in her face went down and her body stopped aching. That didn't happen until the trip was over a week later. Alize and Star suffered similar beatings from Smooth, leaving them with fractured ribs that needed medical attention once they returned to Canada. Dianna, Vanessa, and the rest of Smooth's girls weren't touched. According to the pimps, the decision to get on that yacht could only have come from the bottom bitches. Sierra, Alize, and Star were held responsible because they were in charge when their pimps weren't present. Everything that happened with the group fell on them. The blame was clear. Even when the other girls tried to take accountability for their own choices, it only made Gelato and Smooth angrier. The truth, as the men saw it, was simple. Bottom bitches should've known better than to think entertaining men for fun would ever be acceptable, even on vacation. That was one of the costs of holding the position.

Since then, Sierra kept her distance from outings with the other girls. It was safer that way. If something went wrong, she didn't want to be the one answering to Gelato again.

The woman staring back at her looked composed now, the markings on her left cheek hidden well enough. Her beauty still radiated. A pretty girl who belonged to Gelato Icy. No matter how many years they shared or how deep their connection ran, the dynamics of their relationship never changed. She found herself wondering how much longer they would stay in the game. For years, Gelato had said one day they'd be out, owning businesses and living clean. Yet the way he moved showed no signs of a pimp preparing to leave anytime soon.

Her thoughts drifted to Whitey and Coco, how they'd conquered the game by turning it into business, just the two of them as a real team. Sierra wondered if it would truly be just her and Gelato at the end. She couldn't help but think about what he might be promising the other girls these days. As far as she was concerned, they could be waiting for her to slip so one of them could take the bottom bitch position. Even if she stayed strong until the end, what if the others made it there too?

Would they become permanent sister wives, running his businesses and raising his children together?

She liked Dianna and Vanessa, and part of her thought maybe it wouldn't be so bad sharing Gelato with them, just as she already did. Still, deep down, Sierra had always imagined something different. A nuclear family of her own with Gelato. A better version of the broken home she'd grown up in. A tear slid down her face as the weight of it all settled in. A normal relationship would've been easier than this. She loved Gelato too much and felt lost inside the reality of the life she'd chosen. Sierra leaned over the washroom sink and broke down, letting the tears come. The emotions had been building for too long. Her heart hurt because she loved a pimp. Her thoughts, her reality, her state of mind were tangled beyond order.

She'd have to wash her face again and redo her makeup before seeing her client. But for now, she needed to cry and let it all out.

CHAPTER SIXTEEN

Tuesday, June 26 – 12:02 a.m.

Dianna had been surprised when Gelato showed up at her place two days earlier. What lingered was their conversation about her turn-up habits and Vanessa's complaints about her acting different. The worry came quick. Maybe Vanessa had told him about the day she cancelled on a trick because she was too high. Or worse, about the night she'd been caught taking Percocet in the strip club. But nothing like that came up. Vanessa had only spoken about distance. Her loyalty held. And Dianna still knew she hadn't been fair. She'd been busier lately, but that didn't excuse disappearing on her best friend during the little free time she had. Especially when that time was spent recovering from drug turn-ups with tricks. She'd have to fix that.

For now, her attention stayed elsewhere. Dianna remained occupied with a client she'd been seeing almost every night for the past week. His name was Eric, a tall fifty-year-old Caucasian man who looked his age, grey at the temples with a thinning crown. His chest and belly sagged, though he still carried himself like a man in decent health, pitted skin and all. He owned businesses around the world, multiple homes, and a mansion lined with exotic cars. The two of them were in his two-storey penthouse downtown, where the luxury alone explained how he could afford her rates and still tip heavy.

Dianna and Eric had already gone through plenty of expensive wine and coke, just like they always did before their sessions. They were butt naked, Dianna on top, riding him slow like a surfboard. She moved with purpose, grinding so he felt every inch of her. Eyes closed, not because she couldn't stand to look at him, but because she was lost in the feel of him deep inside. She loved the way his mature hands held onto her curves while hers pressed down on his grey-haired chest. Getting through the session didn't require thoughts of Gelato. Sex with Eric was exactly what Dianna wanted. What she never admitted to anyone was that she genuinely enjoyed her job. Being touched, wanted, and sexually appreciated by all kinds of men gave her a feeling most wouldn't understand. Sometimes she even preferred the older clients over the younger ones, who often didn't know what they were doing. Younger men either tried to be aggressive but came off weak, or had no clue how to deliver real sensual sex. Most times, it was just selfish strokes to a quick nut, and Dianna had to accept it for what it was—part of the job. Aggression was best when it came from Gelato. The sensual kind was a gift the older clients knew how to give.

Dianna's messed-up upbringing with George left her craving older men. She'd grown used to chasing that father figure in all the wrong, twisted ways she was shown growing up. Back when her sex drive first kicked in and she started exploring, George was the one feeding her the answers she thought she needed. Even while she was with her Caribbean man, she cheated with the elderly neighbour because something about older men just felt familiar, even when it was wrong.

Life was good now for a young woman like Dianna with a powerful sex drive. She made her money seeing men who craved her bad enough to pay premium rates, mostly older ones who knew how to please her. The cocaine in her system sharpened every sensation, drawing a graceful moan from Dianna as she moved on Eric. His pelvis rose and fell in rhythm with her motion, matching her pace. He loved the view of her body above him, the weight of her breasts, the glint of the piercings, the way her face gave away how deeply she was enjoying him. His hands slid from her hips to her wrists, gripping them where they rested on his chest, pulling her down slowly. Their mouths met, lips locking, while her lower body kept grinding into him. The kiss was exactly what Dianna needed. Heat climbed fast, spilling over as her moans grew louder, her body betraying the moment she reached her peak.

Eric didn't waste it. He rolled them over to get on top, taking control, then moved down between Dianna's legs. His mouth found her and stayed there as her body reacted instantly. Dianna quivered beneath him, sounds breaking loose while her fingers clenched the sheets, riding out the full pull of her orgasm while he stayed between her thighs.

The moment was over. Eric looked up at her with a smile, and Dianna smiled back. He slipped two fingers into her and brought the milky fingers up close to her face. Dianna eyed his fingers with a smile, tempted to lick them. But before she could, Eric brought them to her lips and slid them in, letting her taste the same sweetness he'd just enjoyed. He had denied himself his orgasm, choosing instead to focus on intensifying Dianna's. But he would get his. He moved on top of her and slid his hard penis into her, this time holding up her thick thighs to drill into her. Dianna grabbed the back of his head to bring him in closer and locked lips with him. She made out with him passionately, knowing there was a chance she would get another orgasm before he finally got his.

Dianna and Eric settled into matching silk robes he'd bought for them. He'd gifted her a small diamond lollipop pendant on a platinum choker on a previous visit, meant to complement the ice cream she always wore at her neck. Dianna refused to wear it. The only chain allowed there was the Icy branding. She never explained what the ice cream really meant or how it tied back to her pimp. As far as Eric knew, she was an exotic dancer providing high-end services independently, and keeping it that way protected the affection he showed her.

Curled together on a large beanbag couch by the bar, they held wine in their hands while a small glass table sat in front of them. An exclusive bottle rested there beside a sleek tray laid out with lines of cocaine, a black card near a small pile to set more, and a golden straw placed neatly for the ritual. Gelato had left Dianna with a good portion of coke that morning and made her promise she'd only use it with a client who asked. She left that baggie at home. Eric always had his own supply ready. With him, it never felt like a paid arrangement. They stayed high, drunk, and close like lovers, not checking the time, letting the night run as long as it wanted. When it was done, Eric wired whatever amount she asked for, and the money eventually made its way to Gelato. And he sat at the end of the equation, tucked behind the good time Dianna let herself have. With Eric, she could be fully herself because he loved to turn-up just like she did. She could get high until she crashed and he wouldn't judge it. He only tried to keep pace. When that strain became too much for his ageing heart, he shifted to other drugs to steady himself. Dianna pushed past the edge of the coke high and into the crash on purpose, already anticipating what Eric would use to balance it out.

"I wanna do some of the other stuff," she said.

"Which stuff, darling?" Eric asked, his mind still swimming in coke.

"The OP stuff. To bring me down."

"Opioids, you mean?"

"Yes, that one." Dianna smiled and kissed him on the lips. Her glassy eyes gave her away.

"Alright. I'll go grab some Percocet from the cabinet upstairs."

"No. I don't want that."

Eric paused. "What, darling? You don't like the Percocet anymore?"

"Yes, I love those. I told you already, I do it all the time now. One of my girls at the club gets it for me." Her mind drifted for a second before she caught herself. "I want the other stuff. The stronger stuff I tried last time."

Eric was the one who introduced Dianna to Percocet. That happened weeks earlier, during their first arrangement after meeting at a strip club in Pickering.

She'd gone too far on cocaine and fell into a fog where conversation was pointless. Eric recognized the state. Wanting to steady her and regain control of the moment, he offered her a Percocet to bring the high down. It worked. Too well. The overstimulation eased into something smooth, almost comforting, and Dianna took that relief as an answer. From then on, Percocet became her way of managing the mental disarray. She knew girls at the clubs who could get it whenever she wanted, and before long, it became routine. Nights with Eric meant pushing the coke high hard, then using pills to land softly.

Eventually, the pills stopped doing the job they were meant for. Dianna found herself taking them even when there was no dysregulation to manage, chasing the body buzz instead. What she was asking for now wasn't Percocet. It was something else she'd tried a few nights earlier. Something Eric hadn't offered, only used himself while feeding his own habits. Watching him take it had stirred her curiosity. The more he warned her off, explaining how dangerous it was and how easily it could ruin someone, the deeper her interest grew. But Eric refused. He told her it wasn't something she should touch. That it was too addictive. Too easy to overdose on. He didn't want to be the one who pushed her down that path. In Dianna's fogged mind, his restraint carried a fatherly weight she'd always craved.

She'd broken one of her hard rules for him the last time, giving him oral sex without a condom in exchange for trying that drug. Eric made her promise it would be a one-time exception, only with him, and never something she'd seek out on her own. She gave him her word. He gave her the smallest amount to snort. That was the first time Dianna tried heroin.

The feeling stayed with her. The warmth. She'd been looking forward to trying it again ever since. The orgasmic buzz Dianna felt off the heroin stayed with her, making it impossible not to want it again. Tonight would be the second time. The first had already set the terms. She took the initiative during tonight's session, polishing Eric's bare penis again and slipping the promise in while he was too lost in the moment to think it through.

Dianna reminded Eric, "The heroin. You promised me, remember? I sucked your dick without a condom, so I already did my part of the deal, babe."

"Oh…that." Eric didn't like the idea of Dianna getting into the habit. "Darling, I don't want you becoming addicted to that stuff. You'll end up depending on it like me. I don't—"

Dianna struck him hard in the chest, wine sloshing out of both their glasses. "Go get it!" she snapped. "You fucking promised me!"

Eric set his glass down and got to his feet without another word. He wasn't about to have Dianna upset with him. If she asked for it, he'd give it to her.

If only she knew.

CHAPTER SEVENTEEN

Wednesday, June 27 – 1:12 a.m.
(Mountain Daylight Time—Calgary, Alberta)

After leaving Diamond's place the other morning, I packed light and caught the next first-class flight to Calgary. Magenta was still doing good when I caught up with her, working steady through the days I left her alone. That was the sign I needed. No babysitting. No chasing her around to keep her on schedule. This was always the setup I preferred. Let my girls choose their days off and manage their own pace, as long as my bread stayed consistent. A bitch should be focused at least five days a week. Sometimes the bookings got heavy and they had to spread appointments through the week with no real day off. When things slowed down, the strip club filled the gap every time.

Smooth caught the next flight to Calgary right after me to check on two of his girls, Asian Ling-Lin and Brazilian Jade. They weren't working at Consational, not premium enough to compete with the girls in there, but they did fine out of hotels, posting on escort sites at Alberta's common rate of $400 for full services. Tomorrow we were flying back to Toronto, and that was when Magenta would start learning the strip club side of the game.

Tonight was party time. We were in a nightclub downtown, the city's popular Tuesday night turn-up. My partners and I did our thing, and the locals ate up the glamour and VIP status we brought with us. Whitey came through with sexy Coco, and our girls held the booth down. Coco led by example, showing the girls how to keep it classy while partying with the big boys. She'd been around us for years, so she knew exactly how we wanted our women representing us in these spots.

Whitey's older brother, Gambit, was with us too. Bald, chubby, Hungarian, Toronto stamped, certified in the fraud department. He was the one who connected me to the right people years ago to get my personal training business set up so I could claim income on paper. Wouldn't surprise me if he had a hand in Consational. Gambit showed up with no girl, like always. He wasn't a pimp, just a major league scammer who'd catch a girl in the club tonight and forget about her by tomorrow.

The club was packed, and our booth sat in an elevated VIP pocket beside the DJ, so all eyes stayed on us. Thirsty bitches. Regular dudes turning into groupies. Even the guys who thought they were guys, until we walked in and changed the temperature. Girls in the lower booths kept looking up like it was a show, and Gambit made sure to flash that VVS full-grill smile at them every so often. Strong jewels were on my neck and wrist, the huge Icy pendant and the Breitling speaking loud. Smooth had his thick Cuban link buss down, no pendant, just weight and presence, and that platinum pimp on a throne medallion sat on his wrist like a stamp, with the Oyster Perpetual Rolex on the other. Whitey's wrist looked like Arctic glaciers, with more ice shining through his Cartier frames and his signature Audemars Piguet.

Latest fashion, clean fits, and all our best diamond pinky rings just to say it without saying it, pimping going on. Our bad bitches were dressed to match the energy, Magenta, Coco, Ling-Lin, and Jade in tight designer pieces and dresses, jewellery catching light every time they moved. They represented us right, swaying and posing like the booth belonged to them too. Calgary's urban culture was close enough to Toronto's, but the locals could feel we were strong hustlers from the big city off the vibe alone. Nobody could stop watching. Girls and groupie dudes crowded near the front of the booth, jamming to the popular tracks like we were the performers.

The booth cost 5K and came with three Hennessy bottles and three Moet bottles. Smooth and I were on our usual stunt game, popping bottles every twenty minutes, keeping the light show circling back to our section for the Instagram and Snapchat flex. We started stunting at 12:20 a.m., minutes after we got there, and it brought another six Henny bottles to the booth. Each bottle was $500, the kind of price that was meant to feel ridiculous. Still, we ordered like it was nothing, stacking more liquor than we could even touch, then tossing two bottles into the crowd just because we could. Gambit was busy too, inviting girls up and pouring drinks like we had unlimited supply, because we did. Whitey and Gambit had grabbed enough Designer-D from one of their quality sources in the city, and our VIP section had its own private washroom. Gambit would slip in there now and then to hit rails, leaving a good pile on the clean counter with a card and a bill sitting there like an open invitation for the rest of us to follow up. So Smooth and I slid into the VIP washroom to turn it up.

With the door closed, the music wasn't as loud. He said to me, "It's almost 1:20, playa. We gon' need another light show."

I snorted four lines off the counter then passed him the rolled bill. "Yeah, man. We definitely gon' get some new bitches by the end of the night."

"Hell yeah, playa. We gon' press up on these hoes wit' the parking lot pimping."

Smooth and I both rented a Rolls Royce for the night, so if the girls in the club were feeling our vibes now then they'd be throwing their panties at us once seeing the cars we pulled up in.

The washroom door opened and Whitey came in with a smile on his face. "I wanna get lit with my brothers!"

"That's what I'm talking 'bout, playa," Smooth said. He did his line then passed the bill to Whitey. "Fix your face and get right up there with the pimp Gods."

Whitey was eager to hit some rails and said, "I cut back on the Designer-D a while ago, but when I'm around my brothers, I gotta revive the liveliness in me. Y'all bring me back to life." He did two rails, then left the bill beside the remaining pile on the counter. Cartier tints hid his eyes, but he was definitely rolling. He'd been in the washroom earlier with Coco, so I figured they were turning up too. Those two had been focused on Consational Spa and hadn't partied with us like this in a long time. Having us in town was their breather from all that business and work.

I patted Whitey on the back, and the Designer-D had me in my emotions. "I'm proud of you, man. Brother, you inspired me to bring this game to new levels. After this summer, I promised myself I'm cutting back on all that fun and focusing on stacking better, getting some business going too. I really wanna build something with Sierra."

"Nigga, man, you be sounding crazy," Smooth laughed. "You talking like this prime pimpin' ain't already a business." He popped the collar on his Louis Vuitton shirt. "We some motherfuckin' gentlemen of leisure, and I'm feeling to give these hoes the business."

We all laughed, then followed Smooth out of the washroom and back into the blaring music. The door spilled us straight into our booth. Coco headed into the washroom with Magenta, Ling-lin, and Jade, no doubt to hit some rails. A sexy dark-skinned girl had joined Gambit in the booth, and they were up at the front spraying Moet into the crowd. Most of the crowd ate up the champagne shower, getting louder in it, while a few people in the lower booths looked pissed about a little of it landing on them.

Pulled a cold Henny bottle from the ice bucket and poured myself a drink. Smooth nudged me and slipped $550 into my hand. He leaned in and said, "Lights, camera, action."

It was 1:22 a.m., so I waved our booth's sexy East African bottle service girl, Sarah, over and handed her $1100. The extra $100 was always our generous tip for the light show services.

Sarah leaned in and asked, "Another two Henny bottles?"

"Yeah." I gave her a nod.

Her eyes flicked toward the ice buckets. "But you guys got so many bottles already, and some aren't even touched yet."

"Yeah, I know," I said low in her ear, voice firm. "Just bring the bottles." My palm tapped her round ass to send her off. Sarah rolled her eyes, but walked away smiling. She probably wanted to fuck me. A quick note went into my head, leaving here with both her and Magenta. Assuming Sarah wasn't in the game meant I could rightfully give her a sample of me in a threesome. If she wanted more of me after that, then getting introduced to the game would be the only way.

Our bitches came back from the washroom and refilled their cups, dancing and enjoying themselves in the booth. They looked sexy, and pride sat heavy in my chest seeing Magenta officially in my stable. The only thing she was missing was the official Icy brand choker, and that came after a solid six months in my stable. Magenta caught my eye and smiled, so a wink went back. She blushed. With Whitey and Smooth taking over performance duty at the front of the booth, Gambit drifted over with his dark-skinned empress and poured her some drinks. She introduced herself to our girls, then to me. Too high to hold onto her name, but the introduction told me enough—she was his girl for the night.

Two Hennessy bottles came from the bar on the far end of the club with sparklers flaring, so I stepped up with Whitey and Smooth at the front of the booth, phone out, catching our fourth 1K light show of the night. Another post for the fans. 4K worth of bottles on a weeknight in Alberta. Smooth filmed too, and the girls had their phones ready. Whitey and Gambit didn't care for recording, they worked the crowd instead, keeping the energy high so our footage looked alive. Everything was set. Sarah, the bottle service girl, pushed through the hyped crowd with both bottles raised, heading for our elevated booth. She got halfway and the sparklers on both bottles died out at the same time. Gone. She disappeared into the moving bodies for a second, and everybody in our booth stopped filming, confused. The crowd didn't care though. With Gambit and Whitey still gassing them up, the party kept rolling.

Seconds later Sarah popped back up at the steps and climbed into our section, bottles in both hands. She leaned into my ear when she saw my face. "Sorry, the sparklers burnt out. They must've gotten wet." Then she slid the bottles into the ice tub with the rest.

Smooth looked at me, unimpressed with the bitch, and I felt it too. I stepped over to Sarah and kept my mouth close to her ear. "Listen up. Take those two bottles back to the bar, get fresh flares on them, and redo our light show."

"What?!" Sarah sounded offended. "You want me to go and come back with the bottles just because the flares didn't last all the way here?"

I nodded.

"I don't know what you think this is or who you take me for," she snapped, already turning like she was about to walk off.

My hand shot out and caught her by the neck, holding her right where she stood while she fought to break free.

"Bitch, who you think you moving sick with?" I said, low and hard.

Out front, the crowd stayed locked on Gambit and Whitey, too hyped to clock what was going on inside the booth. Security did. Three of them rushed up and forced me to release Sarah. Heads started turning, the tension jumped, and the DJ cut the music dead. Sarah stormed out of the booth cursing loud enough to drag all eyes our way.

"Bro, what's up? Everything's alright?" Whitey turned to me, noticing the three security guys around me and more pushing into the booth.

"Security out here trippin' because they caught a whiff of pimping," Smooth replied, proud as ever. "That bitch didn't put respect on our bottles, then had the nerve to get slick with pimpin' Gelato."

I squared up with security, reading their faces and waiting to see what they wanted. They didn't look too sure either, not with a man my size, and Smooth right there behind me.

"Can we please get the manager over here?" one of the security guys said into his radio.

Our girls stayed off to one side of the booth, nervous and quiet. Whitey slid over beside me and Smooth, ready for whatever. All eyes in the club lifted towards our section. People in the lower booths stood up to get a better look, phones already out, hungry for something to post or make go viral. The place buzzed with murmurs, while our booth went tense and still.

Gambit pulled out a couple hundred, trying to defuse the situation with security. He reached toward the one who looked like the lead. "This is for the trouble. Take that and let's move forward with the night."

A voice came up the booth's steps. "What's going on over here?" It was a short older man with tanned skin and a crisp grey suit, the manager, maybe even the owner.

"An incident happened with these men and bottle service," the lead security said.

"What's the problem?" the manager asked, looking between us.

Smooth jumped in. "My man, your bottle service girl didn't put respect on our bottles."

The manager frowned. "What does that mean?"

I kept it simple. "I told her to redo our bottle run with better flares. She got rude about it."

He laughed like it was nothing. "So all this is about flares?"

One of the security guys cut in. "He grabbed her by the neck, too."

Gambit stepped forward with the bills still in his hand, calmer than all of us. "No disrespect to your place, sir. But we don't deserve disrespect either. We paid to enjoy the night properly. We can keep this smooth on both sides if we come to an understanding and move on."

The manager held up a hand. "Alright. Talk to me, gentlemen. What do you want?"

"Have another bottle service girl redo that last run," Gambit said. He counted out what he had, then handed the manager $700. "Give this to the new girl as her tip for redoing the bottle run."

My Breitling read 1:43 a.m., and we were down to fifteen minutes before last call for alcohol. I pulled out $1100 and added it to the stack. "Add two more bottles to the run."

"Make that four more," Smooth said, dropping another $1100 on top.

The manager waved his security out of our booth while he collected the money. Then he said, "I don't know what you gentlemen plan to do with all these bottles you're requesting, but the party ends at 3:00. You've only got an hour to finish your drinks." He glanced at our tub of ice. "I don't know if you're aware, but you cannot leave here with any of these bottles."

"C'mon, boss-man, of course we know that. We do this!" Smooth said, then shouted to the watching crowd, "We just some Toronto playas here to show love to the Calgary city!" He tossed two bottles into the crowd.

The place erupted and the DJ blasted the music again, bringing the club back to life. I would've loved to catch that moment on social media, but a six-bottle light show was on the way. Two more bottles would be flying into the crowd for Snapchat, and at the end of the night Smooth and I would pour whatever was left over our jewellery. Just our way of closing a lit night with pure arrogance.

With the club back in party mode, the manager waved a new bottle service girl into our booth and spoke in her ear. He pointed at our tray, and she grabbed the two Hennessy bottles like she already knew she was redoing the run. Then he handed her only the $200 tip from Smooth and me, and pocketed the $700 Gambit had meant for the girl, sliding it away with the $2000. He threw up the deuces with a grin and walked out.

The booth fell right back into its vibe, with Magenta smiling at me like she'd just watched a real pimp handle business. I winked at her again, then went to the front with Whitey and Smooth to hype the crowd. Down in one of the base booths, Sarah was running a bottle show. Our eyes met and I blew her a kiss, but she turned away with the rudest look. Dumb bitch. *Learn how to keep those flares alive.*

At the bar, our new bottle service girl was setting up the six-bottle finale. Phones were already out in our booth to catch it. Gambit slipped into the VIP washroom with the dark-skinned empress. Something told me he wasn't in there just to hit rails. We'd have to wait for him to finish before we could fix our faces too. For now, three bottle service girls were moving through the crowd towards our booth, each carrying two Henny bottles with huge flames blazing off the tops. Even people who weren't with us knew this one was worth filming.

This was a regular night for my partners and me when we shut a club down. Depending on the occasion, we'd stunt even harder if it called for it.

CHAPTER EIGHTEEN

Wednesday, June 27 – 2:49 a.m.

Vanessa left The Landing strip club by Toronto Pearson Airport upset. Not because it had been slow. She always made good money wherever she worked. She was upset because Dianna hadn't shown up.

Dianna had stayed with a client until 7 a.m., and when Vanessa spoke to her around 11 a.m., Dianna sounded exhausted. Vanessa understood. She told her to sleep the rest of the day. They'd planned to leave for work together at eight that evening, but Dianna was still in bed, so Vanessa went ahead expecting her to catch up within the hour. That never happened. Vanessa worked the whole night without seeing her once. Dianna didn't even respond to messages to say she wasn't coming. Working unaccompanied wasn't the issue. Vanessa got along with plenty of girls at the clubs she rotated. Still, it was different when one of her own stable girls was there. It made the shift feel less like work and more like a game between friends, competing for money while knowing it all fed the same cause. Vanessa handled her night and did what she came to do, but Dianna had stood her up and it felt disrespectful.

Pushing through the heavy front doors of the club in her cute Christian Dior tracksuit with a matching workbag, Vanessa went straight to her black 3 series BMW in the parking lot. The apple-red interior greeted her as she climbed in and hit the start button. One last check of her phone showed Dianna had opened her Snapchat messages and still hadn't replied. Not once. That sat wrong with her. Reading the messages and staying silent felt deliberate. It made Vanessa wonder what Dianna was doing, and whether she was avoiding her for a reason. Calling Gelato crossed her mind, but she didn't want to come off like a nagger. She just wanted to know what was going on.

Vanessa called Sierra, and her voice came through the car speakers. "Hey, babe, what's up?"

"Hey, Skye. I'm just leaving work. You?"

"I just got home from work," Sierra replied. "What's up though. Everything okay?"

"Everything's fine. Just..." Vanessa sighed. "Diamond was supposed to work with me tonight at The Landing, but she didn't show up, and she hasn't responded to my messages either."

"Oh my. Is she okay?" Sierra asked.

"That's why I'm calling you. She opened my messages but never said anything back."

"Yeah, that's weird," Sierra said, knowing Dianna and Vanessa stayed in touch no matter what.

"Yeah...I don't know what to do."

"Okay, give me a sec. I'm gonna call her to see if she answers, then I'll call you back. Okay, babe?"

"Okay, okay." Vanessa ended the call and eased the car out of the parking lot.

Sierra had just got in. Chocolate and Vanilla circled at her feet craving attention, so she pet them both quickly before tossing her Kate Spade workbag down. While she slipped off her Balenciaga sneakers, she called Dianna.

After a couple rings, Dianna answered in a groggy voice. "...Hey, Skye."

"Hey, babe." Sierra kept her tone soft. "You okay?"

"...Huh?" Confusion thickened Dianna's words. "Why? What happened?"

Sierra hesitated, thrown off by how genuine it sounded. "Vanessa said you were supposed to meet her at the club tonight. No?"

"Oh...yeah..." Memory caught up to Dianna. "Yeah, I was going to. But I was with a trick until, like, ten in the morning, so I been sleeping the whole time."

A small chuckle left Sierra. "Yeah, sounds like it."

"I'm so sorry...I hope nobody's mad at me."

"No, it's fine, babe. Nobody's mad," Sierra told her. "But I think Velvet's kinda upset since you haven't responded all night. She might be feeling like you stood her up."

"Fuck..." Dianna exhaled. "I been meaning to message her, but I'm just too tired and out of it."

"Okay. As long as you're okay. Just call Velvet at least. She's worried about you."

"Yeah...I'll do that."

"Alright. Bye, babe."

"Bye, love." Dianna ended the call, then set her phone to silent so it wouldn't disturb her again.

Vanessa got a call back from Sierra, confirming Dianna had answered and was only sleeping. Sierra also said Dianna would call her. Ten minutes passed with no call, no message. Vanessa tried calling herself. It rang out every time. That was fine. She was only five minutes from the condo.

Vanessa stopped at her own unit to drop off her workbag, then went up to Dianna's floor. Standing at Dianna's door, she knocked for nearly a minute. Nothing. She leaned in and pressed her ear to the door, listening for movement inside. Silence. Vanessa's frustration flared and she kicked the door hard, the echo startling her in the quiet corridor. Her eyes cut right, then left, expecting a neighbour to crack their door and stare. No one did. A beat later, the lock clicked. Dianna's front door began to open.

Dianna stood in the doorway in her thick Versace robe, and Vanessa came at her with a whole lot of attitude. "You didn't hear me knocking?"

Dianna had always found angry Vanessa attractive, which made her giggle. "Obviously I didn't hear you knocking, babe. I was sleeping, and that loud bang woke me up."

Vanessa didn't respond. She pushed past Dianna into the unit. Dianna shut the door behind her and locked it.

"Why are you ignoring me?" Vanessa began.

"I'm not ignoring you, Vee," Dianna said, drifting toward the couch and dropping onto it. "I've just been so tired, honestly." The grogginess in her voice backed it up.

"You stood me up, then you been r-bombing my messages," Vanessa shot back, staying on her feet as she moved closer. "Like, what the fuck is up?"

"Oh my God, Vee." A groan dragged out of Dianna. "I'm too tired to fight with you. Let's just go to bed, and we'll talk about it tomorrow."

"Oh, so now you want my company after ignoring me all night?"

"Don't say that, babe. I love your company. Always. I've just been too tired and all."

"Yeah, too tired to respond to me, but you could answer Skye's call, right?"

"You were only messaging me. Skye actually called," Dianna said. The point landed, then her eyes narrowed with a question of her own. "And yeah, what's up with that?"

"Up with what?" Vanessa asked, still carrying the attitude.

"Why'd you run to Skye about this?"

"I didn't run to Skye about anything," Vanessa said, defensive now. "You weren't answering me and I got worried."

"You should've just called me yourself instead of messaging. You know when I'm half asleep I open messages but don't really read them."

"Well, after you spoke with Skye, I tried calling you, and you still didn't answer me."

"I turned off my phone right after." A yawn broke through Dianna's words. "Vee, I've just been tired. You need to relax. Come, let's go lay down and cuddle."

"I'm not laying down with you, Dee. I'm not happy with you right now."

"Oh my God." Dianna rolled her eyes. "You're really mad at me because I've been sleeping?"

"I'm mad because you've been acting different lately."

"How am I acting different?" Dianna fired back. "Because I've been busy, that's why?"

"Turning up on percs with them next bitches in the club and shit," Vanessa told it straight to Dianna. "Word in the club is you've been popping that shit with those whack junkie bitches. You better not start doing other drugs with those stupid bitches. You're even lucky I haven't told Daddy about you popping percs."

"Are you fucking serious?" Dianna's face tightened. "You're a snitch-bitch if you do that, and I'll never talk to you again."

"Yeah, because you care about turning-up on drugs more than being with me." Vanessa's voice rose. "I bet you were in here popping fucking percs."

"Wow, Vee. Did you come here to insult me?"

"No." Tears slid down Vanessa's cheeks, but her words stayed firm. "I came here looking for my girlfriend, but she's clearly not here for me like she used to be."

She turned away and headed for the door.

"Vee, wait." Dianna jumped up and grabbed her arm. "Babe, I'm sorry. Let's go lay down and talk, please."

Vanessa shrugged her off, sobbing now. "No. I'm just gonna leave. You were sleeping just fine without me." She reached for the door, then threw her last words back over her shoulder. "And don't worry, I never planned on telling Daddy about you popping percs. I've always been real with you and never changed."

Dianna wanted to chase after Vanessa, but nothing came to mind that would fix it. Exhaustion sat heavy in her body, pulling her back toward sleep. Letting Vanessa cool off felt safer than saying the wrong thing and making it worse. She locked the front door, went back to her room, and lay down on the bed. The least she could do was send Vanessa a text.

{Sorry bae. I've just been really tired. But just know that I always love you,} and she followed with, *{We'll do lunch or something when we both get a free day this week.}* Then she went to bed, not waiting on a response from Vanessa.

Vanessa got downstairs to her unit and collapsed onto the couch, crying. Dianna's text came through while the tears were still hot on her face. Vanessa opened it, read it, and didn't respond. It did pull a small smile out of her, but it didn't change the ache sitting in her chest. She needed company from someone who mattered. The thought of going back upstairs came, tempting her. Laying with Dianna would've been easy. Too easy. It would feel like giving in too soon to someone who'd been neglecting her.

Gelato was out of the question. He was in Calgary. So Vanessa stared at her phone, weighing the only other option she had. Then she made the call.

"Hey, babe, what's up?" Sierra answered.

"Just here at home. Feeling sad and lonely."

"Aww, you okay, babe? What's wrong?"

"I went upstairs to confront Dianna about ignoring me tonight, and we got into an argument."

"Don't stress it, babe. It happens. I'm sure you two will be fine."

"I hope so," Vanessa said.

Silence sat between them for a beat, then Vanessa asked, "Can I come over to your place?"

"Umm, sure." A chuckle slipped out of Sierra. "I'm not doing much anyways. Was probably just gonna watch a movie and pass out."

"Okay, perfect." Relief lifted Vanessa's mood fast. It had been a long time since she'd hung out with Sierra like that. They used to be at her place all the time on days off. Somewhere along the way, it stopped. Shopping with Dianna and Vanessa was the most Sierra did now, and even that was rare. Nights in, movies, treating each other like real friends, it didn't happen anymore. Sierra always had a reason. Too busy. Too tired. Wanted to be alone. Vanessa and Dianna eventually stopped asking.

A grin touched Vanessa's face as she said, "I'm gonna bring some treats for Chocolate and Vanilla."

"Oh, nice. I'm sure they'll be happy to see you too."

Vanessa went quiet, letting the invitation sink in. A night with Sierra again. Hot, sexy, Persian Sierra. The thought stirred something deeper than comfort.

"Umm..." Vanessa hesitated, then asked anyway, "Should I bring my toys?" Silence followed, and she rushed to soften it. "It's okay if you don't feel like getting into anything. I'm fine with just watching a movie with you."

The question caught Sierra off guard, which is why she didn't answer right away. A smile formed anyway. It had been a long time since she'd been with a woman, and Velvet was a freaky, sexy one who always knew how to turn her on. Sierra giggled at the thought, half amused with herself.

"...Hello?" Vanessa said, checking the line, already regretting how she'd pushed for more.

"Yeah," Sierra said. "Bring your toys, babe. I'll get mine ready too."

"Okay." Excitement brightened Vanessa's voice. "I'm gonna shower then make my way there."

"No, babe," Sierra said. "Just make your way here now. We'll shower together."

They ended the call, and Sierra sat there smiling to herself. Her attention shifted to Vanilla on the couch, hissing violently at Chocolate while he tried to mount her. Sierra laughed at them, then got up to prepare for her date night.

CHAPTER NINETEEN

Wednesday, June 27 – 1:51 p.m.

The only words Sierra got from Gelato that day after the physical incident were in a text. He said he was flying back out to Calgary and would be bringing Magenta down to Toronto. The urge to reply came sharp, to tell him how much money he was wasting. Magenta could've flown down on her own, and he'd be saving the extra cost of his round trip, likely another pointless first-class ticket. Sierra didn't want to start another fight, so she kept it simple and replied, okay. That had been days ago.

Last night with Vanessa had revived something in her. The freaky night was one thing, but breakfast and the conversation that followed reminded Sierra their version of family wasn't as bad as it sometimes felt. Maybe it was its own kind of special. In the stable, the younger women looked up to her, respected her position, and carried themselves around her like she mattered. Vanessa spoke for herself and Dianna when she told Sierra they felt no way about being beneath her. They preferred it that way because they saw Sierra as a big sister.

One expectation came with it. When the game ended, Sierra couldn't change on them. Gelato still had to be shared. That had always been his plan, a family of sister wives. Sitting with Vanessa made it easier for Sierra to accept again, especially after remembering how well she'd always gotten along with the others. Maybe it had been Sierra, too. Maybe she was the one who needed to rebuild the bond after being distant for so long.

Sierra sat alone on the couch with Chocolate and Vanilla cuddled against her when she made the call.

"Hello?" Gelato answered, keeping his voice low.

"Hey, what's up?" Sierra wasn't sure how to start. "Umm, are you busy?"

"Just boarded the plane. Flying back now," Gelato replied nonchalantly. "Waiting for takeoff."

"You with Magenta?"

"Uhh, yeah. She's right here beside me. Why?"

"Oh, okay." Sierra kept her tone nice. "Tell her I said hi."

Gelato smiled, still not understanding. Sierra hadn't cared for the new girl before. "Yeah, I'll let her know. But what's up with you?"

"Nothing." Sierra sighed. "I've just been thinking, and I wanna apologize about the other day. I know I was being foolish. I'm sorry, Poppa. Just know I'm ready to train her whenever you want me to."

"I appreciate that," he said, sincere. "But don't worry about it. I'm just gonna let Velvet handle her."

"Are you sure?" Sierra pressed. "I could do it, Poppa. I don't mind at all."

"I took in what you said that day, and I respect how you stay focused on us, so I want you to just stay doing that. Magenta's gonna hang with Velvet and 'em a lot more anyway. It makes sense to have them train her."

"Okay, but I at least get to meet her first, right?" Sierra needed to hear it.

"Of course. You my bottom bitch, no?"

"Yes, Poppa." Relief warmed her voice. "I'm your bottom bitch. I love you."

"I love you too, mami." Gelato chuckled, turning the last fight into something lighter. "Just don't be hiding no money from me."

A small laugh slipped out of Sierra. "I would never. I only said that in the heat of the moment to piss you off. But I'd never, and you know that. All the cash I made is in the safe waiting for you. And I sent you two money transfers yesterday. You saw that, right?"

"Yeah, I figured you said that nonsense out of anger. Just don't let that happen again. I'm over it though. And yeah, I got the transfers you sent yesterday."

"Okay, good." Sierra didn't have much else to say. The call had gone better than she expected, and she was ready to leave it there.

"How's your face?" Gelato asked.

"Oh." She lightly touched the spot he meant. "It healed up the very next day. After my trick that night, I got home and put a lot of bruising cream on it before bed."

"Okay, good." His tone stayed light. "I also went to see Diamond that day."

"Oh. How'd it go?"

"Went well."

A quick joke slipped out of Sierra. "You know dicking her down doesn't mean you solved whatever issue she had, right?"

"I'm sure that was the prescription she needed." Gelato chuckled. "But nah, for real. I talked to her too. She seemed alright. She knows to chill out on the Designer-D."

Sierra brought up Vanessa's claims that something had been different about Dianna. Gelato told her he already knew. After hearing Vanessa's concerns and speaking to Dianna, it came down to one thing. Dianna had been busier with work and couldn't give Vanessa the attention she craved.

"Yeah, I guess. Apparently they got into a little argument last night, and Velvet was really sad, so she came and slept at my place."

"Oh, wow." Gelato sounded pleased. "So you made time for her and comforted her?"

"Yes, a whole lot of comforting went on with us." Sierra laughed. "But that's not the point. She was really sad and didn't wanna be alone for the night, so I let her come over."

"I'm glad you spent time with her. It's been a while since you hung out with any of them."

"I know. I'm glad I did too. This morning we had breakfast, then hit the gym and sauna together before she left."

"You should do it more often with all of them. Just like you used to."

"Yeah, I'll try, if I'm not too busy. You know my schedule gets crazy sometimes. Plus, I like my alone time." A small pause followed. "And even that, I don't get sometimes, because then you show up."

Gelato chuckled. "Yeah, that's true." His voice shifted, practical. "But, Sisi, the plane's about to take off, so I'ma hit you up when we land. Then you can meet Magenta, okay?"

"Okay, sounds good. I already planned to make today my day off, so I'll go out with her or something."

"Cool."

"Safe flight, Poppa. Love you."

"Love you too, mami."

I ended the call as the plane started taxiing towards the runway. Magenta sat beside me. Our first-class seats gave us more than enough space and a bit of privacy from the rest of the cabin. Part of me wondered if she'd been listening in, but as my bitch who respected my pimpin', her ears were the least of my worries. Besides, she stayed locked into her phone the whole time.

"Who you texting so much?" I asked because she'd been typing away nonstop.

"Oh, just some friends on Instagram and Snapchat," she said, eyes still glued to the screen. "They're commenting on my posts from last night."

"Listen," I said, "I know you got good friends from before me, and they ain't a risk that you gotta cut off. But when they keep messaging you about your posts and all that, don't always be so quick to respond. Carry yourself like you've levelled up, as you shouldn't be easily available to everybody anymore. Ease them into the fan zone."

"Okay, Daddy. Sorry." Magenta fired off one last reply before putting her phone away. She looked up at me with that beautiful smile, and mine came back easy.

Curiosity tugged for a second, who she still kept close, but it wasn't worth pressing. Anybody with even the slightest tie to Marvel was already blocked and deleted. Those were the only names that mattered.

Magenta lifted the big armrest between our seats, then leaned into my space and rested her head on me like she belonged there. "You made my kitty sore, Daddy."

"Good," I said, proud.

After the club, I stayed Designer-Doped up at the Airbnb and couldn't keep my hands off her. We went at it until she was too sore and told me to chill, so I let her rest and held her close instead. Next day, we linked with my partners, the same crew from the party booth, for brunch at a fancy spot. I pulled Magenta into the restaurant washroom for a quick one, then again in the Rolls Royce before we returned it to the rental company. She begged me to stop again, said her pussy was hurting worse than it did the night before. Maybe I caused a tear. I didn't care. I was just glad I got that luxury nut in the Phantom before we made our way to catch the flight.

Smooth planned to stay in Calgary a bit longer. He'd roped in a few square girls from last night's club, so his plan was to keep them close for the week, talk his talk, and see who was really feeling him. I got numbers too, but I didn't bother following up. Getting Magenta back to Ontario came first. I'd tap those lines again the next time I was in Calgary.

Resting against me, Magenta slipped her hand under my Givenchy shirt and felt my bare chest. "Your chest and arms are so buff, Daddy. I was scared for that bottle service girl when you had her by the neck. It looked like you lifted her off her feet."

"I used to live in the gym." A chuckle came out. "Abs ain't as shredded anymore, but everything else still there." Then I made it clear. "And you're keeping your body banging too. No excuses. When I get you in a nice condo, you're staying in the gym."

"If you haven't noticed, I watch what I eat. And I try to do a hundred squats and lunges every other day."

"Yeah, I've caught you a few mornings."

"Exactly. So you don't gotta worry about me getting out of shape, Daddy."

"Good. All my girls stay premium."

Her fingers stayed on my chest as she asked, "So what's the plan when we land in Toronto?"

"You'll meet Skye Icy, my bottom bitch. You two will spend the day together." Saying Sierra's title felt good, especially after that call.

"So Skye's training me?"

"No. Velvet's training you. You'll meet her tomorrow, and you might even start working OT with her tomorrow."

"Okay, and where am I keeping all my stuff?"

"At my place," I reassured her. "By the time you get back from a week of OT with Velvet, I should have a condo in Sauga lined up for you."

"Okay, I'm excited," Magenta said, but of course she had more. "So what about Diamond? When do I meet her?"

"She's been busy these past weeks. You'll meet her when her schedule loosens up. Velvet will tell you all about her. They're close."

"Do you think they'll like me?"

Her questions got cut short when the flight attendant stopped beside us. "Ma'am, please sit up properly and fasten your seatbelt. And you too, sir. We're about to take off."Magenta slid her hand out from under my shirt, lowered the armrest between us, and buckled her seatbelt. I clicked mine in too. The flight attendant moved on down the aisle.

"So you think they'll like me?" Magenta asked me again.

"You'll be fine in the stable, babe. Just relax with the questions so nobody gets annoyed with you."

Magenta blushed and giggled through the embarrassment, then went quiet.

The plane started speeding down the runway and my hands tightened on both armrests. When the wheels lifted, my heart started punching my chest. Magenta's eyes stayed on me, so I turned and gave her a smile I didn't feel. Confusion flickered across her face, then she smiled back, probably remembering that same fake grin from the last take-off and landing.

Truth was, I stayed in first-class because flying scared the hell out of me. Aviophobia. I'd never admit that to anyone, not even Sierra. I already showed enough weaknesses, so this one stayed mine. Even the thought of being packed into the crowded regular section during take-off or landing made my breathing go shallow, then fast. That wouldn't be a good look for a man like me, a pimp who's supposed to stay solid. The extra space first-class gave me was the only thing that helped. In a few minutes the plane would level out, the ride would smooth, and everything would be fine.

GHAD

CHAPTER TWENTY

Thursday, June 28

Maria's outing with Sierra had been yesterday. The bottom bitch title had intimidated her at first, but Sierra's down-to-earth personality, natural leadership, and sense of humour made it easy to relax around her. It helped Maria understand why Sierra held the position. Authority sat on her in a way that still felt familiar, like a woman who could lead and still feel like a friend. Sierra had been the first, and the warmest to welcome Maria into the Icy stable.

This morning, Maria met Vanessa, and that went well too. Vanessa picked her up from Gelato's place at 9 a.m., a light bag of clothes and supplies already in the trunk of her BMW for the week in a hotel in London, Ontario. Maria came down with her own bag packed for the stay, but a few things were still missing, things she'd need for work. Vanessa took Maria downtown Toronto first, hunting for stripper heels, outfits, and a few accessories she'd need for work. Brunch followed at a nice bistro, and the bond kept building from there.

Seeing Vanessa up close made Maria understand Gelato's pride in his premium stable. Vanessa was another beautiful girl. Small and tight in black leggings that showed off her petite bum, a T-shirt sitting neat over perfectly rounded breasts. Maria wore tight jeans that hugged her frame and a crop top with a bra underneath, holding up her heavy set of natural breasts. The ice cream pendant choker at Vanessa's neck didn't go unnoticed. Maria remembered Sierra wearing a similar one with three scoops. Her own would come one day, and she found herself looking forward to it.

Walking side by side through downtown, the two young women pulled eyes. Heads turned. Vanessa clocked it and said, "They turn their heads to look at us because they are thinking with the one in their pants."

Talk between them didn't run out. Nobody had to tell either of them to stop. Vanessa spoke about Dianna, who she hadn't talked to since their argument, and how close they'd been before things shifted. Certain details stayed unspoken. Vanessa didn't mention Dianna popping Percocet. Loyalty still mattered, even with the hurt. What she gave Maria was the safer truth, feeling neglected and unappreciated. Nothing else negative followed. Vanessa hoped the three of them could hang out after the week's work in London. The idea put her in a lighter mood and it came through in the way she spoke. Maria liked that Vanessa talked a lot, so she asked question after question about what to expect in the stable. No fear of coming off annoying. Not with Vanessa.

The drive to London in Vanessa's BMW took about three hours. Maria drove the last hour to give Vanessa a break. As the city got closer, Maria's nerves started to rise. First night in a strip club. First time doing it for real. Questions spilled out of her, one after the next, and Vanessa answered them without frustration.

"Don't stress about remembering everything," Vanessa told her. "We'll go over it again once we're in the club tonight."

It suited them. Maria's anxiety met Vanessa's calm confidence, a balance that made the whole ordeal feel less impossible.

They arrived around 2 p.m. and checked into a hotel off Wellington Road near Exeter. The building stretched wide, four storeys with sections labelled by letters, taking up more than a block. After the front desk at the main entrance, they drove around to the D-section parking lot and entered through its unattended door, stepping straight into the hallway lined with D-section rooms. The executive room was spacious, set up with two queen beds. Food came first. They ordered something to eat before training started. This was Vanessa's first time guiding a new girl, and she'd come prepared with a plan for how she wanted to shape her.

Vanessa had Maria strut the room in six-inch stripper heels for about half an hour, getting her used to the height and balance. Then Vanessa slipped into her own six-inch heels and walked her through a proper stage routine, step by step.

"Don't worry about pole work," Vanessa said. "We'll book a dance studio next week so I can teach you a few moves. For now, focus on stage strutting, moving to the music, and floor play. Just imagine the wall here is a pole. Brace yourself on it and grind on it at times, like a woman in heat."

Her tone stayed firm but reassuring. "The types of tricks you want to attract are elegant ones, and they often don't like girls who twerk and do all that hip-hop, booty-shaking stage show. Nobody's gonna make it rain on your booty like they do in American strip clubs. You want your dancing to be sensual, like a woman in heat. That's how you get clients interested in seeing you privately, and that's how you'll be making your money."

Vanessa ran Maria through tutorial after tutorial until a clean sequence started to form, one that flowed across three popular radio songs. "Tricks always appreciate your stage show more when it's a song they recognize. Top billboard songs are always better to dance to than your own personal favourites."

Next came the private rooms. Vanessa explained what would happen back there, then demonstrated a proper lap dance on Maria. After that, Maria had to practice on Vanessa until it started to look right.

"Listen, babe. You always wanna start slow and gentle with the first song," Vanessa said. "Then you get more touchy and wild in the second song, and so on. For an extra fifty bucks, you can add a handjob to finish off their last song. But make sure you put a condom on them. Never touch a dick with your bare hands."

Playing the client, Vanessa touched and felt up on Maria while she ground against her, moving to the rhythm. Guidance came through her hands, placing Maria where she needed to be, showing her what to do and how to keep the rhythm. Maria followed, trying to make it feel natural. Girl-on-girl contact was new to her. The rush surprised her anyway. Vanessa's hands on her body had Maria feeling exhilarated, pleased in a way she wasn't prepared for. The heat built fast, and lips met before Maria could overthink it. First time kissing a woman, first jolt of that kind of thrill. Training had turned into something it wasn't supposed to be, and Maria felt herself leaning into it. Vanessa cut it off. Focus snapped back into place as she tapped Maria on the nose, playful but firm. "Bad girl. You're never supposed to make out with a trick during a lap dance. They can only get that type of affection in paid arrangements. And even then, I still don't end up kissing most of them. Not when they're ugly and gross."

The lesson moved on. Vanessa went back to the real goal, making money in the private rooms and knowing how to control the game. "Magi, listen. Every bad-bitch got a pussy with a price to turn a trick, but you gotta be a prestigious bad-bitch to game a trick into paying extra for your company and time. The strip club is where you perfect that."

CHAPTER TWENTY-ONE

Thursday, June 28 – 7:30 p.m.

The two Icy girls arrived at the strip club in the early evening so Maria could register and get processed. Vanessa had to re-sign as well, only because she hadn't worked that club in over three months. She suggested to the manager that Maria do her stage show early while the room was still quiet. Most clubs required every girl to perform a three-song stage show at least three times a night. Since Maria was new, the manager agreed to let her go early, and only once. Tomorrow, there'd be no grace. She either got it down on this one shot or made a mistake and learned from it.

R&B played through the speakers while the stage sat empty. The DJ already had Maria's three songs loaded, ready for the moment she stepped out of the changing room. She slipped into a skimpy two-piece with thigh-high stockings. As her first song started playing, Maria stepped onto the stage. Her performance played out in front of only a few men spread across the spacious club.

"Remember, Magi. Reveal your breasts during the second song, then your v-jay after that. It's near the end of the last song that you're fully naked." Vanessa's last words played on repeat in Maria's head.

Nerves hit hard, even with the crowd being so small. The few men didn't scare her. It was the other strippers who had arrived early, watching from the side, curious about the new girl's stage show. Then the music carried her into it. Once Maria started moving, she realized there was nothing to be anxious about. Intimidation loosened its grip. Some of the girls watching were supportive, cheering her on right alongside Vanessa.

"Yes, bitch, work all that sexiness!"

With two years in the game, Vanessa always happened to know a girl or two at every strip club she worked, even when it was three hours from her usual spots. Strippers moved around. Faces reappeared. People crossed paths again sooner or later. Still, tonight wasn't about Vanessa. It was Maria's night, and she'd done perfectly fine on stage. The three-song set only lasted about fifteen minutes, but it felt like a lifetime to Maria. Relief washed through her when it ended without any obvious hiccups. Shyness was the only thing that showed, and that was expected on a first time. Confidence would come with repetition.

Light applause came from the supportive strippers at the end of her set, and it gave Maria a small boost. The few men in the club followed their lead, clapping too once they realized she was new

Bass thumped through the club and the lights stayed low, washing the room in a soft haze. Vanessa guided Maria to a side table tucked off to the edge, close enough to watch the floor without sitting in the middle of it. Vanessa wore a pink one-piece mesh outfit that caught the light when she moved. Maria sat across from her, still holding onto the rush of her stage set. Two drinks sat between them, cognac cut with cranberry. The music was loud, but with Vanessa leaning in close, every word still reached Maria clear.

"Okay, Magi," Vanessa said. "This is our first drink of the night and it should be the only one we buy for ourselves, because we gotta make the tricks pay for our drinks. That doesn't mean you always ask for one or accept every time it's offered. That's how you lose focus. I can't speak for other bitches, but a focused, clear mind runs the best game. I only have a drink every forty-five minutes so I'm relaxed and in the right vibe, but never tipsy. Never close to drunk.

"Remember the next thing we talked about. Never talk to any guy who looks like a pimp. Urban clothes, jewellery, certain swag, all that. You gotta watch it. If you entertain a pimp and he thinks you want him, that's mess you'll stir up for Daddy. Best advice is don't look at or talk to any black guys that show up in here, unless he's at a table with a bunch of white guys and really looks like he's tricking with his friends.

"Always keep your small purse with you. Always keep your total stash in the interior zipper so your money doesn't show if you open your purse for your phone or something. Anytime you get cash, shove it in the purse, then go to the washroom after and put it with the rest in the interior zipper.

"Only take cash here at the strip club. There are ATMs in here that tricks can use if they need more money. E-transfers and all that is fine when you're at an arrangement or something, but the strip club is cash-only. You don't wanna complicate your night with an e-transfer process.

"For tonight, stick to handjobs and blowjobs for extras. Yeah, sometimes you can get away with a quick fuck for six hundred, but full-on sex isn't allowed in most clubs, so you gotta be real sneaky about it. See it this way. If a trick is willing to pay six bills just for a rushed quickie, you're better off getting him to take down your number and making arrangements outside the club. Either his home, or a hotel if you don't feel safe about his home. If he's got that type of money to afford you, he's worth gaming so he spends it right, with quality time and all so he becomes a regular."

The pep talk finally ended, and Vanessa guided Maria over to a table where two men had just arrived, casual in jeans and shirts. As they closed in, Vanessa leaned to Maria's ear. "Go off my vibe and stay with my game."

At the table, Vanessa smiled first. "Hey, how's it going?" She shook both their hands with a gentle grip, traded names, and introduced herself as Velvet before taking a seat. Maria followed with her own introduction. "Magenta." She sat down too.

Both men looked to be in their early 40s, pleased to have the two young women at their table. Paul and Jerry.

"So, how's your night going?" Vanessa asked.

"Not too bad," Jerry said. "Just got off work and decided to escape the wives for a bit."

"Oh, no." Vanessa laughed. "You two are out here being bad boys, huh?"

"Yup," Paul said. "We escaped wedlock for a bit."

Maria slid in smoothly. "Well, you've come to the right place."

"We come here regularly," Paul said. "Don't think we've seen you two working here before. You're both absolutely gorgeous."

Both girls took the compliment well. "I haven't been here in a while," Vanessa said. "I'm usually working in Mississauga. And it's Magenta's first time working at a strip club, so I brought her out here because the men are much nicer in this town."

"Wow, so you're new to this business, huh?" Jerry asked.

Maria smiled. "You just missed my first stage show ever."

"Oh, darn it." Jerry shook his head. "Can't believe we missed the debut."

"What's even better, you could be the first man to take her for a private dance," Vanessa said.

"Yup," Maria added with a giggle. "I'll probably end up remembering you forever."

"I'm up for it," Jerry said, eager now. "How about a drink with us for starters?"

Maria looked to Vanessa.

"Sure," Vanessa said. "We don't like to drink too much, but I guess one shot with you two won't do no harm."

A quick wink followed. Maria smiled back, catching the message. A single shot wasn't going to throw her off, not after how slow they'd paced their first drink through the long talk.

The men called for the waiter to bring four shots of tequila, then they started chatting about their lives while the girls played interested. When the drinks arrived, they cheered and downed them. Jerry took Maria to the private rooms, and Paul went with Vanessa.

Downstairs, a hallway led to ten cubicle rooms lined along both sides. The private rooms. Each one had a single comfortable chair for lap dances, even though everyone knew other things happened in there too. The rooms were private in name only. The doors were transparent glass, and anyone walking past could see inside. Security walked the hallway at random, checking for safety, and catching girls who crossed the club's lines.

Private dances ran at twenty dollars a song, same as everywhere else. Most men knew that before they even asked. As soon as Jerry stepped into the room with Maria, he set his limit. "A hundred," he said.

"Okay," Maria replied. "I can give you five dances, babe."

"Nothing extra, sweetie?"

"I guess I can give you two dances and a handjob in the second dance if you'd like."

"That sounds more like it."

Maria sat reversed on Jerry, who was still fully dressed, moving to a Tory Lanez song playing in the club, one that another girl was likely performing to on stage.

By the second song, she turned to face him, straddled his lap, and asked him to take his dick out while she reached into her purse for a condom.

Jerry said, "Most girls do the handjobs without a condom, sweetie."

"I'm nothing like most girls, hun." Maria said it gently and rolled the condom onto him.

She kept her body moving, grinding on his lap while her hand worked his erect penis between them. Jerry slipped her bra off and cupped her breasts, and she let soft moans meet his touches as she kept her rhythm steady. It did not take long. Before the song finished, Jerry came into the condom. Cut the music. We're done.

Remembering what Vanessa had taught her, Maria told him, "Keep the condom on you and flush it when you go to the washroom."

"Yeah, I know, sweetie." Jerry winked, smiling at her like the seasoned regular he was, reminding her she was the newbie here, not him.

After they got themselves together and made a bit of small talk, Maria and Jerry left the private room and went upstairs. Jerry headed straight for the washroom. Maria slipped into the girls' changing room to wash her hands, then moved the $100 from her purse into the interior zipper pouch.

More people filled the club when she came back out. More strippers moved around the floor. The night was building, and the ambience had turned lively. Vanessa wasn't in sight, and it stood out. Paul had been back at the table long before Jerry, which meant Vanessa had finished downstairs well before Maria did.

A familiar song was already playing, the kind Maria had heard a hundred times on the radio. She caught herself chiming into it under her breath, and that was what pulled her attention to the stage. A sexy little brunette was up there, working the pole like an exotic gymnast. It was Vanessa.

Maria stayed by the wall and watched, taking in how much more advanced Vanessa's stage show was than the one she had done earlier. Vanessa still used the strutting and sensual movement she'd taught Maria, but her routine carried something else too. Clean pole spins. Dazzling transitions. Moves that made her look acrobatic up there. All of it in six-inch stripper heels. At one point, Vanessa spotted Maria across the club and blew her a kiss, hanging upside down with one leg hooked around the pole.

Vanessa's dazzling show left sweat on her skin so she headed straight for the changing room when she came off stage. Maria followed and waited nearby while Vanessa rinsed off in one of the shower stalls. She then stepped out naked with only her purse in hand, kept dry in the stall. A clean towel came out of her work bag, and she dried off before pulling her outfit and heels from a bench. Dressed again, she moved to the mirror to retouch her makeup. Questions kept spilling out of Maria while she watched, praising the routine and asking how Vanessa pulled off certain moves. The admiration made Vanessa smile. Compliments came back the other way too, praising how Maria had handled herself with Paul and Jerry. In the middle of it, Vanessa pressed close and kissed her. Maria embraced it, letting the moment take her.

The changing room door opened and two strippers walked in. Vanessa and Maria broke apart at once.

"Don't mind us, babes. We're up to no good too," the taller one said with a friendly grin as she headed for the counter. "We 'bout to turn up."

"Hey, Velvet. Long time." The other girl knew Vanessa, hugging her before looking Maria over. "Is this hot girl your new girlfriend?"

A blush rose on Vanessa's face and she giggled. "Yeah, I guess."

"You two look good together," the taller one said. "Want to do a few bumps with us?"

"No thanks, babe." Vanessa kept it kind. "We gotta get back to work. It's my girl's first night."

"What's your name?" the other one asked Maria.

"Mari—"

"Magenta," Vanessa cut in smoothly.

A flicker of embarrassment rose in Maria at how close she'd come to slipping. Vanessa gave her a quick look that settled her, like it wasn't the end of the world, just a lesson.

The two strippers introduced themselves by their stage names, and the talk stayed light while they did their lines. After a bit, three more girls came in wearing comfortable street clothes—fresh arrivals getting ready to change. That was enough of a cue. Vanessa and Maria brought the conversation to a close, said their goodbyes, acknowledged the new girls with quick hellos, then returned to work.

Once they stepped back out into the club's live ambience, Vanessa leaned close and spoke over the music. "It's not a problem to tell other girls your real name. Just don't give it to bitches you're only meeting in the club. That's something you share after a friendship, once something's built. There's a lot of shady bitches in this game, so you gotta be careful how much info about yourself you give out."

The night carried on. Vanessa sent Maria off on her own to work a solo guy sitting at a lone table. It went well. Maria took him downstairs for four songs while Vanessa waited. When Maria returned, having done only lap dances, Vanessa explained that sometimes you had to offer the extras even if they didn't ask. Timid men liked to be led to what they wanted.

Maria approached another man and took him downstairs, but she came back up soon after. He'd wanted a blowjob or sex for $100 and refused to pay more. That price would get him neither from an Icy girl. Vanessa was glad Maria hadn't lowered her value and had come back empty-handed instead.

Two young men walked into the club and took a seat at a table. Vanessa moved fast, bringing Maria with her before other girls could reach them. It was a simple lesson, say the prices up front and save yourself a pointless trip downstairs. Some men would be a waste of time, and it was better to find that out at the table. Vanessa led the game with Maria beside her. The men offered drinks, and the girls accepted. It had been a while since their last one. When the talk shifted toward the private rooms, Vanessa leaned in and whispered her price to the man next to her. His face tightened before he answered. Her blowjob was too expensive for him. He repeated the price out loud to his friend, and the two of them laughed.

"Honestly, you're stunning," he told Vanessa, shaking his head, "But I'm not paying two hundred dollars for a fucking blowjob. Especially with a condom. The most I ever paid for a blowjob was a hundred."

Both men turned to Maria, expecting her to offer something better. Maria played it right. She looked at Vanessa and shared the laugh with her. No scrambling, no bargaining. The girls excused themselves and left the two men sitting there, dismissed.

"You did so well, babe," Vanessa said once they were away from the table. "Never let it discourage you when some guy can't afford you."

The Icy girls tried the same straightforward approach with another table, and it went nowhere. Those men were polite about it, at least. They offered to buy drinks, but the girls declined since their last one with the younger guys hadn't been long ago. Another table came next, older men this time, and the tone shifted quick. It landed. Each girl took a client downstairs, and Maria found it easier when the job was just a condom blowjob that lasted no longer than five minutes, without all the extra work of dancing and grinding. Comfort settled in. Flirtation came more natural too, and she successfully exchanged contact information with the older man for future arrangements.

Back upstairs, Vanessa left Maria on her own while she went to do another show. The club was busy now, after 10 p.m., and Vanessa wanted to get her second set out of the way so she could focus on money during the prime hours. If management wanted a third show, she'd do it near the end of the night. This time, Maria didn't stand around to watch. She worked the floor, approaching men and steering the ones who showed promise toward the private rooms. A couple dances and a handjob came easy enough, and by the time she returned upstairs, Vanessa's set had been done for a while. A slim-thick Guyanese girl owned the stage now, moving like she'd been doing it for years. The room was packed. Men filled tables and the bar. Some held the corner pool tables. A few stayed standing off to the side so they weren't clogging the walking space where the strippers moved through, hunting. There were enough men for every girl to eat. Doors kept rotating. The ones who got drained left, and fresh clients kept coming in with new money. It made sense that management wanted the experienced girls performing right now, keeping the energy up.

Maria stood off to the side, taking in the busy atmosphere, when someone crept up behind her and grabbed the ass cheek peering out of her skimpy outfit. *"Hey, babe."*

Maria startled, then felt relief when she saw who it was. "You scared me," she said.

A laugh came from Vanessa, then her focus snapped to something else. "You see the flashy guys over at the bar? Those are the ones you shouldn't talk to or even look at. They're pimps."

Maria stole a glance at the men by the bar. Most were Black, a mix of complexions, their style sharp and mainstream. Extravagant jewellery. The kind of look that read like hip-hop artists. It reminded her of Gelato. One of them was dark-skinned with dreads, and Maria's gaze lingered. For a second she wondered if it could be Marvel, even though Marvel never wore anything that expensive. The man caught her looking and stared back.

"Stop looking over there," Vanessa warned, sharper now. "You could get us in trouble staring at a pimp too long. It's an old pimp charge called *reckless eyeballing*."

Maria turned away fast. "Sorry, babe. I thought I knew him."

"Huh?" Vanessa pressed. "Which one? Where you know him from?"

"The dark one with dreads. I thought it was my ex, Marvel."

"Oh, shit." Vanessa sneaked a quick look, careful not to hold it. "So is that him?"

Maria checked again, quick and controlled. The dread wasn't looking their way anymore, and the brief opening gave her enough time to see it clearly. Different face. Different features. Marvel, to her, looked more like Chief Keef.

"No," Maria said. "It's not him." Relief loosened her chest enough for a small laugh. "What would we have done if it was?"

"We'd get the hell out of here," Vanessa said, chuckling. "Then call Daddy right away."

With the fear gone, the Icy girls slid back into the night and carried on working. Maria kept her confidence up, approaching clients on her own. When there weren't any open tables with two men for them to work together, the Icy girls split up and gamed solo. The go-to method felt safest for Maria, take them downstairs for dances, then offer the handjob extra, which stayed affordable for most. Blowjobs at Icy pricing only got offered to men who didn't seem tight with spending. Lap dances added up, but the work-to-money ratio was rough, and Maria started to understand why Vanessa preferred being straight at the table. It saved the wasted trip downstairs just to hear a man couldn't afford her blowjob.

"A dance is a full song of about three to five minutes, grinding and working your entire body on him just for twenty dollars. A good blowjob lasts three to five minutes, too, but you're only using your head and mouth and come out with two hundred dollars." That was Vanessa's logic, and it made sense. Still, it was Maria's first night, and the dance approach felt like something she could control. She stuck with what was working. More experience would bring more confidence, and then she could cut straight to the bigger money.

Private-room runs stacked up through the night, and one client eventually got bold enough to ask for full-on sex, willing to pay her price. Nerves hit Maria hard. It was forbidden in the club, and getting caught wasn't an option. The man stayed respectful. He liked her enough to take her number and said he'd book an arrangement sometime during the week while she was still in town.

Work kept moving, solo tables, duos, then bigger groups. When large tables or booths filled up, the Icy girls teamed up with the two strippers they'd met in the changing room, approaching together to pull men downstairs for dances. Once alone in the private rooms, that was when prices and extras got discussed. Other girls rarely had the same pricing, and that was exactly why numbers stayed off the table. Saying amounts in front of men would only encourage them to shop the girls against each other, pushing competition and bargaining before anybody even made it downstairs.

The night ended with Maria at $900 in blowjobs and $620 in dances with some handjobs, a strong outcome for a first shift. Vanessa's numbers sat higher, $1600 in blowjobs, $220 in dances with handjobs, and $660 from sneaking in one quickie. Money handled, work done, they left the club and got back on the road. Vanessa kept one hand on the wheel and slid the other into Maria's sweatpants, smooth and fearless, like the drive was part of the build-up. Maria reclined her seat and let herself enjoy it, staying quiet, letting the heat climb without giving it away. The touch stayed steady and knowing, never rushed, teasing just enough to keep her wanting more. Maria's mind had already left the car, fixed on what the night would turn into once they got back to the hotel room.

GHAD

CHAPTER TWENTY-TWO

Sunday, July 1 – 1:14 p.m.

Every night at the strip club got better for Maria as she settled into the flow of work and grew comfortable with her flirtatious style of game. Brave enough now, she'd provided full sex three times. During one encounter, security did a routine walk past the private rooms while she stayed on top of a fully clothed client, keeping it looking like nothing more than a heated lap dance. That was when she realized security only glanced in during their rounds. Unless someone ratted you out for whatever reason, they rarely came down hard over forbidden services.

After three nights of working the club, Maria secured a few clients for arrangement bookings. One booking had already happened last night after the club at a client's home not far from there, and a few more were lined up for the weekdays. Confidence grew fast once she realized some men appreciated her beyond sex, paying hourly rates just to spend time with her outside the strip clubs.

"Once you get into the groove of gaming tricks from the strip club for arrangements, you'll realize that it's just as easy to game any man in any public place who's staring at you like he wants a piece of you," Vanessa said.

Daytime and after-club bookings stayed the plan so they could still work the clubs together every night.

Vanessa stayed busier than Maria during the day because she already had clients in London from working there before. The moment she posted on Snapchat and Instagram that she was back in town, old clients started booking again. Transportation came down to availability. If Vanessa wasn't tied up with her own bookings, she drove Maria to hers. Otherwise, Maria's clients picked her up from the hotel or she Ubered to them. Bringing a trick back to the room was a no-go. An Icy girl didn't take a trick where she rested her head at night.

It was clear Maria would soon need her own car for work, and for the small slice of personal life she was allowed to have. Gelato promised that when her week in London was done, he'd have condo leasing options in Mississauga ready for her, then they'd pass by some dealerships to buy her a car. Maria was happy about that, but what she wanted more was to be officially settled into the Icy stable with her own ice cream pendant. She swore to Gelato she intended to be with the family forever, but his laws were set in stone. If she was so determined to be family for life, then her Icy branding would come with its time of six months. A six month wait was nothing beside the lifetime she swore to. After the Icy brand, Gelato would also consider investing in bodywork if he felt there was any surgical need for perfection.

As for Gelato, he Facetimed the girls every morning they were in London, and they would beg him to come out for a threesome. The idea of having both his sexy young ladies at once always pleased him, though threesomes were something he'd had plenty of, and nothing about that tempted him to rush into a three-hour drive. An hour earlier he had Facetimed them, as expected, and they were just as persistent, urging him to come out for some fun. A hot girl-on-girl show followed to lure him, their bodies moving together with that teasing ease they knew he liked. The sight had him tempted, especially once he found himself giving them a hands-on show in return while they carried on with their steamy display for him. But once all that tension had been released on cam, the urge to make the long drive faded, and he decided he'd wait until next week for his time with Maria and Vanessa. He even suggested that Sierra and Dianna would join the gathering when the time came. It would be Daddy versus bad girls. His wink at Vanessa carried the rest. Just like old times.

After ending the Facetime with Gelato, Sierra came to mind. Vanessa decided to call her with Maria, and they pulled on bras and underwear so they wouldn't pop up on Sierra with a naked surprise. Even so, the thought of giving her one crossed Vanessa's mind.

Sierra answered the video call as she got back to her unit from walking Chocolate, so the little guy went straight on camera for them. Vanilla showed up too, stepping into the frame with quiet confidence. Laughter passed between the three Icy girls as the pets acted up for attention. A bit of small talk followed, then Sierra had to go get ready for an afternoon booking.

Vanessa also had a booking at 3:30 p.m. with a previous client in town, but it was only 1:54 p.m., leaving time before she had to get herself together. One more person stayed on her mind. No matter how much fun she was having working and connecting with Maria, Dianna hadn't been forgotten.

"You still haven't met Dee, huh, babe?" Vanessa asked Maria.

"No. She's the only one left to meet, I believe."

"Okay. We'll Facetime her now too."

"Sure." Excitement lifted Maria's voice. "Let's do it."

Vanessa made the video call to Dianna but got no answer. "She's probably busy," she said to Maria, then sent a text out to Dianna, *{Are you busy?}*

Maria filled the silence "Well, everyone says she's been very busy. So, I'm not surprised."

A response came through a moment later. *{Sorry. I was just doing something,} {What's up?}*

{I'm trying to see you,} Vanessa texted back.

{Aww, babe, I miss you too.}

Sweet words didn't soften it. If Dianna could text, she could've answered the video call. Vanessa asked, *{Are you home?}*

{Yeah.}

{Okay...so answer the video call.}

Dianna didn't respond to the last message, so Vanessa waited a minute. With Maria right beside her, the phone screen wasn't private. Maria could see the pause, could see Dianna stop replying. Unease crept in fast. Vanessa didn't like that the new girl was now catching this awkwardness too, even without knowing the full extent of Dianna's recent behaviour. This wasn't the first impression Maria needed.

Vanessa texted, *{Magenta is right here with me. She wants to meet you.}*

A few seconds dragged by, then a reply came through. *{Okay, give me a sec.}*

Excitement lifted Maria as the moment finally came, but Vanessa stayed on edge. Mysterious silence had a way of changing a room. The video call came in and Vanessa answered.

"Hey, babes," Dianna greeted them. She was lying in bed in a tank top, looking like she'd just woken up. Her eyes were extremely red and glossy.

Maria waved happily at Dianna on the phone screen. "Hey, girl. I finally get to see you. You're so pretty."

"I feel like shit," Dianna said. The words came slow, with a slight slur. "Yeah...you're very pretty too."

Vanessa studied her. "Why do you sound like that?"

"Hey, Vee...you look pretty too...like always." The question got ignored, replaced with sweetness. "I miss you, babe...When are you two coming home to me?"

"We'll be back next Sunday," Maria said. "Then we could all have an outing together."

"I'm down with that...It'll be my birthday."

"Yeah, she knows," Vanessa said. "Daddy says we should leave here early Sunday morning so we're there before the afternoon."

"Aww...are you guys planning to surprise me? A surprise party for me?"

"Uhh, I don't think so. I wouldn't be telling you if that was the case." Vanessa sounded unimpressed with where Dianna's mind was at. "Daddy just wants us to be available for whatever it is you want to do as a family."

"Oh...I'm not even sure, babe." Dianna paused like she was thinking.

Silence held, then Vanessa realized Dianna hadn't been thinking at all. She'd blanked out.

"Seriously, what are you doing right now?"

"Just here...resting. Was with a trick all night...I'm tired."

"Resting?" Vanessa pressed. "Didn't you text that you were busy doing something when we first called?"

"Oh my God. Twenty-one questions?" Frustration flashed, but Dianna still answered. "I was using the washroom." Sweetness came right back to steer it away. "Vee, don't you miss me? You haven't, like...seen me in so long...Aren't you happy we're at least Facetiming?"

"Look how you're slurring your words, Dee. And your eyes." Vanessa didn't let it slide. "You're a mess."

Maria noticed the redness and the sluggish sound too, but she took it as tiredness, exactly like Dianna said. Vanessa refusing to accept it made Maria uncomfortable, like she was watching something private crack open. Vanessa had framed the issue as distance and neglect, but now it felt like more. Maria stepped away to give them privacy and went to use the washroom.

"Obviously I'm tired," Dianna insisted to Vanessa.

"No. You look like you're high on something. Something else."

"Something else? Oh, wow...Something else like what?" Dianna got defensive. "How would you know what being high on something else would look like?

Unless...unless you've tried something else before." She leaned back into the excuse. "I'm just tired... so you need to relax off me, babe."

"Don't even say shit like that because I'm not the one popping next drugs," Vanessa snapped. "And I've known you for some time now, Dee, so I know how you look when you're tired. Your eyes don't get glossy red like that. And I know how you are on D-D too, even when you crash. You're looking completely different and sluggish right now."

"Listen...I'm not 'bout arguing with you, Vee," Dianna said. "Where's Magenta? I wanna talk to her instead."

Vanessa glanced around the room. "Magi?"

"I'm in the washroom," Maria called back from behind the closed door.

"Okay...well, I'm gonna go back to bed," Dianna said, already drifting away. "I'll see you guys on my birthday. Give Magenta my Snapchat and Instagram so she can add me."

"Whatever. Bye." Vanessa ended the video call.

Maria came out of the washroom and found Vanessa seated on the bed with her phone still in hand. A pout sat on her face, her mind clearly somewhere else.

"Are you okay?" Maria asked.

"I'm fine. I just don't know about her anymore," Vanessa replied, sounding small.

Joining her on the bed, Maria kissed her cheek. "Don't stress it, babe. She was probably just tired like she said."

"No." Vanessa wouldn't take it. "I know her. Something's up with her. And it looks like it's getting worse."

A slow rub along Vanessa's back came with Maria's next words. "Whatever it is, talk to her about it when we get back."

"Yeah, I'll try. But we'll probably fight."

"I'll be there to make sure it doesn't turn into that." Maria tried to lighten it. "I'll even wear earplugs if it's meant to be private. I'll just stand there ready to break up the wrestling match."

A short laugh escaped Vanessa. "I don't think we'd ever get physical. Diamond might be bigger than me, but she's a little softie. She's scared to fight." Confidence sharpened her tone. "You probably think I'm boasting, but I'd mess up Diamond if I got really angry. I'm banned from some strip clubs because I beat up a lot of bitches twice my size. I may be small, but I did kickboxing, wrestling, and jujitsu when I was a kiddo. I stopped in my final years of high school because I got into boys and wanted to be more girly."

Then her voice softened again. "And if me and Diamond ever argued around you, you wouldn't need earplugs or privacy. You're our sister now too, so our problems are your problems."

Maria laughed. "That's not exactly what I signed up for, but I guess every family comes with its troubles. Just promise me you won't ever beat me up with your kung fu."

They both laughed, then shared a kiss.

"One time," Vanessa said, warming to the memory, "Daddy got mad at me about something and had me pinned on the wall by my neck. I pulled myself up and wrapped my legs around his neck to choke him. You should've seen his face."

"No fucking way." Maria couldn't hold back her laugh. "What did he do?"

"He let go of me just to pry my legs off his neck. He was screaming at me to let go, and I wouldn't because I was so mad. But he's a lot stronger than me, so he got me off him after a good struggle." Amusement lit her expression. "Then after he fucked me up, he left my place and texted me asking where the hell I learned that shit from."

Maria couldn't stop laughing.

Vanessa glanced at the clock. It was 2:13 p.m. "Oh, shoot. I gotta get ready for my three-thirty trick."

Maria watched as little Vanessa got to her feet and rushed into the washroom. In two hours, Vanessa would be back and they would grab dinner, then return to the hotel to get ready for another night of work. Tonight they were hitting a different strip club in London, just to switch up the scenery.

With nothing to do, Maria grabbed her phone from the side table and lay back on the bed. The notifications were normal, except for one Instagram DM from a non-follower. A non-follower messaging her was not strange. She had fans, and a few potential tricks from the club had been sliding into her inbox lately. Still, this message hit differently. The words sat on her screen:

{Babe, I miss you,} {Please talk to me again,} {I'm lost and crying without you.} It had been delivered an hour ago.

The sender was not clear. When Maria clicked the page, it looked fake, like somebody made it just to reach her. Could it be Marvel? She had blocked and deleted him, and anyone tied to him. She had even changed her Instagram username when she got with Gelato. There was no way Marvel could've known what she'd switched it to. Unless it wasn't Marvel at all.

Maria replied, *{Who is this?}*

Vanessa came out of the washroom and caught Maria staring at her phone, looking bothered. "Babe, what's up?"

Maria snapped out of it and looked up. "Nothing. I'm fine. I was, uhh, umm, kinda hungry."

"Then order food and eat now. I'll tell my trick to order me food and I'll eat at his place."

"Okay." Maria nodded, playing it off. "I'll get two chicken salads from Pizza Pizza. One for now, and one for late night after work. You want me to add anything for you?"

"Yeah. Some barbecue wings for late night would be nice," Vanessa said, already reaching for her own phone to call the client waiting on her.

Maria turned back to her screen to place the order, but her focus kept drifting. She found herself waiting for the next Instagram notification instead.

CHAPTER TWENTY-THREE

Tuesday, July 3 – 12:17 a.m.

Preeme and Jiggy were tucked into a corner of the bustling Million Dollar Club, trading turns over a game of billiards. Jiggy's face was familiar to damn near everyone inside, pimps, dealers, dancers, and regulars who lived in the nightlife. Preeme stayed the opposite. His name carried weight, but few could put a face to it, which let him move through rooms like a shadow while Jiggy stood in plain sight. Both men wore designer fits and jewelry. Preeme had on a Rolex and a thick gold chain with a yellow diamond Raptors pendant, but nothing about it was meant to become his signature. Unlike most hustlers, he didn't cling to one identifiable piece. He rotated Toronto themed pendants, buying and reselling them often, keeping his look clean but untraceable. They were the same age group, and the street respect between them was even. In the live game, Preeme's name rang louder, partly because of who he ran with and how long he'd been stamped in it. Jiggy was Preeme's go to for cocaine, since his overseas connections kept the product premium. But it wasn't only business. Their history went back a few years, to the drug trade, when they linked through a mutual friend on an out-of-town run. Each of them showed up with supply from different routes, and Jiggy's was the one that stood out. After that weekend, Preeme stayed in touch, and Jiggy kept him plugged as a middleman without ever exposing the real source.

Preeme respected the boundary. Jiggy respected the man. In return, Preeme sharpened him up with real game, and that was how Jiggy levelled up in the life he already had one foot in. The friendship stayed quiet on purpose. The few people Preeme kept around only knew him as Lucky-Loo when they spoke about him, never tying his real identity to the name Preeme.

They took a break from the pool game, posted up at the isolated table near the corner lane, and talked business over drinks.

Jiggy asked, "You really want just another half and a quarter? I don't know why you don't just grab the full brick, or a couple, just to have."

"Nah, I'm good, bruh," Preeme replied. "I'm good with the half and quarter. I don't need all that extra weight on me."

Preeme was never the type to buy kilos just to look like a heavyweight. He only grabbed what would last him no more than two weeks, and he adjusted depending on how things were moving. When business was busy, the half-kilo covered him for selling ounces to his young dealers and colleagues, and the quarter let him break it down for out-of-town runs.

"When you want it?" Jiggy asked.

"You got it now?"

"I only got like a half at my place. It's prob' even a few ounces short."

"Okay. Get that to me tomorrow, then. Just don't drag it, I only got an ounce or two left."

"I'll grab it early in the morning and swing by you with it."

"I'ma have the paper ready," Preeme said. "Even though I know you be taxing me high compared to the real low numbers you getting it for."

"C'mon, fam, don't make it look so," Jiggy replied. "I gotta eat too. Plus, I give you the raw, uncut version. I deal with you super bless, fam. I just gotta eat too."

"You already eating, bruh." Preeme finished his drink, then got up to get back to the game.

Jiggy rose too, smirking. "I'm just tryna stack up some bread to your level." He grabbed his stick off the wall and stood by the table, eyes on Preeme as he leaned over the felt, lining his cue up to strike. "Save more than you spend, homie. That's the simplest way to get your paper up."

Anybody who really knew Preeme knew his money ran longer than most street guys. It was even longer than some of his high-rolling pimp friends, because he stacked steady in both lanes and didn't waste his nights partying and popping bottles like most Toronto hustlers. A few drinks and a game of pool was enough for him. When he wanted real fun, it was dirt bikes, jet skis, and low-key moves with Crystal or his tight circle. Cottages, quick getaways, vacations. Anything that didn't make him a familiar face in Toronto's limelight.

12:32 p.m.

Dianna already knew Gelato was coming by sometime today. He'd messaged her the night before to make sure she'd be home. With her regular, Eric, booking her more often lately, Gelato understood that if he wanted to catch her while he passed through to collect money from the safe, he had to check in ahead of time. Her birthday was coming up on July 8th, too, and he needed to hear her plans so he could put things in motion. Truth was, he was after what he always wanted from her, good sex with his thick, blonde babe.

When he arrived about an hour ago, she was already in bed, waiting. The second he stepped into the room with that hunger in his eyes, her phone got tossed aside without a thought. Clothes came off, bodies came together, and there wasn't any warm-up talk to slow it down. It moved too fast for her to tell whether he'd already been on coke or not. By the time he was finished, the sweat was on him and whatever edge he'd walked in with seemed burned off, so even if he'd been high, he felt closer to sober now. Dianna was sober too, on purpose. Knowing he was coming, she didn't risk being at home high or drunk for no reason, not after their last talk about her turn-up habits. Part of her had been hoping for a party with him once he got there, but he went straight to sex. She enjoyed it, even caught her orgasm, but now she couldn't tell where his mood was headed next. Would he offer coke, or keep it moving? An evening booking was waiting, her monthly client from Europe, one she knew she had to attend. Still, a piece of her kept wishing Gelato would tell her to cancel and keep her right there with him for the rest of the night.

They lay under the sheets, still naked, sober now, with Dianna tucked against Gelato as they talked about her birthday.

"I'm not really sure," Dianna said. "I just know I want you all to myself at the end of the night so we can turn up all the way, and you just fuck me until I die."

Gelato laughed. "So you basically wanna die on your birthday?"

"Yes. I want to die with honor by your sword." She laughed too. "An orgy with Vee and the others would be fun, but I really just want to get high and get a concentrated, strong fuck from you, alone."

"Okay, so how about we go on vacation for a few days or something? Just you and me."

"No, no, because I still want to do something with the whole family for my birthday. It's just the night I want to be alone with you. Kind of like how Skye did her birthday with everyone at the nightclub, then ended the night alone with you."

"That's cool. We can do that." Gelato's tone stayed light, but he kept pressing for something solid. "So what would you like to do with the family? You still haven't given me ideas."

Dianna went quiet, but not because she was thinking up birthday plans. Her mind went straight to Eric. Eric had been begging to take her on vacation that same weekend, and a guilty part of her wanted it too. Even thinking it felt dangerous, like she was letting herself drift too close to a client in her head.

Gelato looked down at her and caught the distance in her eyes. "You okay, babe?"

A sigh left her. Dianna eased off his chest and lay back on her pillow, staring up at the ceiling. "It's just...my trick's been begging to take me on vacation that weekend too."

Gelato looked confused, unsure where she was taking it. Dianna met his gaze and, nervous now, added, "But obviously I've got no intentions of spending it with him over you. I told him he can take me the following weekend."

"Okay, and so what's the problem?" Gelato questioned.

Dianna laughed softly to ease the tension in her chest. "Well, Daddy, you know I've never been on vaycay with a trick before, so I don't really know how it goes. Skye once told me about doing a few days with tricks and how she finessed it with long tourist days and all that. That sounds easy. I just don't know how much to charge him for the trip."

"How many days he want?"

"Full weekend. Wants to fly out Friday and fly back Monday."

Gelato ran the math quick. "Okay, so we count three nights, Friday, Saturday, Sunday. And I'm guessing he expects a lot of sex?"

"He really doesn't care for sex like that. He just loves spending time with me. But I'd say maybe two sessions a night."

"Sounds like this guy really likes you," Gelato said, pride sitting in his voice. "So I'd say thirty K total. Ten K a night."

"Wow, that's a lot," Dianna admitted, already knowing, "Eric'll pay it, though."

"Well, fuck, you worth a lot, baby. Don't ever doubt your value. Plus, we gotta milk him for the fantasy of having you on another side of the world. He's asking for exclusive time."

"Yes, Daddy, that's true." Dianna cuddled back into him, smiling. "Okay, I'll let him know."

"I would've said a hundred K if he wanted the luxury of having you on your actual birthday," Gelato added, "But I know he ain't about to cough up that type of bread to fulfill his real fantasy."

"Actually," Dianna looked up at Gelato, "He probably would."

"Really?" He sounded stunned.

"Yeah. Eric really likes me," Dianna reminded him. "He's super rich, and I think he'd pay it like it's nothing. He wouldn't even be weighing it like that."

"Hmm..." Gelato sat with it. "So let's charge him a hundred K anyway, even though it's the weekend after your birthday."

Dianna giggled. "C'mon, Daddy. One thing you taught me is to *demand respect with high value, but also be considerate when you're milking tricks, because we'll get more in the long run if we don't scare them off with aggressive milking.* That's your own words." She added, "But maybe I'll tell Eric fifty K instead of thirty, if you want."

"And you think he'll pay that?"

"Yeah." She kept it simple. "Eric really likes me."

Gelato watched her for a beat. With the question on his mind before asking. "Is he in love with you or something?"

Dianna knew the answer, but she answered careful. "I think so. Maybe."

"How are you not sure?"

"Because I've never asked him that type of question. I just know it from how he is with me."

"Interesting." Gelato heard the way she tightened up around it. "And how do you feel about him?"

The question caught her off guard. She looked away for a second, then back up with the only answer that was allowed to exist. "He's nothing but a trick, Daddy. That's how I feel about him." A smile followed, steady, practiced.

"Okay, good." Gelato settled into it. "Tell him July thirteenth and back July sixteenth for fifty thousand. And he pays your round trip and everything, too." He added, "And I want my baby travelling first-class. Tell him it has to be first-class."

"Of course, Daddy. I'll let him know when I see him tomorrow."

Gelato thought for a moment, then said, "Even if he would pay a hundred thousand, I wouldn't let him take you on your birthday weekend. No way a trick's gonna have you on your special day over me."

"Yes, Daddy, I know." Dianna tucked in close again. "I wouldn't want that either."

Knowing Eric was rich enough to cover every cost and still pay a ridiculous price to take Dianna away on her actual birthday weekend didn't sit well with Gelato. Eric knew nothing about him, and there was no competition on the surface. Still, it hit Gelato's ego to know another man could throw money at the situation like it was nothing, like he could buy the right to override who Dianna spent her special day with. A hundred thousand would've been nice, but Gelato couldn't let a client's money outweigh his status as the most important man in her life. Dianna's birthday was his.

"So, anyways," Gelato said, pulling himself back to the point, "what do you want to do for your birthday, babe? You still haven't decided."

"Well…" Dianna thought, then answered, "I don't really care about the whole weekend, but I want you from Saturday night. Then for my birthday on Sunday we can all do something as a family, maybe invite some friends. Then I get you all to myself again that night."

"Okay, so how 'bout this." Gelato's eyes lit with an idea. "How 'bout we rent a private boat and party on the lake."

"Yes!" Dianna sat up with excitement, the sheet sliding low enough to expose her naked upper half. "We'll have our family there, Smooth's family, Preeme and Crystal. I'll maybe invite some good friends from the strip club."

"Okay, that's the plan then," Gelato said. "A private party on the lake."

"Yes, then after the party you take me home alone for some crazy sex. I want to be handcuffed, tied up, whipped, and all types of wild play."

"Woah." Gelato laughed. "You wanna turn up on some real kinky shit, huh?"

"Yes, Daddy." Dianna smiled down at him. "You gotta do it for my birthday."

"Oh, I've got no problem with that." His grin sharpened. "I'm just wondering where all this need for freakiness is coming from." He squinted at her with a smirk. "Is this what you and Velvet been getting into?"

Dianna laughed. "No, no. I saw it in a porno the other day and it really turned me on. I haven't tried it with Velvet yet, but I'm sure she'll love the idea too. I want my first time with you, though. On my birthday."

"Speaking of Velvet." Gelato sat up too, shifting back to lean against the headboard. "I heard about you two getting into a little argument here a while ago. Are you guys okay now?"

"Everything's fine, Daddy," Dianna said. "Vee FaceTimed me two days ago, and I even got to meet the new girl, Magenta. She's very pretty."

"Good, good." Gelato sounded pleased. He heard his phone ringing from his pants on the floor, so he got up to grab it. The caller ID read: *Velvet Icy*.

"Oh, speaking of the little devil," Gelato said to Dianna, "It's her calling."

Dianna smiled, but a tight worry sat underneath it. The last time she and Vanessa spoke hadn't gone as smooth as she just made it sound, and she didn't want Vanessa saying the wrong thing to Gelato.

Gelato answered with the phone to his ear, playful, "Hey, my baby, Vee. What's good with you and your pretty lil' self?"

"Ain't nothing pretty, nigga!" a man's voice snapped back. "Nigga, I got your bitch, and it's my turn to serve you!"

Gelato's heart dropped. He froze, standing naked with the phone pressed to his ear. Dianna's smile vanished the moment she saw his face change.

Gelato's voice broke, "Wh-who is this?"

"Nigga, it's Marvel. Are you ready to be served?"

"How?" Gelato couldn't make it make sense. "But how?"

"Hold on," Marvel said, the phone shifting like he was moving around.

A moment later, Vanessa's voice came through, thin and shaking. "...Daddy?"

"Vee?!"

"Daddy, help me...Please, come get me!"

"Where are you?" Gelato demanded.

"I don't know." She cried. "I don't know where I am, but they brought me to some house far—"

Marvel came back on the line. "Yeah, nigga, I got yo' bitch. I'ma holla at you in a bit and show you how you can help me, and maybe I can help you. Better not call the cops. Take your serving like a man."

"How are you serving me?" Gelato pleaded, panic climbing into his throat. "It sounds like you took her by force. She didn't choose up to you. That's not how a serving goes!"

"Shut the fuck up, you fake pimp!" Marvel barked. "I'll call you when I'm ready to serve you, my way. If you call the cops, I'll fucking kill her."

The call ended.

Gelato stood there naked, staring at the phone in his hand like it was the only thing holding him upright. His eyes watered.

"Daddy," Dianna asked, voice small, "what happened? Is everything going to be okay?"

And those same questions tore through Gelato's mind, with no answers behind them.

CHAPTER TWENTY-FOUR

Marvel spent night after night rotating through strip clubs across the Greater Toronto Area, and still couldn't find Maria. Not even a whisper that somebody might've seen her somewhere. Social media turned into a dead end too, because she'd blocked and deleted everyone he could've used to trace her page. Every day that passed made Marvel miss Maria more, and the truth started settling in. He loved her. Losing her didn't just hit his pockets, it hit his chest. His relationship with his square girlfriend got shaky from his strange moods and the depression that wouldn't lift. He hadn't taken Maria seriously, treating her like nothing more than his gorgeous, bread-winning working girl. He thought losing her would only hurt the money. He still had drug money to live on, so he figured he'd be fine. Instead, his heart stayed sore. A girl as kind as Maria wasn't something you lost without feeling it. He was a fool to let another man slide in and take her.

One morning, Marvel woke up thinking about Chief Keef. Maria was a big fan. Back when she'd left a comment on Chief Keef's Instagram, it pissed Marvel off. Now the memory made him smile because it felt like a lead. He made a fresh Instagram account so he wouldn't be restricted, then went hunting for the post she'd commented on. It was a close-up of Chief Keef's face, looking high and out of it. Marvel scrolled through endless comments until he finally found what he was looking for: *{My man looks just like you♥.}*

The username attached to it was different from what Maria used to have. The page was private. The profile picture was small, but Marvel still felt that wave of accomplishment when he recognized her. Then the depression rushed right back, because even in that tiny photo, she looked vibrant. He could only imagine the new, extravagant posts behind that private page, living lavish as Gelato's girl.

Marvel sent a message from the new account. He didn't bother identifying himself. He went straight into pleas and apologies, because with what he was saying, she'd know it could only be him. He apologized for not treating her right when he had her and he begged for another chance, telling her how much he needed her back in his life. He wrote about realizing he loved her, and he kept going. Each paragraph went unanswered, but the read receipt kept appearing under each message. He knew she was reading. Maria could've blocked him if she wanted. She didn't. So he pushed harder, sending more messages, exaggerating how he'd been crying himself to bed every night. Then he sent one more, talking about breaking up with his square girlfriend. That was when the typing indicator finally showed.

{Why did you break up with your girlfriend?} was Maria's response.

{Because I love you and want to be with you.}
{When did you break up with her?}

Marvel lied, *{Right before I started looking for you on here,} {I knew I couldn't diss you and be with her still if* *you ever gave me another chance,} {This time it will be just you and me.}*

Time passed before Maria replied, *{You just want me to work for you.}*

{No. I want you to be my girlfriend this time,} {Me and you could build our future,} Marvel said, then added, *{I'll do anything for you Maria,} {I love you so much I'm even crying right now.}*

Maria may have been happy with her new Icy family, but nothing beat being the main girl to a man. Especially a man she shared real history with. She didn't give in to Marvel right away. The idea of him making her his one and only tipped the scale. She kept messaging him, testing how serious he was. Being alone in the hotel gave him the opening to call. On the phone he said all the right things. By the end of it, Maria felt ready to give him another chance. The three-hour drive was one obstacle. Another was Gelato. Maria didn't even know how to leave now that she was in his stable. With Vanessa away at a booking, she could've packed and ordered an Uber. She could've disappeared without a trace. One problem kept her stuck though. Some of her personal belongings, IDs and documents, were still at Gelato's condo in Toronto. Things she needed for real life. Replacing them would be a long, complicated headache. She couldn't just walk away from all of it.

Marvel promised he'd figure it out. He told her to get through one more night and not say a word to anyone. He'd build a plan. He wanted Maria back with him safely. He also wanted Gelato boxed into accepting the loss while still cooperating with returning her belongings. Maria gave Marvel the information he needed to put it together. The move would happen the next day. Until then, she'd work another night in London as an Icy Girl and keep in touch with Marvel in private.

When Vanessa came back to the hotel, Maria stayed on edge. Guilt had her jumpy, always checking her phone and replying to Marvel here and there. Vanessa didn't clock it as suspicious. She assumed Maria was keeping up with new clients who wanted to book her.

At the club that night, Maria kept slipping off to the washroom to use her phone. Vanessa started getting annoyed at the constant breaks. She took it as Maria getting lazy on shift. Whenever she could, she checked the washrooms to make sure Maria wasn't hiding in a stall.

If Marvel was really building a way to pull Maria out, he had to move fast. Vanessa's watchful habits were closing in on Maria's foul play.

Tuesday, July 3 – 3:04 a.m.

The chemistry between the Icy girls in the club felt off tonight. Vanessa stayed on Maria, picking up that she wasn't working with the same enthusiasm as the previous nights. Maria, in return, got annoyed with Vanessa hovering over her every move. They still put up decent numbers for a Tuesday, but the drive back to the hotel went quiet, Maria glued to her phone.

Vanessa asked, "Who keeps messaging you so much at this time?"

"A few tricks I met tonight," Maria answered, quick and flat.

Back at the hotel, the silence followed them into the room. They stripped down to underwear and climbed into bed without their usual playfulness. They turned their backs to each other, forced out a simple "Goodnight," and tried to sleep. Maria got up multiple times through the night to use the washroom, and every time she moved, it dragged Vanessa out of her sleep. It was strange how Maria had her phone in hand every trip, but Vanessa told herself not to make it into something. But as morning crept in, it got worse. Maria started going more often, staying longer, always with the phone. Vanessa's suspicion finally kicked up hard enough that she got out of bed and went to the washroom door. When she tried the handle, it didn't budge. Locked.

"Why is the door locked?" Vanessa asked.

"Do-doing number two, babe," Maria stuttered from behind the door.

"Since when do you lock the door when you're pooping?"

Nerves pushed a laugh out of Maria. "I don't think you've ever tried to come in here while I'm doing number two."

Before Vanessa could say anything else, someone knocked on the room door, sharp and impatient. It pulled her mind off whatever Maria was doing in the washroom. Vanessa went to the door and looked through the peephole, but nobody stood in view.

"Who is it?"

"*Room service,*" a strange voice answered.

Knocking at dawn, a voice she did not recognize, and an empty peephole, it all felt wrong. Vanessa knew better than to open the door. But Maria came out of the washroom and headed over like she meant to swing it open.

"No, don't open it," Vanessa said, stepping into her path.

"It's probably room service," Maria replied, trying to push past little Vanessa.

Vanessa grabbed Maria's arm to stop her. Maria yanked back, hard.

"What are you doing?" Vanessa's voice sharpened, concern rising fast.

"Let go of me!" Maria snapped, fighting the hold.

Maria landed a punch to Vanessa's face that dazed her, but Vanessa didn't lose her hold on her. That sparked a serious brawl between the girls in underwear. Little Vanessa yanked back on Maria's arm, and they both lost balance, stumbling away from the door before crashing to the floor. Vanessa got on top and started dropping punches into Maria's face, making her scream as she threw wild shots back. Vanessa followed with crushing elbows that split Maria's lip and started her nose bleeding. Maria flared her hands up blindly, caught a fistful of Vanessa's hair, and tugged viciously side to side until it threw Vanessa off. She yanked harder to one side, used her weight, and rolled them over, ending up on top. Maria tried to throw down a couple hits, but Vanessa kept her forearms tight over the sensitive parts of her face. Maria then slipped off and made a break for the door. Vanessa shot her legs out and hooked Maria's ankles, taking her down again. Maria hit the floor hard and cried out for help, and whoever stood on the other side of the door sounded eager to get in. Vanessa's mind snapped to the only answer that made sense. Maria was behind it. Whoever was at that door was there because of her. This was serious. Vanessa clamped on from behind, her forearm tight at Maria's throat.

"Please, let me go!" Maria gasped, fighting for air.

Vanessa snarled in her ear, "You're going to sleep, you shady bitch!"

Maria struggled against Vanessa's tight arm around her neck, twisting and tucking her chin, then somehow got her mouth to flesh and bit down hard, trying to draw blood. Vanessa screamed and released her on instinct. The pain was too sharp to bear, and Maria seized the moment. She stumbled to her feet and bolted for the door. Vanessa got up quickly, but Maria had already made it to the door. Her only option now was to dash to the room phone by the bed and call for security. She snatched up the receiver, hands shaking, and blanked on what number to dial for help. The door swung open before she could press anything. Three black men rushed into the room. The tallest came straight at her with a gun pointed. Vanessa dropped the receiver and raised her hands in surrender. He showed no mercy. The pistol cracked across her head and her vision flashed white as she fell back onto the bed.

A hard slap across the face brought Vanessa back. Her eyes opened to a gun aimed at her. Behind it stood the same young Black man. Baggy clothes, a black hoodie, braided hair, and he couldn't have been older than twenty.

"Get dressed," he ordered. "Pack your shit."

With the gun on her, Vanessa pushed herself upright on the bed, defeated. She cried quietly, tears sliding down her cheeks. She then touched her forehead where it hurt most from the pistol-whipping. The feel of the wound and blood on her fingers suggested an open gash that would need stitches.

"I'm hurt really bad," Vanessa cried.

"Shut up and let's go," the goon snapped.

"But where are we going?" Vanessa pleaded. "You can take all the money, just leave me, please."

"Hurry up and get dressed!"

Vanessa slid off the bed and went to the dresser for clothes. The goon didn't take his eyes off her, watching for any move he didn't like. She got dressed quickly, keeping her attention on the room and everyone in it. Maria was sitting on the sofa, ready to leave. The sight made Vanessa's stomach dip, the pistol-whipping settling in as she tried to gauge how long she'd been knocked out for Maria to already be dressed and packed. Beside Maria stood an ugly, dark-skinned guy with dreads, most likely Marvel. He leaned against the wall in a blue tracksuit, holding Vanessa's phone.

"Magi..." Vanessa sought sympathy from Maria. "What's all this about? Please, tell them to leave me."

Maria couldn't look Vanessa in the eye, clearly ashamed. She did deserve the black eye, busted lip, and fractured nose from the brawl.

Instead, Marvel replied, "What's your phone's password? I'll call Gelato for you."

"You're gonna tell him to come pick me up?"

"Maybe. If he gives me what I want when I serve him," Marvel said. "But for now, you coming with me. You're mine now."

"Serve him?" Vanessa knew the game well enough to understand what it meant for a pimp to serve another pimp. But what Marvel had said didn't make sense to her. "How are you serving him? I'm not choosing-up to you, though. I don't want to be with you, and I don't want to leave with you."

"You don't have a choice, bitch!"

"But—"

The goon bucked her head with the gun and said again, "Shut the fuck up and let's go!"

She wanted no further problems with the gun, so Vanessa finished getting dressed in tights, a T-shirt, and sneakers. She packed her bag with everything she needed, including her makeup kit from the washroom, while the gunman followed her every move. When she came out of the washroom, Vanessa noticed the last person in the room. He stood tall by the front door, checking the peephole every so often, keeping six. He looked exactly like the gunman who'd been watching her, baggy clothes, braids, same face. They were twins.

After fully packing everything into her luggage, Vanessa was ready to go. The twin at the door cracked it open to peek into the hall, making sure nobody was out there. He gave a thumbs up, and Marvel led the way. He carried Maria's luggage, with Maria following him at will. The twin picked up Vanessa's luggage and went out too, and the one with the gun motioned for Vanessa to follow behind his brother while he stayed close behind her.

They stepped into the hall. The gun stayed tucked under the gunman's baggy hoodie, pressed into Vanessa's back as they guided her toward the nearest backdoor and out into the parking lot. Vanessa hoped to see somebody outside so she could run screaming for help, but the lot was empty at this time of morning, nothing but parked cars. They walked her to an older-model Mercedes Benz, and the gunman shoved Vanessa into the tinted back seat, wedged between him and his twin. Marvel threw all the luggage into the trunk while Maria got into the passenger seat. They waited for Marvel to slide into the driver's seat.

"You don't have sunglasses I could wear, babe?" Maria asked Marvel when he got into the car.

"What you need sunglasses for?"

"To cover my black eye. It's too noticeable."

"Okay. True." Marvel reached into the centre console and pulled out a set of shades for Maria. He popped the trunk and got back out, then returned with a scarf in his hand. He passed it to the twins in the back seat. "Make sure the bitch keeps this over her eyes the whole drive."

That was when it hit Vanessa that she was really being kidnapped and taken away to Lord knows where. She begged through tears, "Can you please call Gelato for me? Please?"

"Yeah, I'ma do that when I'm ready." Marvel said as he started the car.

The twin began wrapping the scarf over Vanessa's eyes, and her tears soaked into the cloth. Unpleasant thoughts crowded in. Maria had bonded with her like family, and yet this was what it turned into. It felt like a setup, like it had been planned long before Vanessa ever caught on. Maria coming into the stable, attaching herself to them, getting close, and then bringing danger to the door. Vanessa couldn't make sense of why it had to be her, why she was the one being dragged into it. Her mind flashed to Sierra, and to the training Sierra refused to take on. Vanessa wondered if that refusal meant something now, if Sierra had sensed what Vanessa missed, if there had been a way to see it coming and stop it. Betrayal sat heavy in her chest, betrayal from Maria, betrayal from her Icy family, and she still could not understand why this was happening to her. In the darkness of her tear-soaked blindfold, Vanessa prayed through the rosary in her mind, hoping God would forgive her for her sinful ways and save her.

CHAPTER TWENTY-FIVE

Tuesday, July 3 – 10:13 p.m.

A lot of time had passed while I waited on Marvel's call. He had my girl, Velvet. I had been desperately ringing off her phone since the last call I got hours ago, and the only response was a text saying, *{Relax nigga. I'll holla at you soon.} {I'm gonna serve your ass.}* That came in over an hour ago. I tried the old number I had for Marvel from almost a month back too, but the line was out of service. I hit Magenta's number a couple times as well. Her phone was completely off. I thought about reaching out on social media, but she had deleted me off everything. Magenta was the least of my concerns because, as far as I knew, she had probably planned this with Marvel the whole time. The way it looked now, Marvel would be calling to demand an amount of money in return for Velvet. Some loser move, trying to come up off a win. Magenta played her part well, getting into my stable and close with my girls just to make this happen. And here I was, a big pimping shark who got fooled by a shrimp. But the vibes I got off Maria from day one would have never had me thinking this day would come. Her choosing up seemed real, and her connection with me felt sincere. Marvel's behaviour the day I served him felt like a man genuinely frustrated about losing his girl, unless they were all very good actors.

Maybe this wasn't some major plan from the start. Maybe Marvel found his way to Magenta and talked her into switching up on me. A dozen roads could've led here, and everybody around me had their own theory. None of that mattered, though. The only thing that mattered was getting my baby, Velvet, back safe.

I sat on the couch in my condo in shorts, topless, with Sierra beside me in sweatpants and a cropped shirt. She looked just as distraught as I felt. Smooth had caught the first flight back from Alberta when I called, frantic that Velvet had been kidnapped. Now he sat across from us in a full Versace tracksuit with jewellery still on, coming straight from the airport to my place. He and I got going on Designer-Dope the moment he arrived three hours ago, hoping it would dull the stress. Being that high kept me from jumping in a car and tearing up the road. I'd be chasing signs of my baby with nothing to go on. But Sierra didn't see this as the time to be under the influence while waiting on an important call, so the disappointment in her face stayed heavy, aimed at both Smooth and me. Mostly me. I brought Magenta into the stable, and now one of ours was caught up in the fallout of my choices. I felt like shit because there wasn't much I could do but wait and pray Velvet was okay. Designer-Dope became my escape from a reality I couldn't control.

I would've had Diamond here beside me just to make sure she was safe too. But there was no need. She had a booking with one of her regulars, a European guy who came into town for business once in a while and always made arrangements to see her. Diamond would be fine with him tonight, away at a cottage until tomorrow, and hopefully this craziness with Marvel would be handled by then.

I picked up the plate of Designer-D and the rolled bill from the centre table to hit a few more rails, then passed it over to Smooth.

"I think you guys should stop with that," Sierra said, looking displeased. "Angelo, you're out of it. How are you gonna talk properly with this guy when he calls?"

"I'm good. There won't be much to talk about. I'll just give him whatever he wants so he lets Velvet go."

"Well, at least be in the right state of mind so you know what's going on and don't get finessed into more nonsense."

"I do know what's going on," I snapped, getting defensive. "You need to chill."

"No, *you* need to chill," she shot back. "You're ridiculously high right now. It's written all over your face. At the rate you're going, it's gonna have to be me who handles the call."

"So handle it," I said. I was too high, and the last few lines were hitting me with force.

"But why would I have to handle that call?" Sierra asked, unimpressed. "Are you not the man of the family? It should be two men talking, coming to terms. No?"

My foggy mind took a second to catch up, but Smooth put the plate down after hitting his rails and said, "If Gelato ain't feeling to talk to the sucka, I'll handle the call for him."

Sierra looked at Smooth and rolled her eyes. "I don't know about you two right now. This is ridiculous."

That sassy attitude always knew how to get under my skin. In moments like this, I wished I could sober up and take control of my power. Instead, being irrationally high made me grab the plate again and chase another hit. Sierra reached like she was gonna take it but caught the look in my eyes and backed off. Any other time, if I was too high, she might've been able to press me and fully get her way while I was mentally weak on Designer-D. Not tonight. Tonight the high had my emotions unstable, and everything going on had anger and frustration boiling under my skin, tangled up with anxiety and insecurities. My thoughts weren't steady, and it felt safer staying locked into the dimension I was already in than letting myself drift into another.

"Where's Preeme?" Smooth asked.

"Talked to him earlier," I said. "Why?"

"Just asking."

Smooth asking that out the blue didn't sit right with me. I'd told him Preeme said to call if I needed anything, so maybe Smooth was thinking we might need him tonight. I looked at him. "You think we should call Preeme?"

"Maybe," Smooth said, then added, "But what he gon' do, though?"

Now I didn't know what to make of it. We were both high, talking in circles, not lining up with each other. Or maybe it was just me.

Sierra clearly had enough. "You know what, I'm calling Preeme to see if he's around so he can take this call from Marvel. Because both of you aren't making sense right now. Worst case, I'll have to take the call myself if Preeme can't make it."

I nodded so she knew I was good with it. Sierra rolled her eyes at my empty stare and kept moving, already on her phone. She'd made her decision and didn't care about my approval anyway.

I looked at Smooth. He picked up the plate and hit more rails like none of this was real. I couldn't even tell if he felt as high as I did. My mind kept racing, drifting toward a darker matrix of thoughts, one I wasn't ready for. I closed my eyes and forced myself to breathe through the wave of anxiety until it eased and I could grab the edge of reality again. But this reality still wouldn't sit right in my chest. Velvet was gone because of me, and she could be getting hurt right now while I sat here doing nothing.

I grabbed my phone and texted her number, even though it wasn't her holding it anymore. The weakness showed in every word I sent. *{Are you gonna call?} {Please, I'm waiting. Just call me soon so we can figure this out,} {I just want my girl back. So please call me soon.}*

GHAD

CHAPTER TWENTY-SIX

Somewhere in Niagara Falls, Ontario, in an old rundown house was where Marvel and his goons held Vanessa captive. It was a house they sold crack out of in Niagara, and the homeowner was a functioning crackhead who lived upstairs. He always allowed them to use his home as their shop in exchange for free drugs throughout their stay. Tonight, shop was closed, but the crackhead was content with having them use the house for other matters in exchange for the usual free fix of crack. From the moment they got there, Vanessa was carefully led down into the basement before removing the blindfold. She had no clue where she was being kept hostage. The blindfold made the drive feel longer than it was, so as far as she knew, she could've been taken to a whole other province.

During the long car ride from London, Vanessa's other senses had sharpened while she was blindfolded. She listened to every conversation in that car, and by the time they arrived she'd pieced together enough to understand how this happened, and how she ended up being taken from the hotel. It wasn't Maria's intention to put Vanessa in that predicament, but it was still shady for her to get back with her ex-lover, then follow through on a plan that used Vanessa as collateral to come to terms with Gelato. There was a thin, ugly kind of relief in hearing Maria press Marvel to promise that he and his goons wouldn't harm Vanessa while keeping her captive.

But his response offered no comfort. He said, "No promises. We gon' see how this plays out. And hopefully, this bitch don't do none stupid to piss us off."

The basement was where Marvel and the twins dwelled whenever they stayed at the house, a living area, a kitchen space, and one bedroom. Vanessa was kept in the living area and wasn't permitted to move from the blow-up airbed unless she needed to use the washroom. And using the washroom meant being monitored during the short walk to the washroom that had no door, then right back to the airbed. It was in Vanessa's best interest to cooperate and not agitate her keepers, the twins known as Blaze and Flame. They lounged on the couch and looked her way from time to time, making her uneasy, so she avoided eye contact. Her outlook was simple. If she didn't make things difficult for them, or for herself, she wouldn't be harmed, and she'd eventually be released. She stayed isolated on the airbed and did nothing that would invite the sexual desire she kept catching in their stares. She didn't need that level of violation added to the kidnapping.

Vanessa was alone and afraid, and the one person she thought she knew, Maria, avoided her by staying in the bedroom the entire time. Maria obviously felt guilty and ashamed about what was happening, so she couldn't show her face. Marvel went out earlier to get pizza for everyone in the basement, but only because Maria asked him to get Vanessa food, like feeding her would make her less of a bad person in the whole equation. Vanessa didn't have much of an appetite, but she ate anyway so she wouldn't starve herself. The open cut on her forehead had dried up and it would become a bad scar if she didn't get the medical attention needed. At some point, Marvel came out of the bedroom with Vanessa's phone and had Gelato on the line. Vanessa got to speak to him, but only briefly, and nothing came out of the call. That stressed her out even more, sitting on the airbed with no idea what would happen next, only knowing she wanted to go home in one piece. Marvel told Vanessa he'd call Gelato again to officially sort things out, and that would determine whether she went home or became his working-girl by force. Then he went back into the bedroom. Vanessa couldn't understand why Marvel thought she'd ever become his girl instead of running the second she had a chance. If the door at the top of the basement steps didn't have a lock, she would've already tried to escape. Just the idea of belonging to Marvel made her sick, and she expected Gelato to do whatever was needed to get her out of this. This was happening because she followed his lead in life.

The twins played NBA 2K on the big screen when Marvel came out of the bedroom again, this time with Maria. They were stepping out for a bit. It was the first time Maria had left the bedroom since they arrived. She wore sunglasses to cover her black eye, though the swelling across the rest of her face still showed from the beating Vanessa gave her at the hotel. Maria didn't look Vanessa's way. She stood by the stairs waiting on Marvel, while he told the twins they were just going for a walk. Before he left, Marvel told Vanessa he'd call Gelato when he got back. Then he and Maria went up the steps and out of the basement. Vanessa couldn't wrap her head around it. Just up those stairs was her freedom, another world above this dungeon. While she sat trapped in place, they went out for a lovely walk like time wasn't chewing her up.

Vanessa passed out waiting for them to return. When she woke, she had no idea how long she'd been asleep. One of the twins was knocked out on the couch. The other played Call of Duty. From the bedroom, Vanessa caught the muffled sound of Marvel and Maria talking, which meant they had come back while she slept.

Vanessa asked the twin playing video games, "Hey, umm, did Marvel call Gelato yet?"

Flame didn't take his attention off the game. "Nah."

"Is he gonna call him?"

"Yeah. When he's ready."

"But he said he would call when he gets back."

"Yeah, and you were sleeping."

Vanessa didn't know what to say to that. She could only be mad at herself. "Can you please tell him I'm awake now?"

"You asking me for a favour?"

"...Can you?"

Flame paused the game and turned to Vanessa with a smirk. "What's in it for me?"

Vanessa knew exactly what that meant. She looked away and didn't answer, hoping he'd drop it. That wasn't the door she meant to open.

Flame chuckled, went back to his game, and said, "I guess you gon' wait forever, then."

Relief hit first because it ended there. Then the room got more uncomfortable, his desire sitting out in the open. Vanessa needed to shift the awkwardness. "Umm..." She hesitated, but it was a request she had a right to make. "I need some water, please."

"Okay." Flame paused the game again, looked at her, then nodded toward the kitchen.

Vanessa got off the airbed and went over. Fresh Styrofoam cups sat on the counter. Her hand went for the tap, and Flame's voice cut in from across the room. "There are water bottles in the fridge."

"Okay." She put the cup down and grabbed a bottle.

While standing in the kitchen area, Vanessa could hear Marvel and Maria's conversation more clearly. The bedroom door was right beside her, close enough for their voices to carry. They were arguing about what to demand from Gelato. Marvel insisted on money. Maria said that was never the plan. The whole point of taking Vanessa was to trade her back in exchange for the rest of Maria's belongings still at Gelato's place. Vanessa would've taken her time with the water, but Flame was watching from the couch.

When she glanced his way, he said, "Bring the bottle back over here with you. I'm tryna play my game and not have to watch you standing there drinking."

"S-sorry." Vanessa took the bottle back to the airbed, and Flame returned to his game.

Marvel and Maria lay on the bed together fully clothed with Maria curled into him. Their walk had given them a little evening air and time to talk. Marvel stayed on his promise. Commitment. Future. All the right words. Maria had heard it over the phone, but hearing it again in person hit different. He'd been Prince Charming since reconnecting, and that was all she'd ever wanted. Even with her face swollen and the black eye, being back with him had her in high spirits. It just felt ugly that Vanessa was caught in it.

A text from Gelato came in, and it showed how vulnerable he was while waiting on Marvel's call. That alone boosted Marvel's confidence. A month ago, Gelato had him looking stupid when he served him for Maria, which Marvel still didn't understand. Now it was his turn to feel in control.

"So check this," Marvel said to Maria. "When I call Gelato, I'll tell him we want the rest of your stuff and half a millie."

"Half a mill?" Maria stared at him.

"Or is that too much?" Marvel questioned, unsure now.

"But we didn't take Vanessa to get money from him. I don't see why you're changing the plan."

"I been thinking about it. This guy swear he's a big pimp, so I'm gonna serve him for his bitch."

Maria didn't know enough about serving to argue the rules of it. "What if he doesn't have the money?"

"Then he won't get her back 'til he gets that money for us," Marvel said. "These full-time pimps make money for years. He gonna have half a mill, easy. If he really loves her, he'll cough it up. We'll see if these big pimps care about money more than their women."

"Marvo, that shouldn't be our worry whether he cares about her more than his money."

"Yeah, but we still need big money out of him."

"But that was never the plan," Maria urged. "We were supposed to focus on my stuff."

"Baby, trust me. We should get the money too."

"I don't want to do that to him."

"Why?" Marvel's eyes narrowed. "Why you so worried 'bout him? You still like him or something?"

"No, Marvo. Of course I don't. It's you that I love."

"So why you telling me not to get at his money?"

Maria didn't have a clean answer. "I just think we should stick to the original plan and not get carried away."

"Well, I want to serve him like he did to me."

Maria held his gaze, black eye and all. "So this is your ego."

"No," Marvel said, even though his tone didn't match it. "I'm doing it his way. He claims he a big pimp. I got his girl now, so I'm supposed to serve him with a price if he wants her back. That's how it goes."

Maria smirked. "I know you, Marvo. You just wanna flex on him."

"Maybe just a little." Marvel smiled and kissed her. "And I'm kinda pissed he had you working for him. He used you to stack more money for himself."

"Okay, fine," Maria gave in.. "But half a mill is too much."

"I don't care. Fuck that whack-ass, light-skin nigga. I want him to pay."

"Yeah, but I still care about Vanessa. I don't want this to be hard on her. Let's pick a number we know he can pay without dragging this out."

"Quarter milli, then."

"How about," Maria said, "A hundred thousand?"

Marvel paused.

"Please, Marvo," she said. "Make it easy for Vanessa. Do that for me."

"Okay, fine," Marvel agreed.

Maria kissed him. Marvel got up, leaving her on the bed and stepped out with Vanessa's phone in his hand. He was ready to give Gelato what he believed was a pimp's serving.

CHAPTER TWENTY-SEVEN

Preeme arrived roughly ten minutes after Sierra called him. Earlier, when Gelato rang with the news, Preeme made sure he stayed in the city in case he was needed. All he had to do was cut his runs short and drive straight to Gelato's place. When he got there, it was obvious that Smooth and Gelato were high out of their minds, and Preeme understood why Sierra wanted him there to handle the call with Marvel.

The clock read 10:47 p.m., and Gelato was slouched on the couch staring at the ceiling. Sierra sat beside him with her arms and legs crossed, unimpressed with the situation involving Vanessa. And even more unimpressed with the state Gelato and Smooth were in. Smooth sat on the sofa to Gelato's right, lost in his own world, keeping his high mind busy with his phone. They would have been doing more lines if Preeme had not taken the plate and kept it with him. He sat at the dining counter in a red Nike tracksuit with Gelato's phone in hand, waiting for Marvel's call. The serious expression on his face was enough to keep Smooth and Gelato from demanding the plate back. He also had his gun laid out on the counter beside the plate. He was not happy with the weakness the two older men were showing, turning to drugs at a time like this.

Nobody in the unit knew what kind of serving Marvel thought he was about to conduct with Gelato, but the plan was simple. They had to negotiate, and they had to get Vanessa back.

Gelato's phone rang. Preeme checked the screen and announced, "It's Vanessa's number. It's him calling."

Everyone got attentive as Preeme brought the phone into the living room. He stopped between the couch and the sofa so everyone could hear, then answered on speaker.

Marvel's voice came through. "Gelato?"

"Yeah, what's up?" Preeme replied.

"You sound different."

"Homie, what's up? Where's my girl?" Preeme pressed, cutting off any talk about his voice.

"She's right here with me. You wanna talk to her?"

"Yeah."

Marvel passed it over and Vanessa's voice came through. "Hello?"

Preeme handed the phone to Gelato on the couch. Gelato sat up straight, like posture could steady his coked mind. "Baby?" He said into the phone.

"Yeah," Vanessa replied. She was dull and tired of it.

"Are...are you o-okay?" Gelato struggled.

"I'm okay. I just want to go home."

"I'm sorry, babe. Please. I-I will get you back. I p-p-promise."

Marvel came back on. "So now you know she's bless."

Gelato started to respond, but Preeme snatched the phone from his hand and spoke for him. "Okay, what's up? What's all this about? Why'd you take my girl?"

"So I could serve you."

"The fuck you mean?" Preeme couldn't believe it. "Kidnapping a bitch isn't how you knock a bitch off the next man. That's not how pimpin' goes, bruh."

"Well, I'm a better pimp than you because I knocked Maria back off you and also took your bitch, too," Marvel said proud.

"Maria?" Preeme looked at Gelato, waiting to see if he wanted something said about her. Gelato only shrugged, so Preeme kept it moving. "What's up with her? Let me talk to her too."

"Nah, there ain't shit for you to talk to her about. She's super bless with me."

"Okay, so how did you get her back?"

"Yeah, it's my turn to put you on some real game, you stupid pimp." Marvel took his time, talking big about how he found Maria on Instagram, then how he was slick enough to snatch Vanessa too. He wanted Gelato to feel how stupid it was to take him lightly. He finished with, "You need to tighten up your game and not fuck around with real niggas like me. You could end up losing all your bitches." He chuckled. "You see, I told you. I'll get my girl back. She's my bitch and will always belong to me. And now I got your bitch, too."

Preeme could've said, *tighten up your game and return big homie's bitch before you lose your life.* But he wasn't one to lay threats. Instead, Preeme kept playing as Gelato and said, "Okay, so you got your girl back. That's good for you. But what you doing with mine? She didn't choose up to you. You gotta send her back because the way you went about this whole thing is wrong."

"Nah, I'm not sending her back. Not 'til I'm done serving you."

Preeme looked around, wondering if he was the only one in the unit who thought Marvel was stupid. Smooth wore no expression through his high, and Gelato looked like a lost cause. Sierra was the only other sober one who met Preeme's look. She shook her head, finding Marvel to be a headache too.

Preeme said into the phone, "Okay, so go on with your serving."

Marvel kept talking. "I just showed you where you fucked up with your game so you could do better next time. Now I need you to be a gentleman about this serving and help me do good too."

"Just tell me what you want, bruh."

"Okay, listen. I know Maria left some of her stuff at your place. I want you to bring it all back to me."

"That's no prob'. And you gon' send back Velvet?"

"Nah," Marvel said. "If you want your bitch back, you gotta bring me a hundred thousand dollars."

Preeme turned to Gelato, who stared back looking more hopeless than ever. Preeme ignored his expression and gave Marvel the only answer that could solve everything. "Okay, it's a deal. When and where do we meet?"

"I c-can't." Gelato tried to speak, but Preeme tapped his shoulder for him to shut up.

Marvel said on the phone, "I don't want to meet you. Make one of your other girls meet me with everything."

Preeme looked at Sierra. She was nervous, but nodded. Then Preeme noticed Gelato's face tighten with concern. He should've known better than to think Preeme would send her alone.

Preeme said to Marvel, "Okay. I'll have one of my girls bring everything."

"Alone," Marvel instructed.

"Yeah, she gon' forward alone," Preeme assured him.

"With the money and Maria's stuff."

"Yeah, I know."

Marvel couldn't believe he'd scored a hundred-thousand-dollar deal that easily. He was on the other end of the phone grinning uncontrollably. He'd never seen that kind of money in his life, and now he was about to get it in hard cash from a pimp he knew was more certified than him. It felt too good to be true.

Marvel's voice turned stern. "Don't play no games, eh. I'm not fucking around!"

"Listen, bruh, you got my girl and I just want her back, in peace," Preeme said. "I'm gonna have everything brought to you how you want it. I just want you to return my girl to me. Be a man of your word."

"Don't worry, you got my word. I'll bring Velvet with me and meet with the bitch you send. I'll call back in a few hours so you got time to get everything ready."

"Where am I sending my girl to meet you?"

"I'll let you know when I call in a few hours. I'ma smoke a joint and chill out for a bit," Marvel said. "Don't be ringing off the phone. I'll call you when I'm ready."

"Okay. I'll have everything ready soon, so how long will I have to wait?"

"Some time after midnight. Just chill out and wait!"

"Okay."

"Oh," Marvel said, "And after this, we good, right? No beef or funny games, right?"

"Yeah, we good."

Marvel still wasn't convinced. "Just know Maria told me where you live, so don't play games or you're dead. I want this all to go smooth, then we go our ways. I'ma call you when I'm ready." He ended the call.

Preeme turned back to Gelato, and that same look of distress stared up at him. Preeme was about to reassure him, but Gelato blurted, "I-I can't pay that money. I don't ha-have that much muh-muh-money."

Sierra couldn't believe what she'd just heard. "What? What do you mean you don't have that amount of money saved after all these years? Angelo, what the hell are you saying?"

It was a full moon that night.

CHAPTER TWENTY-EIGHT

◆

The moment Marvel said 100K, I tuned out whatever Preeme was saying to him. Hard cash. No fucking way. I'd had the gut feeling from the jump that Marvel was gonna hit me with a ransom for Velvet, and 10K would've been fair for that loser. Not that I wouldn't pay any price to get my baby back, but the truth was I couldn't afford 100K, and I could already feel the next wave of problems loading up behind that. Preeme turned to look at me, but my mind was spinning. Being this high had me fighting to stay locked in the same dimension, my face numb, not even sure what expression I was wearing. Preeme looked away and kept talking to Marvel like nothing was wrong. My eyes drifted to Smooth. He looked too focused, like he was wrestling his own high too. Then I glanced left at Sierra and got no comfort from her, just that hard, piercing stare like she could read what I was thinking. I looked away quick. Part of me wished I wasn't this high, and another part wanted more Designer-D just to disappear. *I need to get the fuck out of here.*

Marvel's demand was about to put my real finances on display for everybody. I'd been moving like a big pimp, but my savings weren't as heavy as people would assume. Sierra had been on my neck for reckless spending, always asking what I was stacking for our future, and now she was gonna crucify me because I didn't even have 100K put away. Worse, my partners were here to see it too. Maybe they didn't have that kind of cash either. Preeme might, since he wasn't into splurging and party life like that. Smooth lived how I lived, so I couldn't picture him sitting on much more than me.

I snapped back when Preeme ended the call with Marvel. Anxiety washed over me. This kind of high wasn't what I was used to, not with my mind running like this. It felt like everybody was staring at me, like they could see every thought on my face. I had to say it. "I, I can't pay that...I don't got a hundred K."

Sierra jumped on it immediately. "What? What do you mean you don't have that saved after all these years? Angelo, what the hell are you saying?"

My eyes bounced from her to Preeme, then to Smooth. Smooth just stared at me dumbfounded. When I looked back at Preeme, he didn't look impressed at all. "Big homie, you joking, right?"

I couldn't speak. My mind was racing so I just shook my head. It ran wild on stupid, peculiar thoughts. *Why did Smooth just give me that dumbfounded look?* That look had me questioning whether he actually did have that kind of money, and whether I was the weakest link in my own circle. Maybe my high was getting the best of me. Insecurity crept in, mixed with envy, the ugly realization that my closest friends might be in a better financial position than me.

"Tell me, Angelo, how much do you have saved up?" Sierra demanded.

"Umm..." I rubbed my head, hopelessly searching for an answer. I took too long, and Sierra pressed me harder. "How much, Angelo?!"

"I'm not sure. Maybe f-fifty cash and like f-fifteen in the bank."

"Oh my fucking God. So that's all you've saved up after all these years, Angelo?" Sierra was on the verge of tears. "Didn't you tell me you had a hundred thousand, about a month ago?"

I knew I'd lied to her then. I leaned forward and buried my head in my palms, humiliation washing over me. I was a failure, and everyone in the room now knew the truth.

"Why?" Sierra cried. "Why did you lie to me? Tell me what's been happening with all the money we've been making?"

"Sisi, I'm s-sorry," was all I could manage.

"Of course you're fucking sorry," she snapped. "Always shopping and spending money recklessly on yourself, and encouraging reckless spending with the other girls. How else would we not be broke?"

"We're not broke," I pushed back weakly. "We just don't have a hundred thousand."

Her sorrow flipped straight into anger. "Are you kidding me?! You've been in this game for so long and you don't have a hundred thousand? I've been with you for eight years, Angelo. Eight fucking years. And you haven't saved a hundred thousand dollars?" She kept going. "Let's not forget you've had other bitches paying you too. And you still couldn't save at least that?" She snapped again. "We should easily be sitting on at least a mill if you weren't always partying and doing stupid shit!"

I kept my face buried in my palms through all of it. The way she was going, I was scared it could turn physical, but I wasn't about to match her energy. I wasn't in the right state of mind, and I didn't have the strength to fight anyone.

Preeme stepped in. "Easy, easy. Just relax and breathe, Skye. I know you're pissed, but this ain't the time for all that. We gotta figure this out together."

"Yeah, Mama," Smooth added. "We here to help y'all."

I lifted my head and looked at Smooth. "You ha-have that kind of money?"

"Fo'sho, playa. You already know I keep my paper growing through real estate," he said confidently. "Plus I invest in stocks. I been telling you about that. Remember when the Bitcoin wave was doing mad numbers? I tried to put you on."

Bad enough my partners, the ones I embraced the game with, were now putting me on game. My main bitch was watching it all and adding her two cents. Like a pimp's serving, the whole situation had turned into a reality check. Sierra was disgusted with me, while my partners were in a better financial position than me. The cherry on top was that my other girl was held hostage somewhere, expecting me to have a hundred K ready to bring her home. My high was wearing off, and rationally I knew I needed to sober up. Being stuck in another matrix still felt better than facing reality.

"Okay, so here's what we gon' do," Preeme said. "Bring the fifty thousand and we'll add on twenty-five each."

"It's in the safe in my room. About fifty-three to be exact." I tried to make the total sound better.

Sierra sobbed. "Honestly, this is just fucking sad."

"How 'bout we finesse that sucka with some counterfeits?" Smooth suggested.

"That would be a smart move," Preeme agreed. Then he said, "But we don't have enough time to get a hold of a hundred thousand in counties. You got someone we could grab that from right now?"

"Nah. I only know one cat who got it like that, but he gon' take a day or two to get that ready for us."

"Nah, fuck it," Preeme changed his mind. "Let's play no games with getting Velvet back. We can't stall and fail getting her home."

"True," Smooth agreed.

Coming down from Designer-D hit fast. Withdrawals kicked in, and my body and mind started fiending for another hit. I needed it. The plate of Designer-D sat right there on the kitchen counter, calling me. I pushed up off the couch. All eyes followed me. I went straight to the counter and grabbed the rolled bill off the plate. I rushed to hit a rail before anyone could stop me. I didn't even bother using the card to set a line. I just snorted at the big pile, desperate. Almost everything went up my nose. My nostrils burned and my eyes watered. Then my face went numb. The brain rush slammed me. I might've been pushing myself toward a heart attack.

"What the fuck is wrong with you?!" Sierra snapped from the couch. "Could you ever be serious and not always have your mind on drugs?!"

Preeme just shook his head, unimpressed. He didn't care enough to stop me from hitting more rails. I figured it was because his gun was on the counter by me, so he didn't want to step to me like that while my mind was gone. Or maybe he'd given up on me. Maybe he already decided I was a loser. But I couldn't be bothered with what he thought of me at that moment. I held out the rolled bill for Smooth, inviting him to get up and join me. He looked away, showing zero interest. It could've been the dope in my system making me overthink, but his vibe wasn't sitting right with me.

A thought hit me out of nowhere. The last thing I'd heard Marvel say before the call ended. He mentioned something about *Smooth*. My heart started racing. Either the heart attack was coming, or my mind was running too hot. Preeme, Smooth, and Sierra paid me no mind. They kept talking while I stood there investigating ugly possibilities in my own head.

"I'ma link Crystal to leave work right now and draw for twenty-five thousand to bring here," Preeme said.

"And I'll call Alize or Star to bring my bread too," Smooth added.

Preeme looked at me by the counter. "Get the fifty thousand out your safe. We need to get shit ready from now."

I nodded, but I didn't move. I wasn't sure I trusted what was happening. The dimension I was in felt unstable, but it also felt realer than reality. I couldn't explain it. Something in me kept whispering that Smooth might be involved in this whole mess. Not my friend at all. A snake in disguise, waiting on my downfall. He'd been stacking extra money through side investments for years, all while encouraging me to party and splurge with him. He might've mentioned stocks before, but I never believed he was really doing it or winning at it. A true friend would've pushed me harder to invest with him, not just drag me into partying and nonsense. I could've straightened out at some point. I could've got on my A-game, if Smooth hadn't kept me thinking we were both living lavish off pimp money alone. I was blinded by the fake friendship.

Tonight felt like another example of his devious ways. He encouraged getting high with me, at the exact time I should've stayed sober. He knew once we started on Designer-D, it'd be hard to stop for the night. Now I was in an addictive state, chasing the high like a cokehead, while he had the willpower to cool off and sober up. Maybe he got me going on the rails just to throw me off my game. The more I ran it back in my head, the clearer it got. Smooth wasn't really my friend. He might've played a role in Velvet's kidnapping. My heart pounded because the truth felt too loud to ignore. I didn't know how to address what I thought I knew. Anxiety climbed up my throat. I stayed by the counter, locked in a state, watching Sierra, Preeme, and the snake among us.

Sierra got up off the couch and cut her eye at me as she headed to the bedroom. "I'll get the money out of the safe because this guy is clearly out of his fucking mind."

"Okay, do that," Preeme told her. "Also get ready, cause me and you will be going for the meet-up."

"I'm, I'm c-coming too," I managed to say.

"Nah. You're high, bruh," Preeme dismissed me.

Smooth added, "Yeah, pimpin'. Me and you should stay back."

I didn't have it in me to argue with Preeme, but I was fed up with Smooth. A piece of rationality told me to keep my thoughts to myself. At least for now. I could address it when I was sober, when my mind was focused, when I had the energy to fight if it got physical. But it still bothered me too much to swallow. I couldn't keep playing oblivious. I had to confront him.

"So, Smooth." I found enough courage to speak. "Where did th-th-th-they t-take Velvet?"

"Huh?" Smooth played confused like it was easy.

I didn't bite. I pressed him. "This was your p-plan with Marvel all along, right? To t-t-take my b-b-b-bitch and get b-bread out of me. You think I don't know?"

"C'mon, son, you playing, right? What the hell are you saying right now?"

Preeme stared at me, puzzled. Sierra came out of the bedroom with the large pile of money in her hands. She looked just as thrown as he did. Even if they thought I was a loser, broke, and high on Designer-D, I wasn't about to be played a fool by the snake in the room.

CHAPTER TWENTY-NINE

Sierra placed the fifty thousand on the dining counter. She took Gelato by the hand and held his gaze. He looked out of it, stuck in some kind of trance. It scared her, but she needed to understand.

Sierra asked him, "Angelo, what exactly are you saying?"

Gelato stared at her and said, "Smooth. He's very *smooth*, man."

"How? Why are you saying this?"

"A-a-ask him. He knows. He t-took Velvet." Gelato's eyes shifted across the room to Smooth on the sofa.

"What the fuck you talking 'bout, playa?" Smooth shot back. "Gelato, man, you tripping!"

Sierra and Preeme exchanged a look, then turned to Smooth. He looked just as lost as they were. "My word on my little boy, I ain't got shit to do with Velvet. Word on my son!"

Preeme pressed him, "Then why's Gelato saying all that? Be real, homie."

"C'mon. The playa just ripped a bunch of Designer-D to his face. He's losing his damn mind. The shit he's saying don't even make sense."

Gelato tried to speak, words breaking apart. "You w-want my money. Everybody w-wants my muh-money. I d-don't give a fuck. I'm n-not stupid. F-fuck all y'all!"

"Calm down, Angelo." Sierra rubbed his bare chest. He wasn't all there, she could see it. She asked again, "Why do you think Smooth took Velvet?"

"Because he w-wants my muh-money. He's a s-snake. Don't t-trust him. I kn-know everything." Gelato's voice fell off into a low mumble. Sierra looked to Preeme for something, anything, but he had nothing to give her. Gelato was getting worse, and the accusation wasn't something they could ignore. Both of them turned back to Smooth. He'd pushed up to his feet now.

Smooth couldn't sit under that kind of heat, especially from the two sober ones. He felt pinned, like they were weighing him with their eyes. Coming down off the coke didn't help either, his nerves turning loud in his chest. The accusation made no sense, and it still hit him wrong. Gelato was his childhood friend. For Gelato to say that, even high, had Smooth in his feelings. He hadn't done anything, and he couldn't find a clean reason for why Gelato's mind had gone there.

He glared across the room at Gelato by the dining counter. "You lost your fucking mind, son. I don't give a fuck how high you is, you shouldn't play me like that, Gelato. I was out in Calgary handling my bitches and you know this. I caught the first flight back down here when you called me about this problem." Smooth had to let it out. "I came to help you because you my brother. If I knew you was gon' turn up and lose your mind like this, I wouldn't have turned up with you, son."

"You f-fuck with Marvel!" Gelato shot back.

"Where the fuck do I know that sucka from? I met him that day with you!"

"S-so-so why he mention your name?" Gelato's eyes shifted to Preeme. "Didn't Marvel say he w-w-wants it all to go to Smooth?"

Preeme had to run it back in his head before answering. "Nah. He said he wants the meeting to go smooth. That was the only time smooth was mentioned. You hearing wrong, big homie."

Gelato kept going. "That's not what Marvel m-meant. I kn-know what h-he's talking about."

Gelato's attention snapped to the Designer-D plate and he started to reach for it, but Sierra grabbed his hand and led him away from the counter. She brought him back to the couch. "No more of that. It's got you thinking craziness." She sat next to him.

Gelato kept his fierce stare on Smooth, who'd dropped back onto the sofa. He didn't move, just glared, coke-weak and stuck on the thought. "No. He w-wants my m-muh-money."

"Listen, Gelato, man, you're fucking crazy." Smooth retorted. "Fuck I want your money for? Fuck it, I'll even pay the full hundred thousand for you, playa." He shook his head, fed up. "Some real whack shit for you to be tripping like this."

Preeme cut in, "You don't need to do all that to prove yourself, Smooth. It's just the dope that got him all fucked up and talking like that."

Sierra watched as Gelato laid his head back on the couch's headrest and stared up at the ceiling. He mumbled to himself and sweated hard. Seeing him like this had her worried for his well-being, and ashamed to see her man weak when he should've been showing strength. She put her hand on his sweaty bare chest to feel his heart pounding fast.

"Preeme!" Sierra panicked a little. "I think he did too much Designer. His heart's racing."

"Get him some water," Preeme said, touching Gelato's forehead to check his temperature.

She hurried to the kitchen and came back with a glass of water, trying to help him drink it, but he couldn't get it down and gagged instead.

"Oh my God! Is he going to be okay? Fuck..." Sierra teared up. "Why is all this happening?"

As Sierra and Preeme focused on getting Gelato to drink, Smooth made a phone call. They couldn't tell who he was on the line with, but the one-sided talk sounded like he was directing someone to grab 100K from one of his safes.

"Homie, what you doing?" Preeme asked Smooth.

Smooth ended the call before answering. "Told Alize to bring the bread."

"You were only supposed to chip in twenty-five."

"Nah, nah. Y'all acting like I ain't got bread and think I'm snaking pimpin' Gelato for his, so I'ma cover Vanessa's ransom to prove I ain't got none to do with her 'napping. I'ma do a solid and take the hundred K loss for Gelato."

"Be easy, homie," Preeme replied. "We know you ain't got none to do with this. It's obviously the Designer that got big homie tripping."

"Nah, nah. I seen how y'all were checking me out. No doubt, y'all believed him for a second. Can't tell me nothing."

"Smooth, relax." Sierra already had enough on her hands. She sobbed, "Please, just stop...nobody said we believed anything he was saying...It was just very confusing...I'm sorry if you felt a way."

Smooth did feel disrespected that the accusations even came up, but it'd been unfair to dump that on Sierra while she was already in tears. Gelato caused the whole confusion, a mess and maybe sliding into an overdose. With the pressure building, Smooth felt the itch to get back on a wave that would numb his emotions. He got up and went to the dining counter for the plate. Preeme moved fast, snatched it from his hand, dumped it in the sink, and ran tap water over it until the cocaine washed away. "No more of that shit. Gelato already all fucked up and we not tryna have to deal with you, too." Preeme picked up his gun from the counter and tucked it at his waist. It wasn't safe leaving it out in the open with Smooth in his emotions and Gelato out of his mind.

Smooth couldn't believe what Preeme had just done. He went back to the sofa, cursing, "You stupid for that, son. Waste of quality stuff. Fuck, man."

Preeme ignored the cussing, but told him, "It's good you sobering up now, 'cause I need you to help me count this paper real quick." He nodded toward the 50K on the counter.

"I, I believe the amount is correct," Sierra sobbed, still trying to get Gelato to drink water. "There's a money counter in the closet."

Smooth stayed salty over the coke, but he felt for Sierra. Vanessa being kidnapped, Gelato spiraling, the shock of how tight the money was, then having to give it up for ransom. That was a lot for a woman in one night. Not something a solid woman like Sierra deserved after years of ambition and loyalty to the game.

"Skye," Smooth said to her, "don't stress too much, Mama. I'ma cover the hundred K Okay?" He added, "Gelato's my brother, and his bread looking tight so I'll help him out. I'm doing it for both of y'all 'cause we family."

"Are you sure?" Sierra asked, relief creeping in at the thought of saving what little they had.

"Yeah, ma', I got you."

"Smooth, that's a lot of money to be throwing at us."

"I got a lot of that. And it ain't none to help my brother." Smooth made a face. "Even though he was just tryna play me foul, he still my brother."

Sierra thanked Smooth, then turned back to Gelato, staring at the ceiling with empty eyes like he wasn't even there. Shame burned in her chest, especially knowing his friends lived lavish too and still kept real savings. Gelato clearly didn't know how to manage the money he made over the years, and it was all spilling out during a crisis, one of their girls snatched for ransom. On top of that, he was falling apart, close to overdosing and accusing his friend of nonsense, all because he couldn't control himself with drugs. Even with all of it, she loved Gelato. His well-being came first right now.

"I'm gonna sit him in warm water to help sweat the Designer-D out of him," Sierra said to Preeme and Smooth. "You guys please have everything ready when Marvel calls to meet up."

"Yeah, Alize on her way here with the bread," Smooth replied

"You really don't gotta do that, bruh. We'll go halves," Preeme said to Smooth. "I'ma have Crystal forward with fifty."

"Nah. I got the bread covered. You just play your part and keep Skye safe at the meet-up."

Preeme nodded. "Say no more, homie."

Sierra grabbed the 50K off the counter and took it back into the room. Then the guys helped her carry Gelato into the washroom and set him in the tub. They went back to the living room while she stayed behind, running warm water to fill it with Gelato sitting in it. Thoughts kept piling up, and as she looked into his vacant eyes, she wondered whether he'd ever change. She wondered whether he'd ever become the man who could build what he kept promising. How much longer he had depended on how much longer Sierra could carry on.

CHAPTER THIRTY

Marvel's call, the one Vanessa listened to while thinking she was hearing Gelato on the other end, happened right there in the basement living area. She caught enough of it to piece together the negotiation. When Marvel hung up, he looked at her and summed it up with a smug shrug. "I guess your pimp cares about you enough to cough up a hundred K. I should've asked for more." Then he went back into the bedroom where Maria was waiting.

Relief settled in, knowing Gelato was willing to pay for her release. It didn't feel extraordinary, though. Vanessa had already earned well over a hundred thousand during her two years under him. Refusing to cover it would've felt like betrayal. Her whole life revolved around Gelato, and the obligations ran both ways. If he wanted her loyalty and her money, then her safety was on him too. Once she got back, she'd be expected to get right back to work, and that same money would end up finding its way back into his hands anyway. She couldn't help weighing what this really was. Gelato cooperating out of love, or Gelato doing what a pimp was supposed to do. His voice never sounded cold when they spoke. The concern came through, real enough to make her believe his heart was in it. At the same time, none of this was random. She'd chosen this life with him, trusted his leadership without question, and this was the kind of consequence that came with that choice. If he felt terrible now, he should. This situation belonged to him as much as it belonged to her, and it forced Vanessa to look hard at the life she'd handed over to him.

Two hours earlier, Marvel told her she'd be released sometime after midnight. She'd passed out on the air mattress, then woke about twenty minutes ago, and by 12:49 a.m. her patience was wearing thin. She glanced at Blaze and Flame, ready to ask about the release, only to see both twins slumped on the couch asleep. Voices drifted from the bedroom, then the sounds of Marvel and Maria having sex, and Vanessa's stomach turned with disgust. At least it meant Marvel was awake and probably hadn't forgotten her. She just had to wait until he was done with Maria. Restless on the airbed in the living area, boredom kept dragging Vanessa's thoughts toward something darker. A violent plan started to take shape. She eyed the kitchen drawers, thinking about a sharp knife, then pictured herself creeping up on the twins and stabbing them fast in the throat while they slept. Quiet. No screaming. No chaos. If she acted swift enough with the knife, there wouldn't even be noise to pull Marvel and Maria out of the bedroom. Then she'd take the gun off the dead twins, and if Marvel and Maria came running out from hearing the commotion anyway, she'd shoot them too. With that kind of power in her hands, Marvel would give up the keys to the lock at the top of the basement stairs, and she'd be free. She even imagined shooting them in the legs first, not just to weaken them, but to make them feel something back for what they'd put her through.

With the plan in mind, Vanessa realized she'd have to know how to use the gun. She'd seen guns in movies, and she once held one of Preeme's when Gelato kept it at his condo. The twins' pistol looked similar. Thinking it through, she figured it probably already had one in the chamber. They were using it to keep her in line, ready to fire the second she tried something stupid. Maybe none of this was even necessary. She was supposed to be released soon anyway. She could've followed through just to spare Gelato the hundred grand, but if she succeeded she'd be running straight into a murder charge. A case for her life wasn't worth it. Not for his money. For two years, she'd done everything in his favor and still ended up here. Getting herself into something worse for him would be foolish. Life was real. Vanessa knew she had to start thinking for herself, and herself only.

The sex in the bedroom kept going, and the louder moans started to annoy Vanessa. She also needed to use the washroom. If she got up and went without the twins noticing, they might wake up and think she was up to something. That was a problem she didn't need. It was only a matter of time before she'd be released, so it was best to keep cooperating with their captivity rules.

"Hey..." Vanessa tried to wake the twins on the couch, but they didn't budge, so she called out louder, "Hey!"

Blaze woke up startled. His flickering eyes landed on Vanessa, staring at him. He collected himself and drew the gun off his waist, acting like he'd been on point the whole time. The movement stirred Flame awake too. "What's going on?"

"I need to use the washroom," Vanessa explained. "Didn't want to go without asking."

"Oh." Blaze looked thrown off. "Yeah, go."

Vanessa got off the bed and went to the washroom by the bedroom. It had no door for privacy, and she knew she was being watched. At least the toilet wasn't in plain view from the couch where the twins sat, so they couldn't see her using it. Through the thin wall, she could hear Marvel's grunting and the slap of skin, clear as day. It felt like there was no separation at all. She hurried to finish, washed her hands, and stepped back out into the living area, where the air felt awkward as the moans carried through and she knew the twins heard it too.Vanessa sat back on the bed, kept her eyes off them, and tried to busy herself with the chipped nail she'd damaged in the hotel fight. It didn't help. The sounds kept going. Then she heard the twins snickering. She glanced up and caught them staring at her, smiling.

"Wh-when am I leaving?" Vanessa forced out, needing to break the moment before they kept looking at her like that.

"I don't know," Blaze said, nodding toward the bedroom. "He'll let us know when he's done doing his thang in there."

Flame smirked at Vanessa. "Do you know what they're doing in there?"

Vanessa felt it was a stupid question, one meant to make it uncomfortable. She answered like it was nothing. "They're having sex."

"You like to fuck, eh," Flame said, like he'd already decided what she was.

Vanessa's heart dropped. She didn't want to entertain his game. Flame had already tried that favour-for-favour angle, and now he was back circling it again, pushing sex talk like it was casual. She shut it down fast. "No, I don't."

Blaze followed right behind him. "But you's a working-ting. You fuck and suck dick all day."

Anxiety crept up, not because of the topic, but because of what sat behind their questions. Vanessa withdrew into herself and went back to examining her chipped nail. The twins kept staring at her like thirsty dogs while the moaning in the bedroom carried on.

When it was clear she wasn't giving them anything else, they leaned in and whispered to each other. Flame stood, and Vanessa's heart started pounding, but he didn't come toward her. He walked past and knocked on the bedroom door. The moaning stopped.

"What's gwanning?" Marvel called from behind it.

"How long you gon' be?" Flame asked through the door. "The bitch waiting to go."

"She could fucking wait. I'm busy."

"Yeah, I know." Flame chuckled, then asked, "So what, we can't get busy too?"

Marvel's voice came sharp and irritated from behind the door. "Are you dumb? How you asking me to grease my girl?"

"Nah, you not hearing me." Flame clarified. "I'm talking about the bitch out here. We can't sort that out?"

"Oh, fo'sho. Y'all do your thuggy." Marvel gave them the green light.

"Don't say a word." Flame gave the door two taps to end the talk. He turned back to his brother with a smile that made Vanessa cringe, and the moaning in the bedroom started up again.

Flame went back to the couch where his brother stood waiting and passed the gun over to him, then took off his hoodie and began unbuckling his pants. The sight pressed the air out of her lungs. Tears gathered before she could hide them as she whispered a shaky plea, begging the moment to rewind, begging something to shift in the room.

"Please." Vanessa teared up, "Please, don't."

Blaze was already down to his underwear when Flame handed the gun back to him and started stripping too. Each movement felt slow and deliberate, like they expected her to watch every second of it. Her stomach tightened. Her hands trembled in a way she could not control.

"Please…oh, my God, please. I don't want to do this," she cried. The words came from somewhere deep and frightened, somewhere she had never let anyone access before. She may have been a sex worker and slept with many men throughout her two years in the business, but even the worst encounters came with consent and a price. Nothing in her life had prepared her for a moment where none of that meant anything. The room felt smaller than it had minutes earlier, the air thick with a threat she could not negotiate or redirect.

Growing up in a stable home with a proper family upbringing, Vanessa had never imagined standing in a space where her safety no longer belonged to her. That was why she took kickboxing seriously, training to protect herself as a woman in a world crowded with predators. Even when she entered the sex trade for Gelato, she refused to role-play rape scenarios for clients. Money never outweighed her need for control. She wanted nothing to do with men who got excited by a woman's fear. Yet this fear was different. It crawled under her skin, settling in her chest like a weight she could not lift. Her mind raced through every choice that led her to this room, to these brothers. Fighting them might earn her a broken bone, or worse, a bullet. Doing nothing felt just as dangerous. She did not know what these guys were capable of. For all she knew, Marvel trusted them for reasons she did not want to understand.

A cold clarity crept through her. She was trapped in a moment where every thought hurt, every memory stung, and every instinct screamed at her with no escape in sight. Her tears fell harder, not from weakness but from the crushing realization that nothing about this life had prepared her for the one thing she feared most.

The twins were both standing in their underwear now, Blaze holding the gun as he ordered Vanessa, "Get naked."

Vanessa begged through tears, "Please...don't do this—"

"Shut up and get naked," Flame snapped, stepping toward the airbed.

Panic sent Vanessa's thoughts spiraling. "I-I'm HIV positive," she lied.

"What?!" Flame backed off and turned to his brother.

Blaze chuckled. "Nah, dawg. You can't tell me you believe this bitch."

"What you mean? She saying she got AIDS."

"She just trying to kowall us so we don't fuck her," Blaze said. "Trust me, she bullshitting. Just strap up if you scared."

Flame went to the washroom and came back with condoms for himself and Blaze. They stripped off their underwear, hard and ready, and Flame moved toward Vanessa again, Blaze following this time and leaving the gun on the couch. Tears streamed down her face as the twins closed in on the bed. She lashed out with wild kicks, trying to keep them away, but it only made things worse. Blaze wrestled for control of her legs, giving Flame an opening to punch her in the head, straight into the dried gash on her forehead, splitting it open again. Pain exploded through her skull. One of them dragged her shirt up over her head while the other tore away her tights and underwear. She cried and begged, knowing it did not matter. They were stronger, and fighting harder would only bring more pain. Vanessa closed her eyes and promised God she would change her life if He helped her get through this.

They held her legs apart, and one tried to enter her. Under the circumstances, her body resisted smooth penetration. The condom's lubricant did little, and he struggled to force himself in. The dry friction made Vanessa scream. It was unpleasant for him too, so he pulled out and spit on the condom before sliding back in.

He started stroking inside her.

Meanwhile, the other twin knelt by her head on the airbed, his dick close to her face.

"Open your mouth and suck it, or I'll keep punching you in the face. And if you bite it, I'll fucking smoke you. Word to my dead guys."

GHAD

CHAPTER THIRTY-ONE

Wednesday, July 4 – 3:14 a.m.

Back at the condo, the hot tub sitting helped Gelato sweat out the excessive amount of cocaine that had him in a delusional state. Preeme and Smooth got him into bed after, and he stayed passed out. Around 1 a.m., Alize and Star showed up with the hundred thousand Smooth had called for. A little after 2 a.m., Marvel called and set the meet for 3:30 that morning. Preeme had Crystal come to the condo as well, so she could go with Star to pick up Vanessa's BMW from the Four Points hotel parking lot in London, Ontario. Alize stayed back at the condo so at least one fully sober person was there to help Smooth watch Gelato. Gelato was out cold through all of it, with no idea the meeting was even happening, and Sierra left glad he'd be fine. She was still unimpressed with him after everything that had unfolded.

Sierra drove her Mercedes coupe on the QEW with Preeme following behind in his Acura TSX. They were headed to the location Marvel gave her, with strict instructions that Sierra meet him alone. Her nerves stayed high the whole drive, not knowing what to expect or how the exchange would go. Preeme being close was the only thing that steadied her. The plan was simple. Sierra would arrive first in a Hamilton hotel parking lot, then call Vanessa's phone and wait for Marvel to answer. Marvel made it clear he'd be pulling up with reinforcement, ready to turn the scene ugly if Sierra tried anything. She promised she'd come alone, carrying nothing but the rest of Maria's belongings and the hundred thousand in cash on Gelato's behalf. All she expected back was Vanessa.

The Admiral Inn was right off the QEW on Dundurn Street in Hamilton. Preeme phoned Sierra and walked her through the positioning. She had to slow down and hang back on the street while he went ahead and pulled into the medium-sized parking lot behind the hotel. There were only a few other cars, and Preeme studied each one to make sure they were empty. He parked in a corner spot that gave him a view of every angle, shut the Acura off, then climbed into the tinted backseat so he wouldn't be noticed. His gun sat on his lap while he kept watch over the lot. Tonight had to go according to plan because any messy activity could have that Acura traced back to him. A rental or a stolen car would've made the role easier, but there wasn't time to set it up. Either way, he was ready.

On the call, Sierra pulled in next and parked a few spots across from Preeme's tinted Acura. Her hand shook as she dialed Vanessa's number.

Marvel answered. "You there?"

"Yeah. I'm here."

"Okay, I'ma pull up just now. What car you in?"

"A white Benz."

"Mmhmm. I'll be there just now. Get out and stand by your car. Be ready with the money and Maria's stuff."

"Oh, okay. I'll do that now."

The call ended and Sierra followed instructions. She wore a sweatsuit even though the night was warm.

Silence and darkness sat heavy in the lot, with only a few light posts throwing any real clarity. Sierra slung the Adidas string bag over her shoulder, two fifty-thousand bundles inside, then wrestled Maria's two heavy suitcases out of the trunk. She dragged them onto their wheels and waited by the driver's side door, already on edge for Marvel's arrival. She kept glancing at the rear of Preeme's Acura, hoping for a sign he was still there. The tinted windows gave her nothing back. Feeling alone, she held her stare a second too long. Then a phone screen flashed once behind the dark tint, quick and faint, and relief loosened her chest. Maybe it was Preeme telling her to stop watching his car. Either way, it was enough to make her face forward again.

An old Mercedes Benz rolled into the hotel parking lot from around the side of the building. It crept toward her slow, and Sierra knew it had to be Marvel. The Benz stopped beside her coupe, leaving space between them where she stood. She could make out the driver, a man with dreads, but the back windows were too dark to see who else was inside. The front passenger window rolled down, and Marvel motioned her closer. Sierra hesitated, unsure what her next move was supposed to be, feeling completely lost.

"Come here!" Marvel called out.

With the string bag of money hanging off her shoulder, Sierra grabbed the suitcases by their handles and dragged them towards the car. She kept checking over her shoulder on the short walk, nerves tight, half-expecting goons to jump out and snatch her too.

She stopped at the open passenger window, close enough to be heard, then asked, "Where is she? Where is Velvet?"

Marvel smiled. The tinted back window slid down, and Sierra caught a glimpse of Vanessa in the backseat, wedged between two men who looked young and identical. The blindfold was what hit hardest. Vanessa didn't even know the window was down or that Sierra stood there looking at her. For a second, it felt unreal. Then the back window rolled up again and the trunk popped open.

"Throw the bags in there," Marvel said. "All of Maria's shit is in the bags, right?"

"Yeah," Sierra replied. "Everything."

Marvel didn't move to help, so Sierra went to the trunk and heaved the heavy suitcases into it. Once they were in, she shut it and hurried back to the passenger side. "Can you let her out now?"

"The money," Marvel said.

"It's right here." Sierra lifted the string bag in her hand.

Marvel's smile widened. He patted the empty passenger seat. "Throw it in here."

"Okay, but..." Sierra didn't trust that smile. "Let her out first, then I'll throw it in. I promise I will."

"Nah. Throw the money in first."

"But how do I know you won't just drive off?"

"Bitch, give me the fucking money or I'ma come out the car, fuck you up, take it, and drive off," Marvel snapped.

Fear shot through Sierra. She looked back toward the Acura, hoping Preeme had heard that from wherever he was. Her mind stalled. She didn't know what to do next, and she needed someone to tell her which way to move.

Vanessa's voice came from the backseat. "Skye, just give him the money!"

Sierra stepped closer to the passenger window so she could see Vanessa between the two men. Vanessa was still blindfolded, but her head was turned toward Sierra's voice.

"Okay, babe," Sierra said, then tossed the string bag through the window. It landed on the passenger seat.

Marvel looked inside and saw the two thick bundles. His smile widened. "This is a hundred-k, right?"

"Yes. I swear," Sierra said, praying he wouldn't make her stand there while he counted it by hand.

Marvel held that grin a beat longer, then stomped on the gas.

Sierra's heart dropped as the old Benz surged away. Tears rushed up so fast she barely felt herself sink to her knees on the concrete. She didn't even register that the Benz had stopped near the edge of the lot. One of the twins hopped out of the backseat and yanked Vanessa free. The blindfold came off. Vanessa's phone and purse were tossed onto the ground beside her. The twin climbed back in and the car ripped out of the lot. Vanessa snatched up her belongings and sprinted toward Sierra, who was still on her knees crying like the deal had just gone wrong.

When the old Benz took off on Sierra, Preeme scrambled from the backseat into the driver's seat and was ready to start his Acura. He'd just turned the engine when he saw them stop right before the exit to release Vanessa. The Benz peeled out of the lot, and Preeme drove toward Sierra, who'd dropped to her knees crying. He jumped out to help her up.

"Skye, stop crying," Preeme said, steadying her. "Velvet's good."

Sierra blinked through her tears and saw Vanessa running towards her with open arms. She let go of Preeme and rushed into Vanessa's embrace. They held each other and cried, Sierra apologizing over and over, Vanessa breaking down even harder.

Sierra cupped Vanessa's face and checked the dried gash on her forehead. Worry tightened her voice. "Are you okay? Should we take you to the hospital?"

Vanessa pulled back and shook her head. She was still sobbing, so Sierra kissed her on the lips and drew her close again.

"Listen, girls, we gotta move," Preeme said, cutting the moment short. "We can't be out here like this. It's sketchy."

"Okay, let's go," Sierra said. She wiped her tears and noticed Vanessa only had her purse. "Where's the rest of your stuff?"

"I left it at the house they kept me at," Vanessa said. "It's just a bag of clothes and work stuff. My IDs and everything I need is in my purse."

Sierra started toward her Mercedes with Vanessa, hand in hand, but Preeme stopped them. "You guys take my car. I'll drive yours."

Sierra hesitated, not fully understanding the switch at first. Then it clicked. Marvel knew her car now, and Preeme wasn't about to let them ride straight back in it if there was any chance Marvel was still nearby. Preeme stayed on point even after the exchange, and Sierra respected it.

Vanessa and Sierra got into Preeme's Acura and drove out of the lot, with Preeme following behind in Sierra's Benz. Once they exited, Preeme went the other way while Sierra drove toward the closest on-ramp to the QEW. After the way he moved tonight, Sierra didn't question it. Whatever he was doing or wherever he was going, he'd proven he had the kind of judgment a woman shouldn't doubt. Sierra could see why Crystal stayed happy with him despite all the crazy stories tied to his name. In the game, nothing beat having a man who knew how to save, work what was brought to him, and turn it into more. A strong mind and steady demeanour made a woman comfortable following his lead. Preeme was a clear example of that kind of man.

Vanessa quietly went through her phone as they drove along the highway. Sierra had a lot of questions, but she couldn't bring herself to ask them. She could only imagine what happened during those hours of captivity, and even that felt impossible. The wound on Vanessa's head said there'd been violence. After the way Marvel moved in that parking lot, Sierra could tell what kind of scumbag he was, which made her wonder if they'd tortured Vanessa or done worse. A darker possibility tried to creep in and Sierra pushed it back down hard. Vanessa stayed withdrawn, scrolling without focus. Sierra could feel the heartache sitting on her, heavy and quiet. Digging into what she'd endured felt like it would only rip her open again, so Sierra reached for something safer.

"Daddy's been really stressed about losing you. He ended up doing so much Designer that he had a terrible breakdown."

"Oh," Vanessa said, deadpan, eyes glued to her phone. "Is he okay?"

"Yeah. He was passed out cold when I left."

Vanessa didn't say anything after that. Sierra had a feeling resentment might be in the mix, so she tried another angle. "We gave Star and Crystal the spare key and they drove out to London to get your car."

"Okay," Vanessa said. "I guess I'll thank them."

Silence settled again. Sierra kept her eyes on the road and asked it anyway, soft. "You gonna be okay?"

Vanessa finally looked up. "Yeah, I guess." Then she went back to her phone.

"Want to hang with me tonight?" Sierra offered. "Chocolate and Vanilla would help cheer you up."

"Babes, just drop me off at home…I'm not upset with you, or anyone…I just want to be alone."

Her voice cracked on the last part. Tears filled her eyes again, and Sierra started tearing up too, because she could feel how deep it went. Whatever Vanessa had lived through left more than a gash on her forehead. Some wounds didn't show. Sierra didn't have to ask to know what her mind kept circling.

Vanessa turned toward the door and cried into the quiet. Sierra gripped the wheel, blinking through her own tears, and let the road carry them forward. The ride stayed silent except for the sound of both women sobbing.

CHAPTER THIRTY-TWO

◆

Sunday, July 8 – 9:51 p.m.

Sometimes I'd replay the night Vanessa declared she was done with my stable. After Marvel released her, Sierra dropped her at her condo and I couldn't even see her. That Designer-D trip had me fucked up, then I woke up ashamed of everything that happened. I remembered it, but I couldn't understand how I'd slipped into a delusional state that felt so real. The next day, Sierra and I Googled my symptoms and found the answer. I'd gone into drug-induced psychosis, a condition that messes with how your brain processes information. It can make you lose touch with reality and believe things that aren't real.

That next morning, Sierra wasn't impressed with me at all. Even though I woke up with her beside me and we still had breakfast together, her energy was different. Distant. For the first time, she had me on edge. I'd lost ground in her eyes, lost some of the respect she'd always had for me as the alpha. It wasn't just the breakdown from the night before, it was what came out with it. After all my years in the game, I didn't even have a hundred thousand saved. My partners did. I'd bought my condo with a twenty percent down payment a few years back and built equity through steady mortgage payments, but that meant nothing when Smooth and the others owned property too and still had over a hundred thousand put away. Smooth didn't even hesitate when the ransom came up, like it was light work. He probably had a million stacked. The last thing Sierra said before leaving that morning stayed with me. "I don't know how much longer I can do this, Angelo. You really need to think about what you're doing with the money we make."

She stayed busy the next few days and I didn't see her again after that breakfast. I needed time with her, needed to pull us back into sync, but every attempt I made got shut down. She wanted rest. The spa. The gym. All valid, but all ways to keep distance. I even tried joining her at the gym, thinking it might help me get back into that routine too, but she wasn't having it. She wanted her space. When she finally called me yesterday, she could hear the worry in my voice and told me she wasn't planning on leaving. She just wasn't ready to see me yet. I agreed to give her the rest of the week and let things breathe. The next time she was ready to sit down with me, I'd come correct. A real savings plan. No excuses. Something I'd actually stick to for our future.

I met up with Smooth by the lake the next day, still coming down from that crazy night. Being the kind of friends we were, we laughed it off, joking about how reckless I'd been. I thanked him sincerely for the large sum of cash he'd put up for me, then he got serious and had a heart-to-heart with me about my long-standing problems managing and investing money. He even suggested that I bring him money weekly so he could save and invest it on my behalf. I shut that idea down, but I promised him I'd step my game up and join him in some real investment plays soon. Moving forward, we agreed to chill on the clubbing, partying, and our usual nonsense. It wouldn't be a good look for me, not while Sierra still had me on my toes.

Preeme later explained what he'd done after Sierra met with Marvel in Hamilton that night. Once they were finished, Preeme took her car and drove around the Steel City for a while. The plan was simple. If Marvel spotted Sierra's car and assumed the girls were inside, he might tail it. Preeme would then lead him somewhere quiet and handle it with gunfire. After that, he'd crash the car, burn it, and have Sierra report it stolen the next morning. But that night, Marvel's old Benz never showed up again, and the cat-and-mouse game never played out.

Preeme and I met at his place two days ago to talk about things that couldn't be said over the phone. He wanted every bit of info I had on Maria and Marvel because, to him, a follow-up was necessary. I was pissed and wanted my get-back, but Preeme was hungrier for it than I ever was. Truth is, I wasn't built for the kind of action he was ready to take, and he felt that in me. Loyalty and family is his street religion, so he decided he'd move without me. That had me uneasy because if shit hit the fan, I could still get dragged into a mess of murder charges. I gave him whatever I knew, even though it wasn't much that could actually lead us to Maria or Marvel. On top of that, Preeme put up his own money to his people in the streets, trying to flush Marvel out or get a name and a location. There was a 10K reward for whoever found Marvel and could line it up for Preeme to pop up by surprise. I respected him for taking it into his own hands, riding for what my baby Velvet had to go through.

But the reality was Vanessa wasn't my baby anymore—Velvet. Vanessa Bartelli went back to her square life and her family home in Oakville. She refused to see me and needed time to herself. Sierra was the one who told me Vanessa went through real trauma during that captivity. She mentioned the deep gash on Vanessa's head and emphasized how broken she was on that drive back from Hamilton. When they got to Vanessa's condo, Sierra finally asked it straight, if she'd been violated. Vanessa nodded and broke down all over again. She got out the car crying her eyes out, and Sierra cried too, watching Vanessa's torn soul disappear into the lobby. That's how the truth unfolded.

After a full day of Vanessa refusing to see me and dodging my calls, only answering a few messages, I showed up at her condo and found it empty. Most of her personal shit was gone. Panic hit me fast, so I texted her, asking where she was, worried something happened to her again. That's when she broke it to me through text. A long paragraph. She told me she was emotionally torn, that she'd made the hardest decision of her life, leaving me because she didn't have the strength to keep going after what she'd been through. She said she loved me, said she wished she could still be my girl, just not in the game anymore. But she knew that wasn't real in my world, so she had to let me go. She promised she'd keep a piece of me forever, said she was keeping her Icy pendant and would keep wearing it. Her love for me would never die. She'd always be Velvet Icy at heart.

I refused to accept it and pulled up to her family home, but I didn't even make it past the front door. Her father spoke through the intercom and told me he'd call the police if I didn't get off his property. Parked in my Range Rover in that huge driveway, I kept begging Vanessa through texts, needing her to come out and see me. She said it was best we didn't see each other again, because it would hurt her too much. All she'd do is cry, and she wouldn't have anything to say. I told her I wasn't leaving unless she came out, at least to say goodbye properly. And she warned me her father was dead serious about calling the cops in five minutes.

Vanessa told me she never informed her family about the kidnapping, but with the scar on her head, the depressed energy, and getting caught crying in her room, they already knew something terrible had happened. Especially with her coming back home after two years. She could be a privileged white girl and still refuse to explain herself to her parents, but it'd be a whole different ball game if police got called over me sitting in their driveway. Cops would press her to tell everything, and her parents would likely bring up what they knew about her stripping for me. Even if Vanessa didn't crack under pressure, they'd take it into their own hands with an investigation that could land me in legal trouble for pimping. Bottom line, I needed to get the hell out of there.

Some days later, Vanessa changed her number and blocked me, Sierra, Diamond, and everybody connected to us on social media. I had to accept that she was gone, so the other day I ended the lease on her condo and didn't even bother hauling out the expensive furniture she left behind. The landlord could deal with that, while I dealt with the heartache. The only thing I took was the empty safe. It was officially game over with Velvet.

I moved through my days in a haze after losing Vanessa. She wasn't the first, and she probably wouldn't be the last bitch to leave me, but her story was the saddest loss I'd ever take. I understood her pain and her reasons. Either way, I had to move forward like a real pimp and tighten my game. I was still Gelato Icy, with pimping going on.

I had also stopped by Diamond's place to update her on everything. She was crushed hearing what Vanessa went through, and she couldn't believe her bestie wasn't with our family anymore, but she took it better than I expected. When it came to the 100K ransom, I left out Smooth covering it. I couldn't risk Diamond seeing me as anything less than the reliable pimp she trusted to pay. That money situation stayed locked away while I worked on getting my shit together. I did give her a light version of my episode, just enough for her to understand why I couldn't get into Designer-D with her that night. Diamond kept working, busy with Eric almost every day and night, and she stayed looking ahead to her birthday.

Today was Diamond's birthday. With Vanessa gone, Sierra busier with work, and me watching my spending to get my money right, I had to cancel the boat party plans. Lucky for me, Diamond wasn't an entitled bitch, and she took the cancellation fine. I couldn't take too much from her birthday, so I still let her blow 20K on shopping—an Icy birthday tradition. Diamond had made good money in the days leading up to it, and Eric gave her a chunk of cash as a gift, so nothing came out my savings. After the shopping spree we had dinner at Casa Loma, then went back to her place to end the night.

We lay naked on the bed after a second round of sweaty sex. Sitting up against the headboard, I reached for the plate of Designer-D on the nightstand. It'd been almost a week since I last turned up, and tripped out, probably the longest I'd ever gone without it. Part of me was skeptical about doing it again after that drug-induced psychosis, but it was Diamond's birthday. She took everything else falling through like a champ, so the least I could do was turn up with her. And so far, it was going smooth. We'd been drinking, doing lines, and fucking the way I was used to, but I kept pacing myself tonight. I ripped a few lines, then Diamond sat up and did the same. The buzz settled nice. A smile came easy with my curvy, platinum-blonde bitch in my bed, but something about her looked off. I hadn't clocked it when I saw her a couple days ago because my mind was on business, not her body. Now, up close, it hit. She'd dropped weight. Not gym weight either. Diamond didn't work out to get smaller, she worked out to keep her belly flat while her curves stayed where they belonged. But this looked like at least 30 pounds gone.

"You lost weight," I said.

Diamond did her line, then passed me the plate, and I set it back on the nightstand. She sniffled, clearing her nose. "Is it a good weight loss or bad, Daddy?"

"Nothing crazy. Just looks like you losing weight."

"You worried I'm gonna lose my ass?" She cuddled into me.

I gripped a chunk of her ass cheek. "It'd be impossible for you to lose *this*."

She giggled and kissed me. Weird thing was she still didn't answer my question or give me any real explanation for the sudden weight loss, but I already knew the obvious. Diamond had been locked in with her trick, Eric, almost every night this past week, so I could picture her turning up on Designer-D with him. That part wasn't a problem. What didn't add up was that I hadn't given Diamond enough Designer-D to cover that many nights, and she didn't lose that much body weight for no reason. Somebody else had to be supplying the dope. More than likely it was the trick bringing his own Designer-D for their nights of extravaganza, leaving her sleeping through the days and barely eating right. I had no idea where he was getting the dope from, and that unknown was the real problem. I preferred my girls doing only what I provided because it was the only way I could be sure they weren't touching laced shit. Lately, fentanyl was a growing problem in the city, with careless dealers mixing it into dope.

Pressing Diamond about it right now would've ruined the good vibes of the night. It was her birthday, and it wasn't the time to turn it into a discipline talk and end up mad at her for breaking program rules. I needed to keep the energy right with the girls still in my stable. I kissed her forehead and asked, "You love me?"

She looked up at me and nodded. "I love you, Daddy. Always."

"So, you're twenty-two now. How're you feeling?"

She chuckled. "Feels like I'm getting old. Soon I'll have grey hairs. And maybe start growing a beard like you."

I laughed. "If you grew a beard, I'd be worried about your gender, not your age."

She laughed too. "I've actually seen some old women with hair on their chin."

"*Da fuck?* Women with beards?"

She laughed harder. "Don't worry, I don't think I'll grow chin hairs. I hardly even grow hair on my legs. I'm smooth like a baby."

"Yes, you are," I agreed. "You're my smooth little baby."

A real smile hit my face, because I appreciated her. Losing Vanessa the way I did forced me to look at myself different. These girls did a lot for me. They trusted me, stayed loyal, and took on risks that come with the game. I couldn't keep moving careless and cruel, not after seeing how fast shit can flip. On top of tightening up my money management, I swore I'd be more patient and understanding with my girls, focus on what I already had, and stop bleeding energy and money chasing new bitches. Sierra had been saying it from the jump. It just took Maria's evil to wake me up the hard way, and I'd rather wake up now than never.

Another kiss landed on Diamond's forehead. She looked up at me smiling, so I moved in and locked lips with her. We sank into the bed, and I got on top between her open legs. My hips slid up and my hard dick pushed right into her. Our mouths stayed locked, kissing like we meant it, while I stroked slow and deep inside her.

We lay there sweaty again. I sat up, reached for the glass of Courvoisier on the nightstand, took a gulp, and passed it to Diamond. The plate of Designer-D came next. A few lines went up my nose while she drank, then we switched hands and set everything back on the nightstand. Most of the earlier buzz was gone from fucking and sweating, but those last lines were thicker than the rest. Deep down, I already knew I'd pay for it. Another round of sex wasn't going to be enough to burn it off.

I settled back with Diamond's head on my chest. She asked me, "You remember that Eric is taking me on vacation next weekend, right?"

"Yeah, I remember," I said. Truth was, I didn't, but it came back the second she said it. "He's down to pay the fifty thousand?"

"Yup. He was asking if I wanted it in cash or wired to my account. He's ready to get that to me before we fly out on Friday."

That was music to my ears. "Get it in cash so we don't have to deal with moving it from you to me."

"Okay, I'll let him know when I see him tomorrow," she said.

Diamond had been seeing this one trick every other night for the past two weeks. If I hadn't put my foot down and claimed her for her birthday, Eric would've had her tonight too. He'd booked her so often she barely had time for her other tricks. Normally I wouldn't even clock that as a problem. Eric was just a trick that paid well. Very well. But sitting there now, it started rubbing me the wrong way.

Maybe I was overthinking. Maybe I needed to get out my head. I distracted myself and asked, "So where exactly are you guys going?"

"Paris." Her smile was proud. "He booked the tickets already. We fly out Friday morning and come back Monday afternoon. And he's taking me shopping before we go, on Wednesday."

"Oh, nice," was all I could say.

"I believe once I tell him to give me the fifty K cash, he'll probably have that for me by Wednesday too."

Hearing fifty thousand again should've had me feeling good, but other thoughts kept stepping on it. Eric was really into my bitch. Doing anything and everything for her. What would stop him from trying to take her from me?

Then again, most tricks my girls dealt with could've bought them out the game if they really wanted to, and it never happened. They were tricks. Nothing more. Still, my mind kept spinning like I was losing my grip on my own confidence. Insecure thoughts. Paranoid thoughts. *Fuck. This better not be another wave of psychosis creeping in.*

I sat up fast, jolting Diamond and knocking her head off my chest. "Are you okay, Daddy?" she asked. My palm pressed to my chest, feeling my heart slam like it was trying to break out. I hadn't even done as much Designer-D as last time, so it made no sense why it was beating like this. Maybe I was doing it to myself. Thinking too deep, feeding the anxiety until it grew teeth. I tried to calm down, tried to pull my mind somewhere lighter before it dragged me back to hell.

"Daddy, are you okay?" Diamond's voice sharpened with worry. She got up and rushed out the bedroom naked, then came back seconds later with a wet rag. Kneeling onto the bed, she dabbed my forehead with the cold cloth. That's when I realized I was sweating hard. Noticing it only made me more aware of my high, and that awareness made everything worse.

"What's wrong, Daddy? Talk to me. How you feeling?"

"I, I," I stuttered, fighting for control. "I'm feeling m-messed up."

"Deep breaths." She kept the rag on my forehead. "Deep breaths, Daddy."

I tried, but the breathing wasn't touching it. My thoughts kept piling up, and right behind them was the fear that Diamond would see me as weak. I reached for the Courvoisier and chugged most of it, but she snatched the glass from my hand and set it back on the nightstand. "That's not gonna help you," she said.

Embarrassment burned through me. This couldn't be happening again. Not in front of Diamond. Still, her energy was different from Sierra's the last time. Diamond looked genuinely scared for me, ready to take care of me, no matter what I looked like right now. The irony of it hit too. I'd dealt with her rough before, the times I caught her crashed on Designer-D.

With thoughts swirling and shame crawling up my throat, I forced the words out. "Babe, I'm s-sorry."

She frowned, confused. "It's okay, Daddy. It's not your fault you're going through a trippy phase." The rag lifted off my forehead and she stared at my face like she was reading it. That stare made me feel even worse. Before I could ask what she was looking for, she said, "I think you're too up. You need something to bring you back down."

I blinked. "Wh-what you mean?"

"Designer-D is an upper, Daddy, so you need something like a perc to bring you down."

Her point finally landed, but I still didn't know what she wanted me to do with that. She hesitated, then, seeing how weak I was, found the nerve to say, "I have some percs. I think you should take one." Her eyes stayed on my face, waiting for a reaction. When my doped stare didn't shift, she added, "It would help you, Daddy. Trust me."

That set off another chain. *Why did she even have Percocet? How often was she popping them without me knowing?* The habit was everywhere in the clubs lately, girls chasing that numb. It was fucked up, but I couldn't snap on her right now. I'd been there myself when my mom died. And getting worked up with my head already spinning would be stupid. That's how I misread Smooth last time.

Then the spiral tried to pull me again. *If I couldn't trust Smooth, could I trust Diamond if she'd been hiding percs?* Shady. *What else could she be hiding? Another man, another pimp, money going somewhere it shouldn't?*

No. I had no proof. Just poison thoughts.

Breathing slow, I fought to anchor myself. My head nodded before my pride could stop it. "Yeah," I said, voice shaking. "G-get the p-percs."

CHAPTER THIRTY-THREE

Dianna tossed the wet rag somewhere on the floor since it wasn't helping Gelato anyway. She went to the bedroom closet for her purse, reaching for the Percocet she believed was still inside. Dianna might've been high on cocaine too, but it felt nothing like what Gelato was going through. It had been a while since she'd had one of her crashing episodes ever since she started messing with opioids, especially heroin. Even though she hadn't done any heroin today, it was like her system had grown used to that heavy downer, dulling the edge of the coke high. Seeing Gelato in this state didn't shake her view of him. If anything, it made her more comfortable tonight. His vulnerability stripped some of that usual dominance and gave her room to float the idea of popping Percs. Dianna's birthday turn-up was starting to look more promising to her liking.

After digging through her work purse, she found no Percocet and could've sworn she had at least three, or even just one left. She excused herself and moved through the condo naked, searching. The washroom, the kitchen, anywhere she might've stashed it. Gelato stayed focused on not slipping into another psychosis episode and didn't even register that Dianna had left the room. He tried to control his thoughts, not realizing that pushing mindfulness in this state was feeding his anxiety and pulling him deeper into the spiral he was fighting.

Dianna returned to the room empty-handed, hands on her hips. She stared at Gelato, still on the bed, looking vulnerable and losing whatever mental battle he was fighting. Dianna wasn't especially concerned about him in that moment. Her mind was on something else, something she'd come across while searching for Percocet.

"You okay, Daddy?" she asked, already knowing the answer.

"I f-f-feel fucked up," he replied, staring at her with a blank look. "You g-g-got that?"

"No. I can't find it."

Disappointment flickered in Gelato's eyes. He needed an escape from the psychotic thoughts, to the point where more coke was starting to sound like a solution. Dianna watched him, weighing how far she could push things tonight. He couldn't think straight. It reminded her of the instability she felt during her own crashes. She doubted he'd have the energy to snap on her for any wild suggestion, not in this state. He hadn't even questioned why she had Percocet or where it came from. He'd been ready to try it. That told her enough. This might be her only safe opening to say certain things to him. The coke in her system gave her courage, and it being her birthday, with him promising to celebrate properly, made her feel bolder than usual. Nervous, she tucked her hair behind her ear and said, "Umm...Daddy, promise me you won't get mad, but I think I got something else that could help you."

"What-w-w-what is it?"

"Something to bring your high down."

"Okay, b-bring it then," Gelato said too fast, then blinked like his mind caught up with his mouth. "What is it?"

"But first promise me you won't get mad." Dianna needed the reassurance.

"I p-promise."

Dianna took a deep breath and tucked a wisp of hair behind her ear again. There was no turning back now. "It's..." She searched for what to call it and stuttered, "It's d-d-down."

Gelato heard her, but in his fight to stay grounded he didn't register what she meant. "Huh, w-what?"

Dianna froze. She debated repeating it, thinking he understood and wasn't going for it. He hadn't snapped yet, but she could feel the questions coming, the kind she wasn't ready to answer. The night was about to flip. She stayed silent, staring at him. Gelato's mind kept circling back over her words, trying to make them fit the moment. Then it hit him. "Huh?...Down? Like, h-h-heroin?!" His face held more shock than anger.

Dianna nodded, her fingers going back to her hair out of nerves. She stared at Gelato, bracing for whatever came next. Her thoughts spiraled too, already scrambling for a way to pull the suggestion back. She'd just exposed her heroin secret to Gelato.

Gelato's mental battle intensified as the meaning landed. Dianna had offered him heroin. That meant she had it, and she'd been keeping it from him. A dangerous drug. A secret. His emotions buckled. He stared at her across the room, her face fallen, and his mind started reaching for more things she could be hiding. The psychosis dug into his insecurities and turned the blame inward. He'd failed with their money. Vanessa had been taken. Now this. Somewhere along the way he'd lost his grip on Dianna so badly that she'd slipped into something like heroin. The thought of helping her flashed, then the fear that it might already be too late, leaving him with nothing but acceptance of her habits.

Sweat ran down his forehead as his thoughts skidded toward another reality he wasn't ready to face. The psychosis was fully on him now. For a second he wondered if she'd mixed heroin into the coke and that was why he was spiraling. But he'd been through this same trip before when she wasn't even there. She couldn't be the cause. He didn't want a repeat of the last embarrassment, talking out loud about the madness forming in his head. He forced himself to breathe. Losing another good girl wasn't an option, not on her birthday. All she'd asked for was a real turn-up with him. How could he punish her for her failures when he'd failed too? He knew he'd let the connection slip in the past, and part of him felt like that opened the door for her to end up here. On top of all that, he'd promised he wouldn't get mad before she said it. He had to stand on that. The thoughts kept racing anyway, piling up until he felt helpless.

Dianna stood there, hopeless, with Gelato staring at her in silence. His face gave her nothing to read, so she assumed he was upset and didn't know how to react. She felt like she'd just ruined her birthday night by even bringing up heroin, thinking his trip had him open to anything. Heroin was a junkie's drug. She should've known he'd be disgusted that she'd touched it, let alone that she'd offer it to him. Dianna dropped to her knees and cried, ashamed. She pleaded with lies. "I'm sorry, Daddy. I only did it once with some girl at the club, like, weeks ago." She sobbed. "I only did it because I was crashing off the D-D and she told me it would help. I haven't done it again since." She kept going, voice shaking. "The bit I g-got now is what she gave me from that last time. I still have it. I'm sorry. Please don't be mad at me. I'm telling you the truth."

Gelato's mind kicked into overdrive, chewing on her excuses while the psychosis tugged at him. He tried to speak anyway, like it would keep him anchored. "So you only d-d-did it once?"

"I swear." Her sobs broke up the words. "Only that one time because I did too much coke and crashed. Please don't be mad at me."

"I'm not mad," Gelato said, and he meant it. Ruining Dianna's night was the last thing he wanted. In his warped state, part of him even believed she was testing him, checking if he'd become more understanding after the Vanessa situation. Keeping her happy felt like survival. Besides, she said she tried it once to come down from a crash at work, and he chose to believe her.

He drew a deep breath, reached for the plate, and did two more lines. The guilt sat in him anyway, tangled up with those insecure thoughts of himself as a coke fiend. Even he knew it made no sense. It would only drag him deeper. He set the plate down and looked at Dianna, still on her knees. The crying had slowed. She stared back at him, trying to figure out if she was in the clear after what she'd revealed, then softened her face and asked, "...Are you okay, Daddy?"

Gelato answered with no expression. "Come, come on t-the b-b-bed."

Dianna didn't fully trust the invitation, but she got to her feet. Gelato reached out to her and forced an inviting smile onto his frozen face. She took his hand and climbed back onto the bed. He wrapped an arm around her and held her close. He needed the physical comfort in the middle of his mental battle, and Dianna gave it to him, cuddling in without hesitation. They sat there holding each other for a moment. Gelato's mind wouldn't stop. Dianna's weight loss came back to him, then snapped into something uglier. *What if she was lying about everything? What if it wasn't one time? What if she'd been doing heroin way more than she admitted?* If she could lie to his face, she couldn't be trusted. The thought soured the warmth in his chest. He let go of her, pulling his arm away like he couldn't stomach the comfort anymore.

"...You okay, Daddy?" Dianna looked up at him, puzzled.

Gelato didn't answer. He didn't want to say what was in his head, not when it could be delusions. Ruining the night felt stupid. Looking foolish felt worse. The thoughts kept getting louder anyway, more real by the minute, crushing his reason. Sweat poured off him. His heart hammered. He opened his mouth and started dragging air in and out, desperate for oxygen. "Please, get me water," he said.

"Daddy, you're scaring me," Dianna said, then hurried out to come back with a glass of water.

Gelato drank the water, but it had no immediate effect. Sierra had forced down plenty the last time too, and it still hadn't helped. He needed something else. Desperate for relief, his mind went back to the heroin. Maybe Dianna was right. Maybe it would level out his high and calm the psychosis. He would've never considered it in a million years, but truth was, he'd never really thought about it at all. In Gelato's head, heroin was off-limits because of the stigma, because that was how men turned into junkies. Now he looked at Dianna and she didn't seem like one, not from trying it a few times like she claimed. If she was telling the truth, then one experiment wouldn't turn him into anything. Not tonight. Not from one time.

He stuttered, "What d-does the heroin do? Like, how's the h-h-high?"

The questions put a smile on Dianna's face. She answered fast, almost eager. "It's an amazing body buzz and it calms you. I don't know how to describe it. You just gotta trust me, Daddy."

Trust. The word made Gelato's mind spin harder. The ball was in his court and he felt the weight of it. If he shut her down, that distance between them would widen. If he tried it, it could pull them back into sync, and if it fixed this ugly coke trip, that was a bonus too. "Okay," he said, voice shaking. "Let me t-t-t-try it."

Dianna couldn't believe how perfect her birthday night was turning out. This was the kind of turn-up she'd wanted all along. She got up and left the bedroom, grabbed a fresh plate from the kitchen, then pulled the small baggie with three grams of heroin from the coffee table drawer. When she came back in, she climbed onto the bed with everything.

She tapped a bit of heroin powder onto the plate, then handed it to Gelato to hold while she reached for the card and the rolled bill they'd been using with the cocaine. She scraped the coke residue off both onto the bedsheet, then used the card to set a thin line of heroin beside the small pile on the plate in Gelato's hands. She brought the bill to her nose and snorted it. "You see," she told him, "You just do it the same way as the D-D."

Gelato nodded, but the nerves in him had him second guessing everything while Dianna set a smaller line for him. She took the plate back and handed him the bill. When he looked at her, she saw the vulnerability in his eyes, and she knew that was part of why she'd been able to talk him into this. He wasn't the strong man he normally was. He needed reassurance. Dianna gave him a slow nod, promising with her face that he'd be fine.

She couldn't hold back her smile when Gelato leaned in and snorted the tiny line of heroin. It was a moment for her. After that, they both took a few sips of Courvoisier, put everything away on the nightstand, and held onto each other as the wave came.

Gelato couldn't grasp what was happening to him. His racing mind slowed down, and the psychotic thoughts stopped mattering. Nothing could stress him. Whatever had been spiraling in his head felt distant now, because the euphoria shifted his focus to pure physical sensation. His body flooded with pleasure in rolling waves, and a smile even formed on his face. After a moment, he remembered Dianna beside him and turned with a drowsy grin. Dianna turned too, kissed his smiling lips, and said, "I'm glad. I'm glad you feel better, Daddy." She felt great as well, but this wasn't new to her. Dianna had been on a different level with heroin, so what hit Gelato hard barely moved her. She eased off the bed and said, "Daddy, give me a second. I'm gonna do it differently for myself."

Dianna left the bedroom naked once again and went to the kitchen. She grabbed a spoon and a lighter, then reached for the small kit hidden deep in the coffee table drawer. When she returned, she sat comfortably on the bed, already settled and ready to do her procedure. Gelato watched her with quiet curiosity, tracking every movement. Dianna wasn't worried about questions or judgment. His mind was still wrapped in the trance of his first heroin high. With him locked in that state, she was free to do her own thing even with his eyes on her.

Dianna opened the small kit and took out a syringe, placing it on her lap. She scooped a bit of heroin from the plate onto the spoon, then flicked the lighter and held it underneath. The powder began to bubble and melt, turning to liquid. Once it did, she set the lighter aside and gently blew across the spoon to cool it down. She brought the needle tip to the spoon and drew the liquid heroin into the syringe. Dianna laid her arm across her lap and tapped her forearm near the bicep, coaxing the brachial vein to rise. She slid the needle in and pushed the plunger, feeding the liquid into herself. When she finished, she withdrew the needle and tilted her head back, letting the euphoria settle in.

Gelato watched it all go down. Even in that lovely zombie state, he registered what had just happened. Seeing Dianna inject herself made one thing clear, it could not have been her first time doing it that way. The small scars in the same area of her forearm said the same. She had been using heroin a lot more than she claimed, and the story about only doing it once at the club was a lie. Under any other circumstances, Gelato would have questioned her hard. Right now, none of it mattered. The trance had him numb to everything except the euphoria and the rush of connection he felt with her. They were together in harmony.

Dianna nodded off, then lifted her head from the tilt and spoke through a slow slur, "When this...feeling wears off...we could do more D-D... then more down...to balance again."

CHAPTER THIRTY-FOUR

Monday, July 9 – 1:55 a.m.

Jiggy stood by the bar at Mississauga's Diamondz strip club, waiting on one of the strippers. Diamondz was never his choice for having his girls work. The place was full of ghetto strippers and shady business, but that grimy reputation was exactly why it stayed popular. It was the go-to spot for sleazy pimps, and the kind of club where a girl could choose up fast once a face felt familiar. Jiggy wasn't there for that. He was there for a stripper who went by Mercy. Mercy wasn't one of his girls, she was a friend he grew up with back in his old neighbourhood, and they had business together.

Mercy was nearly impossible for any pimp to handle. She was truly ghetto, quick to fight a man, and she often kept an illegal gun in her purse. The guys she dealt with usually settled for living off the avails because nobody really controlled her, she ran her own show. Mercy also sold drugs in the club as a side hustle, and Jiggy was her supplier. She already made good money stripping, but she liked the extra cash that came with the dope game. Jiggy showed up tonight because she'd sold out and needed another half ounce.

The club was nearing closing time, and last call for alcohol had already been announced. Most of the girls were either in the change room or finishing up in the private rooms, and pimps were starting to pull up for pickups. Mercy had her own car, so she didn't need a ride from Jiggy. He wasn't here to play chauffeur. He stayed by the bar, finishing his Heineken and watching the room. He knew a few of the pimps posted up inside, and more were outside in the lot, waiting on their girls or just exercising the true definition of *parking lot pimping* in their fancy cars.

Jiggy finished his beer and got impatient waiting on Mercy, so he texted her to hurry up. She replied that she'd just finished with a client in the private rooms and was about to freshen up before changing. Jiggy considered stepping out to wait in his car, but a pimp walked in and pulled his attention. The guy moved like he owned the place, dapping up the faces he knew and throwing his usual screw-face at everyone else, Jiggy included. What caught Jiggy was who it was.

Marvel was really in Diamondz, casual, leaning at the bar and chatting with another pimp like nothing in the world was on his back. The nerve. Preeme had a $10,00 Where's Waldo tag on him, yet Marvel was bold enough to be out in the GTA anyway.

With the club preparing to close and nobody on stage, the music wasn't as loud as it normally was. Jiggy stayed by the bar, pretending to be occupied with his phone while he eavesdropped on Marvel and his friend. Marvel didn't mention kidnapping or ransom. He bragged about his money, talked like he was a major player in the game, and said he was back with Maria, who was making big money in the strip clubs. He flashed his new Rolex and spoke about buying a new car. To Jiggy, Marvel sounded way too confident, like he believed there'd be no backlash to the kidnapping because of whatever agreement he had with Gelato. That also told Jiggy Marvel knew nothing about the finder's reward Preeme had put out to a few trustworthy friends.

Jiggy sent Preeme a message on Snapchat. *{Yo, what you dealing wit?}*

He responded, *{Wudup.}*

{Over here at Diamondz,} {Your boy is here.}

{What boy?}

{C'mon, man. You already know.}

{Word?}

{Yeah,} {Club closing real soon so pull up right now and handle your business,} Jiggy added, *{Then you owe me 10 😊.}*

{Fuck!} {I'm deep OT right now,} Preeme replied.

Jiggy then got a text from Mercy saying she was coming out the changing room and asking where he was in the club.

{At the bar,} Jiggy replied.

{Okay,} {I see you.}

Jiggy looked up and saw Mercy walking over. She wore casual clothes with her work bag hanging off her shoulder. With her reputation as a savage, Mercy was still a stunning brown-skinned girl with a body that matched her face, standing 5'5" and carrying that *badgal Riri* energy. She greeted Jiggy with a hug and said, "Okay, let's go." She led the way, and Jiggy turned to look at Marvel one last time before leaving the bar. The fool was still deep in his conversation, not paying any mind to his surroundings.

Jiggy stepped out the club's front doors with Mercy and caught a few European cars parked up, pimps out there showcasing their presence. He walked with Mercy towards the huge lot around the side of the club where more cars were parked and nobody was campaigning. They hopped into his Range Rover, and that's when Jiggy felt his phone buzzing in his pocket. "Hold up a sec," he told Mercy in the passenger seat, then pulled his phone out and saw the Snapchat messages from Preeme flooding in.

{What is he doing there?} {It looks like he be there often?} {Yo you still there?} {Try to get a better drop on him for me,} {Yo!} {Yo!} {Yo!!}

Snapchat showed Preeme typing again, but Jiggy replied, *{Hold on,} {I'm not in there anymore,} {But I'm with my homegirl who works there. I'ma see if she got details for you.}*

{Bruh,} Preeme responded.

{Don't worry. She's bless.}

{Just don't be mentioning my name to no bitch.}

{Never that.}

{Holla back.}

Jiggy turned to Mercy and said, "My bad."

"No worries." She smiled at him. "I know you gets busy."

"Sometimes too busy, and not busy in the way I'd like to be."

Mercy laughed. "You kill me." Then she got to business. "So, you have that for me?"

Jiggy reached into his centre console and came out with a Saran-wrapped ball of cocaine in his hand. "It's a full bounce, not a half. I didn't have time to ski' it out, so just take the full."

"Now I gotta…" Annoyed, Mercy opened her purse and pulled out a stash of money to count. "You're forcing me to buy more than I asked for."

Jiggy chuckled. "It's cheaper for you to take the full."

She kissed her teeth, playful. "So now you're my accountant?" Mercy handed him a colourful bundle of bills, then tucked the rest back into her purse.

Jiggy shifted the talk. "So, what's gwanning in the club?"

"What you mean?" Mercy asked.

"Any new bitches worth swerving on?"

"C'mon, Jiggy. You know most of the bitches that work this club are whack," she said. "Me and maybe one or two girls are the only ones that actually got our shit straight."

"True. So, nobody new at all?"

"Not that I could think of. Why?"

Jiggy weighed whether to be direct. Mercy wasn't some soft girl, and she knew how to keep things quiet. He figured he could ask without making it hot. "Who's that Marvel guy? You know him?"

"Ohhh, so that's what it's about, huh?" Mercy chuckled. "You want his girl?"

That wasn't why Jiggy asked, but he took the lane she gave him. "Yeah. I heard he got the baddest bitch in the club."

"For your information, I'm the baddest bitch in that club," Mercy said, half serious, half joking. "But yeah, he got a little baddie. I can't even hate."

"How long she been working the club?"

"Started this weekend. I don't really talk to her, but I keep hearing her in the changing room. She got some tricks she usually goes to see in London. Now she's trying to find new tricks in the city by working weekends."

"She been in the game for a minute?"

"Yeah. She used to do telly work." Mercy paused, then added, "I think there's already a rumour going around that she left Marvel and got with a big pimp, and he's the one that got her into working the clubs. Now she's back with Marvel and doing her thing for him."

Jiggy wondered if the full story was really out there. "Who's the big pimp, then? What's the details of that story?"

"I don't think she ever mentioned his name to anyone, or said anything else about him. Must be some secret of hers that she won't share, thinking she's something special. But none of the girls asked much about it because nobody really cares." Mercy looked at Jiggy and chuckled. "Why? Were you the secret big pimp that had her before?"

"Stop the bullshit," Jiggy laughed. "You know I ain't no big pimp. Besides, wouldn't it be weird that I was just at the bar with the Marvel dude?"

"Yeah, I guess," Mercy said. "Or maybe you just keeping it sucka-free." Then she flipped it on him. "But for real, what's up? Is there more to the story that I should know about? Should I stomp that bitch out for you or something?"

"Nah, nah," Jiggy denied. "Ain't none gwanning. I just heard Marvel talking like he got the baddest bitch, so

I got curious." Jiggy kept it light, knowing the less he said, the better for everybody. It wasn't his place to put murder in a woman's lap, no matter how solid she was.

"Didn't you see her tonight?" Mercy asked. "She was the Spanish girl with the mole like Marilyn, wearing purple lingerie and stockings. Goes by the name Violet."

"Nah, I came late. She was probably in the changing room or something."

"Oh, okay. Well, that's her over there with him right now." Mercy nodded toward a couple cutting through the parking lot.

Maria left work in a sweatsuit with a big bag in her hand, walking beside Marvel. They stayed wrapped up in their conversation as they headed toward the old Benz, not giving a look to the Range Rover watching them.

"Yeah, she's cute," Jiggy said. "He always picks her up?"

"Yeah, every night since she started Friday."

"I guess I'm gonna have to come earlier if I wanna swerve her without him around."

"Marvel is a babysitting nigga." Mercy explained. "He passes through all night when she's working, so he'll probably pop up on her anyway. Plus, Marvel used to be in here even before he got his bitch working in here. He's always trying to sell his shit like he don't know I got this place on smash already. He's fucking annoying."

Jiggy chuckled. "She'll be working next weekend for sure?"

"Yeah, I think so. That's her plan," Mercy said. Then she made sure he heard her. "But like I said, Marvel probably gon' be popping up on her all night, then picking her up at the end. She'll most likely show you no interest."

"True," Jiggy said.

"Anyways, I'ma get going now," Mercy said. She hugged Jiggy, then got out of the Range Rover.

Jiggy watched Mercy walk towards her BMW, then observed as the old Benz with Marvel and Maria drove past his Range and out the parking lot, onto Dundas Street. Jiggy got on his phone and messaged Preeme on Snapchat, *{I got some good details for you.}*

Preeme responded quickly, *{I'ma pull up at your place in the morning.}*

{Okay.} Jiggy pondered for a moment and then inquired, *{You wanna just pay me 50K flat and I sort this out for you right now?} {I'll waive the 10K finders fee you owe me.}*

{Lol,} {Nah, nah,} {I'm feeling to do the work myself,} {It's personal,} Preeme declared. *{I'ma pull up with the 10K for you in the morning and take that info you got for me.}*

{Aight, bless.} Jiggy put his phone in his pocket before starting the Range Rover, then driving out the parking lot. That very location would become a crime scene a week from now.

GHAD

CHAPTER THIRTY-FIVE

Monday, July 16 – 2:30 a.m.

For the past three nights, Preeme tried to get the job over and done with. Maria kept leaving the club at random times before closing, and she wasn't with Marvel. When Jiggy asked Mercy why Maria was never around at closing hours, Mercy explained she'd been leaving with a client each night. Tonight wasn't as busy as the others. Jiggy showed up and saw Maria was still around thirty minutes before last call, so he played his part and tipped Preeme. Marvel eventually pulled up wearing his red-faced Rolex, and Preeme was already on the move by then. Minutes later, Jiggy got the Snapchat message that the grim reaper was in position somewhere outside in the darkness.

The car came from a referrals-only spot that didn't check documents too hard. Even so, he swapped the plates for this night so nothing could lead back to the shop. Extra precautions for everyone, but mostly for himself. He was now sitting in the dark Volkswagen Jetta with a turbo transmission; in case there was a need for speed. The windows were tinted for discretion. He wore shades and a baseball cap. In the spacious lot along the side of Diamondz, he parked facing the front entry, only a few spots from Marvel's old Benz. With Sunday closing down, there wasn't the usual parking-lot-pimping going on. Out front was dead. Preeme looked up at the sky and clocked the full moon. His weapon of choice was a GLOCK

23 with an extended thirty-clip. He didn't need a full-auto switch because every shot would be calculated. Preeme meant business.

The Heineken in Jiggy's hand had an extra chill to it, so he sipped it slow at the bar where a few other pimps stood, Marvel included. Maybe it was the full-moon vibe, but Marvel had surprised Jiggy with a nod when he walked in greeting some pimps at the bar. Jiggy took it as nothing more than Marvel choosing to acknowledge him with something other than the usual screw-face, after seeing him around before. As far as anybody knew, Jiggy was there for Mercy. As far as Mercy knew, Jiggy was there to shoot his shot at Maria, which Mercy figured wasn't happening tonight because Marvel had shown up. Mercy came out of the changing room ready to leave with Jiggy and said at the bar, "Ready to go?"

"Hold on, I'm soon done my drink," Jiggy replied. He chugged the rest of his Heineken, then brought the bottle down hard on the bar counter. He made sure not to glance too much at Marvel posted further down the bar, but he nodded at the pimps around him, and did not exclude Marvel. Jiggy led Mercy out of the club.

They pushed through Diamondz's heavy front doors and Jiggy's attention went straight to the side lot. There weren't many cars out there. He expected to spot the Corvette or more likely the Acura, but neither was there. It only made sense Preeme wouldn't roll in his own car tonight, which meant the grim reaper was sitting in one of the random rides parked out here. Jiggy's eyes locked on the only car he recognized, Marvel's old Benz.

He'd been so focused, he almost forgot he was with Mercy until she spoke.

"So, you didn't get a chance to talk to her, did you?"

"Nah." Jiggy knew she meant Maria. "She was busy working the floor, then dude showed up for her minutes after."

"Okay. So what's your plan now?"

"No plan. Just gon' head home."

"Your spot by Lakeshore?"

"Yeah."

"Okay, I'll meet you there," Mercy said, inviting herself. "Don't feel like going to my place. I been fighting with my man."

Jiggy nodded and they walked towards their separate cars. Mercy knew Jiggy had his girls, but she also knew he lived alone, so there wouldn't be an issue with her crashing for the night. His girls were in check, they knew better than to confront him about being with another woman. The only real headache was her man ringing her all night because she wasn't coming back to their place in Scarborough. That was tomorrow's problem. Tonight, she was riding with a genuine street-savvy one.

Jiggy got into his Range Rover, and that was when he spotted the dude in the Volkswagen, shades on, cap pulled low. They shared devious smirks, then Jiggy pulled off with Mercy following behind in her BMW.

Back in the club, Maria came out of the changing room and was ready to leave with Marvel. She said to him, "It was so dead tonight."

"Yeah, I know. Shit's always weird on a full moon."

"It's a full moon tonight?"

"Yeah."

"Hope there are no werewolves out there," Maria joked.

Marvel chuckled, then gave a quick nod to a guy at the bar as they passed, leading Maria out the club. The warm night air hit nice, and Marvel took a deep breath like he could finally enjoy it. Ever since the big ransom payout, life had been feeling good. He was all smiles, holding Maria's hand as they headed toward the side parking lot. His old Benz sat up ahead, and he was already thinking about swapping it for a newer model in a day or two once financing cleared on Maria's credit. Even with that lump sum in his pocket, Marvel knew better than to cash out on a new whip. The payout put him in a better position to invest in his hustle and spend smart.

That smile started slipping as he got closer and clocked the Volkswagen Jetta parked a few spots to the right of his Benz. The windows were dark, but from where he stood, he could see through the windshield. What didn't sit right was the driver's seat laid all the way back. It didn't make sense for somebody to leave a seat like that, unless they'd been posted up in there.

"Hold on," Marvel told Maria, letting go of her hand as he drifted closer for a better look. His heart jumped when he saw a brown-skinned guy laid back in that reclined seat, staring straight ahead. He wore shades and a cap pulled low. The shades hid his eyes, so Marvel couldn't tell if the man was sleeping or watching. The thought of those eyes being open behind the lenses sent a chill down his spine. He backed off quick and returned to Maria by the Benz. When he looked again, the reclined seat started creeping upright. The guy sat up and aimed his face right at Marvel. Hat and shades made it hard to place him, but the vibe was off. Marvel grabbed Maria's hand and pulled her back towards the club, moving fast.

Maria was confused. "What's going on, Marvo? Who was that guy?"

"I don't know, man." Marvel glanced back. The dude stayed in the car, still fixed on him. "We gon' wait inside and I'ma link Blaze and 'em to draw for us."

Marvel didn't think it was life or death, but that new Rolex on his wrist could've made him look like a payday to jack-boys. The last thing he needed was getting stuck up in the lot, especially with Maria right there. The twins were posted at the ghetto motel next to the strip club, pimping out two crackhead girls, so he could get them over quick. They'd be there in minutes and Marvel would feel a whole lot safer with a gun around. As soon as they pushed back through the club's front doors, Marvel pulled out his phone in the lobby and called the twins.

CHAPTER THIRTY-SIX

Sierra left Brass Rail strip club at last call. She'd made good money for the night, as usual, and didn't see a purpose in sticking around with tricks who weren't trying to spend any more. Chocolate and Vanilla were at the door to greet her when she got home, so she pet them both before stepping fully into the unit. That was all the attention they'd get from her tonight. She needed time to herself. Sierra went to the washroom and ran warm water to fill the tub, then headed to the bedroom to get settled, slipping into her cozy Louis Vuitton robe. She mixed bath liquids and salts into the water, then let the robe fall away and stepped in, easing her body into the heat. Eyes closed, she sank into the therapy of it. There was a lot to think about after spending the day with Gelato.

Since Vanessa's kidnapping and that horrible night, Sierra had finally met him for brunch at their favourite bistro by the lake. They talked through what needed to be said. A savings plan was set, one Sierra had full entitlement to, with access that matched the responsibility. She'd always know the total saved, she'd have a spare key to Gelato's condo and access to the safe. She'd also have the final say on approving any new girl for the stable. Sierra stuck to her guns that Gelato needed to focus on who he had left—herself and Dianna. The overall agreement left her content to forgive his failures. Her position wouldn't be just bottom bitch to the stable anymore. She'd be more like his co-pilot. By the end of it, they'd been happy to be together again, riding the good vibes back to Sierra's place.

It was also good knowing $50,000 had come in from Dianna's trip with Eric. That money, along with everything else saved up, had them comfortably above a hundred thousand. Still, they were supposed to be sitting on hundreds of thousands after years in the game. At least they finally had enough to start investing outside of it and let their money grow. Smooth would be the perfect person to help them navigate opportunities he was already part of. There was no need to jump into anything right away. The money was not going anywhere, and it would keep climbing as long as Gelato stuck to the savings plan. They would start investing when the timing felt right.

Besides the talk and the time well spent, Sierra had been able to tell Gelato wasn't his usual vibrant and healthy self. He hadn't seemed coked out or drunk, but something had dulled his confidence. Sympathy hit her hard, and part of why she'd fallen back into him so easily. By the time they'd gotten to her place she'd ended up laid out naked beside him in bed, giving him what he needed. The sex was great, but it was her love and support he'd been reaching for.

Now, reflecting on everything, Sierra wondered if Gelato suffered from some kind of mental illness. After his psychosis episode the night of Vanessa's kidnapping, it was in his best interest to stay away from cocaine, which he'd promised to do. Only God knew if he really would. As far as Sierra knew, he hadn't touched it since.

They hadn't been around each other much, and most of their communication had been through texts, so she couldn't truly know what he'd been up to. Dianna's birthday being just a week ago made Sierra suspect he might've indulged with her, but she didn't ask. He'd either lie and upset her or admit it and disappoint her.

She stayed in the tub and kept thinking, wondering what would become of them if Gelato didn't strengthen up and failed again. At their age, they couldn't keep playing with the game, not unless Sierra was ready to end up like the older women who still strutted through the strip clubs after years of never finding a way out. She'd always believed that by now she would've owned a business or something, and had a child or two with Gelato. That wasn't their reality. And after everything that unfolded that terrible night, their situation was far from what she'd imagined. She loved Gelato and still meant it when she said she'd be his strength while they built again, but deep down she was drained too. Mentally, physically, and emotionally. At this point, things had to get better. It was all she could wish for.

CHAPTER THIRTY-SEVEN

Preeme's plan was to wait for Marvel to get in his car then ambush him with gunfire. That would be the end of it. The only cameras in the area were focused on the front of the strip club, so anything in the side parking lot wouldn't be captured. But the simple plan had already failed. Marvel noticed him in the Volkswagen, and now his guard was up. Still, Preeme had watched him flee in fear, and that suggested Marvel was unarmed. It only made Preeme more confident about how this was going to end. He'd wait. Marvel couldn't stay in the club forever. Closing would flush him back out to that Benz. Even if he called a cab to the front, thinking the danger was only in the gloomy lot, he'd still be in for a surprise once the ride pulled off. Marvel's only real way to stay alive was to call the cops, yet Preeme questioned whether he grasped the danger enough to break street code like that.

Preeme waited for over ten minutes in the driver's seat of the Volkswagen, eyes fixed on the front entry. His gloved hands stayed ready, close to the gun in the door compartment. He watched a few dudes leave with their girls, jump into their cars, and drive off. Then two girls came out and got into an Audi that had pulled up front. As it drove off, the black male behind the wheel stared toward Preeme sitting shaded in the dark Volkswagen as they passed the lot on their way onto Dundas Street. A car left every minute, and still there was no sign of Marvel or his girl. The old Benz waited for them, abandoned under Preeme's watchful eyes.

Finally, Marvel appeared out the front doors holding Maria's hand, and both their heads turned to study the parking lot where the Volkswagen was. At that same moment, a Chevy hatchback pulled in from Dundas Street. The windows weren't tinted, so the identical twins in the front seats were clear as day. They kept their eyes on Preeme behind his tints, then caught him through the windshield as they drove past the side lot toward the front of the club. Marvel waved them down anyway, anxious as hell, even though he was standing out front alone and they couldn't miss him if they tried.

He and Maria climbed into the backseat. The driver did a shaky three-point turn and every head in that Chevy kept tracking the shady man in the Volkswagen. Preeme had to think of a new plan. Marvel calling his goons meant they came armed, guard up. It'd be stupid to risk an exchange of bullets in a public lot. He needed to downplay whatever threatening vibe he gave off, make them ease up. By the time the Chevy finished its turn, Preeme popped the hood of the Volkswagen and stepped out in his dark, worn-out clothing with his phone to his ear. He leaned over the open hood like a man dealing with car trouble and waiting on help. It gave a reason for why he'd been sitting out there so long. He put himself in a dangerous position with his back turned at the hood while the Chevy drove past behind him, but it was the only way to sell it. He had to defuse the tension, cut the chance of a gunfight in that lot. The hatchback rolled by, then hit Dundas Street heading east. Preeme didn't turn to look at them. Even if their heads stayed twisted back watching him, they couldn't see him as a threat after the way he played it.

CHAPTER THIRTY-EIGHT

Monday, July 16 – 9:01 a.m.
(Central European Time—Paris, France)

In a completely different time zone, Dianna had already started her morning with Eric. They'd had breakfast at an amazing French restaurant and were now in a stretch limousine headed for Charles de Gaulle Airport. They were set to catch an 11 a.m. flight and land in Toronto around 12 p.m. EST—losing only an hour on the seven-hour flight.

The time Dianna spent in France was beyond her expectations, filled with exciting adventures and a level of glamour she'd never experienced before. What really blew her away were Eric's romantic gestures. France encouraged courting and he moved like a man trying to win her heart, securing the best reservations and making sure every moment felt deliberate. They'd spent the last night on a yacht with a crew assigned to just them. During an elegant dinner on the deck, Eric presented Dianna with a dazzling diamond ring. He didn't go down on one knee and propose, but he did present it formally as a promise ring and declared his love for her. He wanted a real relationship. Eric confessed his burning love and his need to be her lover. That part wasn't new, but Dianna's response was.

"I love you, too," she'd said, and the words surprised even her. They came out naturally because that was truly how she felt.

Their love for each other carried on in the limo's private cabin as they sipped champagne. Eric's lifestyle was beyond what Dianna had imagined. They weren't heading to the airport for first class. They were going to board the same private jet that brought them to France. Dianna hadn't told Gelato about the jet because she'd been caught off guard by it herself. After that, she had no intention of mentioning it, knowing it would only stir up his insecurities while she was away with Eric. She spoke to Gelato every morning after she'd updated him that she landed safely. The daily calls weren't because she missed him. It was reporting. Truthfully, Dianna was more than fine. She was falling in love with the fifty-year-old man.

Now, seated in the limo, she admired the ring on her right hand when Eric said, "There's something I've been wanting to ask you."

"What is it, babe? You can ask me anything."

"Well, since you're my lady now, why don't you move in with me?"

"Huh?" Dianna had to be sure she heard him right. "Like, live with you?"

Eric didn't answer right away. Maybe he was coming on too strong. What he wanted was to have her fully under his care, so he softened it. "We don't have to live together every day, but you should consider moving into one of my condos."

"But I'm fine at the condo I'm already staying at."

"Yeah, and I don't know if I'm fine with it," Eric said. "I can't come see you there with the roommate you say you live with."

The excuse Dianna had made to keep Eric from coming over could no longer hold now that they were genuinely a couple. It also hit her that she couldn't keep treating him like a client, and she didn't want to. She loved him, and she wasn't trying to deny it anymore. She had no clue what to do with the situation she was in, a bitch in the game falling for a trick. Dianna sipped her drink, stuck in her head, with no idea what to say.

Eric took her silence as a sign she was listening, so he kept going. "I have a condo out in Richmond Hill that I think you'll like. It's a spacious two-bedroom and a den, with the finest furnishing. Granite kitchen counters with marble backsplash and walnut flooring. It's amazing, my love. I want to take you to see it once we land back in Toronto. If you like it, we'll go pick up your belongings right away so you can settle in."

"Uhh…" Dianna hesitated. "I don—"

"We can have the place renovated and furnished however you'd like if you're not happy with the way it is now," Eric added.

"It's not that, babe. I just don't know if doing all this is a good idea." She looked at him, needing something real from him. "Don't you think we're moving too fast?"

Eric set his drink into the cup holder and took Dianna's ringed hand in both of his. "My love, you know the situation I came from. I was married. I was sincerely in love with a woman who couldn't bear me children, then I lost her to cancer after years of a happy marriage. I fell into my drug addictions to cope with my depression, then I sought escorts to satisfy my lust. But through it all, nothing ever felt as right as when I first connected with you, my love.

"You've filled the void in my heart. You've revived the sensual part of me I've been yearning for, for years. I've told you all of this before, just like I've told you many times that I'm in love with you. All I ask is that you don't break my old fragile heart.

"With that being said, I'm willing to sign the condo in your name so you truly own it. That should show you how serious I am about you. I'm sorry if it seems like I'm moving too fast, but, my love, I'm trying to move forward with you." He rubbed the ring on her finger and looked into her eyes. "I don't want to die without the full experience of real love again. I'll put you in my will if you promise me real love."

Dianna stared into Eric's eyes, speechless, and her eyes watered. It was a lot for her heart to handle. A love scenario that only happened in fairy tales, except this charming character wasn't some strong, handsome prince in shining armor. He was an older man who would make everything shine for her. She loved him. Making this fairy tale real would mean ending her life with Gelato. And the guilt of that alone had her breaking. Tears slipped down her face as she closed her eyes.

CHAPTER THIRTY-NINE

Once the Chevy hatchback turned right onto Dundas, everyone inside finally stopped looking back at the strange guy they'd left in the parking, checking his engine. From the backseat beside Marvel, Maria asked, "Who do you think that was?"

"Some waste man."

Blaze laughed from the passenger seat. "That waste man had you bummied."

"Nah, not even," Marvel denied. "I just thought he was some waste jack-boy, tryna jam me for my Rollie. I wasn't tryna get into all that."

"Whatever, broski." Flame mocked him from behind the wheel. "So since that nigga not on piss, should I pull a U-turn and take you back to your car?"

"Nah, nah. I'll come back for it tomorrow morning or something."

Flame chuckled, then asked, "So you gon' crash at the telly with us?" He eased off the gas like he was about to swing into the motel lot.

"Nah, yo," Marvel refused. He glanced at Maria, then looked back at Flame. "Just drop us at my condo. My girl's with me, so don't expect us to sleep in them nasty hotel rooms you be working your crackhead bitches out of."

"Drive you all the way back to your condo in Vaughan? That's fucking far."

"The highway's right up ahead," Marvel said. "Ain't no traffic at this time. It'll be like a ten minute drive."

Flame got annoyed having to drive Marvel across town, so he floored it. The hatchback jerked forward since he was not turning into the motel complex anymore. He stayed on Dundas and headed for the highway. Under the full moon, Dundas was almost empty. No cars in front of them, none beside them. Then high beams flared in the mirror, a car riding close behind like it wanted to climb into their trunk.

"The fuck's wrong with the fool behind us?" Blaze said. "Why don't they just pass in the open lanes?"

"I don't know," Flame muttered, getting more annoyed as the glare kept washing out his rearview. He slid left into the middle lane to give the car room.

The high beams clicked off as it pulled up on their right. Heads turned. Dark-coloured Volkswagen. The same one from Diamondz. It crept alongside them with the window down. The same brown-skinned guy leaned out, hat and shades gone now, face clear. His arm was already outside. A gun was in his hand, pointed straight at Blaze in the passenger seat.

Blaze nervously reached for the gun on his waist. A thunderous blast shattered the passenger window and clipped his head. Pain roared through his skull and his vision blurred. The gun slipped from his grip onto the floor by his feet. Blood flooded his mouth as he slumped forward in his seat. More shots cracked over him, loud and close, and Blaze couldn't tell what they hit after that. He couldn't even place where he'd been struck, only that his face burned and pulsed and wouldn't let up. He fought to stay present, reaching down on instinct, feeling along the floor for his gun. But darkness swallowed everything. He didn't know if his eyes were open or shut. He kept searching anyway, fingertips dragging along the floor by his feet until they closed around the grip. More shots drove into his back. Heat tore through him and punched out into his chest. Breath caught. He wheezed, choking as metallic blood pushed up and slipped into his lungs. Shock hit hard and fast, draining him in seconds. The gun stayed in his hand, but his body wouldn't answer anymore. Blaze sagged over in the seat unable to draw a breath.

Preeme came up behind the Chevy hatchback on purpose. He wanted it to slide into the left lane so he could pass on the right and strike first at the passenger, the one most likely to be carrying a gun. His first shot blew out the passenger window, tore off the man's face, and shattered the driver's window. The passenger folded forward. Preeme shifted his aim to the driver and fired again, but Flame tucked his head between his arms, hands still on the wheel, driving blind. A couple rounds missed. Two caught him in the shoulder. Maria's screams ripped through the backseat. Then a hard crash stole Preeme's attention for a split second. He looked up to see a car smashed into a light pole across the road. Gunfire must've spooked the driver in the opposite lane, and they lost control. The wreck faded behind them and Preeme snapped back to the work in front of him, staying on the Chevy hatchback as it sped. The slumped passenger was moving. Alive. Maybe reaching for his gun. Preeme leaned farther out of the Volkswagen so he could angle his shots down into the cabin, then he drilled the passenger's exposed back with five more rounds to finish him. Everything was happening fast, but it felt like only now Flame decided to gamble. The hatchback swerved toward Preeme's Volkswagen in a desperate attempt to end the mayhem. Preeme stomped the brakes in time to avoid the swipe, but the Chevy still clipped his front bumper.

Both vehicles kicked sideways. Preeme sat deep in the seat, tightened his grip, and fought the wheel until the Volkswagen straightened out. Up ahead, the hatchback kept fishtailing while Flame, panicked and stubborn, tried to catch the upcoming highway ramp anyway. He didn't make it. The Chevy smashed into the guardrail. Preeme stopped behind the wreck and reached into the backseat for his shades and cap before he got out. Under the full moon he walked up on foot, eager to finish it. Flame was slumped over the steering wheel, twisted and wrecked. That wasn't enough for Preeme. He put two more shots into his back to finish what he came to do.

Marvel and Maria were trapped in the backseat. The doors had been dislodged and jammed from the crash, and one window was already blown out. Preeme appeared at the empty frame and locked eyes with them. He looked like the grim reaper. The couple thrashed and clawed at each other in panic with nowhere to go, then the shots tore through the car, more than fifteen, punching into them until their bodies quit moving.

Preeme leaned in and finished it with final shots to their heads. The GLOCK 23 clicked dry, and the slide locked to the rear.

Two passing cars witnessed the execution on the ramp, but they sped off the second they saw him look their way. Preeme climbed back into the Volkswagen and took off the shades and hat again, not wanting to match whatever description those drivers would give. A killer in shades and a cap near Dundas and Highway 427. Preeme drove off fast, leaving the wreck and the bodies behind as he sped toward his final destination.

CHAPTER FORTY

Monday, July 16 – 12:34 p.m.

They stepped off the private jet at Toronto Pearson and into another stretch limo waiting on the tarmac. Part of flying like this meant their crew handled customs before the jet even landed, so they didn't deal with the regular international procedures. Dianna loved every bit of the high-profile lifestyle, and she could get used to it. Now she had the option to.

On the highway, they headed toward Richmond Hill, settled into the private backseats of the limo and sipping more wine. With Eric's own driver up front they didn't have to shy away from doing cocaine lines off the woodgrain armrests. In Paris, Eric had pulled strings to have drugs brought to them each night, and being back home only meant they could turn up whenever they wanted. The plan was to take the turn-up from the limo straight to the condo waiting for Dianna in Richmond Hill. That was where they'd turn down with some heroin.

"Excited, my love?" Eric asked, holding Dianna's ringed hand.

"Yes..." Dianna felt great, riding the cocaine euphoria and picturing the life ahead. She rested her head on his shoulder. "Yes, Daddy."

It was the first time she'd ever called Eric Daddy. It hit strange for a second, a young woman who could pass as his daughter saying it. But he understood it was a new-era thing. He smiled and held her closer. "I promise I'll take good care of you, my love."

"Forever and ever?"

"Forever...even after I'm gone."

They met with a kiss then both smiled in the quiet, taking in that they'd each gotten what they'd longed for. Dianna's mind was made and she had no intention of looking back. She didn't want to return to the condo she was leasing in Mississauga. Eric promised to buy back everything she liked, brand new for her new condo in Richmond Hill, which would own in her name. He would also add her as a joint holder on his accounts and give her access to everything. The only thing she wouldn't have access to was anything tied to his businesses. Eric had the sense to know restrictions were needed, in case Dianna somehow spent millions recklessly in a year. His businesses generated 24.6 million every year, so as long as he kept that secure, they'd always be fine. Dianna would eventually have rights and access to all his businesses once Eric was gone. That was the plan.

Dianna's plan once they arrived at the Richmond Hill condo was to take off her Icy pendant and hand it to the limo drivers, along with the keys to the Marilyn Monroe condo in Mississauga. The drivers would go to retrieve all of Dianna's documents from the secured cabinet in her bedroom, then leave the keys on the dresser with the Icy pendant. Dianna did love Gelato, but she'd found the real love she'd always yearned for, a real father figure.

After the early-morning events, Preeme dropped the Volkswagen rental at a trusted chop shop that ripped cars apart within minutes. They were privately open at the hour he arrived. From there, he took a cab home to get some sleep. Later, during business hours, he called the rental company and reported that he'd crashed the car while drunk. He offered to cover the cost to replace the Volkswagen Jetta with an upgraded model, as long as they didn't involve police. He stressed that the car was completely totaled, and said he'd already had it towed to a scrap yard before police could arrive, avoiding impaired driving charges.

The rental owner was a crook who put on a loud show of being furious about losing a car he claimed was in high demand. With all that disappointment, he settled on thirty thousand. Preeme knew the car couldn't be worth anywhere near that, not with five years on it and over two hundred thousand kilometres. Still, he brought the cash over immediately and settled the score. Back home, he shut his phone off so Gelato, Smooth, or Jiggy couldn't reach him if they caught breaking news and started asking questions. But it did matter what the public knew about the shooting. He stayed on the couch, waiting for City Pulse. He'd missed the noon highlights, but he figured they'd run them again after the boring stories, like they always did. Crystal was in the kitchen making lunch for both of them.

"King, there's not enough mayo left. One of us has to go without it on the turkey sandwich," she said, glancing at him from behind the counter.

At five-three, the counter hid her body, leaving only her pretty Portuguese face and red-dyed hair for Preeme to take in. "I'm guessing I'm the one going without?"

She snickered. "You got it."

Preeme sighed, eyes fixed on the television. His relationship with Crystal was healthier than anyone would expect from a pimp with his reputation. He wasn't the young guy he used to be, the one who treated women like nothing but product in the game. Facing the murder case involving Tanya became the turning point that changed everything. Crystal waited years for him to come home from jail, and it showed him aggression wasn't what kept a woman in check, especially not her. From day one she put up with his guerrilla-style pimping, and when things went south, she still stayed. Crystal stayed loyal to Preeme instead of using that moment to cut ties like his other two girls did. She loved him, followed her heart, and stuck with him. What she got in return for that kind of loyalty was a better man who came home to her.

Crystal finished making the sandwiches and said to Preeme, "Well, I was thoughtful and shared the last bit of mayo with you. So, we each got mayo on one slice of bread."

"Thanks." Preeme's eyes stayed glued to the television.

"Okay, well, are you going to just sit there or join me, King?" Crystal set their plates and drinks on the counter, then came around with her petite body and seated her plumped butt on one of the stools on the other side of the counter, waiting on him.

Preeme didn't look away from the screen when he answered, "Chrissie, please, just give me a second."

The news anchor spoke over images of police at the crash scene from earlier that morning. "Wild gunfire believed to have ended in a horrific crash happened in the early hours on Dundas Street, causing some road closures while police investigate the scene. We have Tommy now live at the scene." The images switched to the daytime live feed. The crashed car had already been cleared, leaving only yellow tape surrounding an extensive crime scene under investigation.

The reporter, Tommy, stood near the tape with his microphone in hand. "Yes, Nicole. I'm here live on Dundas Street where police believe a shooting in traffic erupted and led to the targeted vehicle crashing into the guardrail on the 427 Northbound ramp. As you can see, police have closed off a significant stretch of road and marked the entire area where shell casings appear to be. Police say it seems to have been a wild car chase, something you'd see in a movie.

"Witnesses say the male and female in the backseat were shot multiple times after the vehicle crashed, along with the male in the passenger seat. All three were pronounced dead at the scene. The driver also suffered gunshot wounds, but paramedics found him with vital signs and rushed him to the nearest hospital. He remains in life-threatening condition and could also be facing charges due to an unregistered firearm found in the vehicle. The suspect was described as being in dark clothing and fleeing in a vehicle."

Preeme was disappointed hearing the driver survived. The thought of him cooperating with police to get the gun charges dropped bothered him. Before he could dwell on it, Tommy continued. "In addition to this horrific scene, a driver traveling in the opposite direction at the time of the shooting was struck in the head and crashed into a light pole. Police do not believe the young man had any involvement and say he was an innocent victim of stray bullets."

Preeme mentally tuned out, remembering the car in the other lane that crashed into the light pole while he was shooting at the twins. Guilt hit him hard. It could only have been his bullet that got him. Preeme wasn't about to grieve over an honest accident, not now, not when a police officer came on-screen with information he had to hear. "We've received information that the twenty-three-year-old woman found in the backseat of the Chevy hatchback was an exotic dancer at the nearby gentlemen's club. She had left work with her boyfriend, known for picking her up, and that's when they were targeted by a suspect who'd been waiting in the parking lot. We're interested in a dark-coloured Volkswagen sedan. If anyone has any information, please contact Peel police immediately."

"King," Crystal said from the dining counter, watching him. "Are you going to be okay?"

Preeme nodded. "Yeah, I'm good." As long as the rental owner didn't see the news, connect the dots, and switch up on him.

"Umm…" Crystal hesitated, picking her words. "You think we should go away to a cottage or something for a bit? A nice little getaway for just the two of us?"

Preeme smiled. "Yeah, I like that idea." He got up, went to her at the counter, kissed her forehead, then sat on the stool beside her. "Have everything set so we can leave before the evening."

"Okay. I'll book something that includes dirt bikes and the fun stuff you like," she said. "But let's eat first."

Preeme nodded and reached for the sandwich in front of him. He took a bite and chewed with a small smile, appreciating the turkey sandwich made by the woman he loved and trusted most. Crystal was a real one.

CHAPTER FORTY-ONE

◆

Wednesday, July 18

I caught the news about Marvel and Maria a couple days ago, and the dots started connecting on their own. Preeme's phone being off made it worse, because now I didn't even know if he was okay. On top of that, Diamond was supposed to be back from Paris on Monday, and I hadn't heard a word. I rang her off and sent countless texts all day, but nothing landed, and my worry kept climbing. I drove out to her condo in Mississauga, and the front door being unlocked hit me wrong right away. The place looked normal until I reached the bedroom. Diamond wasn't in her bed the way I'd been praying she would be—knocked out after a long flight. Her keys were on the dresser. Her Icy pendant-chain was there too. A million thoughts came at once, but I forced myself to grab onto the one that didn't crush me. Maybe she was still with Eric. Maybe she hadn't even brought her keys and pendant to Paris, and everything was fine. I held onto that hope even with worry chewing through me.

I wasn't about to lean on Designer-D to deal with it, so I went straight to Sierra's place and waited for her to get home from work. Vanilla and Chocolate helped keep my mind busy until she walked in. When Sierra got home, I laid it all out, and we ran through every possibility we could think of. We agreed to give it until the next day. The next day came and Diamond was still a ghost, so we pulled up the public flights from Paris that landed in Toronto on Monday. None of them matched the times Diamond told me, and every one of those flights showed up without delays. She should've been back. Then the texts stopped delivering. Calls started going to a line that wasn't in service. After that, we realized we were blocked on all her social media. That was the confirmation I didn't want. Diamond left me for Eric. It took a bite out of my heart, my pride, and my pimping. Sierra stayed beside me through the whole day and night, keeping me grounded so I didn't run to drugs to numb it.

Today was a new day, and Sierra was booked with a client all day again, which meant I had to stay strong on my own. I kept replaying the bond Diamond and I built over the two years she'd been on my team, and the more I thought about it, the more betrayed I felt. Once I'd sobered up from that birthday night, the heroin kept nagging at me. She had pushed it on me when I wasn't in the right state of mind, and I let it happen. I never confronted her after, either. She had been lying, acting like it was something she only tried once, but it was obvious she was doing it regularly. I told myself I was focused on building a better bond with her and avoided laying down discipline, especially over something I had already accepted and done with her.

The week before Paris, I even went out of my way to tighten our connection. I used to go long stretches without seeing her, so I made it a point to spend time with her after her birthday, then did it two more times before her trip. Those two other nights I spent with Diamond turned into the same kind of turn-up I knew I should've stayed away from. The psychosis came back, and both times I caught myself asking for more heroin. Diamond always had it right there at her place, like it was nothing. It was part of her routine. And in my intoxicated state, I let myself get pulled deeper into it, letting her lead me through it, chasing a buzz I knew I'd never forget.

All day, I'd been thinking too much and drinking too hard, and the alcohol wasn't doing shit to keep my mind off it. I called for a Designer-D drop. I hadn't bought from Preeme since my first psychosis incident, because he vowed he wouldn't sell to me again unless I could prove it was for the girls to use at work. After that embarrassing episode, I wasn't about to ask him anyway. Chico was a dealer another pimp in the game referred me to. I'd grabbed from him the nights I turned up with Dianna, and his product hit just as clean as Preeme's. Today, I had Chico bring only a gram to Sierra's place, but he knew I was playing myself with that small order. He told me he'd be in the area if I needed more later. I told myself I'd pace it with self-control and stop before night, before Sierra came back from her trick. I ran through the gram before sunset anyway and called Chico back for a quarter ounce. After that, it turned into a storm of lines off the dining counter all evening. Chocolate and Vanilla stopped caring for my attention once they felt me drift into that zombie state. Designer-D was the only thing that mattered, my escape from the heartbreak Dianna caused.

Sierra would be done with her trick by midnight, and the clock read 11:11 p.m., giving me about an hour to straighten myself out. She'd been texting me all day to make sure I was holding up strong, and now she was gonna come home to catch me high on Designer-D. The fear of getting caught is what set it off. Psychosis crept in, paranoia right behind it. Sierra was with a trick, *what if she fell for him and left me too? What was I without my bitches, without Sierra?* One thought stacked on another until I was deep in my feelings, feeling like a weak man. Over the past month, I'd lost myself as the great pimp, Gelato Icy. Without a bitch, I was nothing. I had to fix up fast and not let Sierra catch me in this state, because whatever respect she had left would be gone the moment she saw me tripping out on Designer-D again. Slipping out before she got back started sounding like the smartest move. I just needed something to balance this bad trip.

I wasn't in a state to drive, so I left my Range Rover parked at Sierra's condo and walked to my own, only ten minutes away. On the way, I called Chico to see if he was still in the area, and asked if he also sold down. He did. Then I asked if he knew where I could get a syringe, and he said he could provide that too. Less than five minutes later, he met me at my condo's lobby. Paranoia made it awkward, doing the transaction in his car before I went upstairs. A few coke lines off the dining counter came first, then I stripped down to my boxer briefs and sat on the couch. City lights from the Gardiner Expressway beamed through one side of the living room's glass wall, while the other side sat darker, facing the lake's wilderness. In that moment, the dark side felt like it matched me. The pimp Gods had betrayed me. Diamond was gone, and it happened at the exact time I needed my precious jewels the most. *How was I supposed to shine again as big Gelato Icy?*

Dianna was a shady bitch all along and I should've seen it coming. How did I not see through those clear crystals—fugazi—posing like a gem in the comfort of luxury. The only thing she ever looked forward to was turning up with me. She never cared about any future I had lined up for us, or for her. Dianna worked for me, got taken care of, asked no questions, and stayed hungry for the next turn up. She played her role for the comfortable life, and I was a fool for not seeing she'd eventually leave me for a trick who offered an even softer landing.

Sierra was the last girl I had left. She might've been more to me than a bitch in my stable, but I was scared her love would fade too. I could feel her respect slipping after all the bullshit she'd witnessed this past month. Maybe she already didn't love me anymore, just riding the comfort while waiting for the right trick to scoop her up. Or worse, maybe she'd find a new pimp to choose up to and ghost me. Psychosis kept feeding me those ugly thoughts, then texts came in from Sierra saying, *{I'm done,} {About to make my way home,} {You okay?}*

That shot my anxiety through the roof. I couldn't even answer her, not after I'd left her place on purpose so she wouldn't catch me high on Designer-D. If Sierra saw me like this again, it would stamp me as weak. Or maybe she already knew I'd crumbled, been secretly turning up with Dianna, and she'd been moving around behind my back anyway. Then the thought of Sierra not being with a trick all day hit me like a punch. My mind kept insisting she'd been with a new man, and my heart started racing. I was tripping and tried to check the thoughts, but they felt too real. I tossed my phone onto the couch so I wouldn't reply with some crazy accusation. I knew what I needed, and I needed it now. Paranoia had me thinking the lights from nearby condos were people filming me through the windows for some humiliation online, so I closed every blind. Then I moved through my place looking for a spoon and a lighter.

Back on the couch, I laid everything out on the centre table for my heroin procedure. I'd watched Dianna do it enough times, and she'd taught me the last time, so I knew the steps. Powder onto the spoon, heat until it turned liquid, let it cool, draw it into the syringe. My forearm veins were already thick, but I still tapped the spot the way I was taught. The needle went in, then the liquid followed. And there it was. The feeling my body and mind needed. *Everything wrong just feels so right.*

CHAPTER FORTY-TWO

Sierra made her way home from a client with a handbag full of cash. She had no plans to strut through the strip club in heels tonight. She wanted to get back to Gelato and spend real time together because it was officially just the two of them. It was understandable that he was feeling down after losing Dianna, but Sierra needed him to be the strong man she'd fallen head over heels for when they first met. At least now, with the other girls out of the picture there'd be nobody around to tempt him into turning up. Sierra felt more at ease knowing she wouldn't have to worry about Gelato finding reasons to do cocaine when she wasn't around, and it'd be easier to shape him into the man she wanted beside her. She just had to do her part, earn more, and keep building their savings and investments. Eventually, she'd get out of the game and build a nuclear family with Gelato, finally living the dream she'd held onto for years.

Gelato hadn't been responding to Sierra's texts or calls, so she assumed he'd fallen asleep. The drive from her client's place downtown took only fifteen minutes, and she now pulled into her lakefront condo. The building's garage door opened as she approached, sensing the key in her bag, and she descended into the underground parking. The first level was visitor parking, where Gelato's silver Range Rover sat in the same spot she'd seen earlier. Sierra drove deeper underground to her assigned space on P4, parked, and headed inside to catch the elevator. In a black Christian Dior tracksuit, running shoes, and her handbag, she stepped off on her floor and walked toward her unit. Chocolate and Vanilla were already shuffling behind the door. Sierra opened it carefully so she wouldn't bump into the furballs, and they were right there to greet her. She crouched to give them a little affection, then straightened up, expecting to see Gelato knocked out on the couch. He wasn't there.

The bedroom and washroom were empty, with Gelato nowhere to be found. Sierra dropped her bag in the bedroom and went back to the living room with her phone in hand. She stopped at the dining counter and called him again. It rang out with no answer, and she slapped her palm against the countertop in frustration. The surface didn't feel smooth the way it should've. Something gritty was on it. Sierra looked at her hand. White powder. She brought her fingers closer and caught the smell right away. Cocaine. She hadn't done coke at her place in forever, and she wiped those counters down every day, so it didn't make sense for any of it to be there. The only suspect was Gelato. Anger flared, but the bigger issue was finding him. She fired off text after text, demanding to know where he was, telling him she knew he was high. There was no point hiding. His cover was blown. Minutes passed with no reply. Sierra's temper kept climbing, and she needed him in front of her. She sat on the couch, mind racing through where he could've gone. His Range Rover was still parked downstairs, which meant he hadn't driven. That pointed to a friend, most likely Smooth, picking him up the way they always did when he was on coke. Sierra made the call.

"What it do, Mama?" Smooth answered.

"Hey," she got right to it, "is Gelato with you?"

"Nah. Why? What's up?"

"I'm looking for him."

"Oh." The random call clicked for Smooth. "He's not with me. Ain't seen Playa all day. But don't stress it, Ma', he prob' out there mackin' on a hoe, like he should."

"I highly doubt it." Sierra sighed. "He's out there high on Designer, again."

Smooth chuckled. "Sheit. So you thought he'd be with me?"

"Yup."

"C'mon, you know I wouldn't want him on that stuff either. Not after how he tripped out on me last time."

"I hope not," Sierra said. "Anyways, let me know if you find him."

"Fo'sho, Ma'. Peace-out."

Sierra then tried reaching Preeme, only to find his number out of service. It hit her that he might be laying low after the news about the shooting. Calling Crystal to reach him wouldn't do any good. Maybe Whitey had come into the city and Sierra didn't know, so she called him too. Whitey was still in Alberta, and besides getting updated on important news, he was out of the loop. He had no idea where Gelato could be.

Sierra needed to know where Gelato was. If he wasn't with his close friends, she couldn't think of who he'd be around when he was high and socially awkward. Chocolate and Vanilla sensed her frustration and climbed onto the couch with her, mostly cuddling each other while she sat there thinking. Gelato's Range Rover was still parked downstairs. Maybe he'd gone somewhere on foot, which meant he couldn't be too far. He did have other friends in the area that Sierra didn't know well, so maybe he walked to someone's place because he was too high to get behind the wheel. Then again, Gelato never wanted to be around people when he was so high he couldn't function. Her thoughts kept turning until one idea landed hard. He couldn't drive, and his high had to be bad enough that he couldn't even handle being around Chocolate and Vanilla. A light bulb went off. Sierra got to her feet and grabbed her small purse and keys.

From Sierra's building it took no longer than two minutes to drive over to Gelato's. She did not bother with parking and left her Benz by the lobby's front. If he were home, Sierra had no intentions of staying long. She only wanted to confront him about being high on coke. The elevator ride felt like forever, but every ding brought her closer to the twenty-fifth floor, where she expected to find Gelato high as a kite in his suite. The doors opened and Sierra marched out, already rounding the bend toward his door when the elevator behind her announced, *"Twenty-fifth floor."* She reached into her purse for the spare key he'd given her not too long ago. Tonight she would exercise her right to enter his home unannounced. Sierra opened the door and stormed in, the heavy door slamming shut behind her, the sound loud enough to alert him wherever he was. She stormed down the entry hall, passed the den and washroom, then stopped at the end of the hall where the open-concept kitchen and living room sat behind glass walls. Gelato was there, passed out on the couch. Relief hit first, then anger all over again when she spotted the small pile of cocaine on the edge of the dining counter. It reminded her why she came. Failure. Liar. Cocaine addict. She moved closer to the couch, ready to disturb whatever rest he'd managed after partying on an upper like coke. Then her eyes caught the centre table. A spoon. A lighter. A syringe that looked used. Sierra's throat tightened. Tears welled as she noticed a small baggie with brownish content. It couldn't be MDMA. Nobody injected that. It had to be something that dropped you, something that put him down instead of up. The tears slid free as she sank onto the sofa, overwhelmed by what she was seeing. Gelato had dozed off after injecting heroin.

Gelato's cocaine addiction was one thing, but heroin was beyond Sierra's understanding. It tore at her that he'd fallen deeper down the hole, from coke to becoming a heroin junkie. Not only was he still using behind her back, he'd picked up new habits. Sierra sat there in tears, staring at him asleep on the couch. Every urge to confront him disappeared. A cold disconnection settled in as she looked at the man in front of her, and she wanted nothing to do with him. Not right now. Sierra got to her feet and stumbled away from the living room, sobbing. By the time she reached the front door, tears were streaming from the depths of her heart. She'd walked into something her heart, mind, and spirit couldn't bear. Now she couldn't stop wondering if the man on that couch was the same man she'd fallen in love with. It couldn't have been Angelo "Gelato Icy" Russo, the strong man who came into her life like a gift from the universe on her birthday, dozing off on the couch from heroin.

Love don't live here anymore...

GHAD

CHAPTER FORTY-THREE

Monday, January 7, 2019 – 1:12 p.m.

Snow covered the unpaved parts of Toronto in the chilly winter weather. Preeme and Smooth stood on the rocks by the lake, smoking a blunt and drinking straight from a Courvoisier bottle. Preeme wore a Moncler jacket, zipped down to expose the gold chain carrying his newest pendant of Mayor Rob Ford's fat face, glistening with diamonds. He wore fitted Balmain jeans cuffed at the ankles, tucked into Gucci high-tops designed like boots. Smooth was in a thick mink vest over a Versace turtleneck, wearing a diamond chain that needed no pendant. His signature medallion sat on his wrist, with Christian Dior jeans and Buscemi boots. They were supposed to be celebrating Gelato's birthday. Instead, they stood on snow-covered rocks, smoking and drinking, on FaceTime with Whitey.

Before they came to the lake, they'd gone by Gelato's condo and knocked for minutes with no answer. That part didn't surprise them. They hadn't seen or heard from him in months. When Sierra officially told them about Gelato's heroin habit six months ago, Smooth and Preeme took it on themselves to help however they could. It started with them and Sierra putting together a major intervention with professional therapists, which led to Gelato having to attend rehab programs. None of it stopped him from using. Sierra eventually wiped her hands with him, and it was left to Preeme and Smooth to carry it. Gelato got put on methadone and it became their responsibility to make sure he stayed clear of drugs. That didn't last either. Gelato started avoiding them at all costs. He drifted until he couldn't be found at his condo. He was never home, or he wouldn't answer the door when he heard them knocking. With Sierra no longer in the picture and without a spare key to his place, she couldn't help them keep up with him. The only signs that he was still alive, other than his phone staying active, were the occasional replies to their casual texts checking on him.

Gelato had replied to Preeme's text just the other day. When Preeme asked to see him on his birthday, Gelato agreed. Now it was the same old story. He wasn't answering texts after saying he'd meet Preeme and Smooth at his place that afternoon. It was a stunt he pulled every time they tried to reconnect. They'd hoped this time would be different because it was a new year, and they wanted new results. Gelato's birthday was never small either. He'd always celebrated it big through the years they'd known him. Now he wasn't even the man they remembered. None of them would've thought drugs would be the downfall of a strong pimp in Toronto.

"So what's the plan now?" Whitey asked from the phone screen Smooth held up.

"I don't know," Preeme said, puffing on the blunt. "You think we should circle back to his crib, see if he came home?"

"Man, I don't see no point in that. If he wanted to hang with us today, he would've at least texted back,"

Smooth said, then took a swig from the bottle in his other hand.

"Yeah, that's true," Whitey agreed. "Can't force him to link up on his birthday. The man been M-I-A for months, not caring to link up with any of us. We'd be lying to ourselves if we thought he cared to see us today."

"Straight facts, playa," Smooth said. "We gon' finish up here, then I'ma go do my thang."

With nothing else to say, Smooth and Preeme ended the call with Whitey. Silence sat between them by the lake.

"You think big homie ever gon' come back around?" Preeme asked.

"Nah. I think the boy wrapped up with the game. We gotta stay focused on what we still got going on and stop looking back. Gelato been history, playa. Today just made it official."

A long pull on the blunt bought Preeme a moment. He held the smoke, then exhaled slow. "Nah, bruh. That's still big homie to me, even if he fell off and turned into a full-out dizzy head. I'ma be there if he ever needs me." He took another pull, passed the blunt to Smooth, then started walking off. "I'm off this, man. I'ma holla at you later."

"Yeah, fo'sho," Smooth said. He knew Preeme had too much love for Gelato to accept what it had come to. Smooth wasn't about to waste breath telling him to move on. Smooth took a slow drag of the remaining blunt.

Sierra cruised in her Benz coupe after meeting with a client, and she could not shake the thought of Gelato on his birthday. It was only him on her mind, not the depression or breakdowns she went through months ago. After they officially called it quits, Gelato took back the spare key to his condo, wanting privacy to do whatever he pleased. She knew the real reason, though. He realized she'd taken sixty thousand from the safe, almost half of what was in there. Their breakup ended ugly. Sierra never gave back the money she took, and Gelato answered by violently ripping the Icy chain off her neck, then beating her. Sierra took time to heal physically, and emotionally she had no regrets about leaving him the way she did. Life was better for her now. She stayed in the game without Gelato and started prospering in the ways she used to dream about.

And yet Sierra hadn't left Gelato for dead. When it was all said and done, she told herself she was still making good money while Gelato had no real source of income, because pimping was all he knew. She made sure to e-transfer him just enough to cover his bills, and only that. The least she could do was keep a roof over his head. Anything beyond that was not her problem, and it probably meant whatever was left in Gelato's safe would get burned on his habit.

Sierra knew she had been the prize in Gelato's stable, and this was her time to excel on her own. But the game got lonely after being used to having a man for so long, so she eventually found herself another strong pimp to work with. He was better, kept a good head on his shoulders, and Sierra didn't have to look far to find him.

CHAPTER FORTY-FOUR

Gelato had her bent over the bed and pounded from behind. He might not have been the same 250-pound brute he used to be, but he still knew how to lay it strong. This woman was a bit on the obese side and much older than he preferred, but she deserved what she came for. At the end of the day, Gelato was still getting paid by women. Just on the flip side of the game. He didn't have the luxury of choosing only premium anymore. She was a 52-year-old cougar who might've been considered premium in her time, at least to the rich husband who married her and then stopped making time for her. Now Gelato was her go-to whenever she needed good sex. He enjoyed it too, even if there was a stale odor that stayed on her and bothered him. Making her wash up first didn't change it. Her money was good, and he wasn't turning her down when she called. All he had to do was get her to climax while pushing past the smell, and once he got himself into it he'd finish not long after. The session didn't run longer than fifteen minutes, and that was $150 for his protected services.

Gelato took a quick shower when the client left, then went straight to his work phone to check missed calls and texts from other clients. He answered a few messages and made a mental note to get back to a client trying to book a date next week. His main phone lit up too, and when he grabbed it off the dresser, he saw missed calls and texts from Preeme. Today was Gelato's birthday, and he was supposed to meet Preeme and Smooth at his place. Instead, he worked through the day even though he'd agreed to see them. He didn't want to see them. Gelato had other plans.

It'd been a long time since he'd been around any of his old friends. Things weren't the same after they found out about his heroin addiction. They meant well, all the rehab talk, all the help, all the attention, but Gelato just wanted to be left alone. His life had fallen apart, and in his heart he knew they'd never look at him the same after he became such a fuck up. He didn't feel the need to chase their acceptance anymore. As his values and priorities shifted, he started relating more to people he met through rehab. He made new friends while keeping distance from the old ones. Sometimes the new friends would be at his condo, and everybody would go quiet to act like nobody was home when Preeme and them came knocking. That game got annoying, so Gelato started staying at the homes of his new friends down in the ghetto parts of Lakeshore. That was how he got used to life in the slums again, the same kind of familiar he came from as a kid.

His taste for luxury died right alongside his love for Sierra. She left him and took a good portion of the money from the safe, leaving him with a little over sixty grand. It only took a few months for Gelato to burn through most of it, having fun with his new friends. With the home he had, the clothes he wore, and the cars he drove, he was the rich one among his addict friends, so everything stayed on his tab. He hosted the wildest parties all summer. They always spiraled into sex, drugs, and alcohol with friends who praised him, until things got shaky in November when he was down to his last five thousand.

He went from the name brand pimp everybody knew, to just another heroin-addicted John, without even seeing what his life had turned into. The only thing that mattered was getting high. He couldn't keep up with the Bentley payments, so it got taken. The Range Rover stayed—paid in full from the day he bought it. Sometimes he thought about selling it for a cheap car, just to free up cash and cut the insurance. That huge Icy chain was the first thing he sold when money got tight in November, along with the two smaller ones that belonged to Diamond and Skye. That money went straight into his addictions while he tried to figure out other ways to keep himself going.

It was one of Gelato's new friends that suggested he become a male escort. It made sense. A good-looking man with Black heritage could put himself on the market. He ended up doing better than the Slavic friend who introduced him to it. Gelato might not have been as muscular as he once was, but at 6'2", biracial, and covered in tattoos, he was a boy toy for women looking to play. He marketed himself as high-end, even if it didn't hit the way it used to for the girls he'd managed. Male escorts weren't in demand like women were. The other truth was uglier. Gelato wasn't the upscale provider he told himself he was, not when he was only doing it to feed a heroin habit. What kept him afloat was his looks, and even that was fading under the weight of constant drugs. Protected full services were his standard, and he'd bend the rules for clients he felt comfortable with, especially when the money was right. He found clients through classified sites and worked agencies when independent business slowed down. None of his old friends knew he'd stepped into the male side of the sex trade. That world was foreign to them, and Gelato kept it that way. He lived a new life in silence. With Sierra covering the bills, he only worked a couple days a week for personal money. Getting high with his friends mattered more than anything else. Sex, once something he chased, had turned into a routine income source. Heroin ran his days, his nights, his only desire, his only need.

Gelato sat naked on the hotel bed in Mississauga, getting ready to call his next client. She was a regular who paid well and liked to party too, which kept their bond close. Only a few people knew it was his birthday, and she was one of them. She'd be the only one seeing him tonight. But first, he needed a line to keep his wave going. He went into the washroom and did a few off the sink counter. After months of using heroin at least three times a day, cocaine didn't hit him the way it used to. It was like the heroin kept his system regulated, balancing him out and keeping the psychosis away. After the lines, he was about to leave the washroom and grab his phone, but he paused when he caught his reflection in the mirror. He couldn't help staring at himself, naked, under that harsh light. The Greek gods inked across his chest didn't radiate the same power on a frame that had thinned out. The sleeve of women and creatures on his arms didn't look as commanding without the bulk they once wrapped around. Gelato was down to about a hundred and seventy, coming from two-fifty. The full beard didn't suit his sharper face, and he looked older than he was.

Gelato turned thirty-four today. He wasn't the same man he'd been a year ago. Better or worse didn't matter to him because he didn't sit with the past anymore. Only a few things mattered now, and those things felt under control. Life was going fine. He watched himself a moment longer, then smiled at the birthday boy in the mirror. The coke had him feeling alive.

His primary phone rang and snapped him out of it. Barbie's name lit the screen. He answered right away.

A strained woman's voice came through. "Hey, hon. You forgot about me today?"

"Nah," Gelato said. "I was just about to call you."

"Okay. So we still on for tonight?"

"Yeah, of course. I'm just about to call my guy for some dizzy."

"Okay, get whatever amount you think we could handle for tonight. You know I got it, babe."

"Yeah, I know."

"Okay. See you soon, hon." She paused, then added, "Oh, and happy B-day, my sexy caramel-man."

"Thank you, babe. See you soon."

He ended the call, then rang Chico to order heroin and more coke. Tonight with Barbie was going to get crazy.

When Smooth left the lakeside, he went to a condo in Liberty Village where the new girl was staying. She wasn't exactly new because she'd been in the game for years, but she'd only been in his stable for a couple months. Smooth went up to the unit, and of course he had keys to enter, as a pimp should to the home of his girls. He let himself in and got greeted by the French bulldog—Chocolate. The little guy was always excited to see him, unlike the serval cat on the couch with an attitude. Vanilla knew who Smooth was from back when he used to come around as Gelato's friend. She was the smarter one of the two pets, the one who sensed the foulness and refused to accept it, even after several months. Smooth kicked off his Buscemi boots, hung his fur vest in the closet, then took a seat on the other end of the sectional, far from the crazy exotic cat staring him down. That piercing gaze always had him uneasy when he had to wait in the condo alone for Sierra, but at least Chocolate would hop up beside him and take his mind off the tension. Whether Vanilla liked it or not, Smooth was the new alpha male in their home. The new home Smooth moved them into.

When everything went downhill, Smooth couldn't resist reaching out to Sierra, knowing she was on her own now. She was smart enough to manage herself and didn't need support to carry on in the game. What she needed was an effective alpha male figure, someone a real bitch in the game could rely on, and Smooth understood that. He made sure he stayed available, an option if she ever felt like choosing up to another pimp. Being there as family, the way he'd always been for her and Gelato, was his way in. From there, he flexed how resourceful he could be, and she naturally started coming to him for advice, help, and sometimes comfort when loneliness hit. Sierra respected that Smooth had financial stability and handled money smarter than Gelato did. That made it easier for Smooth to eventually bring her into his stable. Sexy, focused, and experienced, Sierra got titled as another boss-bitch on the team right away, and it worked because she was already friends with Alize and Star. The three girls had solid working relations from strip clubs in the past. It made Sierra's transition into the new stable smoother than Smooth Darken-Caesar would've imagined.

Smooth didn't feel he owed Gelato a pimp's serving because he hadn't taken Sierra from him. She'd already left Gelato and was technically free for the taking. Besides, Gelato showed no signs of caring about anything except getting fixed on drugs. If Gelato's mentality wasn't in the game, Smooth couldn't be bothered respecting him with a pimp's serving. But embedded in the truth was that Smooth still felt wrong, and disloyal to the bro-code, for going after the woman who once belonged to the man he grew up with. He knew Gelato would be hurt if he ever found out. Moments like Vanilla staring into his soul stirred that guilt up. Even so, Smooth told himself it was better Sierra got with him than somebody else. The fact was, if Sierra had chosen up to another pimp, that man wouldn't have given two shits about Gelato, and he would've cut off the money she was sending him.

Chocolate jumped off the couch to greet whoever came through the front door with keys. After removing her Louis Vuitton boots and hanging her long coat, Sierra greeted Chocolate with hugs and kisses. She expected Vanilla to greet her too, then spotted Smooth on the couch and understood why Vanilla wasn't in the mood.

Sierra dropped her bag on the kitchen counter on her way into the living room, kissed Smooth on the lips, then rubbed Vanilla's head. "You gotta stop being so sour when Poppa comes over."

Vanilla's demeanour didn't change.

Smooth chuckled. "I doubt she gon' ever like me."

"Then that's gonna be her problem to live with," Sierra said, and she meant it. Sierra couldn't have been happier with her situation. After choosing to partner with Smooth, her life in the game took a turn for the better. Smooth respected the work she'd put in for years with Gelato and honored her loyalty to the game, acknowledging she deserved a lot. His immediate focus was to get her situated properly, as a boss-bitch should be, so most of the money Sierra brought in got invested right back into her.

Sierra owned the condo she lived in now. Property was all she could've ever asked for after so many years feeling wasted. She finally felt a real sense of achievement, and this was the benefit of being with a pimp who had his priorities straight. Smooth might not have been her physical ideal, but she respected his leadership and the alpha male business model he brought to the stable. He deserved to be paid by his women because even when he indulged, he still made ample money through other channels to reinvest in the family, making sure each of his girls got what they deserved. Whether Sierra genuinely loved Smooth or not, she for sure loved being his bitch.

"Have you eaten, Poppa?" Sierra asked Smooth.

"Nah. Was waiting on you."

"What do you want to eat? I'll cook before I jump in the shower."

"Not hungry for cooked food." Smooth bit down on his bottom lip. "Shower now so I can eat you up in the bedroom."

Blonde Barbie showed up at the hotel room door that evening in a black leather coat and red stiletto boots. Gelato answered in a robe with a sleepy grin. One look at him told Barbie he'd spent the time waiting on her getting high and down. The birthday boy's eyes were glossy red and his movements were slow, but the excitement still came through. Her nose job, lip fillers, and Botox sharpened her European beauty. She slipped off her leather coat to reveal a tight red leather dress that hugged her surgically enhanced body. Standing at 5'9", she carried herself with a sassy walk, her stilettos clicking across the floor. "Hey, Big Daddy." Her distinctive voice strained for a feminine pitch. "You ready for me?"

Gelato nodded, slurring, "I got lines set in the washroom. The dizz' is in the cabinet, with the needle and everything."

Barbie zipped off her boots and marched into the washroom where the lines waited. Gelato stayed there, mesmerized by her runway walk, the sway of her long blonde hair, and the bounce of her hips. Barbie looked flawless, and he adored every aspect of her. Being her service provider did something for him. The one thing Barbie didn't like about herself was that she hadn't completed transitioning and still had a penis. Barbie was a trans woman.

Straight male escorts weren't in the same demand as women, so staying busy often meant being willing to bend. Gelato started out servicing only women. Still, gay men called him a lot, persistent, offering generous pay for the simplest favors. He kept turning them down. Barbie was the first one to break through. She booked her first visit the way any other woman would and paid only to perform oral on him. She came back a couple more times for the same thing, and Gelato was the one pushing for full service. She refused, saying she needed to know him better first. With that play, and with Barbie being gorgeous, Gelato had no problem spending time with her outside of work. They hung out and found they shared the same taste for drugs.

It was on a comfortable night together, faded on drugs and alcohol with money on the table, when Barbie told Gelato she was a trans woman. He'd been wanting her for a while, and the price she offered made him decide he didn't care. The first time they went all the way, it surprised him how good it felt. Barbie still having a penis didn't disturb him the way he thought it would. Being the one doing the penetrating, he told himself he wasn't violating his manhood. With that mindset, and with him staying faded, Gelato kept providing full service every time they met. Then one night Barbie brought a gay friend for a drug party that escalated into an orgy. Gelato felt he hadn't compromised his masculinity because he never took the bottom role and didn't perform oral during it. He stayed in control, got paid, and after that he opened up to taking male clients too.

Barbie came out of the washroom after snorting a couple lines and approached Gelato, who stood by the bed looking completely zoned out. "You okay, Big Daddy?" she asked.

Gelato smiled and nodded. "You...you wanna do some dizzy too?"

"Yeah, in a bit." Barbie slid the straps of her dress down, baring her full breasts, then pushed Gelato back onto the bed. "I want some hard candy first, Daddy." She leaned in for a deep kiss before parting his robe and guiding her thick lips down his body to find his arousal. And like the pornstar Barbie wanted to be, she took him into her mouth with practiced perfection.

CHAPTER FORTY-FIVE

Monday, January 7 – 11:43 p.m.

Preeme was let down by not seeing Gelato on his birthday, so he had spent the day drinking at Jiggy's place. The drinking didn't give him the closure he wanted, so he made his way to Pro Club strip club in Vaughan for the night. There, he quietly accompanied his love, Crystal, in the ambient world the big homie, Gelato, introduced him to years ago. Music blared while half-naked women in six-inch heels worked the room, hustling clients. It was the exact vibe Preeme needed tonight. He took it in from a barstool, the diamond face of Mayor Rob Ford hanging against his chest, catching the club's glow. Crystal had done her stage show not long ago, and they'd been stealing looks at each other all through it. They never spoke in the club or made obvious gestures that would expose their relationship. She knew he was there for her, and he knew she belonged to him.

At the moment, Crystal was nowhere to be seen because she'd slipped off with a client to the private rooms. That part was normal. What didn't feel right was the presence of a certain individual. A young Black man with braids, wearing a cheap jacket over worn-out jeans and sneakers, had just arrived. His eyes swept the place like he expected to see someone, then slowed when they landed on Preeme at the bar. He took a seat at a side table closest to the entrance and scanned the room again.

Preeme had seen that face before, twice, because it belonged to one of the identical twins.

Now the question was whether the twin recognized Preeme from the murder night and could place him today. The twin sat in clear view while Preeme did his best not to look his way. Still, he kept him in his peripherals, tracking every move. A server approached to take his order, and the twin looked annoyed that he had to buy at least one drink to stay inside. He dug into his pockets and came out with a five-dollar bill and some loose change. The server walked off unimpressed, then returned with a bottle of beer, set it on the table, and left with attitude.

From there, it looked like the twin was enjoying himself watching the girl dance on stage. Preeme's intuition kept warning him it wasn't that simple. It couldn't be a coincidence that the twin showed up at this strip club tonight. He hadn't dressed to impress, and he seemed bothered to spend money on a drink, which only raised more questions about why he was even here. Maybe the cheap look and behaviour really was just who he was. Either way, sticking around to figure him out felt stupid. Preeme needed to get out of this situation before it turned dangerous. He also needed his gun, which was locked in the stash box of his Corvette out front. Security in the foyer patted all guests down, so he couldn't bring it inside. That meant the twin shouldn't have a gun on him either. Then another thought hit, though. *How'd the twin get in with his jacket on when coat check was mandatory?* Preeme left his own jacket in the car because he wasn't paying a pointless fee. If the twin got waved through with a jacket, it raised the possibility he got waved through with more than that. With Preeme's gun hidden in the electrical stash spot, it would take time to grab if he had to rush outside for it. To steady his mind, he landed on the only thing that made sense. Security might've spared him the coat check, but there was no way they'd let anyone in with a weapon. If the twin tried anything, it would have to be hands, and Preeme was more than good with his Nova Scotian ones.

The whole time, Preeme kept the twin in his peripheral vision, and he was damn near sure the twin was doing the same. Crystal came back onto the floor after finishing with a client and glanced at the bar to see Preeme was still there. On the surface he looked calm, watching the stage. Crystal knew him too well to believe that. She went into the changing room and messaged him. *{King, are you okay?}*

Seconds later, Preeme replied, *{Yeah,} {Why?} {What's up?}*

{You look uncomfortable,} {Something on your mind?}

{Nah,} {I'm good babe.} He downplayed it. *{I'm just thinking about the old times with big homie,} {I miss him.}*

{Awww♥ Don't be down on yourself babe. I'm sure he thinks of you too.}

{I hope so,} Preeme replied. *{I'm gonna cut out now though,} {I'll see you at home babe.}*

{Ok♥ I love you.}

{I love you too.}

Preeme finished what was left in his glass and got up, heading for the washroom at the opposite end from the entrance. He wanted to see what the twin would do. If he was really here for him, he might follow him in. Preeme stepped into the washroom and posted at a urinal like he was using it. The twin should've shown any second. Nobody came in except a white guy who went straight into a stall. After washing his hands, Preeme left. Back on the floor, he checked the other end of the club. The twin was still there. Their eyes met. Preeme dropped his gaze to his phone and kept walking, sliding past his spot at the bar, then cutting right by the twin's table on his way out. Rounding into the foyer, he gave the coat check girl and the security guards a quick nod and pushed into the small lobby where the music didn't hit as hard. He was about to step through the front doors when he looked back. The twin was coming out of the foyer behind him.

Preeme pushed through the heavy doors and took off outside.

CHAPTER FORTY-SIX

Monday, January 7, 2019

It was six months ago when Flame woke up in a hospital bed hooked up to an IV, handcuffed to the frame. He'd been lucky to survive the horrific shooting that took the lives of everyone else in the car, and unlucky that police chose to charge him with the gun found inside. It took him two months to recover from the injuries from both the shooting and the crash, most of that time spent in the medical unit of a Toronto jail. After that, he spent the remainder of his time on a general-pop unit while waiting for court to decide on the firearm charge. It wasn't Flame's first time in jail, so he knew how to do his time. He also knew a couple guys in there from the streets, enough to get situated. Four months later, he was out. His lawyer got the charges dropped before trial, helped by the sympathy of him being a victim of a tragic shooting and the fact he'd lost friends and his twin brother. On top of that, the gun was found in the passenger area with his twin, and not on him. Yet, Flame couldn't shake the feeling that the shooter roamed free while he sat in jail, grieving his friends and, most painfully, his twin brother. Within the first week of being a free man, he got his hands on a gun and went hunting for his brother's killer.

People in jail always seemed to know more than investigators ever could. Inmates knew the tale about a dude named Marvel, the one who snatched the infamous

Gelato Icy's girl, which led to payback and one man left taking the fall for the gun in the shot-up car. When Flame landed on the unit, plenty recognized him as the guy who went down for it. Word kept moving. Someone mutual with one of Gelato's associates pointed out the only bold shooter in his circle. The name made its way to Flame—Preeme. The name came with its own stories, the kind that stuck in people's mouths. Flame gathered enough to know Preeme was the type of pimp you'd probably only catch at elite strip clubs. Still, not many people knew what he looked like. Most couldn't have picked him out even if they crossed paths with him. Flame had seen his face that horrific night, so he at least knew what he was hunting.

Only a few clubs in the GTA counted as elite, and Flame checked each one after he got his hands on a gun. Security turned him away every time. They wouldn't let him in without a pat-down, and he had no intention of going inside unarmed.

Pro Club was different. The head security guard there was a family friend. One look was enough. He waved Flame through without a pat-down because he understood Flame was carrying for protection after the shooting and his brother's death. Flame took the pass and made the club his spot, coming back in hopes he'd bump into his shooter someday with the advantage of being armed and dangerous. The staff read it their own way, assuming he kept returning because it was the only place he felt safe.

Tonight was another night. Flame recognized the silver Corvette parked outside the club. Based on what he'd learned in jail, it had to be Preeme's car. He also remembered seeing that same Corvette out front of Midway strip club long ago, when he and Blaze were with Marvel hunting for Maria. Flame parked his Toyota rental two spaces down from the Corvette, then went into Pro Club ready to see Preeme.

Flame stepped into the foyer and greeted the head of security with his usual brotherly hug, then breezed past the other guards and the coat check girl without a word. He entered the ambient glow of the club and paused at the entryway as the music blared. His eyes swept the room and landed on a brown-skinned guy seated with his back to the bar. It had to be Preeme. He looked like the gunman from the Volkswagen, the one responsible for Blaze's death. From that distance, Flame couldn't make out the details of the dazzling pendant on Preeme's chest, but he still found himself staring a second too long. Preeme stared back. Flame broke eye contact and slid into a table near the entrance. It was the perfect seat to watch the stage and keep Preeme in his peripherals. A waiter came over to take Flame's order, and irritation flashed through him. He was sick of wasting money on drinks every night he showed up. He ordered the cheapest beer. Tonight would be the last time he ever bought a drink in this club.

When the waiter returned with Flame's drink, he refused to tip. She walked off frustrated. Flame didn't care. He took small sips and kept his eyes off Preeme, locking in on the stripper on stage. He tried to enjoy the show while turning over the truth in his head. Tonight, he was about to make a move that could bury him for life. He'd never taken a life, but love for his twin had him set on shooting Preeme the moment he saw him. Now that the moment was here, Flame didn't feel rushed. He wanted to do it clean, then disappear. His gaze stayed on the stage as he ran through angles. In his peripheral, Preeme was on his phone. Flame wondered who he was texting, and panic crept in that help might be on the way. A third body would complicate everything. The pressure pushed him toward the gun on his waist, toward doing it right there with witnesses and cameras. Heat climbed under his jacket, sweat starting to form. Flame wanted it over. But his nerve wouldn't break. The chance slipped when Preeme stood and headed for the washroom. Flame thought about following, catching him off guard, then stayed frozen at the table. He drank more beer hoping it'd turn into courage.

Preeme came back out a moment later and their eyes met. Flame held him in his sight, refusing to blink first. Preeme started walking his way, phone still in hand. Flame damn near stopped breathing as he closed the distance, then Preeme walked right past him toward the exit. Flame didn't assume that meant safe. Preeme could be setting a play, luring him outside. Everything Flame had heard said the man was sly, built for war, a real killer. Flame couldn't take him lightly. If he let Preeme slip, he might end up the one getting hunted the second he stepped out. Flame stood and followed. Preeme was just reaching the lobby when Flame came in behind him.

Right before Preeme pushed through the heavy front doors, he looked back and registered Flame trailing.

Flame pushed out right behind him, the gun already off his waist. Outside, Preeme reached for the Corvette's handle, but he didn't make it in. Flame's first two shots caught him high, shoulder and neck. Preeme's hand slipped off the door. His body rocked back into the car, barely staying upright. Pain lit through his throat and he clamped a hand to his neck, trying to hold the blood in. Flame drove two more shots into Preeme's chest and pinned him to the Corvette's side. Preeme's breath broke. Blood sprayed out in a cough. Flame kept firing into his chest as he backed away, steady, cold, making sure there'd be no getting back up.

Then he turned and ran for the rental. He jumped in and peeled out of the lot. The cameras out front caught everything, and Flame knew what that meant. He didn't care. He sped off, eyes cutting to the rear-view, watching Preeme sag down onto the pavement. The Corvette's side was punched with holes and streaked with blood where he'd been standing seconds before. It was all over when security finally came running out of the club. They'd held back for their own safety, not about to rush into active gunfire. They saw him right away. Preeme on the ground beside his Corvette, not moving.

Flame did what grief demanded for his twin, Blaze.

CHAPTER FORTY-SEVEN

Tuesday, January 8 – 11:35 a.m.

Gelato woke to his phone ringing over and over, so he reached for it on the nightstand. The caller wasn't saved, but the number looked familiar. He couldn't place it, which meant it was probably someone he'd deleted a long time ago. Hesitant to answer, he let it ring out with the phone still in his hand. He sat up naked on the hotel bed, staring at the screen and wondering who it was, sure they'd call again.

Barbie lay under the sheets beside him and spoke without lifting her head. "You okay, hon?" Just waking up, her voice was deep and groggy, leaning masculine. "Who keeps calling you?"

"I don't know," Gelato said, and a text came through. He read it in his head, word for word. *{It's Sierra. I been trying to call you all morning,} {Listen, Angelo...I don't know where you are in life right now and if you even care about what I'm reaching out to you about, but your friend Preeme is dead. Got shot at Pro Club last night,} {Just thought you deserve to know.}*

Gelato thought about calling Sierra back right away to ask questions, but he didn't want to hear her voice. He searched Google for news on the shooting instead. An article on CP24's website spoke about a man who'd been gunned down beside his Corvette in front of Pro Club. He'd been rushed to the hospital, but wasn't expected to survive. Gelato, just awake and sober, was struck by the news with a wave of anguish. He normally would've started the day with a hit of drugs to enter his world where nothing mattered. This news hit him before he could escape reality. Gelato was shaking and sweating, showing signs of a breakdown. Barbie asked, assuming he was dealing with withdrawals, "Hon, are you okay?" Gelato didn't respond, so she kept going. "Looks like you need a fix, but we finished everything last night. Maybe call your guy to bring more down." Still, Gelato stayed silent, and Barbie touched his sweaty back. He turned to her with tears streaming down his face, like a lost child.

"Baby, what's wrong?" She reached for his forearm, but Gelato pulled away.

The loss of Preeme weighed heavy on his heart, and the reality of it gnawed at his soul. He'd just lost someone he considered a little brother. Someone who always had his back and truly wanted the best for him. Then he thought about what Preeme would think of his big homie if he could see what Gelato had become. Gelato hadn't even made the effort to see him yesterday for his birthday. That would've meant the world to Preeme. Now he was gone.

"Talk to me, hon." Barbie reached for his hand again. This time he didn't pull away, but he wasn't taking comfort from her either.

"What's going on with you?" Barbie asked. "Talk to me."

"Please, just leave me!" he demanded.

"Are you sure?"

"Get out!" Gelato barked at her.

Barbie got out of bed naked and scrambled around, grabbing her things. She threw on her dress and coat, then turned to Gelato, who stayed seated on the bed, crying. Barbie still had no clue what triggered it. She could tell he needed space, so she decided they could talk another day. She walked over and gave him a flat kiss on the lips. "Call me when you're feeling better. I love you."

Gelato nodded, and she turned away to leave. When the door shut, Gelato stayed seated, crying for minutes, not knowing what to do with himself. Then he made a call.

"What's up, man, you alright?" Chico answered.

Gelato struggled to speak through sobs. "I, I, I need something. ASAP."

"I heard the news, man. I know that cat used to be your people." Chico offered his condolences. "Just try to keep yo' head up."

"Bring me something. ASAP," Gelato repeated.

"You want soft, hard, or dizzy?" Chico asked. "Whatever you want, man, it's on me this time."

"Bring dizzy. Or something even stronger. I, I need something stronger than that, right now."

"Fuck, dawg, I dunno about all that." Chico hesitated. "I mean, I could bring you fentanyl, but I don't think that's a good idea. That shit too strong if you ain't done it before."

"Bring it. Please."

"Okay, I'll bring some dizzy, and just a few points of fetty."

"Bring me a ball of that."

Chico sighed, stressed. "I know you going through it, man, but I don't think you should be fucking with the fetty like that."

"Just fucking bring it!" Gelato barked. Then he begged, "...Please."

"Whatever, man. You still over at the hotel?"

"Yeah. I'm still here."

"Be there in twenty minutes." Chico ended the call.

Gelato sat with his phone still in hand, sobbing. In that moment, he wished he hadn't deleted the few pictures and videos of Preeme he'd had saved. All he had now were the vivid memories in his head.

Smooth was at his huge estate in King City, completed just a month ago. None of his friends knew about it because it was meant to be another property flip in a few years. For now, it was the temporary mansion where he spent family days with his boss-bitches. After a long orgy night with Alize, Star, and Sierra, the women were having brunch in the huge open-concept dining room. Smooth sat alone on the living room couch, stuck on the news. A tear slipped down his face now and then, but he fought not to let the devastation swallow him. It wasn't just about the women seeing him cry, they were sobbing too, but Smooth felt a need to sit in the anger moving through him. He didn't know what, or who, caused Preeme's shooting, but it ate at him that the young homie got murdered while Gelato was out there being a junkie without a care in the world. Smooth and Whitey were the last ones left of their brotherhood, and that thought hit him as Whitey called.

"…Hello," Smooth answered, voice shaky.

"Brother…I'm guessing you already got the news," Whitey said. "Remember, I'm two hours behind over here, so I'm kinda late. Chanel seen everybody reposting on Instagram about the shooting at Pro Club, so she called Crystal, and that's how we got the word on Preeme." Whitey's words broke into sobs. "I'm praying, man…I'm praying for our brother."

"He on life support. I'd be lying if I said I believe he gon' pull through. Son was basically dead on the scene. We lucky they even got a sign of life back into him."

"Crystal saying we just need to pray…I don't think she'll ever let them pull that plug."

"Word," Smooth agreed. "But that don't be helping the situation. I know the young playa tough, but I'm sure he'd rather be set free than lay there a vegetable."

"Fuck…This shit's deep, bro."

"I know…"

"I'ma go smoke a dub…I'ma get back to you later, bro. Be easy." Whitey ended the call.

Smooth looked over at the women in the dining room. The whole house felt heavy with sorrow. Responsibility sat on his shoulders, and pressure came with it. He already had Sierra reach out to Gelato with the news, hoping the junkie would care about losing his little homie. Nothing came from that. It felt like there was nothing else Smooth could do for his brothers, all of them falling off in their own way. He raised his voice toward the dining room. "Anyone spoke to Crystal yet?" They shook their heads, and Smooth said, "Someone give her a call. Let's see how she holding up."

CHAPTER FORTY-EIGHT

When Chico dropped off the care package, he told Gelato, "Keep your head up." Gelato did just that with coke lines, then heroin injections to bring himself back down. At the rate he was going, his heart was getting overworked, but he couldn't care less because it already felt torn open by the news about Preeme. Seated on the hotel bed in his robe, Gelato rode a roller coaster of emotions, replaying his life with Preeme. The good times had him smiling through tears, but the bad came back too, the days his empire started falling apart. He cried for himself. Not only did he lose Preeme today, he'd lost himself a long time ago. The drugs weren't helping him escape reality the way they normally would. He couldn't shake the thought that he'd become a real junkie over the past six months. And other than right now, he never stopped to process the raw truth. He stayed clouded on purpose to avoid that shameful awakening. Today it was harder to wash everything away, because that would mean washing away Preeme too, and he just couldn't accept that, no matter how much coke and heroin he used.

Gelato remembered when he first met Preeme, a sixteen-year-old thug working at a pizza shop under a probation order. Gelato was twenty-one at the time, in his prime pimping, and he was a regular who'd show up right before closing. Young Preeme was always fascinated when the bigshot walked in with designer clothes, fancy jewellery, and tattoos. After regularly seeing and acknowledging each other at the shop, the kid finally gathered the courage to ask Gelato for a ride home one night. Gelato liked the kid's energy, so he was more than glad to take him for a drive. That ride home marked the beginning of their bond, and Gelato would spend days hanging out with Preeme like a big brother. Not long after that, Preeme ended up doing time for a shooting in broad daylight downtown. He pleaded guilty as a young offender and got locked away for a full year. Gelato made sure the kid's canteen stayed full, and he even kept up a phone line that forwarded to Preeme's girlfriend at the time. When Preeme got released, his unpredictable mother refused to let him live at home any longer. Gelato took the kid under his wing like family, and young Preeme grew up following in Gelato's pimp footsteps, eventually solidifying his own name in the game.

Gelato had been doing well for himself in those years. He'd basically molded Preeme into the successful man he became in the game. That thought dragged Gelato back to the glory days, the cars, the women, the fashion, and the beautiful pets, Chocolate and Vanilla. There was no denying it was a wonderful life. Now he could only cry about it after losing it all.

Bringing Maria into his family was what tipped the scale to Gelato's demise. He should've taken Sierra's advice and focused on the solid women he already had by his side. In the end, Gelato was doing what a pimp does, recruiting new girls into his stable like he always had. What followed Maria's arrival was beyond anything he could've predicted or controlled. Vanessa suffered because of it, and no matter how anyone viewed the situation, Gelato was to blame. Bringing Maria into the stable, then sending her out of town to work with Vanessa, was his call alone. It wasn't losing Vanessa that ate at him most. It was failing to keep her safe and protected while she was in the game for him. There was nothing he could do to make it right, not after what she'd experienced.

Losing Dianna was the icing on the cake. Not only had she fooled him into trying a new drug that ultimately took over his entire life, but she'd also left him for a man who was considered a trick and nothing more. Gelato felt like it happened because he'd lost his pimp strength down the line, leaving him feeling less like a man after Marvel's interference in his stable. Truth was, he'd never been the strong figure he pretended to be. Beneath the surface, he was weak when it came to drugs, and that weakness led him down the heroin path. Every flaw in him and every addiction dragged his glory down. It cost him the one girl he truly loved. Only God knew where Sierra was in life now.

Gelato leaned on the nightstand with a rolled bill, ready to do a line, but tears dripped onto the coke and dissolved it. He didn't even bother setting new lines. He snorted straight from the pile, taking in more than his nose could handle. A mess, he stayed on the bed with his head in his hands for a long moment, crying and reflecting on his life, the things he should've faced months ago, before ending up where he was today. This wasn't how his mafia-tied father would've expected his son's life to turn out. His mother had always thought highly of her only son, even knowing he was a pimp. If they could see him now, it'd be a disgrace to the Russo name. Preeme wouldn't be impressed with the big homie, either. Regret tightening in his chest, Gelato grabbed his phone off the bed and texted the same number that had sent him the breaking news about Preeme.

{I'm sorry about everything. I really wanted to be a real man for you, but I failed,} {But that's in the past…I'm moving forward and just want to say I'll always love you.}

Gelato's tears streaked the phone screen as he hit send. He was about to set it down when he thought of someone else who deserved a text. No matter how messed up everything had become, one good thing had come out of this new life, and he had to acknowledge her. Gelato texted Barbie, *{You've been amazing to me, and I'm glad we met.} {I love you forever.}*

Gelato threw the phone onto the bed and reached for the bag of fentanyl, his hands steady despite the weight sitting in his chest. He unravelled the Saran wrap and broke off a piece from the marble-sized purple clump, setting it onto the spoon he'd been using for heroin before lighting it. The fentanyl melted slowly, spreading until the spoon could no longer hold it and the liquid spilled over the edges. A small iceberg remained at the centre of the pool when he stopped heating it. Gelato drew all the liquid fentanyl into the syringe, then set the spoon with the remaining solid on the nightstand. He tapped his forearms once before unloading the fentanyl into his bloodstream.

Within seconds, the most intense full-body orgasm ripped through him, followed by a heavy paralysis that pinned him in place. Gelato felt stuck, and it felt perfect. It was his first time doing fentanyl, and the pleasure came so strong it didn't even seem real, like nothing could ever top it again. He fell sideways onto the bed and lay there on his side, nodding off into the darkness. His breathing turned short and shallow. A tightness clamped around his heart, but his body stayed wrapped in ecstasy. He didn't panic. He let the dark take him. He welcomed the light he believed waited at the end.

CHAPTER FORTY-NINE

When Gelato's body was found in the hotel room, police identified him through minor charges from his past. Those records led them to Sierra. She'd once been his surety on an old assault charge involving a girl who hadn't lasted in his stable at the time. Through Sierra, the devastating news spread to the people who'd once been family to him. Loose lips carried it further. Smaller news broadcasts picked it up, then social media did the rest, reaching plenty of people across the city who'd once known the infamous Gelato Icy. In a world where names live longer than people, his name didn't die quiet.

Smooth handled the funeral arrangements with his grief held down and anger simmering under it all. He was hurt, but he was also frustrated with Gelato, not impressed with how far he let himself fall. Still, he stayed composed and handled business because somebody had to. Attendees included Gelato's aunt, Smooth's own family who also regarded Gelato as one of their own, Smooth's stable of women, and Sierra, who showed up carrying a kind of grief she didn't have words for.

The funeral was open to the public, and people made sure to attend, including those from the underworld in Montréal and Toronto. Some came out of love. Some came out of respect. Some came just to see it with their own eyes, because legends aren't supposed to end like that. The room held a strange mix of silence and murmurs, prayers and stares, designer coats and tired faces. Old stories floated under people's breath, the good ones and the ugly ones, all of them tracing back to the same truth. Gelato had been somebody in this city. Even some of his former women showed up, standing off to the side like ghosts from earlier chapters of his life. But there was no sign of Dianna or Vanessa. A social media chain shared the funeral details and it reached Barbie, too. No one knew who she was or what her relationship with Gelato had been, and nobody asked. Like everyone else, she had the right to pay her respects. Whatever Gelato became at the end, whatever people chose to say about him now, he was still a man in that casket. He was still somebody's memory. And all the talk went quiet when the casket closed.

Sunday, May 12

Crystal could've attended Gelato's funeral on behalf of Preeme, but she was stuck at the hospital by Preeme's side. Gelato's funeral took place two weeks after his death. A few days before it, Preeme was taken off life support and doctors confirmed he was stable. After months of attentive care, he was finally on the road to recovery. He was discharged just two days ago with heavy bandaging on his body and neck, and his right arm in a sling until his upcoming surgery. He also went home with medication to manage the pain and support healing. When he left the hospital, nobody but Crystal knew he'd been discharged. A few close friends tried calling and messaging, but couldn't reach him. He never answered, even after he came off life support and was stable. Crystal had told the hospital not to release any information about Preeme to anyone, so he wasn't allowed visitors except her.

Crystal would've been his homecare nurse, but he sent her to Portugal days after he was deemed stable. He needed to make sure she was safe from anyone who might target his loved ones to get to him. The twin was out of the picture anyway, since police found him hiding at a friend's house days after the shooting. All Preeme could do now was pray someone in jail collected the $50,000 hit he'd put out on the twin. As for Gelato's death, it was something Preeme refused to sit in. He'd already shed enough tears in the hospital. Part of his recovery was grieving his big homie, and he was still trying to heal in every way he could.

Preeme was back in the comfort of his own home, but nothing about the days felt comfortable. A personal support worker showed up every morning and night to help him bathe and change his bandages. His upper body and neck stayed in constant pain, and it took a lot of Percocet just to get through the day. His voice was raspy, his throat still sore from the bullet that hit his neck and barely missed his larynx, tearing muscle instead. Along with luck, it was the Rob Ford pendant that kept a bullet from reaching his heart.

Smooth had not attempted to reach out to Preeme through his entire recovery. Preeme found it interesting that Smooth reached out to Crystal many times, then stopped once she told him Preeme had come off life support. From how Crystal described the calls, Smooth seemed more worried about her well-being than anything else. Preeme wanted to address that with

Smooth, so he made a note to have the conversation. It would be today. His legs were fine, so he could move around and get into an Uber to head to Smooth's place. Surprise was the best way to confront a friend you suspected of being shady. It left less room for answers and excuses made up on the spot.

That morning, the personal support worker helped Preeme get dressed in a comfortable Polo sweatsuit so he could head out for the day. She left before noon. Preeme grabbed a leather Armani jacket from the closet and draped it over his shoulders. There was no way he was pulling his right arm from the sling just to work it through a sleeve on his own. May's weather was decent but the pain and the anxiety still gave him chills, so he needed the jacket. He needed something else too. He went to the hidden compartment in his washroom cabinet and retrieved one of his three pistols. The snub-nose revolver was the choice, and he tucked it into the jacket's interior pocket. Now he just had to call an Uber and take some Percocet to manage the pain.

Preeme knew Smooth well enough to predict he'd be at his Sherway Gardens condo on a Sunday afternoon, laid back with nothing serious planned. This visit wasn't about malice or hostility. It was Preeme's way of getting a real, on-the-spot read from Smooth, something that would help him decide if Smooth was still a brother. The gun in his jacket was there because Preeme didn't feel safe moving around without one. He nearly lost his life four months ago when his gun wasn't within reach. Now he lived with post-traumatic stress, the paranoia always close, the anxiety hitting over the simplest things. He swore he'd rather be caught with it than without it. The twin was out of the picture, but Preeme couldn't assume nobody else would try to follow up on his behalf. Besides, he had a complicated past, and what happened months ago was a reminder that other parts of his history could come back to haunt him too. As long as he lived in Toronto, he'd always have to watch his back.

The Uber dropped Preeme off in front of Smooth's condo by Sherway Gardens. There'd been no conversation the whole drive, but Preeme checked the trip details on his phone and left the driver a decent tip. A young woman came out through the condo's lobby doors with a small dog, and Preeme took the opening to slip in without buzzing Smooth—keeping the visit a complete surprise. If it wasn't obvious the woman was just taking the dog out, his anxiety would've flared at her timing. But everything was fine. He shoved his phone into his pocket and hurried inside, gripping his jacket so it wouldn't slide off his shoulders. Doing everything with his left hand, he made it through the front doors and caught the second door before it shut behind the woman. The unfamiliar concierge watched him, noticing he'd entered without buzzing up to a unit. He might've stopped him to confirm he belonged there, but the sling and neck bandages made Preeme look vulnerable. He left him alone. Preeme crossed the foyer and stepped into an elevator that was already waiting. He rode up alone, got off on Smooth's floor, and headed down the hall. Voices and laughter drifted from inside Smooth's unit. Preeme wondered if he'd picked a bad time, then he caught the second voice. Feminine and familiar. It had to be Alize or

Star, both considered family, so his surprise visit wouldn't be an issue. Without hesitation, he knocked on the door.

CHAPTER FIFTY

Sunday, May 12 – 1:35 p.m.

Sierra and Smooth had just finished the shepherd's pie she made for lunch, and they were in the living room enjoying each other's company. She'd arrived at his condo last night after working in Ottawa for a week, and it was only right she got her personal time with Smooth. Her birthday was two days away, too. They were both comfortable, him in a tank and boxers, Sierra in a tank top and booty shorts, talking, laughing, and flirting like new lovers as their relationship settled into a new level of romance. Their bond had grown so much over the past months that even Star and Alize sometimes got jealous of how the two of them clicked during family nights at the King City mansion. Smooth picked up on it, so it was sometimes better to spend time alone with Sierra at his condo, or hers.

The day got interrupted by a knock at the door. Smooth and Sierra looked at each other with the same expression because they weren't expecting anyone. Sierra wondered if Star and Alize had caught wind of them being together and decided to crash it. Smooth had his own thought, that one of his other girls might've shown up unannounced, and that would mean discipline for being out of pocket. He got up from the couch and went to the door, then leaned in to check the peephole. Preeme stood there with a leather jacket draped over his shoulder. His right arm was in a sling, and bandages showed on his neck. Smooth didn't speak. He motioned Sierra over to look, and she saw it too. Out of everybody they'd just named in their heads, Preeme never crossed their minds.

"It's me, homie. You don't recognize me?" Preeme's raspy voice came through the door. He chuckled. "I don't think my face got hit up, bruh."

Smooth signalled Sierra toward the bedroom. He waited until she disappeared down the hall, then said, "Sheit. Looks like you lost some weight. You sound different too, playa." He unlocked the door and opened it with a smile.

"I don't know what weight you're talking about. I've always been skinny," Preeme said. He greeted Smooth with a gentle, one-arm brotherly hug.

Smooth locked the door once Preeme was inside, then said with some enthusiasm, "Good to see you, playa. When'd you get out of the hospital?"

"Not too long ago," Preeme replied with a casual vibe. "Been like two days now."

"Good, good. Glad to see you, man." Smooth started toward the kitchen. "You want something to drink?"

"Nah, I'm good."

"Oh, okay." Smooth redirected towards the living room. "Come sit down, playa. Let's catch up. It's been a while since I seen you, man."

"Nah, nah. I'm not staying long. I was just in the area, so I decided to stop by." Preeme added, "But you right, though. I haven't seen you in a minute. At all."

Smooth paused by the dining counter and sat on a stool instead. He tried to downplay the comment with a laugh, then said, "C'mon, son. Don't play me like that."

Preeme chuckled and stepped up to the other side of the counter. "But fo'real, though. You ain't even check on me."

"How was I gon' do that? Crystal told me she made a safe play by cancelling visits."

"Yeah, true. But you could've reached out with a phone call or something. My number didn't change."

"Once I heard the good news that you were holding up, I wanted to give you time and space to recover right."

Preeme nodded like he accepted it, then caught him with another question. "Speaking of that, don't you think that was kinda weird?"

"What you mean?" Smooth had an idea where it was going, but he played dumb to buy time. "I'm not getting what you mean."

"You were ringing Crystal on the regular, but once you heard I was good again, you didn't follow up with her anymore. And from how Crystal put it, it seemed like you were more worried about how she was than how I was doing."

"C'mon, son. You trippin'." Smooth spoke steady. "I was checking on your girl because we family. I wanted to make sure she was holding up while you were down. I called to make sure she was eating right and getting rest." Smooth added, "Then I was happy to hear you were off life support, so I figured I'd hear from you when you got home. I didn't think they were still gonna keep you that long in the hospital."

Preeme thought about it, then said it plain. "If you wasn't my homie, I'd think you was tryna swerve on my bitch, using sympathy and comfort as your game. Then when you heard I was breathing again, you fell back with your games."

"Don't be thinking like that, playa." Smooth let a little edge show. "We family. I'd never try to run games on your bitch. I ain't no sucka."

Preeme nodded again, taking it in. Then he asked, "So where's your girl?"

"What girl?" Smooth asked, even though his mind was already racing.

"I heard you in here with someone when I was at the door."

"Oh…" Smooth froze. "It was, uh…"

"Alize?" Preeme fed him.

"Nah, nah. It was Star." Smooth didn't take the lifeline. It would've felt like accepting it, and he knew Preeme was already on him.

"Oh, okay. So where is she?"

"What you mean?" Smooth kept his answers simple. "She in the room."

"She not gonna come out to see me before I go?" Preeme scoffed. "I just got out the hospital, bruh. Shouldn't she be out here happy to see me?"

"Nah, playa, it ain't even like that. She sleeping, that's why."

"Sleeping?" Preeme's eyebrow lifted. "I swear she was talking and laughing with you before I knocked."

Smooth scratched his head, realizing he'd slipped up. "Nah, I mean, she in the room. Just chilling."

Something about it didn't sit right. Preeme's nerves were already wired, and the awkward answers made it worse. He needed clarity for his own peace of mind. "Then tell her to come out and see me before I leave. Just outta respect."

Smooth stared at him, scratching his head and looking stuck. He didn't answer.

Preeme's anxiety climbed. He started down the hall towards the bedroom.

Smooth moved fast, cutting him off before he reached the doorknob. "Chill out, son. My bitch naked in there."

Preeme stopped, then knocked instead. "Star?"

"Preeme, I'm busy." The voice wasn't Star's, but it was feminine, and it was familiar.

"You naked in there?" he asked.

"Yes, I'm naked."

"Okay." Preeme glanced at Smooth like he had more to say, then turned back to the door. "I'll wait for you to throw something on, then. My bad if I'm bothering you, but I won't feel right leaving without seeing you."

"Oh my God. Just go!" she snapped. "I'll see you tomorrow or something."

Her answer and the shuffling in the room didn't settle Preeme's nerves. Anxiety kept climbing louder than reason, so he twisted the doorknob and shoved the door open. The bedroom was empty. For a split second, his mind stalled on it, trying to make it make sense, then Smooth blindsided him with a tackle. They crashed into the bedroom together. Preeme hit the hardwood hard and pain flared through his upper body and neck. His left wrist wrenched as he tried to brace the fall with his only good hand. His right arm stayed pinned in the sling, but the pain was still brutal. He couldn't understand why Smooth had turned on him. When his head cleared, Smooth was towering over him, barking, "I told you to chill out, son. Get the fuck out my crib before I gotta hurt you!"

Preeme's confusion burned into anger, then into survival. His hand shot for the jacket beside him. Smooth saw it and froze. The moment Preeme's fingers closed around the gun, Smooth's bravado cracked. He started to lunge anyway, desperate. Preeme read it, raised the barrel, and fired. The loud shot stole the air from the room. Smooth stumbled back, shock spreading across his face as his hand clamped to his stomach. The closet door flew open and Sierra stumbled out, panic spilling out of her. "Oh my God. Preeme, no!"

Preeme stared at her like his eyes were lying to him. His chest went hollow. His throat tightened. "What the fuck?" The words came out rough, almost strangled. He snapped back to Smooth, slumped against the dresser and bleeding into his own hands. Everything clicked at once. The calls that stopped. The ducking and dodging. The slick answers. The laughter behind the door. It wasn't paranoia. It was real.

Rage roared through Preeme and choked out the doubt. He fired again, twice, his swollen left hand steady enough to drive both shots into Smooth's stomach.

"Please, stop!" Sierra cried. "I can explain."

Preeme kept his eyes on her as he forced himself back up, the gun still in his hand. He flicked a look at Smooth on the floor, folded down and clutching his stomach, dragging air like every breath cost him.

"What the fuck is going on?" Preeme's voice came out harsh. "What's poppin'?"

"I'm sorry, Preeme," Sierra sobbed. "But I been with him for some time now, and we didn't know how to tell you. I swear he's been good to me."

"You know this is foul, right?"

"I know," she cried. "That's why we couldn't tell you."

"Bitch, you hella wrong for this." The words came fast, then cracked. Tears sat right there, ready to spill. "You swore to me and Crystal you'd stay independent. I stayed true to you like a brother. I told you claim my name if next pimps ever sweat you about being a renegade. I had your back." His throat tightened. A tear finally broke free and ran down his face. "No way...you disrespected Gelato, you disrespected yourself, and you did that with a new pimp when you knew I had you." He stared at her like he didn't recognize her anymore. "But really though, one of the brothers?"

Preeme turned to Smooth with disgust sharp on his face. "You a real fuckboy, bruh." He shot him twice in the head. Sierra screamed. Preeme stepped in and pistol-whipped her hard enough to drop her out cold.

Preeme picked up his jacket off the floor and draped it back over his shoulders, then stood in the bedroom and processed what had just happened. As the adrenaline eased, the pain came rushing back through his body, and his swollen left hand throbbed even worse from the pistol-whip. His mind went straight to Percocet, but he could not ignore the scene he'd created. Smooth was dead by the dresser and Sierra was knocked out cold on the floor. He had no regrets. The thought crossed his mind to put the last bullet in Sierra's head, but he shoved the gun back into his jacket instead. Preeme chose to spare her. Gelato loved Sierra to his grave, and killing her would've stained the big homie's soul. The only thing that mattered now was getting out of the building safely, then figuring a way out of the mess.

Preeme left the unit and saw a woman down the hall peeking out from behind her door. She had to be the only nosy neighbor after hearing the gunshots. Preeme met her eyes and gave her a calm smile, like nothing happened. He was just another man passing through. With his right arm in a sling and bandaging still visible on his neck, he looked like somebody healing up from bad luck and leaving after checking on a friend. He kept walking without breaking pace.

In Gelato Icy's name, the game called the balance due. Blood cleared it.

GHAD

EPILOGUE

Thursday, May 16 – 2:30 p.m. (Caracas, Venezuela)

Bathed in the warm South American sun, Preeme sat alone on the patio of a restaurant while Crystal got her hair done at a nearby salon. His birthday was just ten days away, but this was not a vacation to celebrate it. This trip had been part of a plan to avoid a subpoena as the victim in Flame's attempted murder case, and even that was not supposed to happen anytime soon. They left early because Preeme knew he would be a suspect in Smooth's murder. The killing was impulsive and unplanned. There was ample evidence to arrest and convict Preeme at trial, especially after he left Sierra alive, knowing she would become a key witness. So he left Canada that same day before the sun went down.

Preeme first landed in Russia, then had Crystal fly in from Portugal to meet him. Within two days, new identifications and passports were arranged through Whitey's brother, Gambit, and they flew out to Venezuela. They planned to live there, and Preeme managed to hide over a million dollars in his check-in luggage to bring with them. For now, they were staying at a five-star hotel, with plans to buy a decent home and eventually put most of their money into legitimate businesses in the country. Over the past few days, they explored parts of their new city, and Preeme met with people referred by Gambit, so they were in good hands.

He felt even better in the care of his love, Crystal, who helped him shower and change his bandaging every morning and night. They had found a reputable surgeon to book his shoulder surgery with, keeping him on the road to a full recovery.

He sipped his piña colada and smiled at the Venezuelan waitress as she brought his food. "Gracias," he said with a polite nod. She smiled back before walking away. It was rice and beef stew with avocado slices on the side, just like the picture on the menu. With his right arm in a sling, he had to eat with his left hand, and he still hadn't mastered using a fork that way. Funny how just days ago, that same non-dominant hand had handled a gun just fine. His phone started ringing as he reached for the fork, so he let it drop and answered the unknown caller. Preeme stayed silent, waiting for the person on the other end to speak first.

"Bro, it's me," Whitey said on the phone. Only he and Gambit had Preeme's Venezuelan number. The call felt off, though. They usually reached him through an app, not direct. Whitey kept going. "Listen, I got someone on the other line who wants to talk to you."

"Who is it? Bruh, I'm not tryna talk to everybody," Preeme replied. His raspy voice was getting better.

"Just hold on." Whitey clicked over, then came back a moment later. "Yo."

"Yeah, I'm here," Preeme said.

A woman's voice came through. "Hello?"

"Who is this?" Preeme demanded.

"It's me, Vanessa. Velvet."

"Huh? Velvet?"

"Yeah. Remember, Gelato's girl?"

"Yeah, I know who you are," Preeme said. "Just surprised to hear from you."

"It's been a while, hasn't it?"

"More than a while. You went ghost on big homie and everyone."

"I know, I know. I'm sorry. I was going through a lot and I needed to get away from everything."

"Oh, okay." Preeme paused. "So what's up?"

"Not much. I actually been doing really good now."

Preeme didn't give her anything back, so Vanessa caught it quick and got to the point. "So, I've been meaning to get a hold of you for a while now. Just days ago, I tried yours and Crystal's numbers, but both were out of service. I knew I wouldn't find Crystal on social media, and definitely not you," she giggled. "So yesterday I went to your condo and found out nobody had seen you or Crystal in days. The front desk even mentioned detectives coming by asking about you, or something like that. I'm not too sure. I didn't ask because the less I know, the better. Today I finally got a hold of Whitey, and now I got you." She giggled again.

Preeme stayed quiet, waiting for the point to land.

Vanessa's tone stayed light, almost happy. "So listen. I had a baby not too long ago. I didn't tell anyone, but I was pregnant with Angelo's baby when I left. And now he has a baby boy. I named him Angel."

A smile spread across Preeme's face and tears rose in his eyes. "Wow. That's a beautiful name."

"Thank you." Her voice cracked into sobs. "I got the news when Gelato passed away. I wanted to make it to the funeral…but I couldn't. I was too broken to get up and go anywhere…I just couldn't." She inhaled, trying to steady herself. "Besides, I was too far along in my pregnancy to be traveling all the way to Montréal anyway." Vanessa gathered herself and forced her voice back into something lighter. "So, yeah, you're the one person that's always been there for Angelo. So, umm, I was thinking, maybe you could be Angel's godfather."

Preeme went quiet. The smile stayed, but it hurt. Tears sat in his eyes, joy and grief tangled together. The news hit him hard, especially with everything that had happened over the past year.

"…Hello?" Vanessa checked the line. "You there?"

"Yeah, yeah. I'm here."

"Okay, so? Will you be Angel's godfather? It would mean the world to me."

"Listen," Preeme said, voice low, "I'ma have Whitey send you a link to download an app. Then I'ma holla at you on there, and we'll figure out a flight to get you and baby Angel over to join me and Crystal for my birthday."

"Hmm…I don't know if I can travel with the newborn baby just yet. I'll have to look into that."

"Well, if we gotta wait some time, that's cool. As long as I eventually get to meet my godson."

"Okay, perfect. I'm so excited. I'll look into it," Vanessa said. "And I'll download the app as soon as I get the link."

"Say no more. I'll keep in touch with you on there."

"Okay, okay. Talk soon."

When Vanessa hung up, Preeme stayed on the line with Whitey and they talked through the news for a moment, both sitting in it, before they ended the call too. It didn't fix what happened to Gelato, but it eased something in Preeme's chest. Angelo was gone, but he left a son behind, and that boy gave the name Gelato Icy somewhere to live. Preeme called Crystal to tell her.

Meet The Characters Beyond These Pages
—Follow along on Instagram—

@GHADBOOKS

Don't forget to leave a review. Your words keep the story alive.